D0063712

FLASH
FIRE

FLASH FIRE

(A Navy SEAL Romance)

DANA MARTON

My sincere thanks to Sarah Jordan for having my back day after day, Diane Flindt, Linda, and Toni for editing, and Clarissa for the perfect cover.

This book is dedicated to all my wonderful readers in my FB Book Club. Thank you for hanging out with me!

FLASH FIRE - Copyright © 2015 by Dana Marton

First Edition: 2015
ISBN-13: 9781940627137
ISBN-10: 1940627133

CHAPTER
ONE

Nothing woke up a man as quickly in the morning as a scorpion in his pants. The world—which at the moment for Light Walker consisted of the arachnid's alarming proximity to his most sensitive parts—snapped into focus real fast.

Walker slowly unfolded from his crouching position at the foot of the balsa tree where he'd fallen asleep. Bomb squads moved with less care. He unfastened his belt, unzipped his fly, then—barely breathing—he gently eased his pants away from his body to make a way out for the intruder.

Most people thought scorpions lived in deserts, but his experience said otherwise. Some species liked the rainforest just fine.

He didn't bother wondering how the damned thing had gotten in despite the fact that his cargo pants were fastened at the ankles. The leeches, scorpions, and other bugs had mystical ways of sneaking past even the best defenses— one of the laws of the jungle.

Instead of reaching in to where the scorpion's legs tickled his skin, he waited. He knew too well the pain of a sting as it spread through his body, and the accompanying blurred vision he couldn't afford right now. He'd been bitten not a week back on his elbow, an experience he didn't care to repeat.

Two days before that, he'd been bitten by a snake. Probably a sign that his luck was running out and he should leave. Another man might have taken the hint. Walker rejected the thought as quickly as it came to him.

"Come on. Out," he said under his breath. "Get moving."

Three inches long, coffee brown, and carrying a world of hurt in its stinger, the scorpion inched up on his lower abdomen like it had all the time in the world.

Walker maneuvered his shirttail in front of the little sucker until it climbed onto the fabric. Once the scorpion was off his skin, he reached for the knife on his belt and used the blade to flick the damned thing into the bushes that stood a dozen feet to his right. "Adios, amigo."

Then he drew his first full breath of the morning. "*Hijo de puta.*"

As the Mexican jungle sang its lively song around him, he shoved the knife back into its ballistic nylon sheath that hung to the side.

The knife was just the right size and, due to the light aluminum handle, just the right weight. The Mark II combat knife—a classic since Vietnam—and its six-and-a-half inch, double-serrated steel blade had saved his life more times than he could count. Guns had an unfortunate tendency to run out of bullets, or jam, but a good blade never let a man down, for a damn fact.

He fastened his pants, then stretched his stiff muscles. He swore under his breath one more time as he looked after the scorpion.

Could have turned out a lot worse.

He scanned the ground to make sure there'd be no further nasty surprises. The silver-embroidered black sombrero he'd stolen the day before leaned against the tree next to him. He even checked under that.

When he was sure his small area was clear, he folded his six-foot frame into a low crouch again and leaned his back against the balsa tree, the same position he'd spent most of the night in, waiting for the convoy, and—most importantly—the noseless man.

Walker rubbed the last remnants of sleep from his eyes. Hot, humid air filled his lungs as he inhaled the distinct smell of a rainforest—the smell of things growing, flowering, decomposing—the smell of life and death all mixed into one.

Controlled breath in. He checked his watch. Controlled breath out.

He rubbed his hand over his face. He'd fallen asleep. *Shit.*

He was damned lucky the convoy was late.

They couldn't have come already. No way would he have slept through the trucks' passing. He was a light sleeper. For the most part, he existed on quick combat naps, a habit he'd developed in the navy. If the trucks had come, he would have been awake and alert at the first sound that wasn't part of the jungle's usual music.

The first hint of human intrusion wouldn't come from truck engines but from a slight change in the bird song, in the tone of the monkeys' screeching. The rainforest had its own alarm system to warn of predators.

The local indigenous tribes—Tzeltal and Tojolabal—the proud descendants of the Maya, could read the jungle noises like a news report. Walker knew the basics, the different cries for snake, jaguar, man, different again for an approaching storm.

He listened for the slightest change of sound around him.

Monkeys called good morning to each other above, in high-pitched, manic shrieks. The bugs produced the background sound, their unending song rising and falling, almost like listening to waves crash against the beach. Moisture dripped from leaves above to leaves below, lending another layer to the symphony. Nothing unusual.

Walker let himself relax.

A million shades of green that existed nowhere else on earth but in rainforests surrounded him. Leaves glistened in the sun like jewels. Lianas cascaded from above like an emerald waterfall.

A toucan poked its head from a tree hollow—probably had a nest there—its large green-orange beak a new splash of color.

"What's up, Sam?" Walker asked the bird. They knew each other from the day before when Walker had first come here to scout out the clearing.

The toucan flew off. Not into morning chit-chat. Walker could relate.

Parrots flashed between the branches—red, blue, yellow—like flowers dancing in the air.

Some people found the jungle beautiful and returned to it over and over as if to a lover. Walker wasn't here to enjoy the scenery. Where another person might have seen paradise, he saw a killing field.

After two years of careful planning, today was the day: the beginning of the end. He was ready.

He checked his guns—first the SIG P226, twenty-round magazine loaded with 9mm Parabellums; then the semiautomatic rifle, an M14 with a twenty-round detachable box magazine and five-hundred-yard effective firing range.

He stuck with weapons he was already familiar with from his navy days. He needed the dependability, something tried and true. Between the two, they

3

gave him forty shots before reloading. He carried extra magazines in the side pockets of his pants.

He checked his watch again. The convoy was over an hour late.

Eyes narrowed, he looked to the south, not that he could see far through the dense foliage. Maybe the information that the schedule had been brought forward by three weeks was just bait in a trap. Somebody could be setting him up.

Even as unease had him shifting his weight from one foot to the other, the jungle's music changed to a different, harsher tone. He gripped the M14 and assumed a battle-ready stance. His surroundings came into a sharp focus. He breathed deeply, evenly. *Here we go.*

Another full minute passed before a low rumble from the distance finally reached his ears. The sound disappeared the next second, then returned, then amplified.

He kept low and held still in the cover of the achiote bushes that stood between him and the dirt road passing about ten feet ahead, winding through the small clearing chosen for the ambush.

The trucks were coming from the direction of the Guatemalan border, heading north, deeper into Mexico, a well-traveled drug-smuggling route.

One minute ticked by, then two, three, four before a beat-up Jeep appeared in the lead. Walker bided his time and waited for the two trucks he knew would be following.

The sound of rumbling motors grew as the vehicles neared, drowning out most of the jungle noises, except for the rush of wings directly above Walker as half a dozen birds took flight with sharp cries. He felt none of their panic, just the opposite. As he touched a hand to the dog tags hanging under his shirt—one his, the other his brother's—a deadly calm descended over him.

The Jeep rumbled toward the far end of the clearing, lurching over tree roots and rocks. Then the two flatbed trucks came out into the open at last. In the back of each truck, about half a dozen men sat on top of the heavy tarps that covered the shipment they guarded. Each man held an AK-47—assault rifles not to be underestimated.

One out of nine of the nine hundred million firearms in existence was some kind of a Kalashnikov, and for a good reason. But a weapon was only as good as the man wielding it, and Walker was damned sure he'd had better weapons training than any of the jerkwads he'd be facing today.

They'd be sweaty and tired, having spent the last four days in the back of the trucks. Their legs would be stiff from all the sitting, their minds at their least alert during the journey. They were almost at their destination.

They had made it through the border. At this point, they'd expect to be in the clear. They'd expect that tonight each would be drinking cold beer at a cantina, then going to sleep in a real bed with a lively whore who'd work the kinks out of his muscles.

If they were thinking of anything, they were thinking of that, and not what dangers the jungle could still be hiding around them.

Walker scanned them carefully, one by one. According to what scant information he had, the noseless man usually covered his face with a bandana. Several of the men had sweat-soaked, twisted bandanas around their necks, but none had his face covered. And they all had their noses, as far as Walker could tell from his cover.

He swallowed his disappointment and anger as the Jeep in the lead rolled forward.

Three, two, one... Walker counted silently. Then the front bumper hit the trip line.

Boom!

The ground shook as the vehicle blasted up into the air in a fiery explosion, crashing back down a second later and shaking the ground again.

The two trucks lurched to a stop, armed men jumping from the cabs, shouting, shooting randomly at nothing, keeping in the cover of the doors, while the rest bailed from the back, dropping to the ground, pulling behind and under the vehicles.

Walker sprayed them with bullets, dropped and rolled, then rolled some more, his path carefully planned and calculated, so as the men returned fire, they hit nothing but trees. *Five down.* He shot, rolled again. *Nine down.* He shot and rolled, over and over.

Two men—realizing that they were trapped in the clearing—jumped back inside the first truck and rammed the burning Jeep, desperate to get away. Metal screamed against metal.

Walker shot them through the truck's windshield, shards of glass flying, blood spraying the cab. When the second truck tried to back down the jungle road, Walker drilled a bullet into the middle of the driver's forehead.

The handful of remaining men scattered, scampering behind bushes, running away into the trees.

Walker dashed after them.

He didn't enjoy killing, but he didn't dread it either. He spent the next couple of hours tracking and hunting the cartel soldiers down one by one, until the last bastard was dead at his feet in a bleeding heap.

E. effing K. I. A. *Enemy Killed In Action.*

Walker headed back to the clearing, scratched to shit and covered in blood, but nothing life threatening. The worst damage was his busted cell phone—smashed into pieces in the side pocket of his cargo pants when he'd crashed into a rock. He shouldn't have brought the damn thing. No reception in the jungle anyway.

He thought no more of the men. His focus was on where he stepped. The scorpion was enough for the morning; he didn't want an encounter with a poisonous snake. He walked with an even stride, no emotion about the massacre, no guilt.

He didn't replay the ambush in his mind, didn't analyze it, didn't celebrate the win, didn't regret the loss of life. He simply gave no further thought to the attack he'd carried out. He moved on to the next task.

He dumped the bodies from the cab of the first truck and lined the vehicle up for the pulley system he had hidden high in the canopy. Once he had the truck in position, he pulled back the tarp, lowered the pulley from the tree, hooked it up to the pallet that held over two hundred pounds of raw heroin in plastic bags, then he ratcheted the entire pallet up and out of sight.

He moved to the second pallet and hoisted that, then the third, then the fourth. He did the same with the four pallets on the other truck, working until the entire shipment was hidden in the rainforest canopy high above.

Every muscle in his body burned, sweat dripping from his eyebrows, by the time he strode back to his hiding spot behind the achiote bushes where he'd spent the night. He grabbed the sombrero, shot a few rounds through the black felt with his SIG, then carried the hat back to the clearing, and wiped his bloody hands on the brim before he dropped it.

He went in search of the convoy leader next. The man had been in the Jeep, had been thrown clear in the explosion. Walker had noted earlier the spot where the guy had fallen, and now hurried straight to the mangled body.

He reached into the bulging breast pocket on the guy's camo shirt and pulled out the roll of hundred-dollar bills held together with a rubber band. Around fifty banknotes, five thousand dollars of bribe money, just in case the convoy bumped into some kind of law enforcement that hadn't been paid off in advance.

Walker shoved the roll into an empty side pocket of his cargo pants, then checked the rest of the men for their loose bills and pocket change. Leaving the money to rot would be a waste.

He checked the faces too, carefully, but every one of the fuckers had a nose. He swore under his breath.

Then he found something he hadn't been looking for, in the footwell of the second truck: a woven palm leaf basket, about two feet wide and a foot tall, lid fastened on with black electrical tape.

Probably snakes—either headed for the exotic animal trade or some voodoo doctor somewhere. He hated snakes, dammit.

Slowly, carefully, he used his knife to cut the tape, then he wedged the blade under the top of the basket and raised it an inch, then another until he could peer in. He saw green, with dots of yellow here and there—feathers. He released the breath he'd been holding.

He dropped the lid back on, then lifted the basket out of the truck. One of the men had been smuggling parrots as a side business. At a couple of hundred dollars each, the nearly two dozen birds jammed into the basket meant a veritable fortune around here.

"Let's liquidate some assets." Walker tossed the lid aside.

The birds—yellow-naped Amazon parrots—were too stunned for a moment, blinking at the bright light and him. Then the bravest hopped up to the basket's edge and took flight with a wild cry, his wings brushing Walker's face. And the next second, the basket was empty.

Or nearly so. Among the bird droppings and lost feathers on the bottom, a baby parrot blinked curiously at him. The chick was flightless, would probably be flightless for another couple of weeks, judging by the length of its tail and wing feathers.

Walker thought of the small-animal sanctuary at the edge of the jungle, run by an elderly do-gooder British couple. *What the hell.* He scooped up the parrot and put it into his left breast pocket where the chick immediately snuggled in as if into a nest.

The tiny bird felt warm and alive there—almost as if Walker had a heart again.

"You shit in my pocket and our friendship is over," he grumbled to the chick as he moved forward.

A deadly silence filled the air. The explosion and following gunfire had scared the wildlife away. Even the bugs kept quiet. The scene around him that had been the picture of paradise not long ago was now a snapshot straight from hell, corpses littering the clearing.

He'd annihilated the enemy, while all he had were scratches. He was the indisputable winner of the battle. Yet, if he felt anything, it was bitter disappointment underscored by the cold, dark anger that lived in his bones and never went away.

Where in hell was the noseless man?

The guy had been there when Walker's brother had been killed. Which meant the bastard would know Ben's killer. Walker wanted a name.

But he wasn't going to get it here today.

He swore as he turned onto an animal track and walked away without looking back. He didn't much care what would happen to the bodies he left in his wake.

Back when he'd been in the navy, he used to believe in valor and honor and all that bullshit. Now he just believed in being better armed and better prepared than the men he planned on killing.

The list was long. He'd barely gotten started. He had a lot to do—including finding the noseless man—and only a week to do it.

CHAPTER TWO

Mexico City, Mexico

The men loading the coffin into the back of the hearse in the US embassy's courtyard took their time and handled it with care. Sweat beaded on their foreheads, ran down their cheeks, but they didn't rush. Even as the July sun radiated brutal heat from above, they kept every move careful and dignified, as befitted the occasion.

DOD Investigator Clara Roberts watched the scene through the open door of the embassy's back hallway, looking past the marine corporal who stood in the opening.

"Anybody you know?" she asked the marine, keeping her voice down.

Behind her, her retrieval target was dozing in a chair, the flaxen-haired college freshman's legs sprawled halfway across the corridor, drool gathering at the corner of his lips. Bobby Lekker looked beat, but was otherwise in pretty good shape, all things considered.

At least he wasn't going to the airport in a hearse.

The marine corporal's somber gaze swung to Clara. "No, ma'am."

He was about to turn back, but then he paused and added, "Repatriation of remains. A tourist. He died in a Jet Ski incident while on vacation. Third repatriation this week. The other two were car accidents. Flown back to the States the day before yesterday. Rough summer so far this year. We don't normally see this many bodies."

The marine stood ramrod straight as he spoke, shoes at top shine, uniform in impeccable order, his hair regulation cut. He was as exact as if he'd been drawn by a mechanical engineer, with the help of a caliper and a bow compass.

Clara fully approved. She liked order and orderly people. He was the exact type of man she would be attracted to if she had time to be attracted to a man. He looked clean-cut and dependable.

Someday...

She stifled a sigh. She had a lot of other things to take care of before she could focus on her personal life. Romance was not on her twelve-month schedule.

Not that she had her entire life mapped out in a spreadsheet. But she did have one-year, five-year, and ten-year plans, both for her private life and her career. She liked knowing where she was going and when and how she was going to get there. The very idea of people meandering through life gave her the heebie-jeebies.

She turned her attention from the marine back to the coffin that would probably be on her flight. The thought didn't bother her. She'd done repatriations herself. While her job was search and rescue, there had been times when she'd reached her target too late and could only fly back with a body.

The remains of US citizens who died abroad were repatriated via the various US embassies, a streamlined procedure that took the grief of their families into consideration. The deceased were afforded all respect and dignity. The staff wasn't just shipping boxes. The embassies had a system in place, and the people who ran it cared.

As Clara watched, the men closed the back door of the hearse and the car rolled away.

Within another minute, a black SUV pulled up with tinted windows, the Great Seal of the United States emblazoned on the front door in gold—a majestic eagle holding arrows in his talons on one side, an olive branch on the other.

The marine reached for her suitcase. "I'll take that, ma'am."

"Thank you, Corporal."

She couldn't wait to get back home. Tomorrow was her father's first chemotherapy treatment, and she planned on being there with him. She wished she could do more, like donate a kidney or bone marrow, *anything*. There was absolutely nothing on this earth she wouldn't do for her father. But she couldn't do anything about prostate cancer.

Clara and the lost-and-found college student, who had disappeared in Acapulco on a birthday trip with friends, would get a marine escort to the airport. Then she would hand-deliver the delinquent frat boy, in exactly six hours and seventeen minutes, to his worried parents, who'd be waiting at Reagan National Airport in DC.

Clara had her schedule mapped out for the rest of the day, and she planned on sticking to it: hand over Bobby, then go home to her condo to drop off her luggage, shower and change. After that, she'd drive to her parents' house to spend the night. She wanted to drive her father to the hospital in the morning.

She needed to get the schedule of his future appointments so she could go with him as many times as possible. She could take a leave of absence from work, if necessary. She liked her job—the investigations let her use her analytical skills, took her to interesting places, and she got to save people—but family would always come first.

As the marine stepped outside with her suitcase, Clara called back to the sleeping kid. "Time to go home."

Bobby Lekker blinked awake slowly and stared at her for a long moment before he pushed to his feet.

He'd cleaned up using the embassy's facilities, but the shadows of the three weeks he'd spent in a Mexican jail were still in his eyes as he lumbered toward her. He wore the jeans and T-shirt Clara bought him—nothing special, but he'd been ridiculously grateful.

"Thank you," he said again, his sleep-laden voice filled with emotion. "I'm sorry I caused so much trouble." He hung his head. "My dad's gonna kill me."

She gave him a reassuring smile. "Your parents are going to be extremely happy to see you. I promise."

She was about to say more, but the clip-clop of high heels behind her made her turn. One of the embassy secretaries hurried toward them, a young woman in a sharp black suit and matching heels.

"Miss Roberts? You have a call, ma'am."

All of Clara's good feelings evaporated in an instant, startled right out of her. *God, don't let it be bad news.* Not something about her father. He didn't have another doctor's appointment today, did he?

She called to the marine who was halfway to the car. "I'll be right back."

Then she hurried off after the secretary, who was already heading back into the maze of hallways that led to the administrative offices of the embassy.

Clara's heart beat faster. "Who is it?"

But as she hurried down the hallway, her hand knocked against the cell phone in her pocket, and she knew a sudden moment of overwhelming relief. Her father—or her mother—wouldn't call her at the US embassy in Mexico City. They would call her on her cell.

She slowed for a beat, relaxing her jaw. Then, with her next thought, her muscles tightened again. Why would *anyone* call her here? She cast a questioning look at the secretary, who still hadn't told her who wanted to talk to her.

The woman waited until they were out of hearing distance from the corporal and Bobby, and even then, she kept her voice so low, Clara had to strain her ears to hear her. "The Department of Defense is on the line for you in the bubble room, ma'am."

Clara blinked.

She'd sent in a case update last night so Bobby's parents could be immediately notified that he'd been found. Why would her boss, Karin Kovacs, call her? Bobby Lekker's case was straightforward. Clara had pulled off her target recovery without a hitch. She'd located and retrieved the kid within forty-eight hours of her arrival to Mexico.

All that time, his parents had been worried that their son had been kidnapped or worse, Bobby had been sitting in a small village jail for dancing down the street naked. The local police had misspelled his name, so when the first searches were run, he hadn't come up in the system.

The secretary turned down the corridor. "This way, ma'am."

They reached the small windowless room, the walls foot-thick metal to keep anyone from listening in. Most embassies had a microphone-proof "bubble room" where top-secret conversations could be conducted without being compromised, but Clara had never been inside one. Her job didn't involve any state secrets.

She tried not to gawk too much as she glanced around. A round table stood in the middle of the room. An old-fashioned desk phone waited on the desk, with a single blinking red light.

As the secretary walked away, Clara stepped inside and closed the door behind her. The space was small, the ceiling low, leaving her feeling vaguely claustrophobic. Before she could start thinking about what would happen if the door locked on her, she picked up the receiver and pushed the button next to the blinking light. "Clara Roberts."

"I'll be connecting General Roberts, ma'am," a friendly voice said on the other end. "Please hold for a moment."

Then the general's deep voice came on the line. "Clara?"

Alarm shot through her as she gripped the phone. "Are you okay, Dad?"

Her father was a retired general, the head of the Civilian Personnel Recovery Unit, a new, experimental department at the DOD where Clara worked. *Not* through nepotism. She'd been recruited independently, recommended for the position by her supervisor in her previous job at the FBI, long before it was known that General Roberts would be leading the department.

"I'm fine, honey," he said.

"Is it Grandma Lucy?" Her eighty-year-old grandmother, her father's mother, lived at an Alzheimer's facility.

"She's doing well. I talked to her this morning," her father told her, but then he hesitated, which was very much out of character and did nothing to dispel Clara's alarm, especially when he added, "I need your help."

"I was just about to leave for the airport. I'll be home in a couple of hours. I can head straight over instead of going to the condo first."

Was something wrong with her mother?

Before she could ask, he said, again, his tone hesitant and…something else. "Someone I know disappeared in Mexico recently."

Clara waited for more. Finding and retrieving US citizens missing abroad was what her unit, Civilian Personnel Recovery, did. But this was not how cases were assigned. Case assignments came from her boss, Karin Kovacs, accompanied by the case file and a brief strategy meeting at the office.

The general was the big boss, because the new department needed someone with status, someone the rest of the DOD wouldn't just roll over, someone who could negotiate with the higher powers as needed. So General Roberts handled that, while Karin ran the day-to-day operations of the department and managed the investigators.

CPRU investigators worked on one case at a time. Technically, they couldn't take on a new case until Karin signed off on the previous case, until all the paperwork was completed and all the reports filed.

Bureaucracy was an indelible part of any government work. Rules, rules, and more rules. Which suited Clara pretty well. She was a rules and regulations kind of girl, probably because she'd grown up as a military brat.

Life was much easier when you knew what was expected and had the ability to perform to those expectations. Rules made life dependable.

"Someone else from the embassy can escort your current recovery target back to DC," her father was saying, his voice still off. "I'll make the arrangements." He paused, and in that brief gap, she identified the odd emotion in his tone: misery. "I'd like for you to stay where you are, if possible."

Her brain scrambled to work out what was going on. "Will you be sending me the case file here?"

"No case file. It's a personal matter. What I'm about to tell you is strictly confidential."

From our own department?

Before Clara's brain could catch up, her father went on with, "The recovery target is Rosita Ruiz. Last seen on July first in Furino, in the state of Chiapas. Long black hair, black eyes, five foot four inches tall, about a hundred and ten pounds. She has family in Furino that she was going to spend the summer with, a cousin, Melena Ruiz."

Her father rattled off a street name and number.

Clara committed the information to memory, then asked, "Age?"

He hesitated once again before he said, "Eighteen." He paused. "Nearly."

Clara stared at the desk with a cold feeling spreading in her stomach. *Why are we talking about this in the bubble room? Why is this an off-the-record case?* "May I ask how you're connected to the search target? It might help the investigation."

Maybe it had something to do with the military. Military secrets. Espionage? Why wasn't the CIA investigating?

A personal matter, he'd said.

She clenched her teeth. Her father was her hero. She didn't want to hear what she feared she was about to hear. She stared at the phone, at the rows of buttons, wishing for one that stopped time right then and there.

She did receive a small reprieve. For several long moments, silence stretched on the line. Then her father took a deep breath on the other end.

"I've done something incredibly stupid." Undisguised despair underscored his last words. "I'm sorry, Clara."

Her heart sank. The bottom of her world fell out. She felt like that astronaut in the last movie they'd seen together, her cord from the spaceship snapped, spinning alone in space.

"How?" If this was true, then everything she'd believed in so far had been a lie, and she had trouble comprehending that. "I have a right to know."

"I'm sorry," More miserable silence. Then, "The day the doctor told me the cancer came back. Your mother had that benefit gala at the Ritz. She's the committee chair, and she was receiving an award, had to go. I was going to go with her, but she told me to stay home and rest."

Clara tried to remember, but her mother chaired a number of committees and received awards regularly for her charitable works, most having to do with veterans and children of veterans.

"The diagnosis caught me off guard," her father was saying. "We were both reeling. We were going to tell you in the morning. After she left for the gala, I decided to sit by the pool. I suppose I was having myself a pity party. I had a couple of beers."

Because he wouldn't want his wife to see him upset. He'd want to be strong for her to the end. So he used what little alone time he had to let his fears and disappointments out. Clara wasn't going to blame him for that. But anything else...

"It was Friday night," he said. "Juanita had been there to clean earlier in the day. A young lady showed up, saying she was Juanita's niece. She said she'd been helping her aunt and left her school bag in the laundry room. She needed her books to do homework over the weekend. I let her in."

Clara stared at the empty wall. She knew Juanita, her parents' new housekeeper. "Rosita Ruiz is Juanita's niece?"

"I'm not going to say that I was too drunk to know what was happening. You deserve more than excuses."

Damn right. Hot, blind anger swirled through her, an emotional tornado that left devastation in its wake. How could he betray his wife and daughter like that?

"I don't remember much," he said. "I'm sorry. That sounds like an excuse too."

But Clara clamped onto it. She could have sworn on her life that her father wasn't capable of something like this. "Maybe nothing happened. Did she say something happened? She could be lying."

But he said, his voice dejected, "Apparently, I took pictures with my phone."

Her heart broke then and there, because *that* certainly rang true.

Her father snapped pictures of everything. Photography was his only hobby. He had a shelf full of expensive cameras and, in addition, he always had whatever latest phone took the best pictures. Clara used to joke that they were the most documented family in the world.

But she was far from a joking mood at the moment. She was numb. Then a new terrible thought wedged itself among the other terrible thoughts that were already circling in her mind, and shock pushed the words from her mouth before she had a chance to reconsider.

"Have you done anything like this before? With other women?"

"No." He sounded pained. "Never."

"How can I believe you?" she whispered, her heart breaking a little more.

She closed her eyes for a moment. She didn't want to hear excuses. And maybe he knew, because he didn't give her any.

She swallowed. She couldn't deal with the revelation, not right now. So she focused on the assignment she was being given. A seventeen-year-old had disappeared. Clara had to treat this as any other assignment.

Except that she hated the recovery target with a hot, burning passion.

"I'll do my best to find her."

"Juanita is really worried," her father said. "Her niece told her what happened between us but made it sound as if we had some whole twisted relationship. Juanita has come to me to beg me to find the girl. If I don't, I'm afraid she'll go to your mother."

Clara clenched her jaw. Something like this would kill her mother. Meredith Roberts was madly in love with her husband. She would be crushed beyond recovery. She hadn't dealt well with the cancer coming back.

She'd been worrying so much, she made herself sick, and she had a weak heart to begin with, the result of some exotic virus she'd caught when Clara's father had been stationed in Africa at the beginning of his military career, years before Clara's birth.

To have a much-wanted child, her mother had risked pregnancy and labor, even knowing the stress on her heart might kill her. She'd survived, but she had a delicate constitution ever since Clara could remember, which never stopped Meredith Roberts from championing every cause and trying to save the world.

Her husband admired her deeply and loved her endlessly. He would have given his life for his wife at a moment's notice—for his wife or his daughter. Clara had never doubted that for a second.

This whole Rosita situation was a non sequitur. Someone else's life.

Suddenly, Clara lost her grip on who her father was, felt as if she no longer knew him. But if she knew one thing, it was that she was going to protect her mother.

"I'll find the girl," she heard herself say. *Think of it as nothing more than your next case. Forget the personal connection.*

Then her father was talking, but, her brain a beehive, Clara missed most of it. "Sir?"

Just in that moment, she couldn't call him dad.

She normally called him *sir* in work situations.

His office wasn't on the same level as Clara's. She reported to Karin Kovacs and not him. Clara and her father had little interaction at work, which they'd always kept professional, both wanting to avoid even the shadow of any favoritism in the workplace.

He repeated the information now, giving her the rest of the details of the case.

She blinked hard, then looked up at the low metal ceiling and kept blinking so she wouldn't cry. She couldn't go back to Bobby Lekker and the marine corporal with tears in her eyes. *I'm a professional.* Deep breath. *I can and will handle this with full professionalism.*

Her father finished the briefing with, "You will not be filing an official report."

She cleared her throat. "No, sir."

"You report straight to me."

"Yes, sir."

"Time is of the utmost importance. Two weeks have passed already since the disappearance. Juanita didn't find out until Rosita missed their weekly phone call. Then she waited for progress from the local police for another week before giving up and coming to me."

"Who will be my in-house connection?"

Clara would need research done, not to mention remote access to various law enforcement databases. And the state of Chiapas was several hundred miles to the south of Mexico City. She would need plane tickets, rental car, lodging—travel arrangements usually made by the office manager, Elaine Fisher. Elaine, at the very least, would definitely have to be involved.

But her father said, "No in-house connection. I am wiring you funds personally."

She swallowed. *No in-house assistance.* Which was completely against the rules. Then again, none of this made any sense.

"Okay. As far as the department is concerned, I've caught a nasty virus and I'm in a local hospital, hooked up to IV. I need rest, so I won't be checking in with work. It'd be best if I didn't talk to anyone until the mission is completed."

"Thank you." The general's voice was filled with emotion. He cleared his throat. "I arranged for a local facilitator in Furino. His name is Light Walker. Don't do anything until you talk to him. He said he can meet you at the village guesthouse around Thursday."

Tomorrow.

Okay. Doable. "Is he with the local police?"

"The local police are not to be trusted. You'll need to fly under their radar."

"Yes, sir."

So the facilitator was a civilian. Her department normally worked with whoever the local investigator was on the given case, usually the local cops. Unless the local cops were completely corrupt.

"Walker will help you with whatever you need," her father said. "He'll take you around and make sure you'll safely get where you need to go."

Sounded like a local travel guide to make up for her not having office backup on this case—a substitute Elaine.

Silence stretched on the line. Her father had finished with the instructions and was probably unsure about what to say next. To have him be unsure about anything was beyond surreal. Clara felt as if he was a different person suddenly, a stranger she no longer recognized.

She drew a ragged breath. "Don't tell Mom."

All her life, when everything had always been in upheaval—the dozens of houses they'd lived in, the countless schools she'd attended, the revolving door of friends—the one constant had been the living, breathing love that filled her family.

Her parents loved her and each other. And she loved them. One maybe a little more than the other. She loved her mother too, but from the first moment Clara could remember, her father had been her knight in shining armor, the hero in the uniform she respected who made her feel safe. As far as she'd been concerned, he could do no wrong.

Until now.

Suddenly she was so angry, she was choking on it. She hated him at this moment, and she felt guilty for the emotion, then even angrier at him for having to feel guilty. Because she couldn't hate him. Because he was dying.

Prostate cancer was one of the most curable cancers. Most men recovered. But not all. Her father's cancer was back, and this time, the diagnosis was dire. He'd been given six months, with chemo and radiation. That alone was so incredibly unfair it made her want to scream.

And now this.

He'd served in five wars and earned countless medals. But if the indiscretion came out, his reputation would be forever tarnished. The moral failure was all everyone was going to remember him for. This was how her mother would have to remember him.

"I'm not asking for your help for myself," he said.

She blinked at the phone.

She'd been focused on her mother and herself, but suddenly she saw the wider implications. The Civilian Personnel Recovery Unit only existed because of General Roberts. If his involvement with Rosita got out and caused a scandal…If the general had to resign, Civilian Personnel Recovery could be disassembled as quickly as it had been created.

He'd been looking for a replacement since the day he'd found out he only had six months to live, but he didn't have anyone selected yet, just a loose list of possible candidates.

Plenty of higher-ups at the DOD questioned the need for CPRU's existence. The army had Personnel Recovery for military members and Department of Defense contractors who went missing abroad, but those were people the government had sent into harm's way, and their recovery came out of the army's budget.

The argument had been made, over and over, that US civilians who went missing abroad had taken their chances going there in the first place. Why should taxpayers be responsible for helping people out of trouble they had gotten themselves into? If they couldn't take care of themselves, they should have stayed home.

Of course, the counterargument was that, A: the United States government should provide protection to its citizens regardless of location, and B: kidnapped citizens could be used as leverage by terrorist organizations, so the problem was really a matter of national security.

Clara silently ran through what little information she had on the case, as her father said, "The DEA has an office near Furino, in Mercita. If you run into trouble or find that Rosita's disappearance is somehow drug related, you'll find help there."

US law enforcement nearby was a comforting thought. The Drug Enforcement Agency worked with the Mexican government in the war against drugs as close allies. They had several offices in Mexico, but still…

"I'd rather not reach out to official US channels."

"Your safety is more important than my reputation," her father said firmly, then cleared his throat. "First step is to find out whether the girl is still alive. If she is, we need to see if the situation can be solved by something as simple as a transfer of funds. If the case is more complicated than that, we'll come up with a strategy at that point. You are an investigator, not a SWAT team. I want you to observe all precautions."

"I will."

She wanted to say a lot more, but swallowed it all back because none of it would have been particularly helpful.

Silence stretched between them.

"I'm sorry," her father told her again.

But Clara couldn't give him absolution.

All she could give was a promise. "I'll find her."

She clenched her jaw and put the receiver back in its cradle, because she couldn't say what she'd always said: *Good-bye. I love you, Dad.*

Her eyes burning, she walked to the heavy door, opened it, then hurried back to let Bobby Lekker know about the change of plans. She didn't have much time. She needed to get going. The sooner this whole horrible incident was behind her, the better.

She had to find Rosita. Whatever Clara had to do, she could *not* fail.

CHAPTER
THREE

Town of Furino, Chiapas State, Mexico, 4 days later

Clara doubted she'd make it halfway to the door, if the men caught her spying.

The dim, one-room cantina ten miles from Mexico's southern border reeked of booze, smoke, and sweat, the haphazardly arranged tables and chairs—none of which matched—the very picture of chaos. The scene was an affront to Clara's senses as she sat in the darkest corner. The place made her scalp itch.

Three freaking days wasted.

But no matter what it took, she was going to make progress today.

She'd snuck into the cantina during a loud argument—every man on his feet, gesturing wildly and waving weapons. Her dark baseball hat pulled over her face, she'd skirted the wall and hurried to the farthest table in the back. Since then, she'd been doing her best to stay invisible so she might overhear something resembling a lead.

Her cases tended to progress smoothly from point A to point B and beyond. Not this one. She'd been waiting for Walker since Wednesday night, renting a room at the dilapidated, rooster-infested guesthouse across the road.

At least the cantina was chicken-free. Mostly woman-free too. Dressed for undercover work in a plain T-shirt, faded jeans, and a pair of well-broken-in cowboy boots, Clara was hoping anyone who wasn't looking too hard would mistake her for a boy.

Where in hell was her facilitator?

How could her father hook her up with someone so unreliable?

Clara hadn't talked to the general since the embassy. She tried to keep her feelings bottled up on the subject. But she'd called her mother to ask how her father's first chemo treatment had gone, and to tell her that she loved her. At one point, she would have to deal with her father's mess, but she was determined to find Rosita first. She wanted to hear straight from the girl what had happened.

As she kept scanning the room, her gaze snagged on the largest of the men. The others called him El Capitán. He could have walked straight out of an old Western: ammo belts crisscrossing his round belly, silver pistols by his sides in silver-studded holsters, black boots, black pants, black shirt, black sombrero—all embroidered with silver thread.

His greasy mustache hung to his double chin, bracketing a cruel, fleshy mouth. Clara strained to hear—without appearing to listen—what he was saying.

The captain sat about fifteen feet from her, four empty tables between them. She could only see him in profile, but then, as if sensing someone watching him, he swung his head toward her. His beady brown eyes fastened on Clara. He stilled for a moment before flashing a yellow-toothed grin.

"Gringa! When did you come in?" he shouted over in heavily accented English. "Come here. Let Pedro look at you."

Clara bit back a groan. So much for her disguise of a boy. All eyes were on her suddenly, narrowed, disapproving gazes, and more than a few predatory leers.

"Come on, gringa. I don't bite." The captain's lips stretched into a toothy, suggestive smile. He winked. "And when I do, you'll like it."

She'd seen the captain before from her window at the guesthouse, always with at least a dozen well-armed thugs around him, people scampering out of his way on the street. If she had to make a guess, she'd guess he was the baddest bad guy in Furino.

She must have hesitated too long, because he pushed heavily to his feet and walked toward her, his boots shaking the rough-hewn wood floor with each step.

His smile didn't reach his eyes as he stopped in front of her table. "What brings you to Furino?"

"Writing a book about the Mayan sites." She reached down behind the cover of the table as if to scratch her leg in a nervous gesture, pulled her Glock from her cowboy boot, and lay the gun on her lap.

Bringing a weapon into the country, even a pocket knife, was illegal, but her father had arranged for a small Glock through the marines at the US Consulate in Merida, along with a temporary embassy ID that would grant her diplomatic immunity if she was caught with the firearm.

She didn't want to use the gun. She was to avoid doing anything that would bring her to the attention of local law enforcement. Hopefully, she wouldn't have to shoot. She had a fair idea that this was just a pissing contest, Pedro exerting his dominance.

The man reached for her. He didn't waste time on asking; he went straight to taking what he wanted. "You give Pedro a kiss, and I buy you a drink."

He wiggled his moustache, his fat fingers closing around her arm and biting into her skin as he roughly yanked her to her feet.

But by the time they were chest to chest, she had her gun at his double chin.

Something dark and dangerous stirred in his eyes as he stilled, a cold and calculating expression hardening his features.

She'd underestimated how high his blood Neanderthal level was. She saw death on his face as clearly as if the words *judge, jury, and executioner* were tattooed on his pockmarked skin.

Should have let him kiss me.

Instead, she had initiated a deadly confrontation. *Back down. Turn it around.* They stood in the darkest corner, his large body blocking sight of her and her gun from his men. He hadn't lost face. He could still let this go. They could still have a laugh over the misunderstanding. He could decide he liked her for being spunky.

She plastered a smile on her face and opened her mouth to diffuse the situation, but the back door banged open and a scrawny kid burst in, yelling for Pedro, then yelling something else in Spanish so rapidly Clara had no hope of comprehending a word.

Pedro dropped his hand from her arm. "You wait here until I come back."

If doom had a voice, she'd just heard it.

But as Pedro walked out, Clara sat back down instead of running. He could find her anywhere in town. She couldn't exactly blend in and disappear in a place the size of Furino.

And she wasn't going to run, in any case. She had come here to retrieve a disappeared person. She was going to take Rosita home. Then she was going to let her father handle the rest however he wanted to handle it. At that point, her job would be to stand by her mother.

She pushed those thoughts aside and refocused on the cantina. She needed to keep in investigator mode. *Don't think about the personal connection.*

From what she'd overheard so far, Pedro was Furino's "godfather." Clara doubted much went on in town he wasn't involved in or didn't give his permission to at least.

Now she just had to establish some kind of rapport with the guy and get him talking. She slipped her gun back into her boot. *Let's not remind El Capitán of that little misstep, shall we?*

She waved over the waitress the men called Margarita. "Could I have a bottle of tequila with two clean glasses, please?"

The order would take most of the pesos she'd stuffed into her pocket before coming over, but she needed something to break the ice with El Capitán.

The waitress cast Clara a baleful look. The women who served the men at the cantina also took the time to sit on the men's laps and fondle them, and periodically take a customer in the back. Maybe Margarita thought Clara would be competition.

But after a glance at the swarthy bartender, who gave a barely perceptible nod, the waitress said, "Sí, señorita."

In Mexico, most cantinas didn't allow women unless they were prostitutes. But since El Capitán had said he'd be back for her, Clara was safe from removal for the moment.

As Margarita sashayed her petite but voluptuous figure back to the bar, Clara made no comparisons between the waitress's exotic feminine allure and her own tall, flat body. Nobody would ever call her a sensuous beauty. She dealt with it. She had other admirable qualities.

When Margarita brought her order, Clara cleaned the glasses on her T-shirt, then lined them up neatly with the bottle.

She scanned the room again. Her facilitator could advise her on the local criminal element. She resisted grinding her teeth.

She'd gone to work at Civilian Personnel Recovery specifically because the missions were lone-wolf operations. She did not, as a rule, work with a partner. And she most certainly did not work with partners who made appointments *around* Thursday.

The amount of time she'd wasted waiting for that idiot...

At least she'd talked to Rosita's cousin and found out more about the circumstances of the young woman's disappearance. And she'd gone to the Mayan ruins, plus walked around town to play up her cover as a travel writer, acting like the average American tourist. She'd used the time to get the lay of the land. And she'd made a game of picking out the main local players—none of whom inspired any confidence.

The majority of the town's shady-looking characters seemed to end up at the cantina at least once a day. *Unsavory-character Grand Central.* If a crime had been committed in Furino, these were the men who'd had a hand in it.

Most of the banditos sitting around the tables seemed capable of kidnapping. Or straight-out murder. Aggravated murder wasn't out of the question either.

Her local connection, if he ever showed, should be able to give her some real understanding of the local criminal power structure. She hoped he was good at what he did, even if he was just some hippie who'd come down for the spiritual Mayan sites located around the small town of Furino, then stayed for the tequila and the weed.

She'd run into a few of those already. One Canadian guy ran a bicycle rental; another old hippie from Jersey sold tie-dyed T-shirts with Mayan symbols superimposed over psychedelic swirls.

She expected her facilitator to be a mellowed-out travel agent slash travel guide who could help her with the maze of dirt roads that weren't on any map and didn't show up on her GPS. The area had a number of indigenous villages without names, logging camps, and temporary shanty towns where people fleeing South America stopped to rest on their way farther north.

She hoped the guy was on his way instead of permanently delayed somewhere, pushing up agaves. Anything could happen to a man, or a woman, down here.

Clara pulled her baseball hat deep over her face and listened to the resumed conversations around her.

The talk centered on the local armadillo races and Chiapas FC's chances in an upcoming soccer match at Tuxtla Gutiérrez. The two events seemed to hold equal importance for the patrons.

She looked for patterns: who talked to whom, who deferred to whom, who watched whom with suspicion. In the past hour, she'd identified five distinct groups, each with its own captain, with El Capitán being the overall head honcho.

Drug runners? Gun runners? Human traffickers?

Before she could figure it out, the front door banged open, and she turned that way, still hoping for her travel guide, finding herself staring at a mercenary who looked like he'd just stepped out of one of those high-testosterone video games.

Okay. Wow. Because...wow.

A machete strapped to his back, a semiautomatic slung over his shoulder, a handgun in the side holster, and an army knife on his belt, he walked into the cantina with a swagger that said he could beat any man in town and could take any woman to bed. If he wanted.

He was taller than the locals, his hair a few shades lighter, a couple of days' worth of bristle covering the lower half of his face. He wore army boots, cargo pants, and a black T-shirt that did nothing to conceal a distracting amount of muscle. White flashed as he chomped on the cigar between his teeth, his eyes covered by sunglasses.

Clara slid down in her chair and backed farther into the shadows as she watched him. So Pedro wasn't alpha dog of the local pack. *This* guy was most definitely the top predator in Furino. His body language seemed completely relaxed, yet power emanated from his every pore.

All around, hands surreptitiously migrated to the tops of the tables, as if making sure the newcomer didn't accidentally misinterpret any move as someone going for a weapon.

The mercenary claimed the empty stool at the far end of the bar. He didn't ask for a drink. The bartender poured him one anyway. He didn't so much as crook an eyebrow at a woman. But Margarita went to sit on his lap and rubbed against his well-built chest like a cat. She just about purred.

The waitress's lustrous mahogany hair tumbled to her waist in waves, curling and swinging all over the place. She looked wild and free. Clara touched a hand to the strict bun tucked under her baseball hat.

The mercenary tossed back his drink with one hand while putting the other one on Margarita's bare knee, running his palm up her thigh, under her short red skirt. He bent to her neck and nibbled her. Or maybe whispered something into her ear, because Margarita laughed. And then he was laughing too, a throaty sound of pure seduction.

One second, Clara was glaring at them with annoyed disapproval, and the next she suddenly felt her own skin heat, as if the man was touching her, his callused palm running over her naked skin. A long-neglected part of her body tingled, waving a flag. *Hey, remember me?*

At the bar, Margarita flattened her palms against the muscles of the mercenary's chest and caressed them, moving lower and lower.

Clara blinked. What the hell was wrong with them? Then she clenched her jaw. What the hell was wrong with *her?*

It had to be the heat. A dozen fans whirled overhead, swirling the hot, humid air without providing much relief.

The mercenary chatted on with the bartender, as if being publicly fondled was par for the course for him, certainly nothing to remove his sunglasses over.

Appalling. Both his behavior, and that Clara would feel hot and bothered from simply watching the outrageous bastard.

Then he finally slid off his glasses, and the next second his unerring gaze pinned Clara, and it was too late to turn away or slide down in her chair, because he'd caught her watching him.

He gave a knowing smirk as he shooed the waitress off his lap and patted her curvy behind. He never looked at the woman again as he sauntered toward Clara, six feet of pure muscle and laser-focused attention.

The scene should have been the opening shot of an action movie—light glinting off hills of muscles, determination in every masculine move, a cocksure grin. Casting directors all over Hollywood would have peed their pants at the sight of this guy.

He dropped into the chair across from Clara, his muscled thighs spread. She clamped her own thighs together. His white teeth flashed in the dim light of the cantina as he chomped on his cigar and took stock of her.

"Are you lost, Cupcake?" His I'm-a-bad-boy-and-you-know-it voice scraped along her nerve endings. He was definitely American. East Coast, if she had to guess from his accent.

Her grandmother used to say there were men the devil put on earth to test good women. Clara was tempted to ask the guy whether he'd just zip-lined in from hell.

"Go away," she said instead.

His smile was worth a thousand words, most of them dirty. His voice dipped. "How can I, when your eyes begged me to come over?"

She rolled said eyes so hard, she might have caused permanent damage.

One: she hadn't begged in her life.

Two: the only thing she wanted was to hit him over the head with the bottle of tequila between them on the table. She was trying to keep a low profile, and he was drawing every eye to them.

He smiled around his cigar. "What's your name?"

DOD Investigator Clara Roberts, she badly wanted to say to wipe the superior smirk off his face. "None of your business."

His eyes were a brilliant multicolor green like the rainforest, alive and full of secrets. He let his gaze travel over her chest from left to right, then from right to left with undisguised disappointment.

He tsked. "No tits, no manners." He shook his head. "You should try to have at least one or the other. A pair of great tits covers a multitude of sins."

When his gaze reached hers again, the very fires of hell glinting in his eyes, he said magnanimously, "Don't worry about it, Cupcake. You look like the brainy type. Believe it or not, that appeals to some men. I think I read that on the Internet." He edged his chair forward until their knees touched under the table.

A tingle ran up her thighs at the contact. She shifted her legs away from his. "Please leave."

"I can't. You need me." He flashed an infuriatingly cocky grin. "Walker."

A who?

Her mouth dropped open. *Light Walker? The hippie travel guide Walker?* The one she'd been picturing with long, thinning hair, wearing a tie-dye shirt?

Why on earth would her father send his daughter to a man like this?

29

Before Clara could figure out what to do with Walker, Pedro stalked back into the cantina. El Capitán was yelling obscenities over his shoulder to whomever he'd been talking to outside. Then the door swung shut behind him, and his gaze swept the room and settled on Clara.

His mouth twisted into a snarl as he strode toward her. "You're coming with me." He narrowed his eyes at Walker. "The puta is mine."

Walker rose in a measured move and stood toe-to-toe, nose-to-nose with the captain, all easy like, displaying none of Pedro's bustle. The cantina fell silent around them. The hostile looks they exchanged said the two men knew each other, but there was no love lost between them.

Clara wouldn't have minded knowing what their relationship was exactly.

Pedro's eyes narrowed another notch. "I don't have time to argue. Don't get into the middle of this, gringo."

Walker hesitated only for a second, then his expression hardened as if he'd come to some sort of decision.

"I'm pressed for time myself," he said around his cigar and pulled his knife from his belt in a lightning-quick move, shoved the blade into the man's abdomen, and yanked up hard.

Clara had no time to react other than jumping to her feet. Her gore rose from the wet sound of the blade being pulled back. She stared wide-eyed as the captain grabbed his belly to hold in his guts, a stunned look on his pock-marked face.

And suddenly she could smell the contents of his stomach.

Oh God. She swallowed hard so she wouldn't gag. She needed to look away, but she couldn't.

She'd never killed a man. Unlike in action movies, most law enforcement officers never killed in their entire careers. She'd certainly never seen a man disemboweled. Light Walker, on the other hand, hadn't so much as blinked.

Before she could fully recover, Walker shoved the man onto the nearest chair, then reached across the small table, practically pulled Clara over it as he hauled her against him. He spit out his cigar and slanted his lips over hers in a primal gesture of claiming, his left hand all over her butt, while his right hand wiped then put away the knife and went for the semiautomatic to hold the room at bay.

Her head—and her stomach—were still reeling when his lips pulled away from hers as abruptly as they'd swooped in.

"Chica's mine for the night. Whoever wants her tomorrow, you work that out amongst yourselves," he said to the den of thieves in general, then sauntered to the back door without letting go of her.

Pedro sat slumped over in the chair, a pool of blood spreading on the floorboards under him. His men rushed to his side. Since the altercation had taken place in the dark corner, they probably hadn't fully seen what had happened.

And Clara didn't want to be there when they figured out the particulars. She didn't protest when Walker pulled her through the back door. Stunned speechless, she followed him.

Her "facilitator" wasn't a hippy travel guide. He was a stone-cold killer.

The door swung closed at their backs, and Clara squinted into sunshine as Walker dragged her down the rickety wooden steps, his arm a metal band around her middle. The level of noise behind them in the cantina doubled, then tripled, a beehive that had been disturbed. The shock of Pedro's sudden death was wearing off at last.

"Now what?" she asked, not that she was admitting that Walker was calling the shots. Maybe for the moment. But any second now, she was going to get her act together and take charge.

"Now we run." Walker let go of her waist, grabbed her wrist, then sprinted forward, crossing the dirt road that was lined by derelict houses on each side, the cantina and the guesthouse the best of the bunch.

He dragged her toward the jungle that began a hundred feet or so behind her guesthouse, and she did her best to keep up, wondering if she could outrun an army of drunken bandits. And whether the bandits were any worse than the man she was running with.

To be completely honest, she wasn't entirely sure if she was being rescued or kidnapped.

CHAPTER
FOUR

Clara gasped as she stumbled on a root and went down, for the third time, banging her knees. She ignored the stinging pain and pushed to her feet, then lurched after Walker. They'd entered the rainforest on a foot trail, but Walker had pulled her into the bushes after twenty feet or so.

This close to the village, plenty of trees had been cut by the locals, so the canopy was thin instead of forming an impenetrable umbrella. The availability of more sunlight meant plenty of bushes that slowed their progress. The nearly impassable undergrowth seemed like a completely different jungle from the comfortably wide tourist trails that led to the Mayan ruins—the only part she was familiar with.

Since the gun in her right boot rubbed painfully against her ankle, she stopped for a second, grabbed the Glock, and stuck it into her sports bra. She would have preferred having it in hand, but she needed both hands free as she fought her way through the undergrowth, branches slapping at her.

Walker headed up an incline, and she followed, grabbing protruding roots for support, then flailing when the thick layer of leaf mold crumbled under her feet and she slid back. He waited for her at the top and reached out his hand, yanked her up next to him, then pointed at a nearly invisible animal trail that led down the other side.

"We have to go faster." And he broke into a run.

She ran after him, stumbling on the uneven ground, catching herself on a leafy branch. "This can't be safe."

She had no idea what plants were poisonous to touch. And what if she stepped on a snake?

He cast a look back over his shoulder without slowing, just as gunshots sounded behind them. "It's safer than a bullet in the back."

He had a point there. She ran faster, trying to catch up.

Gunshots sounded again, this time from closer.

"We need to get off the trail." Walker darted into the undergrowth again.

She followed, tripped after a handful of steps, heading face-first toward a broken branch that looked to be at the right height to put out an eye, but at the last second, strong hands closed around her shoulders and hauled her up. Then Walker wrapped his fingers around her wrist and drew her after him.

"When I duck, you duck. When I jump, you jump."

As he sped up, she needed all her strength and concentration to keep up with him. They vaulted over roots, logs, tree stumps, while branches swatted her in the face. Then something dropped on her shoulder, but even as she screamed, her heart stopping midbeat, the next oncoming branch swept the tarantula away.

Aww! Ick!

She manically brushed her shoulder with her free hand, every inch of her covered in goose bumps.

"When running from people who're trying to kill you," Walker advised as he kept dragging her, "it's better to stay quiet. Generally speaking."

He was melting through bushes, while the lianas did their best to hang on to Clara. She swallowed back any complaints. She focused on just hanging on for another few minutes, until they could stop to catch their breath.

Breath-catching didn't seem to be in Walker's vocabulary, however.

When, after twenty minutes or so, they suddenly found themselves on top of a cliff over a rapidly flowing river—a thirty-foot drop—he jumped without pausing, without warning, dragging her with him.

Nonononoonoooo!

One second, she had solid ground under her feet, the next she was airborne, flailing. Walker let go of her hand.

She hit the water the wrong way, and it hurt. She immediately went under. The current rolled her for long, desperate seconds.

Did he *want* to kill her?

Because she was drowning.

Which way was up, dammit?

Then his arm clamped around her waist, and he dragged her to the surface. "Swim!"

She wanted to shout right back at him, but her mouth was full of dirty river and God only knew what parasites and disease, so she spat and coughed as she fought the current that rushed them forward.

Her cowboy boots, filled with water, pulled her down. She kicked them off, one after the other.

She felt lighter and a smidgen more optimistic after that, for about a split second. Then she caught a better look at the river, narrow enough so the vegetation hanging in from each side obstructed the view. Visibility was maybe fifty feet, if that. As the water swept her along, she had no idea where they were headed from one minute to the next.

All she could think of was what usually happened in situations like this in the movies.

Don't let there be a waterfall straight ahead.

She swam toward shore for all she was worth. Until Walker grabbed the back of her shirt to hold her in place.

"Save some energy," he shouted to be heard over the rushing river. "Getting out will be a lot harder than getting in. Don't try to swim straight for the shore. Angle yourself slightly and go with the current. Let the water do the work."

That he had enough breath to talk seemed superhuman. She gasped for air and angled her body, stopped struggling.

Oddly enough, she made more progress with less effort. She was actually reaching closer and closer to shore.

Of course, the water still trapped her. The river was no longer hemmed in by tall cliffs, but the bank towered at least three feet above current water level. No way out. So for now, she concentrated on not going under.

A full hour must have passed before they reached a stretch of low shoreline. Even here, the jungle stood like a wall of green on both sides. The dense stand of bamboo was as effective as a fence.

Since the river created a break line in the canopy, more sunlight meant thicker undergrowth once again. They had to fight jumbled roots and impenetrable vegetation while being rolled forward, their grasping fingers finding purchase, then losing it, over and over again.

Walker caught a handful of overhanging lianas first, then caught Clara by the upper arm, guided her to a fallen tree that lay half on land and half in water.

For long minutes, all she could do was cling to the log, the current pressing her upper body against it, while she spit water and gasped for air. Then, once she caught her breath, she inched toward shore handhold over handhold.

When she finally made it out, she dropped onto her back in the first available spot. *Thank you, God.*

"You okay?"

"Alive." She hated how weak and winded she sounded. The muscles in her arms and legs burned with exhaustion.

Breathe. It's over. Breathe.

But long moments passed before her heart stopped its mad cartwheeling in her chest.

She filled her lungs and lay there, staring at all the green above while her shaky muscles recovered. Dappled sunlight filtered through the canopy.

They hadn't drowned. *Okay. Good. Okay.*

She'd panicked in the water for a moment when she'd thought the river was winning.

And now she thought: Was that how her father felt? Was the *thing* with Rosita a desperate gasp for life, the way Clara had gasped in the strong current for air?

She pushed the idea aside, along with the need to make excuses for the father she still loved, despite everything. Her eyes burned. She blinked.

Walker stood over her with an assessing look on his face. "We don't have time to stop and take a nap."

He wasn't even breathing hard. His clothes were plastered to his hard body, showing off impressive muscles. He still had his machete and his rifle, his knife still at his side, his handgun safely holstered.

He radiated the kind of tough, uncompromising competence she desperately needed at the moment.

Was he really going to help her?

Her father thought he would. But maybe Walker had changed—a lot— since her father had known him. His conduct at the cantina didn't inspire

Clara's confidence. She needed to consider what she'd do if he was no longer one of the good guys.

She needed to know what kind of man he was, someone she could count on, or someone she should get away from.

"Are you undercover something?" she asked as the thought occurred to her. "CIA? FBI? Some antiterrorism unit?"

He raised an eyebrow. "Are you trying to decide if it's okay to shoot me if I get in your way?"

When she didn't respond, he said, "You don't have to worry about any blowback on my account. If I ever disappeared, nobody would come looking. But I hope we'll be friends."

His grin was pure sin. If she was Catholic, she would have been making the sign of the cross at the way he was looking at her.

She thought of how he'd disemboweled Pedro without the slightest emotion. It was safe to say friendship was unlikely. She had certain minimum requirements.

She stuck with the truth. "I hope we won't be enemies."

He made an odd sound, as if he was swallowing a chuckle.

She sat up and pulled her Glock from her sports bra, checked it, then she shoved the gun into her waistband for easier access, grateful that she still had it. If she'd left it in her boot, she would have lost her only weapon in the river. She did lose her cell phone. And most of her pride, but she'd worry about that later.

Walker pulled up his shirt and wrung out as much water as he could, flashing hard abs ridged with muscles. She tried not to look, but she caught sight of a couple of scars anyway, and a corner of some kind of a tattoo farther up his rib cage.

"Are you ex-special ops?" Plenty of mercenaries had that kind of past.

He didn't answer as he covered up.

"Delta Force, Army Ranger?" she tried to guess, then thought about how good he'd been in water. "Navy SEAL?"

"Maybe."

"Maybe which one?"

"The strongest and the bravest."

No false modesty there. She gave up on getting a real answer out of him and tried listening for their pursuers. All she could hear was the river. "I think we lost the banditos."

He nodded. "Doesn't mean we can stop for afternoon tea, Cupcake. The nearest road that'll take us to civilization is a five-hour trek from here. We have to reach it before dark. Otherwise, we'll have to sleep in the jungle."

She was on her feet before his last word was out. She was *not* sleeping with snakes and tarantulas. "I'm ready."

The look he flashed her reflected serious doubts. But he reached for his machete and led the way once again, hacking away. She hung back far enough so she wouldn't be decapitated by a backswing.

Impenetrable walls of green surrounded them, branches and lianas constantly touching her. Visibility was as little as three feet in places. They could, at any moment, come face-to-face with a jaguar or a giant snake or a weapon-wielding bandit, without any prior warning. Sweat rolled down her neck, and not just from the heat and humidity.

Luckily, things soon turned for the better. Once they were away from the river, under a thick overhead canopy again, the bushes and ground vegetation thinned out. Forging a path with the machete became easier.

She kept up with Walker, watching nothing but where she put her bare feet. Of course, the rocks and roots managed to scrape her soles anyway. She figured she had maybe another mile in her before her feet would start seriously slowing them down.

But Walker stopped after another minute or so by a tree that had branches nearly reaching the ground and large round leaves the size of his two hands put together. He nodded at the tree with satisfaction as if he'd been looking for it, then hacked off two leaves with his machete.

"You need to cover your feet." He handed the leaves to her. "Sit."

While she did, he untucked his pants from his boots, then cut off both pant legs below the knee. Then he dropped to his knees in front of her.

If the touch of his long, capable fingers on her feet made her hyper-aware, she sure as anything wasn't going to betray herself with the slightest flinch.

He layered the fabric of the pant legs with the rubbery leaves and wrapped her right foot up first, then the left. He undid his shoelaces next, and peeled off two strands.

"Useful special ops tip," he said as he used one of the strands to tie her footwear securely together in a crisscross pattern. "Use parachute cord instead of shoe laces. They're multi-ply, so you always have string handy if you need it. And the material is practically indestructible. I used one before as a fishing line. Saved my life."

She liked the practicality of the idea as much as she liked his confident competence. Murderous mercenary or not, Light Walker came in very handy in the jungle. She wasn't so petty that she couldn't give him credit for that much at least.

"Thanks," she said as he repeated the procedure on her other foot.

When he was finished, he stood and stepped away from her. "Try them. How do they feel? Too loose and they'll fall off, too tight and you'll lose circulation to your toes."

She stared at her primitive footwear as she rose and took a few steps. "Just right." The makeshift coverings were actually pretty comfortable. "What's with the leaf?"

"Water barrier. Let's go." He was moving forward already.

She noted his expert use of the machete. He wasn't blindly hacking away. He was continuously adjusting the force and the angle of the blade, depending on whether he faced soft lianas or harder branches.

His movements were precise and economical. Unhurried. And kind of nice to look at. If there was such a thing as masculine beauty, Light Walker had it. She saw no sense in denying that his body had been incredibly finely built.

Not that she was gawking. She only looked because she had no other choice, since she was walking behind him.

She put one foot in front of the other. Having "shoes" was a hundred percent better than not having them, but the soles of her feet were still sensitive where they'd been scraped up. She wished she'd protected her feet as soon as she'd crawled out of the river.

As if reading her mind, he said, "Sooner would have been better, but I wanted to wait until the pants dried. Wet cloth would rub your skin raw."

Right. He knew stuff. Useful stuff. In general, she was attracted to competence, but she refused to be attracted to him, for obvious reasons. She simply said, "Thanks," as she followed him.

They hadn't walked twenty minutes when he suddenly halted, raising his hand in warning. She stopped in her tracks and scanned the dense foliage around them, but saw nothing dangerous, no slithering snakes or giant spiders.

Then a branch snapped up ahead. Other, shuffling, sounds followed. Something large moved in the undergrowth, hidden from view by all the greenery.

Walker switched the machete to his left hand and pulled his gun with his right.

Clara held her breath, her heart hammering as she reached for the Glock in her waistband. Had the banditos somehow cut ahead of them? Or was it some kind of a predator? Were they upwind or downwind? She couldn't tell. The hot, humid air seemed to stand still.

They waited until the sounds weakened, then disappeared. And then they still waited another two or three minutes after that. Finally, Walker gestured with his head to move forward, putting his gun away.

"What was that?" she whispered as she followed him.

"Could have been something as harmless as white-tail deer, but there are jaguars in these parts." He kept moving. Stopped. Pointed to the ground. "Wild boar."

As she spotted the brown pellets, she swallowed hard, her throat suddenly tight.

Walker continued forward with a shrug. "It's gone now."

As she followed, she thought about sharp tusks that could gore a man. Or a woman. She'd already seen a disembowelment today, and she was pretty sure one per day was her limit. One in a lifetime was one too many, really.

In fact, if she could, she would have dearly preferred to return the memory.

She scanned the dense foliage around them. She hadn't been that worried about animals beyond snakes and spiders. She knew jaguars were indigenous to the region, but also knew they were pretty rare these days. *Wild boars.* She hadn't thought about those.

Walker held a thorny branch out of the way for her. "Be glad we didn't come across any caimans in the water earlier."

She stared at him as she stepped through. "Caimans?"

He released the branch and moved forward. "Most rivers around here are full of them."

She kept up, making a mental note to never ever let anyone drag her into any kind of body of water again while she was in Chiapas. Her swimming days were definitely over.

Jaguars and wild boars and caimans. Oh, and poisonous snakes and spiders.

For the next mile or so, she expected sudden death at any second. But the human body could not keep up that kind of freak-out endlessly, so eventually she relaxed enough to think about other things.

Walker's wide back and the shifting muscles under his tanned skin that glistened with sweat provided ready distraction. Then she caught herself. Was she seriously ogling him now? *No way.* So she forced herself to look at nothing but the ground in front of her feet. Probably the most sensible course of action, in any case.

She walked like that until her tongue stuck to the roof of her mouth from thirst and her muscles trembled from exhaustion. She was a regular at the gym, but a mad dash through the jungle over rugged terrain was nothing like running on the treadmill. She hated to appear weak in front of Walker but decided to put common sense before foolish pride.

"Could we take a break?"

To his credit, he didn't seem annoyed or judgmental at her lack of stamina as he checked her over. "Are you hurt?"

She tried to roll the tension and the soreness out of her shoulders. "Just tired and thirsty."

A slow rain drizzled over them, little more than mist, not something they could collect for drinking.

He checked their immediate surroundings and pointed to the base of a nearby tree that was overgrown with lianas. "Sit right there."

She did, then inspected her footwear that had miraculously held together. She ran her fingers over the binding. "Is this something you learned from the local tribes?"

He shook his head. "The Tojolabal walk around barefoot. Their soles harden up from a lifetime of doing that, so they can walk over any terrain. And they see every thorn and poisonous leaf and snake and bug without having to really look. Their brain just registers the stuff and signals to their feet to avoid it. They evolved to suit their environment over thousands of years. It's pretty damn impressive to see in action."

She took his word for it.

He searched around for a moment, then separated a finger-thick liana from the others above her head, sliced it through with his machete, and handed her the end that hung down. "You can drink this. We can rest ten minutes, but that's about it."

He folded his hand over hers and directed the dripping end of the liana above her lips. "Open your mouth."

She did, trying to ignore how suggestive the whole exercise was. She even stuck out her tongue as the thin sap began flowing, drip by miraculous drip, tasting like very lightly sweetened water.

He thumped onto the ground next to her, selected another liana and cut it for himself. "Slow, but better than nothing."

She didn't talk. She didn't want to waste a single drop, wanted every bit of moisture given to her by the plant.

Minute after minute ticked by as they drank, not stopping until their jungle water pipes ran dry at last. Even the misting rain had halted, as if the lianas had been connected to the wispy clouds over the tree canopy.

She closed her eyes for a moment, more exhausted than she'd ever been. And, okay, a little discouraged. She was on a side trip that had not been in her plans, wasting time here instead of investigating. And Walker...

As she turned to him, her shoulder bumped into his. She thoroughly resented her sudden awareness of how close they were sitting, and the fact that she found his physical strength intimidating from this close up. The idea that she was at his mercy at the moment didn't make her happy either.

She had no idea where they were, or how to survive the trek in front of them. She was lost in the jungle with a ruthless mercenary she didn't trust.

And it was all his fault that she was in this situation.

She was hot, hungry, and irritated. Frustration bubbled up inside her, and she wiggled a few inches away from him. "Did you really have to stab Pedro?"

Walker stared at her. "Why in hell would you go into the cantina?" He seemed as unhappy with her as she felt with him. "You look fifteen in this outfit. You *want* to be gang-raped? You couldn't have waited for me at the guesthouse?"

Outrage steamed her brain. "I've waited *three* days. *Around Thursday*, you said. Do you know what day it is?"

He gave a one-sided shrug, his massive shoulder muscles shifting. "Who has time to check the calendar when people are shooting at you and snakes are biting you in the ass?"

CHAPTER
FIVE

Clara stared. *A snake bit his ass?* "Poisonous?"

Walker nodded, a notch more subdued. "I lucked out. I was at a Tojolabal village, and Baku, the local shaman, happened to be visiting."

"He had antivenin?"

Walker's expression said, *I wish.* "He chewed a bunch of jungle leaves and wild tobacco into a paste and spit it at the wound. I had to lie on my stomach for twenty-four hours while he chanted over me and blew smoke at my ass."

She glanced at the body part in question. His cargo pants were wet once again and molded to indecently firm flesh. She clasped her hands together in front of her and looked back into his face.

Amusement glinted in his jungle-green eyes.

She filled her lungs. God give her patience. To think that if her father hadn't asked her to wait for Walker, she could have begun her investigation full steam on day one. Who knew what leads she would have found and where they would have taken her? Maybe far away. Preferably up north. She would never even have met Walker.

As he shifted toward her, forcing her to shift back, she reached for her professional core—something the man clearly didn't possess.

"How fast do you think you can you take me back to Furino?"

"You need to give Furino a break."

"I'm here to find someone who disappeared in Furino on July first. The town is crucial to my investigation," she said, unsure how much information he had about her case.

Walker remained unimpressed. "Should have thought of that before you made a mess of things at the cantina."

43

She wanted to hit him. But she didn't lose control, as a rule. She was a calm, reasonable person. She barely even shouted as she said, "*I* made a mess at the cantina?" She took a moment to further compose herself. "I should be arresting you."

He fixed her with an I'd-like-to-see-you-try look. "One, I don't appreciate being unappreciated. Two, you have any jurisdiction down here?"

She growled.

He gave her a considering look. "That's almost sexy."

She started to growl again, caught herself, switched back to glaring. She put enough ice into that glare to sink the *Titanic*.

"The growl was better," he said. "Had some real nice heat to it. Made me think there might be hope for you yet." He looked her over, making her aware that her clothes were just as wet and plastered to her body as his.

Her jeans had been too tight to start with, but now her thin T-shirt might as well have been painted on her for as much as it concealed. She pinched the material in the front and pulled it away from her torso.

Time to shift focus. "Who are you working for down here?"

Whoever it was, her mission was more important. Walker would have to accept that and make time for her.

He ignored her question as his gaze moved over her torturously slowly, stopping entirely at times in its meandering. She resisted the urge to cross her arms over her chest. She would not allow him to think that he was getting to her.

"How well did you know Pedro?" she drilled him, focusing on the job she was here to do. "What do you know about him?"

He watched her without responding.

"You are supposed to be helping me," she reminded him.

His lips flattened, as if he wasn't overly happy about that. But at long last he said, "Pedro mostly worked in human trafficking."

"Not drugs?"

"The cartels have that handled. They keep reins on the trafficking too, but indirectly. Pedro was affiliated with the Xibalba, one of the two main cartels in the area. He kicked money up to them, and in exchange, they let him run his business the way he saw fit."

"How big a business is human trafficking?"

"Bigger than it should be, but compared to the four hundred billion dollars' worth of drugs that comes through here each year, human trafficking is small potatoes. Except for the violence it brings."

"More violence than what comes with drugs?" She tried to grasp what exactly she was facing.

"The cartels keep the drug business low-key and the violence down," Walker said. "The war against drugs put heroin transport via ship and plane out of business. A ship or airplane is easy to pick up on radar, easy to target. The land routes are all the cartels have left. They don't want to draw attention to Chiapas. They lie low here as much as they can."

He paused, then continued. "Up north, the level of violence is way higher. What violence you see here is mostly the robbery, rape, and murder of migrants. Since they're coming through illegally, they can't go to the police. And even if they do, most of the time, the police will rob them the same as the criminals."

Exactly the kind of information she needed.

"So if the cartels focus on the drug trade and keep a low profile around here," she said, "then it's likely that the young woman I'm looking for, Rosita Ruiz, was kidnapped by people like Pedro's banditos."

Walker thought for a moment. "Or some random street thug. Two weeks ago, a group of street kids gang-raped a woman walking home from work after dark."

Clara had heard the story from French tourists on one of her treks to the Mayan ruins. The four perpetrators—the oldest nineteen, the youngest sixteen—were still the talk of the town, now sitting in jail. She'd seen plenty of criminals through her work, but the case shook her.

"A sixteen-year-old should be just a child," she murmured. Then sighed. "Children are supposed to be innocent. A sixteen-year-old shouldn't even know about rape."

"They do what they see around them. Childhood is a privilege not everyone in poverty-stricken regions receives."

She couldn't argue with that, had seen plenty of poverty-stricken regions on her previous missions. "The police seem to have acted quickly and efficiently."

"They're quick to prosecute street kids. Then they sit on their thumbs when it comes to the cartel bosses." Walker nudged a giant green beetle with his boot, diverting it from heading toward Clara. "You think these kids had something to do with Rosita?"

She shook her head. "They came across their victim in a dark alley and jumped her, but made no attempt to kidnap or kill her. Rosita disappeared in broad daylight. These kids couldn't have kidnapped her on foot, dragged her down the streets without being seen. Why leave her cell phone in the open car? Why leave the car? She had the keys with her."

Walker watched her. "Tell me exactly how she disappeared."

"She went to the market with her cousin. They got back home and went inside. Rosita realized that she left her cell phone in the car. She went back out to get it. She never returned. When the cousin went to look for her, the car door stood open, the phone still inside, Rosita nowhere to be seen."

"Could be a crime of opportunity." Walker nudged the beetle again, and it flew off. "It's a small town. People could have heard an American relative was coming to visit the cousin. Then someone saw Rosita alone and grabbed her in the hope of some easy ransom money."

Clara had already considered that. "From what I've seen in other cases, small-time criminals usually go for express kidnappings."

Express kidnappings were popular in South and Central America. They involved either grabbing someone quickly, contacting the family and asking for immediate transfer of funds, or simply taking the person from ATM to ATM until all their money was withdrawn.

"Rosita had no ATM withdrawals after her disappearance," she told Walker. "Her purse with her wallet had been left at her cousin's house. And nobody from her family received a ransom request; both her aunt in the US and her cousin in Furino confirmed that."

She pulled her shirt away from her chest again, trying to help it dry faster. "I've done some research while I was waiting for you to show up."

She didn't bother to keep the reproach from her voice. He'd wasted her time, and she wasn't ready to let him off the hook just yet.

"Over a hundred thousand people are kidnapped in Mexico every year. A thousand or so are reported to the police. Sometimes the police *are* the kidnappers." She paused. "How much do you know about the cops in Furino?"

"About as corrupt as the average." Walker's tone turned pensive. "I don't know. I don't see it. The corrupt cops are either on the cartel payroll, in which case they kidnap enemies of the cartel and take them to the cartel to be dealt with. Or some crooked cop makes a spur-of-the-moment kidnapping on a dark country road, if the opportunity arises, for quick cash."

He shook a fallen leaf off his arm. "Kidnapping an American is a hell of a lot of hassle. Their disappearance actually gets investigated. The embassy puts on pressure, the media gets all excited. Only about a hundred and fifty US citizens are kidnapped in Mexico each year. You have a better chance of getting kidnapped back home than here."

Clara turned her head so she could look more fully at him. Odd that he'd know the statistics so exactly.

"Have you investigated this kind of thing before? What do you do for a living down here?" she asked again.

"Why is that important?"

"I'm trying to determine whether or not I can work with you."

Instead of responding, he let his gaze glide over her again. "You know," he said when he finished scrutinizing her. "Everything is way too sensible about you. Take that shapeless T-shirt. And the lack of makeup. Guys like women who take the trouble to look good for their men. Some mascara, some cleavage."

His gaze stopped on her mouth. Stayed. "The lips have potential."

She had no illusions that the flair of interest and flash of heat in his gaze was real. She wasn't a looker on her best day. Turning on the heat was a kind of evasive maneuver for him. He brought it when he wanted to shut her up.

If she'd been a man, he would have told her to fuck off. But with her being a woman, he probably figured a hard come-on was the fastest way to make her back down. He was half-right. She wasn't used to this kind of focused attention from men who looked like him.

She had jungle on her face, in her hair, and probably in places she didn't want to contemplate. She was drenched in sweat and covered in dirt. She looked like the chicken that crossed the road, was hit by a car, then dragged, pounced on by a large cat, chewed up and spit out, then shot from a cannon.

While Walker actually looked better dirty, the outrageous bastard. The smudges of mud only accentuated his perfect muscles and lent him an even more pronounced aura of rugged, dangerous sexiness.

Truthfully, she'd never met anyone quite like Light Walker, not with this kind of raw, unapologetic masculinity. But she wasn't the swooning type, so he was plumb out of luck if he thought he was going to control her with the testosterone slash pheromone cloud he seemingly produced at will.

"I think you needed this jungle trek," he told her. "It'll loosen you up a little. In Furino, there's an old hippie from Jersey who sells T-shirts to tourists. He says the universe gives us experiences to make us better people."

Her hands twitched. *How bad a breach of protocol would it be to strangle him with a liana?*

He must have read the murder in her eyes, because he said, "Don't tell me you're the kind of feminist who can't appreciate friendly suggestions for improvement."

She rolled her eyes. "How old are you?"

"Thirtyish."

Of course. Because giving an exact number would have gone against his grain. She shook her head. "How are you still alive? The only explanation I can find is that none of the women in your life ever owned a gun." *Or a cast-iron frying pan.*

"You sound grumpy."

When she didn't respond, because what she wanted to say…well, she'd been raised better than to say it, he went on with, "Maybe you're just hungry. I could probably rustle up some grubs before we get going."

Yuck. "The Jamie Oliver of the jungle."

He offered a half grin. "The big white grubs taste like chicken. Or we could have roasted tarantulas. It's a delicacy with some of the tribes."

The image of giant hairy spiders flashed into her mind, and she was on her feet the next second. "Spiders and lunch should never be mentioned in the same sentence. Ever. That should be international law."

He kept grinning as he stood with feline grace next to her. Then he reached for his machete and began clearing a path for them.

"Clearing" was a deceptive word, Clara decided an hour later. Their path was by no means actually clear, only passable. With effort.

While she felt as if she'd just crossed the continental United States with Lewis and Clark, he looked unfazed. He kept pushing forward. She had no doubt he could do this for the next two weeks without taking a break.

He hacked at the jungle, wielding the machete with the same efficiency he'd used to disembowel people. A man programmed to destroy whatever or whoever stood in his way.

She wasn't a fan.

Walker was not only a cold-blooded killer but a loose cannon. Partnering with a loose cannon was the fastest way to get killed.

As soon as they reached civilization, she was going to finish debriefing him on the local terrain and power structure so she could figure out the best way to run a clandestine investigation under local conditions. Then he could go back to doing whatever nefarious things he did, flashing muscles and swaggering while he did them. If they actually had to work together, they'd probably strangle each other.

No matter what her father wanted, no way was Clara going to partner up with Light Walker. He'd suggested a tarantula for a snack, for heaven's sake.

They were never, ever, ever going to work together.

***

Walker was impressed by the woman, and he wasn't easily impressed. She'd been limping for the last couple of miles but did not complain about her feet. When Walker had offered to carry her on his back to speed their progress, she'd refused. She was determined to make it on her own. She wasn't a wimp.

He didn't like the idea of her feet getting damaged, however, and he was beginning to consider carrying her whether she liked it or not, but then they finally reached the road at last.

He flagged down the first vehicle they saw, a beat-up blue pickup. The old-timer farmer was headed to Mercita, the nearest large town, and he agreed to take them, so they piled into the back.

Walker made himself comfortable as they rode away from the jungle, then passed banana farm after banana farm. Since he'd seen all that a thousand times before, he watched Clara as she sat next to him. Despite some obvious shortcomings, she wasn't bad to look at. Long legs, for one. Long neck too, very kissable looking. And he hadn't lied earlier about her lips.

Too bad her mouth was most often flattened into a line of displeasure. She was altogether too severe: the look in her gunmetal gray eyes, the line of her nose, the set of her shoulders. He figured her for about twenty-six or twenty-seven years old, twenty-nine tops. If he didn't know she was DOD, he would have guessed FBI. She had the tone of a government agent. He didn't much care for that.

And she was definitely as flat as a tortilla. Every time his gaze dipped to where her breasts should have been, the song "Brimful of Asha" by Cornershop, the song about every man needing a bosom to rest his head on began playing in his head.

On the other hand, she'd kept up with him in the jungle. He hadn't thought she would. He'd fully expected that they'd have to spend the night in some makeshift shelter.

She couldn't have dropped into his life at a worse time if she'd planned it. *A freaking DOD investigator.*

What he knew for sure was that he had no time to waste on her mission, as worthy as it might be. Which left him with a dilemma. Was there a way to use her—either as a distraction or bait—to further his own agenda? Or should he simply get rid of her?

Five years ago, he wouldn't have used her. Two years ago, using her would have seriously bothered him. Now he'd do what needed to be done. She'd come here on her own. She'd willingly put herself into the middle of the giant clusterfuck that was Chiapas.

While he decided that made her fair game, she cast him a look of open suspicion, asking, "What are you thinking about?"

"What I should have for dinner."

"Prison food," she said, apparently still upset over Pedro.

At least she had a sense of humor, a point in her favor. That sexy growl too.

But the disapproving looks she shot him…As if she had tested him, and he had failed miserably, let her down in some way.

Except he hadn't. He'd saved her life. But were any words of gratitude forthcoming? No way. Despite the sense of humor, her overall personality wasn't that great, really.

She had the soft presence of a fish hook in the eye.

A lot had changed in the few days since Walker had agreed to help the DOD. He'd received that tip about the convoy coming three weeks early.

He'd taken care of the shipment of raw heroin, then a couple of other things. The pieces on the chessboard were being moved into position one by one.

The borderlands' power structure was about to blow up. Things Detective Cupcake didn't understand and wouldn't be allowed to find out about had been set in motion. Walker was at the epicenter of the trouble, but *she* didn't have to be. She could still survive.

If he'd been able to come up with a way to use her to further his own agenda, he would use her, but he couldn't think of anything. She'd just be in the way. It'd be better for everyone involved if she left, he decided.

"I need to go back to Furino," she said again.

Dog with a freaking bone.

"You should go straight to the airport and go home," he told her.

She cast him a withering look. "I am going back to Furino, with or without your help. Just to be clear."

Stubborn was all over her, in the rigid set of her shoulders, the tilt of her jaw, the glint of her gunmetal eyes. Weird eyes. They would look ridiculously innocent in her unguarded moments—few and far between—then sharp and judgmental as anything when she focused on him.

"You're supposed to help me," she said.

"Not going to happen." He planned to scare her straight, then send her packing.

She fell into a resentful silence, and he let her.

As the pickup reached Mercita—a rundown border town of about twenty thousand people—they passed a recently renovated factory building on the right. XPTM Pharmaceuticals, the banners proclaimed. Other signs celebrated the upcoming grand opening the following week.

"That'll be good for jobs," Clara observed.

Walker said nothing as they passed the building, then block after block of similar places, some with the lights on, others abandoned.

Chiapas was one of the most poverty-stricken states in Mexico, and every bit of that showed in the borderlands, in both the weather-beaten buildings and the malnourished people, many of whom belonged to the indigenous tribes, eking out a bleak existence from sustenance farming.

The pickup slowed for a traffic light. Walker banged on the top of the cab and shouted, "Gracias, amigo," to the old guy behind the wheel, then he vaulted over the side.

He walked away without looking back, without helping Clara down. If she thought he'd be holding her hand through her investigation, she needed to reevaluate.

She caught up with him a few seconds later. "Where are we going?"

"To my place. We're not going back to Furino until I find out how Pedro's death played with the others."

Killing Pedro today hadn't been on his agenda. Yet the move had been made, and it was the kind of move that could mess up his carefully laid plans if he didn't play things smart. He had to adjust a couple of things, shift his plans. All because of the woman currently glaring at him.

He'd barely set eyes on Clara, and she was messing up his life already. He needed to learn a lesson here. He shouldn't have agreed to help the DOD.

He strode down the litter-covered street and led her to a narrow four-story brick building. The front yard was graveled, the back overgrown with weeds. Faded red shades covered the windows; a weather-beaten sign, BRUNHILDA'S, hung over the front door.

Clara tried to peek in. "You live above a restaurant?"

"Kind of." He led her around to the back, pointed to the rubber hose that snaked among the weeds. "We can clean up here."

Then he pointed at the outhouse at the back of the small yard that Brunhilda had kept even after she'd had plumbing put in. "Bathroom."

Most women would have at least flinched, if not outright refused. Clara hurried off toward the outhouse with purposeful strides.

Because he was a man, his gaze hesitated on her legs and the sway of her slim hips as he took off his shirt and turned on the hose.

He let the water run a bit until it cooled, then he aimed the spray at his chest, then hair, soaking himself, washing off the grime of the jungle. He washed his shirt next, then put it back on. The light material would dry fast in this heat.

He thought about the call he needed to make.

When Clara returned, he left her with the hose and walked into Brunhilda's through the back door, dripping. He ignored the ongoing business, used the bathroom in there, then the old-fashioned rotary phone on the wall in the hallway.

"Walker," he said when the call was answered. "I need to talk to Santiago."

He waited until the man on the other end talked to someone else, walked off, came back.

Walker listened to the guy's response, then said, "I'll call again in two hours. Maybe he'll be back by then."

He needed to see Santiago. Which meant a trip to the Xibalba cartel compound. Who knew, with some luck, he might run into the noseless man there. He had no idea where the man was, so the Xibalba compound was as likely a location as any.

All Walker needed was ten minutes with the guy. Hell, even five. He was pretty confident he could get Ben's killer's name out of the bastard.

He looked up as he hung up the phone, saw Clara at the back door, and hurried toward her with a muttered curse.

"Who did you call?" She tried to peer into the house over his shoulder, open curiosity sitting on her face.

He turned her around and pushed her outside, closed the door behind them. "When I want you to know something, I'll tell you."

Which would happen—never. He wanted her to know absolutely nothing about him or what he was doing here.

Her face and hair were wet. She'd lost her hat in the river. The blond locks that had been previously tortured into that tight little bun at her nape now swung softly around her shoulders.

She wasn't beautiful. She wasn't even pretty. But he was beginning to find her sharp-with-intelligence eyes and her pursed-with-disapproval mouth interesting.

She'd held up under duress so far. A lot better than he would have predicted. That intrigued him. Where did that toughness come from? Why was her hopeless mission so damned important to her?

But while he had plenty of questions, he made no attempt to discover her secrets. She wouldn't be around long enough for any of that to matter to him.

The only thing he wanted from her was for her to leave, with as little fuss as possible. First thing tomorrow morning, preferably. He had dangerous places to be and ruthless criminals to see.

He turned toward the fire-escape ladder to his left and stepped close enough to pull down the rusty metal ladder. He went up without looking back at her. "Yank it up behind you."

She did as he asked, which boded well for their continued cooperation, as brief as it was going to be.

He went up all the way to the top of the ladder, then climbed the window frame another level up, unlocked the padlock on the shutters, and ducked in through the small, round window of the attic, gun in hand just in case.

He stood blocking her out until his eyes adjusted to the low light and he could see that the room was safe.

Then he tucked his gun away and stepped forward. "Come in."

And he wondered, even as he said the words, what in hell he was doing. He'd never brought anyone here before. The attic was his secret hiding place.

He'd known Clara less than a day and he'd already broken one of his own rules because of her. As he watched her climb in, he swore he wasn't going to break any others.

CHAPTER
SIX

Walker breathed in the hot, stale air of the attic. The accommodations were meager: a tarp-covered mattress on the floor—in case the roof leaked—mosquito netting, a rickety table, a washstand with an empty bowl. Dust and more dust, dead bugs in the corners.

"We're spending the night here," he said, then waited.

She didn't cry him a river.

Clara scanned the dim space, her spine straight, her shoulders back, an impassive expression on her face. "I've been in safe houses before. I've been on stakeouts. It's not always ideal," she said, as if sensing his thoughts. "I can handle unpleasant things."

"Wouldn't know it from the way you screamed in the jungle when that tarantula fell on your shoulder." His ears were still ringing.

Her impassive expression dissolved as she shot him a look of pure death ray.

Apparently, she didn't like being reminded of her girly side. Did she think it made her less of a hard-hitting DOD investigator?

He walked to an ancient wooden chest in the corner, rummaged through it until he found a pair of cowboy boots about her size, scuffed but serviceable.

He handed them to her.

She looked the boots over. "Whose are these?"

He shrugged. "Stuff was here when I moved in."

He searched some more and threw her a pair of shorts that were probably going to destroy what little peace of mind he had left, but they were the only thing in her size. "You're going to fry up here in long pants."

While she changed pants and footwear, he turned his back to her and hung up his rifle and machete, then put his handgun on the table. Having no chairs, he folded up the tarp and sat on the edge of the mattress. He kicked off his boots, took off his socks. In a moist environment like this, letting his skin dry was the best defense against swamp feet.

Instead of sitting next to him, she sat on the folded-up tarp four or so feet away, probably thinking she was out of his reach.

He watched as she took the Glock from her waistband and stuffed it into her right boot, rubbernecking to take in the details of the room. She crossed her long, bare legs in front of her.

The shorts had been a bad idea, he could tell that right then and there. They were a light material, red, an inch-long lace edging the hems. Combined with cowboy boots, they created an interesting effect. In his pants.

He had enough control over his dick to ignore that, but he couldn't ignore her entirely. She'd have to be dealt with one way or the other. She didn't belong here—neither in his safe room, nor in this part of the country. She stuck out. She'd gotten tangled up with Pedro. If Walker hadn't shown up, she probably wouldn't have survived the day.

Not his problem, really. He had his own difficulties. Yet he *did* owe the DOD a favor. So he decided to hear her out before he sent her on her way.

"Tell me exactly who you are and what you're doing here. From the beginning."

As long as she was talking about herself and her case, at least she wasn't asking questions about him.

"DOD Investigator Clara Roberts," she introduced herself formally.

He'd expected someone different. When word had come down from the DOD, it'd only been that an investigator would be arriving and Walker was to offer assistance. He'd expected a guy, a grizzled old-timer, but realized his mistake as soon as he'd walked into the cantina. He knew a US government employee when he saw one. She'd stuck out like a kitten in a caiman nest.

He'd been pissed. Why in hell would they send a woman? Alone at that.

Then again, the DOD had no idea what Walker had set up, that the border region was about to go up in flames. And even if the DOD had sent a man, no matter who came, Walker would have done his best to turn the person around and get him to leave.

She was saying, "And you're Light Walker, doing…" She paused. "What exactly are you doing here?"

If she asked that question one more time, he swore to God…"Just Walker. I can't help you."

Anger and disappointment flashed across her face. "You said you'd think about it."

"I just did." He shrugged. "Something else came up."

"You are my local facilitator." She practically growled the words.

He liked her growly voice. He was beginning to regret that they had no time for him to make her growl and moan under different circumstances. The woman needed loosening up, and he wouldn't have minded being the man who stirred her up a little. Or a lot. The thought of her long legs wrapped around his waist definitely held appeal.

Except, while he was contemplating talking her out of her pants, the look in her eyes said she was contemplating shooting him.

He needed to get her the hell out of town. Not that he thought she was going to be reasonable about it.

"I work for Civilian Personnel Recovery," she said with a slight uptilt of her chin. "It's a new department at the DOD."

Just what the world needs, another freaking government initiative.

She must have read the thought on his face, because she shot him a withering look. "As I said, I'm here to recover Rosita Ruiz. US citizen."

Disappeared on July 1st, from in front of some cousin's house, she'd said in the jungle.

Walker thought for a second. At the beginning of July, he'd been smuggling guns across the border to Guatemala. "Have you uncovered any eyewitnesses to the kidnapping, Detective Cupcake?"

The death ray flashed from her eyes. "I'm an investigator, not a detective."

He held back a grin. "Let's not split hairs so early in the game."

She toned down the death ray, but only just. "Rosita's cousin was the only family member home at the time of the kidnapping, but she was inside the house. She didn't see anything. Nobody else came forward either as far as the cousin knows." Clara paused. "I wish I could see the police reports, but I'm going to steer clear of la policía for now."

Maybe she wasn't completely clueless.

He decided to give her a little more specific information than he'd shared with her before about the local cops. Once she accepted that Walker wasn't going to help her, he didn't want her to turn to the cops and get burned. "The chief of police is Carlos Petranos's brother-in-law. La policía is an extension of Carlos's private army. They protect him from his enemies."

She blinked, then her eyes widened. "Carlos Petranos as in cartel boss Carlos Petranos?"

One and the same. "As you said, it'd be better if la policía didn't know that you are in town to investigate anything."

"I've been playing tourist." She pulled a half-dry square of folded paper from her back pocket, then opened it and scooted closer to show him a photo of three high school girls mugging for the camera, inside a typical American mall. The picture looked like it'd been printed off a social media site. "That's Rosita in the middle."

"How old is she?"

"Eighteen." Clara set the printout on the floor next to her to dry, then tugged on the lace of her shorts in a futile attempt to cover another inch of skin. "Almost."

He watched her. There was more there. "Who asked for US government help? The girl has family down here. She disappeared here. Her relatives would go to the local law, corrupt as the cops are. For the right bribe, they would look into it."

Clara inspected her new boots as if she hadn't heard his question.

"Is this some kind of a special case?" he asked.

She said nothing. Then, "It's a personal case."

Her evasive maneuvers piqued his interest. "Is Rosita a friend of yours?"

She remained silent.

He thought for a second. "Not friend or family. You wouldn't have to print a picture from online if she was your niece. You'd have your own photos. And I'm not sensing the kind of urgency from you that comes with 'my brother's kid is missing.'"

He thought some more. "She's connected to someone at your department." He paused. "But not to another investigator, or he would have come himself."

The connection had to be a man. Clara had been uncomfortable with Rosita's age, as if *almost* eighteen was too young for something, and Walker had a fair idea what that *something* was.

He liked puzzles. "Your supervisor's teenage girlfriend," he guessed. "He probably has a wife."

Clara clenched her even, pearly teeth and watched him with angst first, then speculatively, as if trying to determine how much to tell him.

"She's connected to...*someone* I work with." A small sigh escaped her that he didn't think she was aware of. "There is a lot at stake," she finished, her normally self-assured tone tinged with desolation.

"How long have you worked for the DOD?"

Couldn't be long. For one, she was young. Two, she didn't move or talk like a seasoned investigator who'd spent a decade in the field. She clearly had potential, but she wasn't there yet. She needed the kind of experience that came with time, which she wasn't going to get if she got killed down here.

"Over a year," she said.

Babe in the woods. And the woods around here were dark and dangerous, teeming with deadly predators.

"And before that?"

"I was a forensic accountant at the FBI. Recruited straight from college. I tracked down criminals through their financial records."

He could see her as an accountant. Straitlaced could have been her middle name. Investigating from behind a desk was the safe way to do it, for sure. "Why did you leave the Bureau?"

"None of your business."

He held her gaze. "Keep in mind that you desperately need my help."

"I can handle this without you." She looked like she was trying to talk herself into believing that. She squared her shoulders and kept her voice full of confidence. "I just need you to brief me on the area, the power structure, certain people I need to look out for, basic local background. Then we go our separate ways."

A reasonable suggestion. So hearing himself say, "No," surprised him.

He barely knew her. She meant nothing to him. Yet he wanted her safely away from here. Apparently, the last, deeply buried shred of his conscience had chosen this moment to float to the surface. Inconvenient little shit.

Her eyes narrowed at his refusal of help, and she looked as if she was about to growl again, but, to his disappointment, caught herself. "What's your connection to the DOD?" she asked instead.

"No connection. I owed someone a favor. A small favor," he added. "So let's not stretch it. If you don't die on my watch, I'm going to consider the debt paid. Which is why I'm not letting you go back to Furino tonight."

The sooner he put her on a plane back to Washington, the better. In fact, maybe a visit to Jorge was in order. That would scare her out of Chiapas for sure.

She watched him in silence. He didn't expect it to last. It didn't.

"You shouldn't have killed Pedro." Her voice tightened with disapproval. "I wanted to talk with him."

"Pedro doesn't talk with women."

Her expression turned smug. "We talked before you got there."

Unlikely. When Pedro saw something he wanted, he took it. He would have dragged her out of that cantina. By next week, the DOD would be sending Investigator Number Two to look for Investigator Number One's body.

"How did you get away from him?"

Her smug factor doubled. "I outdrew him."

Walker quirked an eyebrow. Nobody outdrew Pedro, which was why Walker had gone for the knife.

Pedro had only had eyes for the rifle. If Walker had gone for that, or reached for his SIG, Pedro would have gone for his fancy pistols. But since Walker's hand merely moved to the front of his belt...

Pedro simply hadn't seen the knife as the primary threat. He was an old-fashioned gunslinger. He would reach for his gun first, a hundred times out of a hundred.

Sitting on the mattress, Walker went for his knife again, meaning to only touch the blade flat against Clara's collarbone to test her. But she had her Glock aimed at his heart while his knife was still two inches from his target.

Shit. Okay, then.

Definitely more to her than meets the eye.

He bit back an impressed smile, returned his knife into its sheath, and looked her over with renewed interest as she shoved her gun back into her boot.

A man's—or woman's—chosen weapon said something about the person. Her Glock 19 was the reduced-size version of the Glock 17, a popular weapon for concealed carry. Semiautomatic, 9mm cartridges. Handy in many ways, not the least because it was compatible with Glock 17 magazines. An all-around solid, reliable gun. A sensible, dependable weapon for a sensible, dependable woman. He had a feeling it'd been carefully evaluated and selected.

And it wasn't for show only. She was definitely fast with it.

"But can you hit what you aim at?" he asked, because that was the only thing that mattered.

Her tone didn't hold a hint of bragging, the words said matter-of-factly as she told him, "Third in my FBI class."

Not bad. He'd been fourth in SEAL training. And some of the guys he'd competed against had gone on to become professional sharpshooters.

He kept his eyes on Clara. So she was a good shot. And she'd outdrawn Pedro.

Thank God she didn't have boobs. A woman with a quick draw and serious curves might have tempted him into doing any number of really stupid things.

*** ***

Clara sat in silence as she mulled over her situation. The attic room was a hovel, no two ways about it. But it was serviceable. And she would eat broken glass before she would complain, before she let Walker think she couldn't handle it.

He'd tested her with the place, had waited for her reaction. She was glad she hadn't given him any. He'd tested her with the knife attack as well. She hadn't failed that either.

But by no means did she think she had the upper hand. She couldn't let her guard down for a second.

She had only one major problem with the attic: that it wasn't bigger. The man took up a lot of space, not just physically but mentally. She wasn't crazy about them being in such close quarters. She found it impossible not to be aware of every breath he drew, every move he made. She didn't like a thing about him.

She watched him while he muttered something under his breath about everybody needing a pillow.

He fit the bare-bones attic room. Probably not his only hidey-hole. She had a feeling he pissed off seriously bad guys on a regular basis.

She couldn't pin him down, and that unsettled her. He was ex-special ops and came with her father's recommendation—two points in his favor—but what she'd seen of him so far wasn't reassuring.

Maybe he'd been a good man once, but good men went bad all the time, molded by their environment.

"How long have you been in Chiapas?" she asked.

"Too long."

"Are you a mercenary?"

"Isn't everybody? You do shit for other people, and you get paid."

"Do you work for criminals?" she clarified. She needed to know at least the basics about him. She should have asked her father, but at the time, her mind had been too preoccupied by his confession.

Walker gave a one-shouldered shrug. "Define criminal."

Which meant *yes*. Not that she hadn't already known that he was a criminal, since she'd seen him kill a man. She still had no idea what she was supposed to do about that. As he'd said, she had no jurisdiction down here.

On the one hand, he seemed easygoing to the extreme—way too laid-back for her taste. But on the other hand, he'd taken down Pedro with lightning speed and precision, in a sudden burst of stone-cold, professionally executed violence.

She didn't know how to reconcile those two facets of him.

Something teased at the back of her mind. Something about his behavior that was familiar. Which made no sense. She was pretty sure she'd never met anyone quite like Walker.

Then it came to her in a flash. *Large predators.*

She'd been on an African safari once, while in high school. Her father's first deployment had been to Africa, and, years later, he took the family back there on vacation.

Clara remembered the lions the most. They were idle ninety-nine percent of the time. A pride of lions spent most of their day lying in the shade. They conserved their energy for the hunt. And when they hunted, they were lethal killing machines.

Like Walker.

He was a dangerous man. She'd be ill-advised to forget that even for a second.

"What I need from you is—" she began, but a loud creaking coming from below interrupted her.

Rhythmic creaking. Like a bed when people were…

A woman moaned.

Clara's gaze flew to Walker.

He flashed her an amused look. "You have something against sex?"

She clamped her mouth shut. Just hearing him say the word "sex" caused tingles in unmentionable places.

The corner of his mouth twitched as he waited for her answer.

She was so *not* discussing sex with a murderous mercenary. She drew a deep breath. "I take it Brunhilda lives above her restaurant."

"That's not Brunhilda."

How would he know that? "How many women live here?"

"A couple." He cleared his throat. "A dozen, last I came around."

"Why do a dozen women live at a restaurant?" She'd never heard of live-in waitresses.

"It's not so much a restaurant as a…different kind of establishment."

A man's lusty laugh sounded from below.

"How can this narrow little house hold a dozen women and their husbands?" A terrible suspicion formed in the back of her mind.

Walker's lips twitched again. "The men come and go."

She clenched her teeth so tight, the enamel was probably cracking. He'd brought her to a *brothel*.

"I can't find the words." She stared daggers at him.

"Don't hurt yourself trying."

He lay down on the mattress and folded his arms behind his head, which made his biceps bulge all over the place in distracting ways. With his arms up, the hem of his T-shirt rode up his abdomen, revealing a three-inch band of tanned skin and rippling muscles, a smattering of hair above his waistband.

Clara drew her gaze up to his face. A drop of sweat rolled down between her breasts. The heat was insane up here.

As if on second thought, he shifted to one side of the mattress to make room for her. "Since we can't go back to Furino today, we might as well take a nap."

A lion at rest.

She blinked. "I'm not sleeping with you in a brothel."

The way he raised his eyebrow was more suggestive than the average Vegas lap dance. "I didn't think you approved of the…*other thing.* But if you're game, I'm game, Detective Cupcake."

"Go to hell," she said through clenched teeth.

He flashed her a resigned look. "Probably sooner than later. But there's no harm in trying to have a little fun on the way."

The heat inside the room was a corporeal thing. And it all seemed to emanate from his body. She felt breathless. And burning. Like she needed to take her clothes off.

She reached to the hem of her shirt and tucked it firmly into her shorts, even if that made her feel even hotter.

She glared at him with full resentment. Since he didn't look the slightest bit abashed, she gave that up, scooted back the folded-up tarp she was sitting on as far as it went, and leaned against the wall behind her.

As a man, Light Walker was…She was clearly out of her depth with him. The very fact that he'd managed to get her to see him as a man made her want to growl with aggravation. She was extremely professional under normal circumstances. She needed to get back to thinking of him as just her facilitator.

She knew how to deal with men professionally. In the personal arena, not so much.

The first serious boyfriend she'd had was in college, a popular basketball player. Josh was a jock, and she couldn't believe he was interested in her. He was her entry to a social life, friends, parties, to feeling normal and not like a nerdy outcast.

She'd pretty much worshipped the ground he walked on. She'd given him her virginity without a second thought. She'd done most of his math homework. She'd been thinking love and forever. Until she'd overheard him talking to his buddies in the hallway.

One of the guys on the team was complaining that the head cheerleader was playing hard to get, making him jump through hoops.

Josh laughed at him. *"That's your problem right there, going after the head cheerleader. You want tail, you go after the ugly duckling, my man. They all look the same in the dark. You don't need to do the dates and the flowers and the gifts. But you get to fuck whenever you want. And they'll thank you for it. Why take the hard way when there's an easy way?"*

Clara had stood there on the other side of the spring art display, feeling eviscerated, diminished, used. Not two feet from her, half the basketball team was laughing at her behind her back. Because she was ugly and pitiful, and too stupid to know that someone like Josh could never be interested in her for real.

On the plus side, she was a quick learner. She hadn't trusted the advances of a man since. Not that there'd been that many who tried to advance. She'd had two semiserious relationships since college, both deeply unsatisfying.

She didn't have time to date. She was a general's daughter. There were a lot of eyes on her. She focused on her career. She barely had time to breathe. She wanted to make her father proud.

Time was running out for that. *Six more months*, the doctor had said.

Her heart clenched. She closed her eyes.

She'd planned on taking time off, spending as much of those six months with her father as she could, going to games, and on walks, making happy memories for later. Instead, she was here, and one of her last memories of him would be her standing stupidly in the embassy's bubble room while he admitted to adultery.

She shifted on the hard floorboards and opened her eyes that were suddenly burning. She needed to find Rosita and get back home.

Walker seemed asleep. His toned body was completely relaxed, at ease. And beautiful.

Made one wonder why there weren't more statutes of sleeping men. A definite oversight on the part of the artistic community.

She could hate his guts but appreciate his shape. She was good at compartmentalizing. And she needed to compartmentalize him right now. She had no time to waste on ogling the lion at rest.

She pushed away from the wall and sat up straight. Her rental car, her clothes, passport, wallet, and laptop were at the guesthouse in Furino. She only had the clothes on her back with her, and her Glock.

On second thought, Walker was right. Mercita was probably safer for her than Furino. Probably most everyone in Furino knew that she was staying at the guesthouse. If the banditos blamed her for Walker's actions, they could easily find her. She had to give them a few days to calm down. But she needed her things.

She glanced toward the window, at the nearly dark sky.

Mercita was a decent-size town. She should be able to get a cab somewhere around here.

She could get in and out of Furino under the cover of darkness without being seen, be back here before her insufferable facilitator woke up. She wasn't going to take a nap in the middle of an investigation, for heaven's sake.

But Walker had told her that he wasn't going to let her go back.

Maybe he'd forgotten that she had a gun. Except, the situation wasn't so dire yet that she'd shoot him.

Since she had nothing else to do, she entertained a few idle thoughts about how to escape the man.

She only needed an hour, but she couldn't lock him in the attic to keep him from coming after her and dragging her back before she reached the bottom of the fire stairs. Technically, the louvers over the window could be locked from the outside, but they were just made of wood. He could kick his way out easily.

She couldn't handcuff him to something, because she had no handcuffs and nothing to handcuff him to up here.

She didn't have any sleeping pills either. Not that she felt good about the thought of drugging someone.

Same with trying to knock him out. It seemed almost as overboard as shooting him. More his style than something a conscientious investigator would contemplate. Yet as a last measure...

"Quit watching me," he said without opening his eyes, startling her. "I can't sleep like that. If you're plotting how to seduce me to get your way—"

"I was plotting how best to hit you over the head."

His eyes popped open, and zeroed in on her. "You were thinking about killing me?"

She sighed. "Killing people is not everybody's first response to every problem. But I do wish I could tie you up for an hour."

The second the words were out, she knew she'd made a mistake.

Heat bloomed in his eyes. He raised a dark eyebrow. "The feeling is mutual."

What was it with the damn heat in this attic? She found it difficult to draw breath. She turned away from him and closed her eyes, pretending to go to sleep.

Minute after minute ticked by. His breathing evened again. Having no other option, she tried to catch some rest but couldn't nod off. She looked at Walker. He seemed to be out completely. Maybe she *could* sneak out and be back before he woke up. How would she know unless she tried?

She eased to her feet and stole to the window, proud that she didn't make a single floorboard creak. She swung one leg out.

"No," came the command from behind her, the voice managing to sound firm even while rusty with sleep.

One leg in, one leg out, she turned toward the bane of her existence. "I don't even have a change of clothes here." Or a toothbrush.

"We'll replace your stuff tomorrow."

"I have my laptop at the guesthouse."

He shot her a look of disapproval, his eyes too sharp for a man who'd just woken up. "You shouldn't have brought a laptop. Any sensitive information on it?"

She stared at him. Who went anywhere without a laptop? *Never mind.* People who ran around in the jungle, getting shot at and being bit by snakes in the ass.

"I sign into my work files through the Internet." She wasn't an idiot. "The only files on the laptop are about the travel book I'm supposedly writing here."

She hesitated for a moment. She didn't need his permission to go. She was perfectly capable of making her own decisions.

67

Walker said, "You never asked me earlier why I told you that Pedro didn't talk to women."

She swung her leg back in, then turned fully toward him and leaned against the window frame. "Okay. Why?"

He held her gaze. "The women in Pedro's company were usually gagged."

Oh.

"El Capitán liked it rough—chains and gags," he added. "The more unwilling the woman, the better. He could drag out the torture for days. When he got tired, he had one of his men take over while Pedro watched until he got his second wind."

The blood ran out of Clara's head. "Do you think Rosita—"

But Walker shook his head. "I would have heard. Pedro liked bragging."

"But if he didn't take her, then who?"

Walker looked up at the ceiling, which was just the underside of the roof tiles. "It's not the right time for you to be here."

She used her best acerbic tone to respond. "I'm sorry if my investigation is an inconvenience."

He looked back at her. "Rosita is most likely dead. Go home in the morning, before you end up in a shallow grave next to her."

"I don't run away from my investigations."

"Listen, Detective Cupcake." His tone turned cutting. "You're out of your depth here. This is not some DEFCON video game."

"And you're misogynistic. You can't deal with the fact that I'm a strong woman."

"You can't poke around down here on your own." He shook his head. "And you wouldn't like working with me."

"That's not exactly a newsflash. I've hated every move you've made so far, and pretty much every word you've said." She was fresh out of polite, and she didn't care.

His green eyes, like the jungle, threatened to swallow her. Then his gaze sharpened. Hardened. "I could scare you into leaving."

She held her ground. "You could try."

Little by little, the attic filled with tension. That the bed in the room below them began its rhythmic creaking once again didn't help matters.

She did her best to ignore the sound and the throaty moans that followed. "The fastest way to get me out of your hair is to help me find Rosita. Give me a starting point. One lead. And then you can be done with me."

If Walker disliked her as much as she disliked him, that should be enough motivation.

He watched her for a while, then seemed to come to a decision. He sat up in one sinuous move, muscles shifting all over the place. He pulled on his socks, then his boots. He stood and lifted the mattress, eased up a floor board, and pulled out a Beretta.

He held out the gun to her. "For backup."

She accepted the weapon.

"Do you have a knife?"

She shook her head.

He grunted, obviously thoroughly disgusted, and handed her one.

"You have an extra magazine for your Glock?" He passed her one without waiting for her answer. Then he put a hand grenade into his own pocket.

At her questioning look, he simply said, "M67 fragmentation grenade. Lethal within a fifteen-foot radius."

He covered up his secret compartment, grabbed his SIG and an extra magazine, and headed for the window.

She moved to follow him, a little stunned at the sudden arms acceleration. "Are we attacking the bandits at the cantina?"

"We're going down the road," he said without looking back at her, "to see a friend."

CHAPTER
SEVEN

Walker shook off the remains of his dream as he walked down the street with Clara. He'd slept maybe five minutes before the noise of her trying to sneak out woke him, but he'd dreamt. He and Ben, as kids, running around like the troublemakers they'd been, playing in the empty industrial lot behind their parents' house back in Maryland.

The abandoned factory had been their childhood playground. They'd played fort, had their treasure hunts, literally climbed the walls. And all through that, his little brother, always following, trusting. *"Wait." "Help." "I want to do that to." "Pull me up."* Always wanting to do whatever Walker was doing.

But then the bright images of the dream morphed into something much darker, as always lately: a giant chessboard with severed human heads scattered across the board. Thankfully, he'd woken before he reached the dream's end—the part he hoped to hell he'd never dream again.

Maybe Jorge knew the noseless man. Walker had been looking for the guy quietly, but time was running out. He had to ask around, up his game, even if asking too many questions could expose him.

"Who is your friend?" Clara wanted to know, nothing but bright and optimistic as she walked next to him on the sidewalk that was radiating back the day's heat. The street was busy, people going about their business. "Why are we visiting him?"

"To look for Rosita," Walker said. *To scare you straight*, he thought. *To scare you out of Chiapas.*

He wanted her gone before his meeting with Santiago in the morning. He had no time to babysit her, and to leave her to her own devices was the same as leaving her for dead.

70

Jorge's Garage stood four blocks over, the parking lot backing to railroad tracks. He ran a busy chop shop disguised as an auto repair store. Sometimes he sent car parts down south by train.

On northbound trips, the human traffickers packed every available nook and cranny with immigrants, but southbound, the railcars had plenty of empty space to smuggle other things. The chop shop wasn't a major operation, but Jorge's guys could feed their families.

The auto shop was a plain, cement-block building, three bays with steel rollup doors, currently all closed. Walker watched the roof, putting himself slightly ahead of Clara as they approached. As soon as it was clear that they were heading for the shop, the top of a head and the barrel of a rifle popped up at the roof's edge, outlined against the moonlight.

Walker squinted at the distinct shape of the AR-15. The rifle was a good, lightweight semiautomatic—the same rifle as the Mexican border patrol used. Jorge had probably bought the gun straight off them. The sad truth was, corruption was rampant all around. Almost everything and everyone could be had for money.

Walker stopped, and when Clara stepped up next to him, he put a hand on her elbow to make sure she stayed with him. "Don't draw unless you see me draw. In fact, don't even look like you're thinking about drawing."

She gave a tight nod, tension radiating from her pores. But she stood her ground. He hoped to hell she'd behave. She didn't look stupid. On the other hand, she *had* gone into the cantina.

He flashed her a stern look, then called up to the roof in Spanish. "Is Jorge around?"

"Who wants to know?" came the answer, a voice he didn't recognize. Then again, Mexican border gangs had a pretty high turnover.

"Tell him it's the guy who cut off his ear," Walker called back.

Next to him, Clara's back stiffened.

A moment later, a tall black man appeared on the sidewalk at the corner of the building, carrying another AR-15. He didn't look familiar to Walker either. He waved at them to approach, holding his rifle ready.

Walker moved in front of Clara.

"Stay a step behind me. Use me for cover," he said under his breath, then strode forward as if he didn't have a care in the world, even if he was pretty sure at least one or two other weapons were trained at them beyond the two rifles he could see.

He walked up to the guy waiting for them, a narrow-faced, sharp-eyed twenty-something who scanned him first, then Clara, spending enough time on her legs to annoy Walker, so he cleared his throat.

The guy flashed him an I'm-holding-the-AR-15-and-I-don't-have-to-give-a-shit-about-your-opinion look, but then jerked his head toward the side of the building, and the three of them went around the back.

Two more guards stood between the back door and half a dozen pickups parked in a half circle for protection. The guards looked to be brothers, early twenties, same spikey hair, same hint of a mustache. One of them nodded toward the rusty metal barrel next to the door. "Weapons."

A deeper voice called out from inside the building in Spanish. "Francisco, you ain't the man to take this particular pasty-assed gringo's gun, trust me, hermano."

Jorge's voice was followed by the man himself as he appeared in the doorway.

He looked Walker over with a shuttered expression, switching to English that he'd learned in a Texas prison back when he'd been a lowly drug mule. "What the hell happened with Pedro?"

Nose flattened by multiple fractures, Jorge was a full head shorter than Walker, but built like a battering ram. He'd been born to the boxing ring. He was all solid muscle and he knew how to use it. At one point, he'd been the Chiapas lightweight state champion.

He'd bought the car repair shop and set up a legit business from his winnings. He'd been *this* close to an honest life when the gang came for him and pressed him into joining. Now he was the leader. He'd gone too far to go back.

His black muscle shirt showed off some of his tattoos, both arms inked to the tips of his fingers, his neck up to his chin and his ears. One ear and one half ear, technically.

Jorge's ink represented his family, his gang affiliations, his time at various prisons, his kills, his girlfriends, his wins in the ring and his losses. They were a visual biography of the man, if one knew how to read them.

Walker did. Tattoos were their own language down here, and being fluent in gang signs could mean the difference between life and death.

"Pedro got frisky with my girl," he answered Jorge's question and caught Clara looking at one particularly lovely piece of art on the guy's neck, a giant eye with a fork stuck in it, blood spurting from the socket.

Jorge noticed her too. His gaze dropped to her slim hips and those long legs that her red shorts left bare. The flare of interest in his eyes said he liked what he was seeing. A slow grin spread on his face. "For what it's worth, I wouldn't let Pedro have her either."

Walker was beginning to rethink the shorts. He draped an arm over Clara's shoulders to head off any trouble. To her credit, she played along and pressed herself against his side.

He felt a bit of softness. Maybe she did have something under her shapeless T-shirt. As intriguing as the thought was, he had to file it for later.

Jorge was looking her over once again. Suddenly, his eyes narrowed. His gaze snapped to Walker. "She a cop?"

All weapons in sight swung to point at Clara.

She froze. But she did not draw. Another point in her favor. She didn't panic under pressure.

Walker kept his relaxed stance. "On vacation, hermano. From back home. She's got nothing to do with anything you do down here," he said all easy like, glad that Jorge was the kind of guy who'd hear him out first before shooting.

There weren't many like him left in the borderlands. People these days were more apt to squeeze the trigger first and ask questions later.

Jorge nodded after a long, tense moment, accepting that Walker was vouching for her. He waved the gun barrels back, then led them inside.

The shop smelled like tire rubber and motor oil, the windows blocked with plywood, and only half the overhead lights lit, leaving the place dim. About two dozen guys loitered around inside, some standing, some lying on mattresses lined up by the wall, all armed to the teeth, every eye on the visitors. Walker knew about half of them, and nodded at them as they called out greetings.

He looked back at Jorge. "Any hits yet?"

"Hernandez's crew tested us the night before last. We beat them back." Jorge's mouth tightened. "Lost Marco."

Marco was Jorge's little cousin, barely sixteen. Walker shook his head. "I'm sorry, man."

73

Jorge's eyes grew cold. "We took out three. Next time they come, we take out the rest. I got a little surprise set up."

He led them to his office, then closed the door behind them and pointed to two rickety chairs.

He watched Clara, but asked Walker, "What brings you here, hermano?"

"Looking for a girl."

That brought the earlier grin back to Jorge's face. "Cop babe ain't enough? You sure your greedy gringo ass can handle another?"

"Don't you worry about what I can handle," Walker shot back in the same easy, macho tone. Then he turned serious. "I'm looking for Rosita Ruiz. American. Seventeen. Went missing on the first of July in Furino."

Clara pulled the photo from her pocket and put it on the desk between them without a word, pointed a finger at the girl in the middle.

Jorge looked at the printout without touching it, then leaned back in his chair. "Never heard of her." His eyes narrowed at Walker. "What makes her important enough for you to give a flying fuck?"

"Favors are owed."

Jorge rubbed his chin. "Pain in the ass."

Wasn't that the truth? Walker nodded. "What's the word on the street?"

"About what?"

"Anything. I've been out of circulation for a while." He'd spent most of last week in the jungle, setting his plans in motion.

Jorge shrugged. "Everyone's tense. The Tamchén pushed through a big load three days ago. Makes the Xibalba twitchy. Especially since the Xibalba shipment is late."

The two cartels coexisted in the region in fragile peace. Walker hoped *fragile* was the keyword. Not something he could discuss with Jorge, so he returned to his reason for being there. "No word about an American girl getting nabbed?"

Jorge scratched his chin. "Two American college girls were killed at one of the tourist bars a week ago. But they were blond Anglos and a couple of years older than your chica. Police was all over that."

"They caught who did it?" Walker asked out of idle curiosity. He liked to know who was up to what.

"Nah, man. Nobody touches Chapa's boys."

Jorge wasn't lying. Walker knew policemen who'd taken people out of witness protection and hand-delivered them to Chapa for torture and execution. Chapa was above the law. Far above the small-time local gangs like Jorge's too. Chapa was second in command of the Tamchén cartel.

But even Chapa didn't usually go after foreigners unless they meddled in his business. Doing something like that was plain asking for aggravation.

Killing the two American college kids, in particular, made no sense. A lot of the girls coming up from South America ended up sold into the sex trade, and a pair of pretty blondes would bring in a healthy premium. So if the girls had come to Chapa's attention, why kill them instead of selling them? Why waste the profits?

Chapa was a money man, a greedy piece of shit. This didn't sound like him.

Walker pushed aside the thought. The college girls weren't his problem, and it was too late for them in any case.

"If you hear anything about Rosita," he said, "leave word with Brunhilda. I'll check in with her. I don't have a cell phone right now."

Jorge pulled the desk drawer open, rummaged through two dozen cell phones, picked one, and tossed it to him. "Number's on the sticker on the back. What happened to the last one I gave you?"

Walker shrugged. "Lost it somewhere. Thanks, hermano."

He glanced at Clara. She hadn't said a word, but she was taking everything in. She didn't look rattled by Jorge and his gang, she looked…ready. Her back was to the wall, her feet braced slightly apart. Her hands were relaxed, at her sides, in position to go for her weapons as needed.

Little wonder Jorge had her pegged in two minutes.

She was new to the job, obviously green, but she had potential, Walker thought again.

He turned back to Jorge. "Got any in the shed?"

"Four," Jorge said without the slightest sign of emotion.

"Chicas?"

"Two."

"Mind if we look?"

Jorge's gaze cut to Clara, stayed there. "If you think your girl can handle it."

"She'll be fine."

Clara moved toward the door.

Walker stayed back. *One more thing.*

"Seen anyone around who's missing a nose, by any chance?" he asked Jorge under his breath, low enough so Clara wouldn't hear.

Jorge lifted an eyebrow.

"Long story," Walker said.

"Name?"

"Don't know."

"Who does he work for?"

"Whoever pays him. Like me. No permanent affiliation."

"He stepped on one of your jobs?"

"Something like that."

"I'll let you know if I hear anything."

Jorge didn't walk them out; he asked one of his men. He was still alive because he was smart like that. When you were in the middle of a gang war, you didn't leave cover.

The shed stood in the back of the property, ten feet by ten feet at tops, wood-plank side, corrugated-steel top, just a few feet from the railroad tracks. Flies buzzed in and out through the gaps.

Walker pulled the neck of his T-shirt over his nose as Francisco opened the padlock and threw the door wide.

The stench hit them like a fist in the face.

Clara gagged quietly behind him.

Walker didn't look at her. He yanked on the chain that turned on the overhead light and took in Jorge's latest pickings.

None of the four bodies was particularly fresh. There was a guy with his throat cut, from farther down south, based on his features. He definitely didn't look Mexican. A ten-year-old boy with bruises on his face lay diagonally over the first guy's body. Then, in front of them, a twenty-something woman who'd been strangled. The rope was still wound around her neck. She had blood on her thighs.

Walker looked away from her and focused on the girl who lay just inside the door, facedown: slim body, long dark hair—about the right age for Rosita Ruiz.

He moved closer and gently rolled her over with the tip of his boot. He looked for a long moment before he stepped back. At Francisco's questioning look, he shook his head.

Francisco turned off the light, closed the door and padlocked it again. Then he walked back to the garage, leaving them where they stood. The smell didn't encourage lingering.

Walker started across the lot, away from the putrid stench, back toward the road. Clara followed him, her stride not entirely steady, but she wasn't about to pass out either.

Too bad. He'd hoped to rattle her into leaving.

She kept pace, walking at his elbow. "So Jorge is in a gang war? That's why we brought the arsenal?"

"If a pickup load of rival gang members showed up, I wanted to be ready."

They reached the road, turned toward Brunhilda's, and walked side by side on the litter-covered sidewalk, passing women on bicycles and kids carrying groceries. The normalcy of the scene stood in stark contrast to what they'd just seen. They walked in silence, trying to adjust.

The temperature was a cool high eighty. It only got hotter than that down here in the summer. A lot hotter. They had to count their blessings for days like this.

"Are all your friends criminals?" Clara asked after a while.

"I don't have friends. And as far as criminals go, Jorge is better than most."

"Meaning what?"

"For one, he doesn't kill for fun. He'll go after a rival, but otherwise, he's all right. Comes from his boxing days. You want a good match in the ring. You don't put on the gloves for any weak punk."

Clara seemed to think about that for a moment. "Why did he think I was a cop?" She looked herself over, examining her shorts and boots. "Is it the clothes? It's typical tourist wear."

"Boxers, in general, are pretty good at reading body language. Your life depends on it in the ring." He tried to explain. "You're too straitlaced. Not a relaxed bone in your body. Someday, if we meet under different circumstances, remind me to take you out for some tequila and salsa dancing."

For a moment, he could see it, and damn if he didn't like what he saw. But she made some kind of a grunt that suspiciously didn't seem like a sound of appreciation. Oh, well. She was right. He definitely wasn't the right guy for her. Or for any honest woman, for that matter.

His female acquaintances tended to come from a different world lately. Speaking of which…One of Brunhilda's girls was already out for the evening, working the next corner.

"Hey, Walker." Carmen smiled at him, swishing her hips, then flashed a questioning look at Clara.

Carmen was voluptuous, her curves barely contained by her low-cut shirt and short skirt. A definite contrast to Clara's tall, lean form. But while Carmen oozed some kind of a sensual, sexual vibe, Walker's gaze barely hesitated on her before skipping back to Clara.

Clara was interesting in other ways. Her vibe was of quiet self-confidence, thoughtfulness, her eyes always filled with curiosity and intelligence. One thing for sure, she hadn't bored him yet, and he'd spent more time with her at a stretch than he'd spent with a woman in a long time.

"Hey, Carmen." He kept on walking.

Clara rolled her eyes at him after they passed, but didn't comment on him being on a first-name basis with a hooker. "How does Jorge's gang fit into the bigger picture?" she asked instead.

"Furino is a small town, under the thumb of some old-fashioned banditos who run the human trafficking, working rural areas. The gangs make a living in the bigger towns off robberies, or have their chop shops like Jorge. Both the gangs and the banditos work with the permission of the cartels that control the gun and heroin trade."

"Sounds like a sizable criminal presence in the region."

"Which is why you need to leave."

"When I have Rosita."

He took her elbow to make her look at him. "Rosita's body might have come to Jorge's shed last week. Or the week before. He might not remember. He has no reason to make a close inspection. You have to face the facts. If she hasn't turned up yet and nobody's asked for ransom, she's dead."

"Then I'll locate the body for repatriation." Her gunmetal eyes sparkled with resolve. "What does Jorge do with the dead, anyway? Why does he keep them in the shed? Who are they?"

Walker dropped his hand from her elbow. "The trains that use the tracks behind Jorge's place come up from as far south as Costa Rica. They come through Nicaragua, Honduras, El Salvador, Guatemala, and pick up immigrants along the way. Some fall from the roof of the train, weak with starvation or exhausted. Others are pushed. Often by the smugglers."

She frowned. "Why does Jorge collect them?"

"The town doesn't have the money or the manpower for proper burials. The bodies go straight to the town incinerator."

Her steps faltered. "Like garbage?"

He shrugged, swallowing the bitter taste in his throat. He would not think about his brother now.

He filled his lungs with the street's hot, exhaust-infused air. "Any bodies that fall in Jorge's gang's territory, they gather up, then truck them up to the convent of St. Lupe once a week. The nuns bless them, then bury them."

The mercy trips were Jorge's way of making up for some of his darker deeds, Walker suspected. Most of his gang had the cross tattooed somewhere on their bodies. Most of them had been raised in Catholic households. Their mothers were probably burning candles for them somewhere.

Jorge was as stone-cold a killer as Walker had ever seen, but he'd held on to something, apparently, a deep-seated need for absolution that Walker had given up a long time ago. He'd gone too far. He couldn't do enough good deeds in a hundred years to make up for all the bad he'd done and was about to do in the next couple of days.

He didn't particularly care anymore if the things he did were right or wrong. He didn't want absolution; all he wanted was release from his nightmares. *Five more days.*

He needed to find the noseless man before that time was up and everything exploded.

Next to him, Clara's stomach growled. Walker could go a day or two without food. Hunger didn't much bother him. But when a street-vendor truck drove by, he flagged it down. He bought enchiladas and water, and they took the bag back to Brunhilda's.

The place was full-on busy now instead of entertaining just the earlier handful of patrons. The way Clara tried hard not to look in the windows as they went up the fire escape ladder made Walker laugh.

"There are two bathrooms in there with nice big tubs," he told her, "but they'll be filled with people all night. We can clean up in the morning when the clients are gone and the girls are sleeping. The bathrooms will be empty then."

Clara muttered something under her breath he had a feeling he didn't want to hear.

They went up and disarmed, down to one handgun each for easier movement, then took turns using the outhouse. While she was busy, Walker used the cell phone Jorge had given him, and called Santiago to set up a meeting for the next day. Then they washed up with the garden hose again before eating their dinner up in the hot, muggy attic.

"How are you connected to Jorge?" she asked between two bites.

"He owes me a couple of favors."

Curiosity came into her eyes. "Why did you cut his ear off?"

A dab of sour cream sat in the corner of her lips. The sudden impulse to lick it off took Walker by surprise. When she didn't have those lips pursed in disapproval of him, they didn't look half-bad. Especially her bottom lip that was fuller than the top one and creased in the middle. He wouldn't say no if she wanted to put those lips on him.

Out of the blue, his body tightened.

He cleared his throat. "We met under strained circumstances."

She raised an eyebrow. "Like what?"

She was no GI Jane by any means, but there was a doggedness about her that was beginning to worry him. She might be a rookie investigator, but so far she'd stood up to everything he'd thrown at her. He was beginning to have a dreadful suspicion that she might be more difficult to get rid of than he had first anticipated.

He swallowed the curse pushing to his lips, and instead asked, "Do you ever just mind your own business?"

"I'm an investigator. My job is to ask questions."

He stilled and narrowed his eyes at her as an uncomfortable thought popped into his head.

He watched her closely as he ran through everything she'd done and said so far, tested it for holes in her story. Then he put the question to her straight. "Are you investigating me?"

Maybe the Rosita Ruiz case was bullshit. A setup.

Clara smothered a snort. "If I was sent to investigate you, you'd be in jail already and the paperwork for your extradition to the US would have been filed by now. I saw you commit murder."

"Dog with a freaking bone," he muttered under his breath, but relaxed his shoulders.

She was right. If he was her target, no way could she let something like Pedro's death slide. She would have taken him in and used a murder charge as leverage to try to make him confess his other sins.

"About two years ago, Jorge was sent to kill me," he said to change the subject. "As his gang initiation."

She choked on her enchiladas, then coughed as she stared at him.

He pushed her water bottle closer to her. "I knew him from the boxing circuit. I knew he was a good kid. We talked about it."

First fought like dogs, then talked when Walker had finally pinned him down.

Clara didn't look convinced. "If he didn't complete his initiation hit, how are you both still alive?"

"I did the gang a favor."

"Kill someone?"

He grinned at her. "Now that's just plain presumptuous." He shook his head. "A different kind of favor."

"So you just go around doing favors for people all day long?"

He shrugged. "It helps to have a few markers out. When I need something, I call them in."

"How did he make gang leader in two years?"

"Promotions in gangs are not like in corporate America. No slow slog up the corporate ladder. When a member is strong enough to gain control, he takes it." Hell, two years was practically forever, the way those kids kept getting killed.

Jorge was a pragmatic kind of guy. He did what he needed to survive. He'd say he liked staying on the winning side of history. History was written by the survivors.

"His neck tattoo," Clara said. "Was that how he got to be on top?"

"No. He didn't stab anyone in the eye with a fork. Brunhilda did." Walker grinned.

Then he decided to tell Clara the whole story. "Jorge lost his mother early. His father was a black-hearted bastard who used to beat the shit out of him. Brunhilda fed Jorge more than once when he was a kid. When he got older, right when he was beginning to do well with boxing, he started liking one of Brunhilda's girls, used to hang out over here. His father found out. He was mad that Jorge was giving the girl money instead of giving it all to him. He beat that girl nearly to death. Then Jorge showed up, and his old man pulled a gun on him. Brunhilda came in from the back and as the guy turned, she stabbed him in the eye with a fork. I think he's buried somewhere behind the outhouse. As a precaution. That way the smell couldn't give him away."

Clara sat in silence for at least five whole blessed minutes without interrogating him, digesting the story. Then she asked, "Were you on the boxing circuit?"

She didn't seem to be able to help herself.

"Not the official one. A few matches here and there in cantinas."

Fighting in those impromptu matches was how he'd gotten accepted down here. People gave him a chance because they'd seen him fight. Or because they'd made money betting on him.

Little by little, they'd begun trusting him. Then small jobs started coming his way. Then bigger jobs. Until he was now finally next to the people he needed to be next to.

"When do you think I can go back to Furino?" Clara asked as she finished her food.

"Best would be never."

She frowned. "Let's see how things stand tomorrow. I'll call the guesthouse in the morning and ask if any banditos have been looking for me. Honestly, I don't see why Pedro would be blamed on me. I didn't do anything."

He watched her, trying to decide on his next course of action. His first choice would have been putting her on a plane, but she wasn't ready yet to cooperate. Jorge and his shed hadn't scared her off.

His plans for Furino definitely would. But Walker wanted to spare her Furino.

There were things that shouldn't be seen, that could never be unseen, that would haunt a person for the rest of his life in nightmares. Walker knew better than most. He didn't wish that on her. But it didn't look like she would give up unless she was taken to the extremes.

He kicked off his boots, peeled off his socks, then lay back and stretched out on the mattress. The attic had no power, no light fixtures, so as soon as the sun dipped below the horizon, they were shrouded in darkness, save what moonlight peeked in the open window. He shifted to the side and made room for her.

She lay down on the folded tarp instead, her back to the wall, facing the window. She put her gun within easy reach, then wiggled around as if trying to find a comfortable spot. Good luck with that.

In any case, not his problem. "Suit yourself."

She watched him. He could almost hear her thinking. He wished she'd stop, knowing it'd end with more questions.

"Do you really smoke?"

She'd been wondering about *that*? He said nothing.

"You haven't gone for a cigar since the cantina. And you're less…brash."

She was observant, he gave her that. "Are you asking if I'm putting on a play titled *Fuck with me, and I'll fuck with you harder*?" If it was a play, it was based on a true story.

She flashed him a look that was somewhat schoolmarmish and at the same time surprisingly sexy. "You can't scare me with swearing. I grew up on army bases. Military brat."

He bit back a smile. He closed his eyes, signaling that the Q&A session was over, but as minutes ticked by, sleep refused him.

She stopped moving around eventually, then her breathing evened. He opened his eyes and turned his head toward her again. He didn't seem to be able to help himself.

She was a soft heap on the tarp. Sleep made the angles of her face disappear. Maybe she was only unguarded when she slept. Better than him. He couldn't relax even in his dreams.

He let his gaze travel up her long legs. The shorts—edged with that thin band of lace—fit her a little too well. They were certainly nothing like her no-nonsense jeans that, pre-swim in the river, had had a crease going down the middle of the pant legs as if she'd ironed them.

Good riddance to those.

With her hair loose and those shorts, she looked like a different woman from the one he'd met at the cantina, and for some reason, it pleased him that even in as little time as they'd known each other, he'd left his mark on her.

His gaze moved up and over the lean curve of her hip. Her shirt had ridden up, and he could see two inches or so of skin above her waistline in the semidarkness. She had soft skin. He'd grabbed her enough in the jungle—by the wrist, arm, elbow—to know.

In fact, thinking back, maybe he'd grabbed her more often than had been strictly necessary.

His gaze hesitated on the patch of bare skin. And he felt a sudden impulse to run his fingers over it. To taste it.

"*Chica's mine for the night,*" he'd said at the cantina, and now he suddenly wished it were true.

He shook off the thought. He was a man, and she was a woman in his bedroom, that was all. No need to read anything more into it. He made an effort to shake off his growing lust and forced himself to look higher up, at her face.

She had a good face: open and honest, tall forehead, straight nose. His gaze dipped to her mouth. He swallowed an annoyed grunt.

He'd never brought a woman up to the attic. The whole point of hidey-holes was that nobody knew about them.

Yet he hadn't hesitated to bring her.

How did that happen?

When he'd gone to Furino to meet whomever the DOD sent, he'd been determined to send the guy right back home. When he'd spotted Clara, at most he'd been willing to drive her to the nearest airport to make sure she got on a damned plane.

But here she was, sleeping practically within reach.

Since when did ex-accountants win when they went up against ex-Navy SEALs in a battle of wills?

She'd handled Jorge and the shed well, which partly exasperated Walker—it would have been so much easier if she'd just folded—but also earned his grudging admiration.

She was determined to find the missing girl. Hell, he could relate. He would never forget the long months he'd spent searching for Ben.

He understood her drive, but he couldn't help her. They were working at cross-purposes. She needed a couple of weeks to turn up and run down leads. And he was about to blow up the place.

CHAPTER
EIGHT

The temperature dropped enough overnight to sleep but was rising again by the time Clara woke, alone, her muscles stiff from the hard boards. A moment passed before she recalled where she was and how she'd gotten here, then, the very next second, the rest of the previous day came to her, and she remembered Pedro's untimely death.

Walker had killed her prime suspect.

The man was out of his ever-loving mind.

And now that he'd thrust her investigation into a tailspin, he seemed to have little intention of helping her. She'd been dealt a rough hand with the guy. He was undisciplined, overbearing, impulsive, murderous…

She sat up and stretched.

She was a professional. If she couldn't work with Walker, she'd work around him. How much trouble could he be?

His machete and semiautomatic were leaning against the wall, so she didn't think he'd gone too far. Maybe out to get breakfast and—oh, please, dear God—coffee. She was willing to wait ten minutes for him, but no more than that.

As soon as she cleaned up a little, she had to go back to Furino. She needed her things. The guesthouse was on the last street in town. If worse came to worst, she could sneak in through the back, without anyone seeing her.

She would talk to Consuela, who ran the place. If any bandits had been by, asking questions, Clara could come right back here. If nobody had been looking for her, she could stay and move her investigation forward.

She hadn't given up on finding out where the bandits' hideout was. If she couldn't follow Pedro there, she'd follow another bandit. Even if Rosita wasn't there now, Clara might find some sign that the girl had been there earlier. Then that would be a new lead.

She pushed to her feet, ready to search out one of the downstairs bathrooms Walker had mentioned. The outhouse, with its stunning assortment of spiders and weeds growing right inside, was more like the Little House of Horrors. And while the garden hose was better than nothing, she wouldn't have minded having the basic necessities for her morning routine, like soap and a mirror.

She climbed out the window and went down the fire stairs, determined to make progress today. First of all, she was going to—

The sight that greeted her when she reached the first landing had her stopping in her tracks. Her eyes strained to pop out of her head, but she couldn't look away from the room below the attic. The breath caught in her lungs.

Holy Jungle Jesus.

Walker stood in the middle of the room, stark naked.

He was casually talking to a woman—the one who'd been standing on the corner the evening before. *Carmen*, Clara suddenly remembered the name Walker had called her when he'd greeted her.

Carmen wore a very short, very sheer slip, with no underwear, as far as Clara could tell—another lush beauty like Margarita at the cantina, all soft curves and cascading ebony hair.

She had sensuously full lips and voluptuous breasts that would well overflow a man's hand. Her dark nipples and areolas showed clearly through the slip. Clara pushed out her chest in a subconscious gesture, before she caught herself and sternly ordered herself to stop.

And Walker...*Walker...*

She seriously needed to look away. She couldn't.

He was built like...*Huh.*

All thought process came to a grinding halt as her eyes roamed over hills of perfect muscles. His biceps were...His abs...*Oh, dear Lord.* And then the long, sinuous muscles of his powerful thighs...

She'd seen men like him, or almost as hot, in movies. Never in real life. The three boyfriends she'd had...Looking at Walker, she couldn't even remember their names.

She was so not shallow. She hated that she was just about drooling. What was wrong with her?

87

Then something else caught her gaze past the physical perfection. His scars.

He had suffered a serious cut on his left thigh in the not too distant past. Two old bullet wounds decorated his hip, then a few smaller scars on his upper arm.

He also had tattoos on his left side, near his heart: a trident and three letters, BEN.

A name?

An acronym? Body Excellent Naked?

Maybe it was a club. The image of a roomful of men all built like Walker flashed into her mind and fried her brain. She blinked to restart her circuits.

He shifted as he chatted with Carmen, and Clara got to see him from a slightly different angle.

She stifled a sigh. Neither the scars nor the tattoos detracted from his sheer masculine beauty; they added another layer.

Carmen and Walker matched. The dark-haired woman was über-feminine, every man's dream. And Walker had the kind of body that made ovaries sing in rapture. Sing, dance, and do backflips. Women probably rubbed against him like cats, like Margarita had done at the cantina.

Not Clara, though. She was in control of her physical desires, thank God.

She wasn't a fan of out-of-control anything. She liked to plan for her moments of passion. Make sure everything was perfect. That there'd be no interruptions. That the sheets were freshly ironed. That birth control was there and ready. Being intimate with a man was a big decision that required prior thought and planning.

Still, the sight of Walker naked…She had to close her eyes before she could step back. And then she nearly tripped. She grabbed the railing, thankful that she hadn't fallen and drawn attention.

She eased back up the stairs step by step, then into the attic through the window, and collapsed in a heap on the folded tarp she'd spent the night on. She was breathing hard, for heaven's sake.

She curled her fingers into fists. She was *not* going to be attracted to Light Walker. She refused the idea. *Not* going to happen.

He was…disorderly. And extremely uncontrolled.

Everything that he was went against everything she believed in. Principles. Honor. His showing up on Saturday when he'd said he would meet her on Thursday.

But Walker naked…

Her eyes fluttered closed. Then they flew open as a wild thought slammed into her brain: *Did he just have sex with Carmen?*

Had the iron bed been creaking? Had that been what had brought her awake? Clara couldn't remember.

*Or…*Was he *about to* have sex with Carmen? As in right now?

Clara sat up, ready to bolt. No way could she lounge around up here and listen to *that.*

Then she heard steps on the fire stairs, and she threw herself onto her back again. She closed her eyes, pretending to sleep. She couldn't bear facing Walker. At least not until he put some clothes on.

He came in, moved around. Minutes passed before the small noises he was making ceased.

What was he doing? Where was he standing? How close to her? Was he looking at her?

"Did you like what you saw?" His voice held laughter.

She swallowed a groan. Of course, he'd seen her.

He chuckled. "You can open your eyes now."

She did, fraction of a millimeter by fraction of a millimeter. *Whew.*

He wore a fresh pair of cargo pants. And nothing else, although he held a faded T-shirt in one hand. Entirely too much tanned skin and muscle showed still.

She dropped her gaze to his bare feet.

He had big feet.

Her cheeks flushed with heat as she sat up.

"Did you have fun with Carmen?" she snapped at him.

He humped down onto his mattress and crossed his legs, Indian style. He watched her with amused curiosity. "Are you asking if I had sex with her?"

"You were naked."

"I took a shower."

"Where were your clothes?"

"Julieta came in while I showered and took them to toss them in the wash."

Julieta in the shower, then Carmen on his way out. Didn't the man just have stamina to spare?

Not going to think about that. Clara drew a deep breath and looked him in the eyes as she pushed to her feet. "I need to go back to Furino. I've wasted too much time waiting for you. I need to find Rosita and get her home."

He stood. And then he stepped toward her, leaving only a foot or so of distance between them.

Her mouth went dry.

His jungle-green eyes were entirely too bright, too devilish, but there was nowhere else to look. She didn't dare drop her gaze to his half-naked body.

"Why don't you have a partner with you?" he asked. "How can you come to a place like this without backup? Don't cops and FBI agents and whatnot always work with a partner?"

"I'm not a cop or an FBI agent."

"Do the DOD investigators in your department always work alone, or are you alone because it's an off-the-books mission?"

She'd never specifically told him that this was an off-the-books mission, but since he'd figured it out, she didn't waste energy on protesting.

"No partners," she said. "We find disappeared US citizens abroad that local law enforcement couldn't locate. We have no jurisdiction. One person coming in unobtrusively and asking questions works better than a whole team showing up, rubbing the local's incompetence in their faces. You don't want to cause resentment that would stand in the way of cooperation."

She paused, then explained a little further. "Mostly our job is combing through paperwork and reinterviewing witnesses. In some third-world countries, the police get little or no training. There might be one policeman who covers a dozen villages, and he'll prioritize his neighbor's disappeared cow on which nine or ten people might depend for survival, over some foreign tourist."

"So you bring expertise," Walker said.

"Right. And if we locate the retrieval target in dangerous circumstances, at that point, local law takes over. We work together. Mostly, our work is pretty tame."

Although, there had been a recent case when a US businessman had disappeared in Venezuela, and the investigator in the case, Miranda Soto, had to face off with the Venezuelan army to get him back. Glenn Danning—super geek turned super tycoon with a body hotter than a sun plasma eruption— had liked the rescue so much, he'd married her. Miranda was currently on maternity leave. So really, the adventure ended well.

"But in this case," Walker said, "the Furino cops don't even know you're here investigating."

Clara nodded. "I can handle it."

She liked being an investigator. Like her father, she was serving her country and protecting its citizens. Ever since she'd been a little kid, she wanted to be just like her dad. Her dad had been her shining hero.

And now...

A tight feeling settled into her chest.

She was so mad at him and disappointed in him. And she couldn't be. They had a few more months left. Wasting that little time on being angry was stupider than stupid.

She had to work through her feelings before she went home.

But before she could go home, she had to track down Rosita.

"I'm going to find the girl. It's my job. I don't leave a mission unfinished. I've been trained for this."

Walker didn't look impressed. "Training is good, but it doesn't make up for experience. You shouldn't be here alone."

"I'm not. I have a local facilitator." Maybe reminding him that he was supposed to be helping her would start him down on that path.

He considered her for a long moment, then another, as if thinking hard about something. "I need to go somewhere this morning," he said at last. "I want you to stay here until I get back."

"I'm done waiting for you. I have an investigation to conduct."

He shook his head. "You wait until I get back, and you get my full cooperation for the rest of the day." He held out his hand. "Deal?"

Why was she feeling as if she was about to make a deal with the devil? She ignored the hand. Too much naked chest, way too close. No way was she touching him.

"I have to go to the bathroom," she blurted, and made a run for it.

"Hey, Detective Cupcake," he called after her.

Half-in, half-out of the window, she turned.

He tossed her the T-shirt he was holding. "Take a shower. And give your clothes to one of the girls. They'll run them through the laundry."

She grabbed the shirt and ducked out, ran down the steps. Since the room below was empty, she went through the window. And wondered how long she would have to live to forget the sight of Walker's naked body.

She guesstimated a hundred years past never.

* * *

The Xibalba cartel compound was on the other side of town. Walker left Clara at Brunhilda's while he went to meet Santiago, working out on the way how he'd handle it if he ran into the noseless man at the compound. More than anything, he wanted that.

He caught a ride from a guy he knew, the sixty-something owner of a taco stand Walker frequented. His own old Jeep he'd driven into Furino the day before was still back there. He could pick it up later today.

Mercita was a typical Mexican border town, overgrown, crowded, multicultural. Half a dozen languages could be heard on the streets, some of them ancient Mayan dialects.

While some states barely had a few hundred indigenous people left, Chiapas's tribes were still healthy, Mayan faces smiling on every corner. Indigenous people made up about a third of the state's population. Most lived off farming, but there were more and more of them in town now, those who'd been forced off their lands by the oil or logging companies.

Walker scanned the familiar landscape as he finished his bottle of water, then he dropped his head against the headrest and closed his eyes to catch a catnap. He'd been up, tossing and turning from nightmares half the night.

Of course, as soon as he nodded off again, the nightmares returned.

In the dream, he entered the room with the burnished Mexican tile floor in that checkerboard pattern. The stench of death filled the air, the only sound the flies' buzzing. Two chairs flanked a scarred wooden table in the corner. Frayed, flower-patterned curtains covered the open windows, billowing in the breeze that failed to penetrate the putrid air.

His gaze was riveted to the floor. A dozen severed heads had been placed on the tiles in a haphazard pattern, as if someone had been playing a board game. No bodies in sight. Blood splatters all over, as if the heads had been kicked as well as dragged.

Then he recognized sun-streaked blond hair, the cleft chin, the green eyes of his brother. *Ben.* Nausea washed over Walker along with dark desperation as he lurched forward. He didn't remember falling, but he was suddenly on his knees.

Then Ben's eyes livened, sharpened, and he looked at Walker. "Help me, brother," he begged.

Walker startled awake, feeling as if a black hole had opened up in his chest. He swore under his breath, and shivered despite the heat.

A few seconds passed before he registered the pickup, the driver, the houses they were passing. He dragged air into his lungs, then blew it out audibly, as if that could blow away the remnants of his dream.

Little by little, the bloody images did recede.

He watched the street. They were nearing the convent.

"Could you stop at St. Lupe's?" he asked the guy behind the wheel. "I need to step in for a second."

St. Lupe's provided health care and education free of charge for the most unfortunate, the largest and sturdiest building in sight, all solid brick laid by early missionaries.

When the pickup stopped, Walker jumped out and hurried up the steps, then pushed the heavy door open.

The region had seen an uptick in malaria lately. Inside the sick ward, people lay on mats on the floor, crammed in, dry-lipped with fever. Nobody had bothered to separate the men from the women. Kids lay mixed in with the adults. A month-old baby wailed in her dying mother's arms.

A familiar scent of smoke caught Walker's nose. The place had started out as a chapel, before a much larger church had been built. A dozen candles, and possibly some incense, burned in front of a fresco of solemn saints in the back.

A harried, middle-aged nun was washing faces with a wet cloth and handing out medicine, mumbling prayers as she went from patient to patient. The sick called out for her from every direction, "Sister Sak Ch'up! Sister Sak Ch'up!"

Not her real name. Sak Ch'up literally meant *white woman* in Mayan.

As Walker reached her, she glanced up, and a smile relaxed the worry lines on her forehead.

"It's you. Thank God. I thought they were bringing in more sick. I wouldn't know where to put them." She wiped the sweat off her forehead with the back of her sleeve.

The people of the tribes preferred St. Lupe's to the hospital. The hospital wouldn't let the shaman add his medicine to whatever the doctors ordered. Most of the missions didn't either, but Sister Sak Ch'up was an exception, overlooking the loincloth and feather necklace. She'd been known to sneak the old man in behind the mother superior's back so he could do his dances and his chants. The good sister was of the opinion that it helped if the patients believed in the cure.

Come to think of it…Walker looked around. The smoke he'd smelled when he'd come in was slightly pungent, different from candle smoke. And then he saw the source, brown toes peeking from behind a curtain.

"Baku," he called toward the hiding spot. "How have you been, my friend?"

The shaman stuck out his head first, then stepped out into the open with a toothless smile as he recognized Walker. He brought out the smoking roll of wild tobacco leaves from behind his back as he pranced over.

He was around fifty, and probably the oldest man in his village. Leathery skin, wiry build, ancient eyes that were hypnotizing.

He hesitated for a moment, then pulled a pouch from his belt. "Brunhilda," he said softly as he handed the pouch to Walker.

Walker looked inside. Nothing but a bunch of dried flowers. Maybe for tea, or to diffuse in oil and use on her skin. He shoved the gift into his pocket. "I'll make sure she gets it."

Baku nodded. He didn't ask if Walker had been well, just looked him over, looking all the way inside him, and nodded with resignation, silently acknowledging that while Walker wasn't injured, the darkness in his soul they'd spoken about in the past hadn't improved either.

"I have to visit the jungle spirits," the shaman said with a frown. "I am finished here." But as he passed by Walker, he blew smoke over him and murmured something under his breath in an ancient language.

The pungent cloud wrapped around Walker, while the guttural sounds of the incantation seemed to sneak down his throat as he took a breath. Something tickled inside his chest, leaving him uneasy. He'd never been superstitious, but on his trips to the tribal villages, he'd seen Baku work what could only be called magic.

Walker had seen him call a storm, seen him turn a baby inside the laboring mother's womb with a puff of smoke and a brief spell. Baku had talked to Walker about Ben, about things that had happened when they'd been children, things Walker had nearly forgotten, things Baku had no way of knowing.

As the old man disappeared through the door, Walker turned back to the nun and caught a sheepish, apologetic expression on her face. He smiled to make sure she knew he wasn't judging her. How could he? He'd gone to Baku for help himself.

He lowered his voice. "I'm looking for a noseless man. Has anyone like that come in?"

The sister shook his head. "You are not looking for him to harm him, are you?"

"All I want from him is information," Walker said truthfully. He didn't add, however, that he was willing to use any method to get that information. He figured the guy's fate was in his own hands. Tell Walker what he wanted to know, and nobody had to get hurt.

Sister Sak Ch'up relaxed. "He hasn't come through here. If I see him, I'll send word."

A while back, when Walker had escorted a shipment of guns to Guatemala, he heard a story told of a mercenary who was hired for a job but messed it up, brought in the wrong kind of people. These *wrong kind of people* were all beheaded at an abandoned farmhouse. The mercenary lost his nose as a reminder to pay better attention in the future.

The man who told the story was killed the same day at the gun exchange, so Walker couldn't ask him for more information. He'd been hunting for the noseless man since.

Sister Sak Ch'up moved on to her next patient.

Walker noted the medicine bottle she held. A hundred pills at most. Roughly two days' rations, considering the number of people in the ward. "Is that the last of the quinine?"

She nodded, her gaze somber, but not without hope.

Walker had never seen her dejected. He reached into his pocket and pulled out the roll of US hundred dollar bills he'd taken from the heroin convoy in the jungle for this purpose. He put it in the woman's free hand and folded her fingers around it. "A small gift. Please use this to buy pills and more mosquito nets."

Tears flooded her clear blue eyes.

He looked away, embarrassed. "I better get going."

Then he turned and strode away, hoping to head off the effusive gratitude the sister heaped on him whenever she got half a chance. She shouted her thanks after him anyway, and called on God to bless him.

Walker ducked out the door. He wasn't comfortable with attracting God's attention.

He got back into the pickup, and it moved on, past the shanty houses of the poor, then wood dwellings, then adobe homes as they passed into more affluent neighborhoods. After a few blocks of that, they started seeing boarded stores again, and empty, weed-choked lots. He had himself dropped off a block from the Xibalba cartel's compound and walked the rest of the way.

He stuck a cigar into his mouth and lit it. He carried only a single gun, his SIG, tucked into his waistband in the back. Coming armed to the teeth would say he was worried. Coming unarmed would say he was stupid. Neither was the impression he wanted to make.

The heavy-set, thick-necked guard at the compound's entrance recognized him and opened the eight-foot-tall cast-iron gate.

"Gracias." Walker strode past the man, chomping on his cigar. "Santiago around?" he asked in Spanish. "He said he'd be here around this time if I stopped by."

The guard pointed toward the main house without a word, an oversized traditional Mexican villa with yellow masonry walls and red tile roof, archways supporting the tiled front porch that kept the sun from the windows.

Six other buildings, a lot more simple and utilitarian, surrounded the front yard that was packed with vehicles, an elaborate blue-and-yellow-tiled fountain in the middle.

Snipers were posted on the tallest roof. Another guard stood at the main house's entrance, in front of the three-inch-thick oak doors that were reinforced with iron bands.

Nobody was missing a nose that Walker could see. He passed two black Hummers on his left, the fountain on his right, then reached the stairs and hurried up. "I'm here to see Santiago."

The guard let him through the thick oak doors with a nod.

The inside of the house was cool and cavernous, the floor covered in the same orange-hued tile as the porch, the furniture Mexican antiques, appropriate to the splendor of the villa.

Santiago was pacing the room to the right, yelling at someone on his phone. He glanced at Walker, then turned away and kept on yelling. Then threatening. Then issuing orders.

Something to do with a late shipment.

Santiago was about five-eight, short black hair slicked back. He was a clean-cut type of guy, wearing a light linen suit and an expensive gold watch. He could have passed for a doctor or a lawyer. Or a successful businessman. Which he was, in the criminal world. Hundreds of millions of dollars moved through his hands every year.

He threw an impressive fit. The power he held in Mercita and the surrounding area underlined his every word. The bandits and the gangs were no altar boys, but Santiago was several levels up from Pedro and Jorge. He was a cartel guy. At the top of the food chain. Nobody but Carlos Petranos, the cartel boss, was above him.

Walker waited.

Then Santiago finally finished and shoved his phone into his pocket. He dropped his chin, as if refocusing on a different issue. His gaze filled with a new blast of fury. He seemed even more pissed now as he watched Walker than he'd been on the phone.

"What the hell?" he spat the words at last, his tone incredulous. "Pedro? Over some fucking gringa?"

Walker relaxed his posture, dropping his shoulders, shoving his hands into his pocket. "Ever seen me lose my head over a woman, amigo?" he asked around his cigar, in a tone bordering on bored.

The man considered him for a moment. "Don't fucking amigo me. Pedro's crew is calling for your head."

Walker shrugged. "I came in of my own free will."

"Which is why you weren't shot on sight." Santiago slammed his palm on the doorframe as he walked out of the office, into the foyer. His tone turned machete sharp. "Why?"

The hard look on his face made it clear that Walker only had one try to get his answer right.

Walker didn't so much as blink. "Pedro was a traitor."

Santiago watched him in silence as a muscle began to tick in his left cheek. "I would have known."

Walker kept his face impassive. "Let me show you something."

And just like that, another game piece moved forward on the chessboard.

CHAPTER
NINE

They drove into the jungle using an old logging road, taking two four-wheel-drive pickups, seven goons in the back of the first, eight in the back of the second. Santiago sat in the cab of the first pickup next to Walker. Walker was driving. A basic safety measure on Santiago's part.

Walker's hands were busy with the steering wheel, out in the open, while Santiago's were free to reach for his weapon if needed.

Humidity was nearly dripping in the air. Only the open windows made the cab bearable. And still they were all sweating.

"You spent the night in Mercita?" Santiago asked, wiping his forehead with a rumpled handkerchief.

Walker nodded, keeping an eye on the gaping potholes in the dirt road, a few deep enough to swallow a wheel.

An annoyed grunt came from Santiago. "What do you know about the hit on Jorge's garage? What's this sudden new beef with Hernandez?"

Surprise had Walker looking over at the man. "Last night? He got hit again?"

"Lost three of his men. He's a friend of yours." That last bit wasn't a question.

"I was nowhere near the fight."

"He needs to let this one go."

"That'll be hard for him." Jorge was a born ring fighter. When he got punched, he punched back harder.

"Hernandez's crew handles security for the factory," Santiago said. "Bigger things hang in the balance."

Walker kept his eyes on the road ahead. *Bigger things.* Murder and misery on a scale even he could barely imagine. Unless he could stop it. He had four days left.

He pointed through the windshield. "The clearing is about half a mile ahead."

"Here would be a good place to stop then." Santiago scanned the jungle. "Pull off the road. We'll walk the rest of the way."

He hadn't risen as high in the ranks as he had because he was stupid. Being second in command of the Xibalba was no small accomplishment. Carlos Petranos wouldn't have picked anyone but the best of the best as his right-hand man.

Santiago wasn't about to drive into a potential ambush. He might trust Walker enough to check out his tale, but not enough to throw all caution to the wind.

They got out and walked down the dirt road in grim silence, the men surrounding them holding their weapons ready for any possible surprise. But other than a few obnoxious monkeys, their short trip wasn't disturbed.

They smelled the clearing before they reached it.

Santiago, still wary of a trap, gestured to Walker to step out into the open first. Walker strode forward and scanned the blackening bodies. They hadn't improved in the past couple of days.

After a moment, Santiago's men spread across the open area, securing the clearing. Then Santiago came up to Walker at last.

His jaw was tight, his eyes black with fury as he looked over the dead men. Animals had gotten to them, but the damage wasn't so bad yet that the cause of death couldn't be easily determined. The corpses were riddled with bullets. The scene spelled out an ambush and a quick but bloody battle. Spent shells and cartridges littered the ground everywhere.

Santiago pulled his gun and pressed the barrel under Walker's chin in a move that Walker could have prevented but didn't. He'd expected as much.

The man's eyes flashed murder. "Where is my shipment?"

Walker kept his posture relaxed and gestured toward the edge of the clearing where a black, silver-embroidered sombrero was stomped into the dirt, full of bullet holes and covered with blood.

Santiago lowered his gun and swore again. "You should have come to me with this right away."

"That was the plan. Then Pedro found out I knew. First thing I heard when I reached Furino was that he had a hit out on me. I had to deal with that, or I wouldn't have made it to you."

Santiago's sharp gaze didn't waver. "Do you know where my shipment is?"

"By the time I came across this place, everybody was gone."

Santiago watched him, then nodded abruptly and put his gun away. He clapped Walker on the shoulder. "Gracias, amigo."

"De nada." Walker nodded back. Then he let his gaze roam the clearing. "When did Pedro get this big?"

Santiago's eyes narrowed. The muscles of his face stiffened all over again as he looked at the bodies. "He wasn't this big."

Walker waited, let the man work it out for himself.

Santiago didn't make him wait long. "They're all in on it."

Walker swore. "I guess I better start watching my back."

Santiago turned from the scene of the massacre, chin down, like a bull about ready to attack. "Don't worry about it, amigo. This will be taken care of today."

He raised his hand to signal to his men to follow him, then strode back toward their vehicles.

When they reached the pickups, Santiago clapped Walker on the shoulder again and said in front of all his men, "You've done the Xibalba a favor. I won't forget it, friend."

Walker nodded, ready to go. He needed to get back to Clara. Because, sure he'd told her to stay put and wait. But what were the chances that she'd listened?

***

While waiting for Walker to return and take her to Furino, Clara ate the leftovers of her dinner then spent her morning mentally organizing and reorganizing all the available data on the case. She went through, word for word, her initial conversation with her father, then with Rosita's cousin, Melena. Then everything she'd learned from Walker so far. Thanks to him, she had a fair idea of the local players now, as far as criminal activity went.

Did she really need him going forward?

She made a mental pros-and-cons table in her head.

Pros: he knew the area, he personally knew at least some of the players, people were more likely to talk to him than to her, and in a violent confrontation—if things came to that—he'd make a great backup. She'd seen him with a knife, and she had no reason to believe that he would be any less competent with a gun.

Cons: he was unpredictable, he was a mercenary who hired himself out to criminals, he did what he wanted, when he wanted, and would never accept her as being above him in the chain of command.

Bottom line: If she worked with him going forward, he would have to be carefully managed. Except, she was pretty sure he was the most unmanageable person she'd ever met.

Deciding factor: Was she more likely to find Rosita with or without him?

With him, was the obvious answer, which meant Clara had to find a way to work with the man. Even if she wished she had other options.

She'd been hoping that the kidnapping had been drug related. The DEA had an office here. Clara could ask to see their files. They could provide backup if needed.

After giving the matter much careful thought, she was pretty sure she could work with them without having to reveal Rosita's connection to her father. Clara worked for civilian recovery, and Rosita was a US citizen who'd disappeared here. Nothing about Clara's looking for the girl should be suspicious.

But nothing about Rosita's disappearance had indicated an involvement with drugs.

Clara had three other main possibilities to consider: either Rosita was kidnapped for ransom, for trafficking, or in a random act of violence.

She hated that last option the most, but she had to consider that maybe there wasn't some greater purpose behind the kidnapping. If not the rat pack of young boys who now sat in jail, then some other hoodlum saw Rosita, grabbed her, raped her, dropped her body in the jungle.

A simple street crime. A crime of opportunity. Extremely difficult to investigate. Chances for a positive outcome: miniscule.

The kidnap-for-ransom option wasn't much better. If the girl had been kidnapped for money, a ransom would have been demanded already, unless she'd died somehow as a result of her kidnapping—say, while trying to escape. So if she'd been kidnapped for ransom, Clara pretty much assumed that Walker was right and the girl was dead at this point.

However, if Rosita had been kidnapped for trafficking, she was likely still very much alive, and time was of the essence. Tracking her down would become more difficult with every passing day as she was transported farther and farther away from her last known location.

Since Walker seemed to have known Pedro, aka el Capitán, he had to have some knowledge of the trafficking business. Like where the women were shipped from here. Or if Walker didn't know, his friend Jorge would. He picked up the dead trafficking victims. Jorge definitely merited a second look.

The waitresses at the cantina were next on Clara's list. They had three things going for them: they must have overheard all kinds talk from the banditos, they were probably safer to approach, and since they were women, they might be sympathetic to a missing seventeen-year-old girl. They might actually give Clara some information. Even if not about Rosita, then other local gossip that could prove useful.

Especially since she couldn't look at police reports. If she had access to those, she could see if there'd been any similar cases in the last couple of months. Maybe she could discover some trends, some clues in the paperwork that could point her in the right direction. But she couldn't see those reports, so the women at the cantina were her best bet. Not that they'd volunteer information to a stranger, but the right number of dollar bills might make a difference.

Clara put on her boots. She didn't have any brilliant insights or breakthroughs, but she had the next step or two mapped out—all she needed right now. Step by step, she was going to locate her retrieval target.

She climbed down the fire ladder, then went into the house through the back. Everything was quiet. The girls were probably still sleeping. She walked to the wall phone, making a mental note to give Brunhilda money for the two calls she planned on making. She dialed her grandmother's Alzheimer care home first, Serenity Acres. She never let more than a day or two pass by without checking in, no matter where she was.

The call rang straight to the room. And rang and rang.

While Clara waited, she checked out the bookcase next to the phone. The shelves held mostly romance novels, judging by the covers, in English, German, and Spanish.

Then Grandma Lucy picked up the call, and Clara turned her attention from the books. "Hi, it's Clara."

Silence on the other end.

"Your granddaughter," Clara added, as her stomach dropped. On her bad days, Grandma Lucy no longer remembered her family.

"Which one?"

Clara's stomach dropped a little more. "I'm the only one, Grandma. Clara. Remember? We talked on the phone the day before yesterday." Or maybe a visual would be better. "I came and saw you two weeks ago. We sat in the garden. I had that red shirt on you gave me. Remember?"

More silence.

"Grandma?"

"I had lunch with the pope today," Grandma Lucy said at last.

Clara closed her eyes and sighed.

Then her grandmother said, "Oh, fine, I'm kidding. How are you, honey?"

And Clara leaned against the wall, shaking her head, relief coursing through her. "You can't do this to me."

Grandma Lucy said, "While you're glad I haven't gone completely bonkers yet, tell me what's wrong with your father."

Clara tried not to groan. She'd just been played by her eighty-year-old grandmother. Seriously.

She proceeded with caution. "Why do you think something is wrong with dad?"

"He's been sounding off-kilter lately, but nobody tells me what's going on."

They had good reason. If they told Grandma Lucy about the dire cancer diagnosis, she would be worried sick, then in two days, she'd forget it. If they wanted her to know, they'd have to tell her again, and she'd go through the initial shock and pain over and over again.

So instead of bringing up cancer, Clara said, "He's fighting the DOD for continued funding. You know how it is to work for the government."

Grandma Lucy harrumphed, not sounding as if she completely bought the story. "Are you still in Mexico? How is it?"

"Hot. I'd like to go home."

"I'd like a vodka martini."

Clara smiled. "How are things at Serenity Acres?"

"Other than half the people forgetting to put their clothes on before they come out of their rooms? No-Undie Monday, and Whip-it-out Wednesday, we call it."

Clara grinned again. "But you like it there, right?" She knew her grandmother needed the around-the-clock care, but she still felt guilty over having her there.

"It's more exciting than sitting home all by myself would be," Grandma Lucy admitted. "At least it's not a Vegas-style place like where your Aunt Betty is."

"Vegas-style?" Clara blinked as she pictured gambling tables in the common room.

"What happens in your pants, stays in your pants," Grandma Lucy quipped. "They're low on staffing."

Clara closed her eyes. She seriously didn't want to think about it.

They talked some more, and she was grateful beyond words that her grandmother was having one of her good days. She wasn't confused or scared. She knew where she was and who her family were, knew that they loved her. And Clara got treated to a little of her grandmother's old spirit, the sassy, funny Grandma Lucy she wanted to remember.

But then her grandmother turned serious. "If he's sick again…He's not too sick, is he? Every night when I pray, I try to make a deal with God. I say, *God, take me, not him.*"

Clara's throat constricted. "Everyone is fine. Nobody is going anywhere."

They ended with smacking kisses into the receiver and Clara's promise that she'd visit Serenity Acres as soon as she was back in DC.

After she hung up, she filled her lungs and refocused, then dialed her father's cell phone number.

"Are you all right?" was her father's first question when she identified herself.

She was glad to hear his voice, and acutely aware that there was a merciless end date stamped on how many times she'd be able to talk to him.

"I'm fine. I just talked to Grandma. She is having a good day. You?"

"Better than I deserve." He sounded tired, bordering on weak, making her heart clench as he asked, "Is this a secure line?"

"No." While she didn't think Brunhilda's phone was tapped, she planned on talking in generalities, without mentioning any names.

"Just give me a brief update, then," he said, apparently thinking along the same lines.

She began with general background. "The local criminal element consists of two cartels on top, then the city gangs and the small-town banditos, then other small-time crooks, pickpockets, and people who run tourist scams and the like."

"Most likely perpetrator?" her father asked.

"I think Rosita would be beneath the cartels' notice. And if she's been kidnapped by a small-time crook, ransom would have been demanded long before now. But the banditos are heavily involved in the human trafficking that goes through the area. Furino seems to be under their control."

"Strategy?"

"I've done some surveillance. I had brief contact with one of the major players, but that's no longer a viable venue." She didn't want to go into the whole incident of Pedro getting disemboweled, not over an unsecured line.

"Juanita said you called her."

Clara had called Rosita's aunt right away, before leaving Mexico City. "She didn't have any usable information. She was very distraught."

"She seems better now that she knows I sent someone to look for her niece." He paused. "Are you with Walker?"

"He showed up yesterday, finally." She hesitated a split second, then decided truth was the best way to go. "I have some doubts whether he's the right facilitator for me. But I've decided to try working with him for now. You trust him?"

"I do," her father said without having to pause to think.

"I think he might have changed some since you last knew him."

"People don't change. Not at the core."

You did, she wanted to say. He'd been the most honorable, most loyal, most ethical man she'd ever known. And then came Rosita. Clara's brain hurt as she tried to reconcile the father she knew, with the idea of hooking up with a seventeen-year-old.

Her heart hurt too, so she slipped back into investigator mode.

"How do you know Walker? Just give me the nonclassified part."

"Not much of that," her father said after a moment. "Walker was part of a joint operation between the Army Special Forces and the SEALs a few years back. Let's just say he distinguished himself in an extremely difficult situation. He more than earned my respect."

Huh. She would have liked to know more but accepted that she couldn't ask questions about the mission. She went into another direction. "Is that how he came to owe you a favor?"

"No." Her father paused. "I helped him with something that had to do with his brother."

She wished she had more details but knew her father wouldn't elaborate.

"He's a loose cannon." There, the truth as she saw it.

But her father said, "I need to know that you're safe. He can do that for you. I don't want you to come to harm. Consider that the prime directive."

Just then he sounded like the loving, caring father he'd always been.

She closed her eyes. She filled her lungs with air. "How is Mom?"

"Gearing up for the First Gulf War veterans' benefit auction."

Of course she was. Her mother had never met anyone she didn't want to help. She was a good person. Beyond good. She didn't deserve betrayal. Clara's heart ached for her.

She talked some more with her father, but it was an uncomfortable conversation. Neither of them seemed to know how to handle their current situation.

She thought about that after they eventually hung up. Then she put those thoughts away. She'd sort out her feelings about her father when she got back home and she could talk to him in person, ask questions. Right now, she had to focus on finding Rosita.

Sitting around and waiting for Walker went against her best judgement. Passing time usually did not improve the outcome of retrieval missions. The longer someone has been missing, the slimmer the chances of live recovery were. And Clara had been given the case way too late already.

Pedro, the banditos, and human trafficking swirled around in her brain. She needed to find out more about the traffickers, where Rosita might be at this stage if they'd been the ones to kidnap her.

And she knew a man within walking distance who might be able to answer those questions: Jorge. She could interview Jorge first, while she waited for Walker.

Jorge had no reason to harm her. He thought she was Walker's girlfriend. All she wanted from the guy was some general information on trafficking.

But as Clara was about to leave, a Teutonic Valkyrie who had to be Brunhilda stuck her head out from a doorway down the hall, toward the front of the house. "Coffee?"

Clara hesitated only a second. "I'd love a cup."

She could afford a five-minute delay. Questioning Jorge would go way better with caffeine in her system. She hurried forward.

Large blue eyes, a generous mouth, Brunhilda was close to six foot tall and well over two hundred pounds. She cursed the heat in a mixture of German, Spanish, and English, her blonde hair braided and coiled on top of her head in a crown. She was a startling sight, like something one would see on stage at the opera. Clara half expected her to burst into a Wagner aria.

Instead, the woman led her to a small kitchen and seated her at the table. "I'm Brunhilda." She started brewing coffee. "Walker?"

"Gone off for the morning. I'm Clara."

Brunhilda flashed her a pensive look. She sipped her own coffee in a poppy red nightgown barely covered by a matching robe, her voluptuous figure on unselfconscious display.

Clara tried not to look at all that silk, fancier than anything she'd ever owned. Personally, she preferred simple, breathable, comfortable cotton sleepwear. She tended to go for the most practical choice in any given scenario.

Brunhilda smiled. "You're the first Mädchen he's ever brought here. He likes you muy bueno, ja?"

"How long have you lived in Mexico?" Clara responded to the question with a question, because she had no idea what to do with the woman's revelation about Walker.

Brunhilda had shared the information with a soft look on her face, like a mother talking about an errant son. *Ah, the first girl he brought home. Sigh.*

The moment was fairly surreal.

"Ich come aus Hamburg five years ago. I was a Bibliothekarin, ja?"

Clara shook her head.

"Oh, was ist das? Librarian," Brunhilda translated the word.

Clara nearly choked on her coffee.

"I shock you, ja?"

"A little."

Brunhilda's smile said the woman appreciated the truth. "Ich ende wo ich beginne. I end where I start. Meine Mutter was stolen von Albania when she was sixteen. I was born in a place like this in Hamburg."

And then she told Clara how she'd been taken from her mother and adopted at ten. How the older couple, both teachers, made sure she had her schooling.

Brunhilda's smile widened. "I worked muy hard at the Hamburg library. Then every year, I take vacation. Ich liebe Mexico." She said *ich liebe* in perfect German, then *Mexico* the Spanish way, with the x sounding like an h. "The food, the music, the muchachos...Muy macho." She gave a wicked grin. "I fell in love, ja?"

Clara sipped her coffee, trying to figure out how a German librarian ended up a Mexican brothel madam.

"Two decades with Guillermo." Brunhilda sighed. "Paradise. Then mine Guillermo dead. Kaputt. I was muy sola."

Lonely.

"And you, um, work too?" Clara couldn't help asking. Brunhilda had upset the spreadsheet in Clara's brain that had librarians in a different column from ladies of the night. She needed to create order again.

Brunhilda offered a wide smile, then slapped her pillowy thigh. "Some hombres need a dainty girl to make them feel macho. Other hombres want to climb Mount Everest. Jedem das Seine. To each his own." She laughed, a free, throaty sound.

The next question tumbled out of Clara's mouth while her brain was still too stunned to function. "And Walker?"

She winced. She hadn't meant to ask that.

But Brunhilda laughed again. "Walker doesn't need to do anything to be macho. Nada. Nicht."

Did that mean that he didn't sleep with anyone here? Clara wouldn't have asked if her life depended on it. She absolutely did not care.

"Walker ist Walker," Brunhilda said with full motherly approval. "When there's Schwierigkeit, trouble, he comes. He asks nada in return. Sometimes he sleeps in the attic. People know he's our amigo. Nobody hurts my girls, nadie," the woman said with affection.

Clara stared.

Light Walker, DOD facilitator, all-around mercenary, cold-blooded killer, protector of fallen women. The man defied categorization. Which was probably why she felt so off-balance around him.

"Does he come often?"

"Nein. He comes and goes like the wind. Unruhig."

Clara raised an eyebrow.

"Restless," Brunhilda translated, even as her cornflower-blue eyes turned speculative. "You know him long?"

Clara shook her head. "He's just helping me with something. I'm looking for a friend who disappeared around here. Rosita Ruiz. Seventeen. Have you heard anything about a young woman like that?"

She pulled the printout from her back pocket and showed Rosita's picture to the woman. Maybe one of her clients had been involved. Maybe he'd bragged.

But Brunhilda shook her head after a moment. "Nein. Did she come up from the south?"

"She came down from the US to visit family in Furino."

Surprise crossed Brunhilda's face. "Und the traffickers took her, ja?"

"I'm not sure," Clara admitted, and it occurred to her that Brunhilda might know as much about sex trafficking as Jorge. So she settled in with her cup of coffee and launched into her long list of questions.

Brunhilda was more than cooperative. She told Clara that while the area was active in the sex trade, Mercita was no Tenancingo.

Clara was grateful for that. The first thing she'd done when she'd been assigned the case had been to look up sex trafficking, and Tenancingo had been the first thing that came up in her search. Tenancingo, up north, was the sex-trafficking capital of the world, one in ten inhabitants working in trafficking.

Generations of men had gone into the business of forcing women into prostitution, mostly for customers in the US. The women were trafficked up to major cities as far as New York, then distributed to the countryside, to farms to service migrant workers.

And Tenancingo was just one town. There were places almost as bad in nearly every Mexican state. Twenty thousand women were trafficked across the Mexico-US border every year so their bodies could be sold.

"But the traffickers don't take Americans," Brunhilda said with a thoughtful expression. "Too much trouble."

Walker had said as much. "Do you think maybe one of the cartels took her?" Clara asked.

She couldn't imagine what for. The human traffickers made a lot more sense to her, but both Walker and Brunhilda were more familiar with local conditions than her, so she wasn't about to completely ignore their opinion.

Brunhilda tipped her head from side to side as she considered, a doubtful expression on her face. "Nein. When the cartels take people, they're rivals, und people who stole from the cartel."

She made a slashing motion in front of her throat with her hand to indicate what happened to the thieves.

Clara nodded and finished her coffee. So not the human traffickers, and not the cartels. Then who? One of the gangs? Walker hadn't thought so. But Clara had to consider any possibility at this stage.

"I'm going to head out for a while."

Even as she stood, she was mentally listing her options once again, hoping the list would trigger some brilliant insight, that something would suddenly jump out at her.

Cartels. Banditos. Gangs. Random.

She'd expected to be back in Furino by now, but Walker still hadn't returned. Right now, right here, she could only follow up on one of the possibilities on her list: gangs.

She needed to see if Jorge would be willing to talk with her. According to Walker, Jorge wasn't given to senseless violence. But he probably knew a lot about the rival gangs who were. Sure, going to Jorge with Walker would have been better. But Walker wasn't here, and even when he was, he seriously dragged his feet when it came to helping her.

111

Bottom line: she was the investigator on this case. She needed to investigate. Walker might blow his top, but she'd deal with him.

Clara thanked Brunhilda for the coffee, then headed out to see if she could scare up a lead without getting killed.

CHAPTER
TEN

Walker pulled over the pickup Santiago had lent him, and parked it by the curb outside of Brunhilda's.

His stomach growled. He'd been gone longer than he'd intended. Longer than Clara had patience for, apparently. As he watched her walking down the road up ahead, he felt a number of things. Surprise wasn't one of them.

He got out, breathing in air that was hot enough to scorch his lungs, then swore under his breath and hurried to catch up to her. Which part of "stay put" didn't she understand?

At siesta time, the street stood mostly deserted—too damn hot to be outside. Even the telephone poles looked wilted, the lines sagging. The heat didn't seem to bother Clara as she marched on—a woman on a mission and a half.

She had a strong, confident stride. Those long, lean legs that her shorts did little to hide certainly drew the eye. As far as curves went, however, she was about as voluptuous from behind as from the front—meaning not at all.

Yet she still managed to draw Walker's full attention. Made no sense. He'd never been into lanky. But the closer he got, the more he wanted to put his hands on her.

All over.

He wanted to put his mouth on her too. And he wanted her to put her mouth on him. He wanted her, period. But he wasn't going to do anything about it. The sudden blast of lust that shot through him only confirmed that it was time to send her packing.

He caught her by her pointy elbow. Which she immediately slammed back in a textbook self-defense move that would have knocked the air out of an unsuspecting person.

Walker evaded on instinct, a decade of hand-to-hand combat experience kicking in. The next moment, he had her turned, his arm around her middle, pulling her body flush to his to keep her in place and keep her from doing damage to either of them.

So much for him trying to keep his distance. "Where do you think you're going?"

As she recognized him, she stopped struggling, but her eyes shot Patriot missiles. "Let me go."

He didn't want to, for reasons he didn't want to probe too deeply. She fit surprisingly well against him. He liked the feel of her. Enough to want to keep her there, her body pressed to his. Enough so that his dick stirred in his pants.

A single swearword slipped through his teeth, hopefully too low for her to hear.

He'd worked hard on telling himself he wasn't interested. He had to keep reminding himself that he liked women with curves and without complications. He hadn't been looking to get involved with anyone, and certainly not with someone like her—a freaking DOD investigator.

Clara Roberts had caught him off guard. Not many people had ever done that.

He dropped his arm from her waist and stepped away before she could feel his growing hard-on and ask what the hell that was about. He jerked his head toward Brunhilda's. "Let's go back."

And because she looked like she might argue, he wrapped his fingers around her wrist, then turned and led her back to Brunhilda's, around the house, only letting her go on their way up the fire stairs.

He went through the window and turned to face her as she climbed in after him. He watched her lift one bare leg over the windowsill after the other, and wished once again that those long legs were wrapped around his waist. His idiot brain had to go there every damn chance it got, apparently.

Shit.

The timing was ridiculously bad. Beyond bad. Impossible.

"I thought I asked you to stay right here while I was gone," he said, his voice coming out more clipped than he'd intended.

She drew a deep breath and changed her expression from angry to coolly professional, oblivious to his X-rated thoughts of what the two of them could do up in the attic for the rest of the afternoon.

"I know you think Rosita is dead," she said. "But if that's the case, I need to at least find confirmation."

He watched the steady resolution in her gunmetal-gray eyes. Then his gaze dropped to the stubborn set of her mouth. He liked people who had resolution. He liked her strength, and that she was sticking with her cause no matter what.

Clara Roberts had backbone. And she wasn't easily scared. Which, at the moment, actually worked against him, since he was trying to scare her out of the state.

He swore under his breath once again as he turned from her and strode deeper into the attic. He'd take her to Furino tonight, but the entire afternoon stretched before them, and spending all that time with her up here was a bad idea.

In any case, he had business to take care of. And he clearly couldn't leave her behind again and expect her to stay put.

"I'll take you to the town incinerator. You can show Rosita's picture to the operator."

Instead of falling at his feet with gratitude, she asked, "Is that where unclaimed bodies go from the morgue?" Then added, "I already checked with the morgue when I got here. They haven't received any unidentified bodies that fit her description."

He shook his head as he turned back to her. "Most unidentified bodies don't make it to the morgue. They only take bodies there that have a high chance of being claimed. If someone is suspected of being a migrant, without any papers, likely a victim of trafficking, they bypass the morgue and go the quick and cheap route. Nobody is going to claim them anyway. Cold storage at the morgue costs money, and they don't have enough capacity to begin with."

So he wouldn't think of his brother, he asked, "Would you rather have lunch before or after the incinerator?"

She didn't look overexcited about that offer either. "I want to talk to Jorge again. Actually, that's what I need to do first."

"Jorge got hit last night. He lost three guys. He won't be entertaining visitors today."

She stared at him.

"Lunch," he reminded her, then added, "If you want my advice, the incinerator is the kind of place best visited on an empty stomach."

But she said, "I've seen dead bodies before. I'm hungry. Let's grab something to eat on the way."

Walker kept his gaze on her. She was pretty tough for a fairly new investigator with a background in accounting. Scaring her off should have been easy. Right at the outset, the incident with Pedro should have done it. If not that, then Jorge's shed for sure. Yet she was still here.

"After the incinerator," she said. "I'm going to Furino, with or without you." Then she added, "You promised to help me. You said you'd take me back."

"I consider keeping you alive helping you."

As a further gesture of goodwill, he didn't tumble her onto the mattress. But the temptation was there.

The attic seemed too small all of a sudden, and way too hot, but it was definitely too early to go back to Furino. They had to wait a couple of hours, at least, before it'd be safe. Not that he couldn't think of a dozen ways to distract her in the meanwhile, as he looked at her—all riled up, her eyes sparkling with heat.

At least, a dozen ways. Actually, make that two dozen. All of them at the very top of the stupid scale. Frankly, he wasn't sure who was distracting whom. His focus had definitely slipped since he'd laid eyes on her in the cantina, a lamb encircled by slobbering wolves.

She was too fresh, too innocent, and entirely too earnest, not nearly cynical enough for the Mexican borderlands. She should have become a schoolteacher. Or stayed an accountant.

At first, he'd been simply annoyed that she'd come, at the exact wrong time, and that he would have to waste time on dealing with her. Then Pedro had come for her. And Walker had known that he would never let Pedro have her.

When he'd kissed her after taking her from Pedro, he'd kissed her for showmanship's sake, to mark her as his to the wolf pack.

And now he wanted to kiss her again. "Let's get out of here."

***

Clara was glad to be out of the weird mood of the attic. There was something off about Walker, but she couldn't put her finger on it and decided not to waste her time trying. Most likely, he just had his knickers in a twist because she wouldn't follow his every order like an obedient little puppy.

They ate lunch at a busy roadside stand, then drove to the dump that stood outside the city limits east of the city.

The Mercita dump was the most ghastly place Clara had ever visited. Other than mountains of regular waste one would normally see at a place like this, the dump also took in the bodies of dead pets and diseased farm animals.

As they passed by a dozen or so maggot-covered cows on their way to the main building, Clara was seriously rethinking her decision to eat on the way over. Her lunch sat in her stomach like a bucket of stones. The stench that permeated the air was unbearable. The dump was a hundred times worse than Jorge's shed.

"I'm going to have to soak in bleach water for a week to get the smell out of my hair and clothes," she muttered as she followed Walker. "Or maybe just burn my clothes and shave my head."

He stopped to look at her.

"The burning clothes part has potential," he said in a low tone.

Was that heat in his eyes?

She blinked. She had to be mistaken. She wished he'd stop with the come-ons he used only to knock her back a pace, because even though he didn't mean them, they left her a little breathless.

She wanted to kick him in the shin, but the uneven ground was covered with garbage, and she didn't want to risk losing her balance and falling into something nasty.

He seemed to know where to go, so she followed him, trying to hold her breath and look neither left nor right.

He led her straight to the back of the building where a ten-foot tall incinerator threw off volcano-like heat, the air shimmering around the giant cast-iron furnace.

The short, wrinkled man who operated the fiery monster greeted Walker as if they knew each other.

They'd probably had some business together in the past. Dirty business seemed right down Walker's alley. Since he clearly had rapport with the man, Clara let him ask the questions, while she stood there quietly, doing her best not to gag from the smell or faint from the heat.

According to the operator, the incinerator was fired up every single day. But he denied burning human bodies, casting nervous glances at Clara.

He had smudges of dirt on his face, whole clumps of it on his clothes, which didn't stop Walker from clapping him on the back. "We're just trying to find a friend who's gone missing."

Clara did her best not to look judgmental, even while the giant cast-iron door of the furnace creeped her out, the thought of bodies tossed in there like garbage sending a shiver down her spine despite the heat.

The man gave a sullen shrug as he watched her. "It's not any different from cremation. There's no one to claim the remains anyway."

She kept her opinion to herself on that and pulled the photo from her pocket. "Have you seen her by any chance? She would have come in sometime after July first."

The old man gave a reluctant but careful look. "I don't think so."

"You have anybody in the back right now?" Walker asked.

The man shook his head. "Not that I know of."

They talked another few minutes, but it was clear the incinerator was another dead end.

As they were leaving, Walker asked if he could take a couple of old tires from a pile. The operator told him to take all he wanted.

"What are those for?" Clara asked as Walker heaved three tires into the back of the pickup.

"They could come in handy," he replied, evasive as always.

Seriously. She didn't know why she even bothered asking him anything. But she did pose another question, "Do you think the furnace operator was telling the truth? He was kind of wishy-washy, wasn't he? Although, I'm pretty sure he wishes more than he washes," she added.

The corners of Walker's lips twitched. "I don't see why he would lie. If he had useful information, he would have traded it in the hope that we'd pay him."

Clara found herself agreeing with that assessment as she got into the pickup. "Are we heading to Furino next?"

Walker slid behind the wheel, started up the truck and drove out of the dump. "I have one more thing to take care of in Mercita."

He drove down the single-lane road leading back to the city.

After another mile, Clara could almost breathe again. "Where are we going now?"

"I need to pick up something from someone who owes me a favor."

She didn't bother rolling her eyes. *Here we go.* Another delay. He seemed to be allergic to going anywhere in a timely manner.

One more trip. That's it.

She would allow him one last stop, then she was going to Furino if she had to steal the pickup from him. Decision made, she settled comfortably into her seat.

Walker only drove for maybe twenty minutes before stopping at a construction site. "You stay here."

"How long is this going to take?"

He shrugged.

She glanced at the key in the ignition.

He grabbed it, then pocketed it.

Because he expected her to make a remark, she didn't. She even bit back the groan-growl working up her throat. Instead, she asked, coolly professional, "Could I use your phone?"

He raised an eyebrow as he opened the door to get out. "Who are you calling?"

"Rosita's cousin. When I met her yesterday morning, I told her I'd give her a follow-up call today."

Follow-up was a good practice with witnesses. They never remembered everything at the initial interview, and they might not take the initiative to call if they recalled something else later. Giving them another call yielded new information more often than not. And by asking Melena to recount again what she'd told Clara yesterday, Clara could also see if there were any inconsistencies in the story.

Walker reached into his back pocket, tossed her the phone, and left her with, "Lock the door. Under no circumstances are you to get out."

Because she hadn't meant to get out in the first place, she clicked the lock, looking after him as he strode toward a trailer behind a couple of front loaders.

He walked like a soldier, constantly scanning the area, his hands loose at his sides, ready to go for his weapon at a moment's notice. He walked with power, and a little swagger. He was so damn masculine, it hurt her eyes.

He was a ruthless mercenary.

He was the type who could never give her a straight answer.

She was pretty sure he'd never toed a line in his life. In fact, he swaggered over lines without slowing.

That she was physically attracted to him while pretty much hating everything about his personality annoyed her so much she gritted her teeth. And yet, she couldn't draw her gaze away from him until he disappeared behind the trailer's door. Only then did she turn to inspect the rest of the work site.

The construction looked early in the process, mostly moving around dirt. Here and there rocks stood in the path of the equipment, some as tall as ten feet. A couple of men were drilling holes into the rocks. Probably for explosives.

The workers paid her little attention past a few curious looks. They went about their work in the midafternoon heat.

She dialed the operator and gave her Rosita's cousin's name and address. The call was connected in just a few seconds.

"Hi, this is Clara Roberts, Rosita's friend. We talked yesterday. I was wondering if you might have remembered anything else, or heard anything new from anywhere," she said in her best Spanish.

"No. I told you everything I remember." The woman paused. "Sorry."

"I'm really worried about her," Clara said, and wondered why Melena didn't sound worried.

"I'm sure she's fine."

"So you have a suspicion about where she might be?"

Maybe the girl had run off with a cute boy and asked the cousin to keep it secret from the aunt. If that was it, Clara was going to be seriously angry for the time and resources wasted.

"No," the woman said.

Too quickly?

Again, she was showing little emotion.

Maybe the cousins weren't that close. According to the aunt, Rosita hadn't been back to Furino since the aunt had taken her to the US.

"If you think of anything, could you please leave me a message at the guesthouse?"

The woman promised, then ended the call quickly.

Clara dropped the phone onto her lap and looked outside.

The aunt was out of her mind with worry, the cousin wasn't worried in the least, not now, and not the first time Clara had talked with her. Was that significant? The aunt had been raising Rosita for years, so it was natural for her to have a much closer attachment. Maybe that explained the discrepancy in their reactions.

Clara thought about that some more as she watched the big machines push dirt around. The ancient pickup had no AC. Dust swirled in the air outside, but she kept the windows rolled down as she went through the entire case again from beginning to end, every little detail that she knew, no matter how insignificant.

Her brain was nearly fried by the time Walker returned an hour later. The sweat stains on his shirt only made him look manlier and sexier, while she was pretty sure hers made her look disgusting.

She hoped she stank. He deserved it.

As he got in, instead of apologizing for putting her at risk for a heat stroke, he handed her what felt like four small bricks of Play-Doh wrapped in a dirty rag. "Hold on to this, and try not to fling it around."

She squeezed her eyes shut for a moment and sighed in resignation. "C4?"

"Nothing makes a man feel like a man more than playing with explosives." His chiseled lips curved into a slow grin. "Well, maybe one other thing."

She'd seen a few of his challenging grins, and plenty of his infuriating grins, but this was the first time she saw his smile fully reach his eyes, and the effect was breathtaking. Behind the hardened mercenary, she could suddenly see the boy he'd once been, and her heart turned over inside her chest without warning.

Stupid. Stupid. Stupid.

She was sure that not only had he broken countless hearts, but he'd stabbed a few too. She would have to be beyond idiotic to let her heart anywhere near Light Walker.

She must have had an odd expression on her face, because he said, "Hey, don't look so scared. C4 is actually pretty stable. You could juggle with it and nothing would happen."

He probably *did* juggle explosives.

Sweet Jungle Jesus.

She needed to put the man under the column heading "Men NOT to Fall for under Any Circumstances." And then she needed to lock the spreadsheet and password-protect it.

CHAPTER
ELEVEN

Walker needed to put off the Furino trip just a little longer.

They took the C4 back to Brunhilda's, then he made a few more phone calls, just checking on people, getting a feel for what all the players were doing.

He wanted to make sure that tensions in the criminal underworld were escalating, that nothing happened that might defuse the pressure he'd spent the last month building.

Where he could, he also asked about the noseless man, but nobody had information. He was beginning to consider that his original intel might have been faulty. He had a hard time accepting that possibility. He couldn't reconcile himself to the idea that he might never find Ben's killer.

He didn't leave for Furino with Clara until late in the evening, when he thought it would be fairly safe.

A police car flew by them on the road as he drove, then another, sirens on full blast.

Clara looked after them. "What's going on?"

"Some trouble in Furino. We'll see."

They drove in silence for all of two minutes before Clara started up her questioning again. "Where did you go this morning?"

"Here and there."

"Who did you meet?"

He stifled a groan. She was relentless. No matter. A quick trip to Furino and she'd be begging him to take her to the airport at Tuxtla Gutiérrez. He could do that, could make it there then back by midnight the latest, then he would move the next piece forward on the chessboard. He had an important delivery to make.

"What did *you* do while I was gone this morning?" he asked, to redirect her attention.

"Chatted with Brunhilda. She labors under the false impression that you're a good man."

He bit back a grin. "*Good* can be an objective classification."

"Not really," she immediately objected. "Good is what's moral, right, legal, and or beneficial to society. As in, the exact opposite of bad."

"And people just fit neatly into those categories?"

"Pretty much."

"How convenient for you."

She frowned. "I don't like it when you mock me."

He didn't like it that she was still here. But that would be remedied shortly.

"What made you leave the military and choose the opposite path?" she asked.

"Opposite?" He quirked an eyebrow. "You mean because serving one's country is good and being a mercenary in Chiapas is bad?"

She nodded.

"Maybe I was never good to start with."

And she said, without stopping to think, "You're not horribly terrible."

He shook his head at her. "You say the nicest things." He held her gaze for a moment. "You're not trying to get into my pants, are you?"

She growled.

He felt his mouth twitch. And, of course, there was a twitch in his pants. She was entertaining. He had to give her that.

"I think I want that on my headstone," he told her. "*He wasn't horribly terrible. Has a nice ring to it.*"

Not that he expected a headstone. Most likely, he'd catch a bullet in the back someday, possibly someday soon, and be left to rot in the jungle like he'd left Santiago's men in that clearing. Karma and all that.

"There are worse people out there," she said in an earnest tone. "I think you have *some* scruples, some lines you wouldn't cross."

"Not that many."

"I don't think you'd kill innocent people. Women or children. I don't think you'd shoot a dog for barking."

He glanced at her. She was looking for his redeemable qualities. It'd been a while since anyone had thought he was redeemable. He certainly didn't entertain such illusions about himself. She was a damn strange woman.

Because her words caught him off guard, he made a joke of them. "Ah, you're warming up to me. You know what comes next."

"Bitter disappointment?" she deadpanned.

A bark of laugh escaped him. "First you warm up. Then you fall head over heels. Next thing we know, you'll be begging to have my babies."

His chest clenched for no real reason as he said the last words. He rubbed the heel of his palm over his breastbone. Probably heartburn.

"No," Clara said, completely serious now. "I don't think we suit each other that way."

What in hell was she talking about? Of course, they did. They'd suit in bed just fine. Those long, lean legs wrapped around his waist would be pure poetry. He could make those gunmetal eyes soften. Did she think he couldn't?

"We live in different worlds," she said.

Okay. She'd been thinking in the abstract, not specifically about sex. Well, she was a woman, with one of those overcomplicated brains. In her case, probably even more overcomplicated than most.

There was no point in thinking about sex with her anyway, no matter how appealing, since she'd be leaving tonight.

He decided to turn their conversation in a different direction. "So with this civilian recovery thing…What's your success rate?"

She sat up straighter. "One hundred percent." A frown pulled her brows together. "Not all were live recoveries. I've had three body recoveries. But all three had been killed before I was even assigned the case," she added quickly.

Her record sounded immensely important to her. She was going to hate having Furino ruin her spotless streak. He almost felt sorry for her. Well, hell, it couldn't be helped.

"Your boyfriend doesn't mind that you're never home?" He had no idea what made him ask. He stared into the approaching darkness through the windshield. He was *not* fishing for information. How stupid would that be?

"If I had a boyfriend, he would be fully supportive of my career," she said with full confidence.

Of course, he would be. A big fat lie. Any man who had her would want to keep her naked and under him, and far away from any danger.

Shit. Walker pressed his lips together. He did not need to think about her naked. Of course, now the image sat there, front, and center in his brain.

Lanky wasn't that bad, actually. He had no idea why he hadn't realized that before. Lithe and tall kind of went pretty well together. Especially when topped off with gunmetal eyes that could go from unforgiving to sparkling with amusement in a blink.

"Maybe I should visit Rosita's cousin again," Clara was saying, her tone pensive, her mind obviously back on the case. "There's something off there. She isn't that overwrought. She said, *I'm sure she's fine.* She wasn't all that excited when I offered to help find Rosita in the first place."

Walker thought about it. "Some people are more emotional than others."

But Clara didn't look convinced. "Nothing about this case feels right. Something's off, but I can't put my finger on it."

She cleared her throat. Looked away. "For one, the man Rosita was involved with…He's not the type for a liaison like this. From what I know of him, I just can't see it. I've seen him with his wife. They're great together. When he looks at her…"

"Maybe Rosita seduced him."

She winced. "I thought about that, but it feels wrong to think it. Like I'm blaming the victim. He's the grown-up in the situation, and she's the teenager."

"Do you know how long the affair went on?"

"From what I understand, they were only *together* once. But she made it into a big story, like a full relationship, to her aunt, so her aunt thinks it was a full-blown affair."

"Have you considered that Rosita told the truth to her aunt, and your guy is lying?"

She watched him silently for several seconds. There were major undercurrents in her eyes, in her body language, but he couldn't decipher them.

She said, "I don't think my guy is lying."

He thought over the possibilities. "So, A, he's a jerk slash predator who seduced a seventeen-year-old. Or, B, she seduced him, maybe for kicks, or for whatever other reason."

The *whatever other reason* stuck in his brain. "Maybe she seduced him so she could blackmail him. It pissed him off, and he made her disappear."

"No."

Her absolute resistance to the idea was all over her face, in the outraged tone of her voice and stubborn tilt of her chin. She looked stricken at his suggestion. Whoever the guy was, she respected and liked him.

More than liked him?

Walker bristled. Then he swallowed his sudden annoyance with the thought and shook off the idea. Clara wouldn't like a married man. She had very definite ideas of good and bad. She had strict principles. He respected her for that. He'd been like that once. Before Ben's murder.

He said, "Maybe Rosita slept with the guy to get him attached to her, then faked her disappearance down here. Maybe a ransom note is on its way. She's making him sweat first."

"Not this long." Clara sucked in her bottom lip then released it. "She disappeared on July first. There are phones, email. It's not like they have to send the ransom note with pigeon post."

She had a point there.

They sank into silence, each lost in thought, until they came across the first barricade, half a mile outside Furino.

A dozen cops lined up by the side of the road.

Clara stared at them, her posture stiffening. "They could be looking for you, you know. You killed a man in town yesterday, in front of two dozen witnesses." She swallowed. "Maybe you're right. Maybe coming back to Furino right now isn't the best idea."

None of this was a good idea. But Walker trusted the fact that nothing around here ever worked the way it was supposed to.

*On the other hand…*if the cops had a warrant for his arrest…He'd seen a Mexican jail up close and personal before. He didn't care to repeat the experience.

"If they ask me to step out of the car, duck. I'm going to gun the engine and make a run for it," he said as he rolled up to the barricade.

The cops looked right at him but didn't stop him. They waved him through instead, and Walker let out the pent-up air from his lungs.

"*You've done the cartel a favor,*" Santiago had said. Looked like the favor was already being paid back. Obviously, the cops had been told to back off Walker.

Clara was gaping at him as he drove off. "How is that even possible?"

He grinned at her. "It's good to have friends in high places."

"Criminal places or government places?" she asked.

"Around here, it's all the same."

An ambulance whizzed by them, sirens blaring.

Clara watched it tear down the road. "What do you think happened?"

Walker shrugged and drove in silence. He rolled his window down and listened. No gunfire peppered the night, a good sign. Looked like he'd timed their drive right. The armed confrontation was over, cleanup in progress, but not yet finished.

They drove by more police cars as they reached Furino. Nobody bothered him. Then they saw ambulances and beat-up old fire trucks.

They were close to the middle of town when they saw the first bodies. Town police were busy bagging and tagging in the light of their high beams, gurneys waiting and ready.

He slowed down next to one of the cops. "*Qué pasa?*"

The man waved them on without looking up or answering.

Walker drove to the other end of Furino, toward the guesthouse where Clara had been staying. That section of town seemed the worst hit. Blood congealed on the street in dark pools, bullet holes peppering the guesthouse's front door, two of the windows shot out. Yet, as battle beaten as the place looked, the cantina across the road looked worse.

The bandits' favorite hangout had been reduced to little more than smoldering remains. Walker saw his Jeep in the side parking lot, burned out. He swore. He'd liked that car. It'd taken jungle roads well. But a single look told him the Jeep was beyond salvaging. He'd have to go see Jorge for another.

Emergency vehicles surrounded the place: three police cars, two fire trucks, and two ambulances. A dozen bodies lay on the ground, all blackened, some still smoking, as if they'd been recently dragged from the building.

Margarita, the buxom waitress, was coming on to one of the cops, caressing his arm. She'd probably shot someone. Walker had no doubt she'd get off and didn't waste time worrying about her.

He stopped the pickup, and they got out. He watched Clara stare at the bodies being gathered up and zipped into body bags, her face a carefully schooled mask he suspected she'd developed for work.

He walked up behind her, noted the slight tremble that ran through her, and felt like shit for making her see the carnage. But he had tried to get her out of here before things had come to this. Now he was out of time, and they had to do things the hard way.

He put a hand on her shoulder. "Looks like the gang wars reached Furino. Listen, you have to get out of here. It's the wrong place at the wrong time. Rosita Ruiz is probably as dead as these men. Will tracking down her body make that much of a difference? Are you willing to die for it?"

"I need to find her," she said without looking at him, staring straight ahead.

The sight was truly gruesome, turning even his stomach. The cantina had been a war zone at one point today. A man sprawled in a pool of blood, half his face missing.

Guns had carried the day, but the machetes must have come out too, because he could see several unattached body parts. A severed hand lay next to what might have been a foot. Then half an arm, chopped off at the elbow, a clean cut. People kept their machetes sharp; no sense having it any other way.

Walker looked back at Clara. He didn't like the way her lips thinned. He'd brought her here specifically to show her this, to shock her, but now he turned her away from the sight until she faced him.

"You need to stay alive so you can save more people," he told her, as logical and reasonable as he could be, because she was most likely to respond to that. "If you stay, you're going to end up in one of those body bags."

"Rosita might still be alive."

His hands tightened on her shoulders, frustration filling him. "Have you taken a good look around this place?"

She drew a slow breath. Didn't look back at the carnage.

Good. He hoped the images had been burned into her brain. "How about we go into the guesthouse, gather up your things, then you get out of here?"

She raised her gaze to his. Then she pointed at the blue Ford Fiesta by the curb, tires and windows all shot up. "That's my rental."

"I'll drive you to Tuxtla Gutiérrez."

She drew a deep breath.

He hated the haunted look in her eyes, even if he'd worked hard to put it there. She looked ready to go, finally. But before he could push his advantage, his cell phone rang in his pocket.

He picked up the call.

"You in one piece, you pasty-ass gringo?" Jorge asked on the other end.

"So far. You?"

"Bulletproof, hermano." Jorge gave a dark laugh. "You in Furino? You really caused all that shit?"

"Just got in. Cops are bagging the bodies. What do you know about it?"

"They say Pedro fucked up. Santiago figured it out. He ordered you to take out Pedro yesterday. Then Santiago's boys hit the rest of the Furino teams today."

"People say all kinds of things."

Walker had been pretty sure Santiago would take credit for unmasking Pedro as a traitor. A shipment had been lost. Even Santiago had a boss. Shit happened on his watch, he needed to fix it before the boss got angry. He needed points for at least figuring out who'd taken the shipment.

In any case, word was out now that Pedro's death had been a sanctioned kill. Which meant nobody could come after Walker for it. That included not only the police, but whatever was left of Furino's bandits. He breathed a little easier.

"Santiago said you lost good men last night," he told Jorge. "I'm sorry, man. I hear you've been told not to hit back at Hernandez. That's tough."

Silence followed his words before Jorge said, "The angel of death is on the wing. There's no telling when and where he'll land."

Meaning, if Jorge saw an opportunity, he was going to take it.

Walker had expected no less. "Let me know if you need anything. I have a friend who has some extra explosives. He owes me a favor."

Jorge gave a dark laugh. "Yeah. Thanks. But these guys, I want to beat the life out of them with my bare hands. More satisfying that way." He paused.

"So, a gesture of goodwill for a gesture of goodwill. Listen, hermano. I might have something on the chica you asked about."

Walker stepped away from Clara to make sure she wouldn't overhear. He had no intention of telling her of any new developments that might keep her here.

"What is it?"

"I put out the word to friends and family, and something came back. I have a cousin in Furino. His seventeen-year-old daughter went to school with a Rosita Ruiz many years ago. She says this Rosita's parents died and her aunt took her to the States."

That had to be the same girl. Furino wasn't that big. But how Rosita had gotten to the States made no difference. "Anything else?"

"Ruiz was her mother's second husband. Her first husband was Petranos. She had a son with him, Rosita's half brother. Carlos."

Everything inside Walker went still. His fingers tightened on the phone.

"Carlos Petranos?" he asked under his breath so only Jorge would hear.

"You need to stay away from this, hermano."

A hundred thoughts pinged around in Walker's brain like ricocheting bullets. "Yeah," he said absently, his mind shuffling puzzle pieces.

"About the other thing," Jorge went on. "The noseless guy. I got nothing on that. I'll keep asking."

"Thanks."

"You try and stay alive, all right?"

"I'll take a stab at it. You do the same."

He ended the call and shoved the phone into his pocket.

Carlos Petranos.

Rosita Ruiz's half brother was the head of the Xibalba cartel. Santiago reported to Carlos, in fact.

Walker swore under his breath. He stared into the night and saw all his carefully laid plans crumble.

Rosita Ruiz was a curve ball that could ruin two years' worth of hard work on his part. He put all his frustration into a single, succinct swearword that he hissed under his breath, then he turned to look at Clara, who was watching the body bags being loaded.

He had a very bad feeling about Rosita Ruiz's disappearance.

And to confirm his suspicions, he needed Clara's help.

Which meant he couldn't let her go. He swore again.

He watched her for another moment before he walked back to her, swallowing the regret that bubbled up his throat. She should have left while she'd had the chance. He'd told her to go. Hell, he'd damned near begged her to leave.

She should have listened.

"Anything important?" She watched him with trust in her eyes, thinking he was there to help her.

Her problem, not his. "Why don't we go inside?"

She nodded briskly and followed him.

They walked inside together, straight into a large dining room that held a dozen tables with chairs. The family who ran the guesthouse—mother, grandmother, three teenage daughters—greeted them, but they were too busy cleaning up broken glass, all wielding either brooms or pans or garbage cans.

"Did anyone get hurt?" Clara rushed to ask, sounding genuinely concerned.

"No, señorita," the younger woman, Consuela, in her early forties, replied.

The older woman was her mother, the three girls her daughters. Walker knew nothing more of them. They weren't players in any of the criminal enterprises in town, so they didn't concern him.

"We clean up quickly," Consuela said, apologetic, as if somehow the shootout had been her fault. "No worry. Dinner in twenty minutes, sí?"

"Why aren't they more upset? How often does this happen here?" Clara asked quietly as she took the stairs up to her room.

"Not that often. But they've seen enough to become resilient." Walker followed close behind, thinking over what he was about to tell her.

Clara too fell into silence for a few seconds.

Then she repeated his earlier words, "Wrong time, wrong place," as she walked down the upstairs hallway and stopped in front of the last door.

She pulled a key from her pocket, unlocked the door, and stepped into the room. Walker followed and locked the door behind them.

He'd stayed at the guesthouse for a week when he'd first come down here and was familiar with the rooms. They were all the same: bed, table, nightstand, and dresser. The two communal bathrooms were at the end of the hall, one for men and one for women.

"Why don't you sit down?" He leaned against the door.

He waited until she lowered herself to the edge of the double bed. She looked a little lost, for the first time. The scene outside had gotten to her. She should have left when he'd first told her. But the fact remained, she was still here.

The question was, was he willing to sacrifice her? Then again, maybe the question was, why was he even thinking about this still, as a self-professed conscienceless bastard?

"Who called?" she asked as she folded her hands on her lap.

"Jorge." He paused. "How about we both lay our cards on the table?"

"Does cards on the table mean that you're actually going to answer my questions now? Because I have a few—Wait." Her head snapped up, her body language changing from numb shock to hopeful. "Did Jorge call about Rosita?"

Walker shoved his hands into his pockets. "Rosita Ruiz's half brother is Carlos Petranos, head of the Xibalba cartel."

Clara leaned forward, her mouth dropping open. She closed it as she stared at him, her eyes growing wide. "Are you sure? Nothing like this came up in my investigation."

"I'm guessing it's not common knowledge. Rosita and Carlos have different fathers."

Clara nodded, her eyes unfocused, as if her brain was churning through this new bit of data, trying to figure out where it best fit into those damnable spreadsheets in her head.

Then she blinked, determination sharpening her gaze. "So now I have a definite lead. I'm going to follow it. Thank you."

She smiled at him, blissfully unaware that she'd very likely just signed her own death warrant.

She had no idea what she was getting herself into.

And he felt sorry about that. But not sorry enough. He shut out all doubt, all emotion as he filled his lungs. "So this is the plan—"

CHAPTER
TWELVE

Clara inhaled the mouthwatering aromas that filled the guesthouse's dining room, but she couldn't relax as she sat at the table. For one, the massacre outside had spoiled her appetite. And even without all that, her mind was too busy. She finally had a clue. The fact that Rosita's half brother was head of a cartel was significant. Possibly a game changer.

Carlos Petranos. She had a serious clue at last, and Walker seemed ready to help. With the gang war in Mercita and the violence in Furino, she was ready to stop pretending that she didn't need him. She was a big enough person to admit that she was out of her depth here.

He'd been about to tell her his plans up in her room when Consuela had interrupted to let them know that dinner was ready. Since they couldn't talk openly where they could be overheard, Clara accepted that her curiosity wouldn't be satisfied until later.

They were the only guests, but the family hovered in the background, along with a handful of chickens and an evil-looking black rooster. The back door always stood open, so the poultry went in and out as they pleased. If a crumb fell onto the floor, they were there in a flash to clean up. Maybe that was why Consuela let them in.

Clara put a forkful of empañadas into her mouth on autopilot, her mind going a hundred miles an hour.

She swallowed her food and drank, then looked at Walker over the rim of her glass. He'd said cards on the table. Had that meant personal cards too? Cards unrelated to the mess they were in? Best way to find out was to ask. "Where are you from?"

"All over."

He really was allergic to being specific. Which didn't stop her from pushing. "Where did you grow up?"

He wiggled his eyebrows at her. "Who says I've grown up?"

She rolled her eyes. "Obviously not mentally."

He puffed out his chest, not that it wasn't distractingly wide already. "I'm glad you've noticed that I've grown up in body."

"It's not going to work," she told him as she set down her glass.

"What?"

"You using sexual innuendos to distract me when I'm doing something you don't want me to be doing."

His chiseled mouth curved into a smile, the kind that reached his eyes. He had to stop doing that.

"I haven't really used sex yet," he said. "I'm pretty sure I could sidetrack you, if I put my mind to it."

She didn't protest the point. They both knew he was right.

"You're from the East Coast," she said instead, pretty sure from his accent. "Me too. I grew up in DC."

"Big political dynasty family?"

"Is this your way of asking whether my daddy got me the job at the DOD?"

He raised an eyebrow. "Touchy subject?"

"New England or Mid-Atlantic states?" she asked instead of answering. "Cards on the table."

"Grew up mostly in a small town near Abingdon, Maryland," he said. "But I traveled around."

"You think you'll ever go back?"

"Nothing to go back to."

"No family?"

He shook his head. "No family left, and not much of the town left worth bothering with either. It'd gone downhill the past decade. Drugs moved in. The criminal element pretty much took over."

His expression was neutral, as if he wasn't affected by his hometown's demise, but she caught tension in his tone—something subtly dark and menacing—and wondered what that was about.

"You were in the navy, right?" Her father had told her earlier, but she didn't want to say that, so she said, "I saw your trident tattoo."

He raised an eyebrow. "You looked that carefully, did you?"

Heat crept up her neck. "More of a cursory glance." She cleared her throat. "So you were a SEAL?"

She would have been lying if she said she wasn't impressed. Navy SEALs were tough operators, the US Navy's principal special ops force, part of the Naval Special Warfare Command and the United States Special Operations Command. She knew SEAL stood for Sea, Air, Land. They'd parachute into places like rivers, swamps, deltas, coastline areas like the Persian Gulf where water depth barred submarines and large ships. They could pretty much operate in any kind of environment, the insertion team of choice for small-team commando missions.

No wonder he hadn't been scared of the jungle. She tried to think back to the few times her father had mentioned the SEALs, and wished she'd paid more attention. "What does B E N mean? The letters under your trident tattoo? Is that a navy acronym?"

His expression closed, hardened. She expected him to end the conversation, but after a tense stretch of silence, he said, "He was my brother."

Oh, Ben. As in a name.

"That's a pretty regular name, isn't it?" she asked. "Compared to Light."

"I was named by my flower-child hippie grandmother. I was the first grandchild. By the time Ben was born, more reasonable minds prevailed."

She opened her mouth to ask where his brother was now, then remembered Walker's earlier words. *He was my brother.*

Was?

Her father had said that Walker owed the DOD a favor because they'd helped him with something regarding his brother. "What happened to Ben?"

Walker's expression remained shuttered. "Do you ever stop asking questions?"

"Curiosity is an indicator of intelligence."

He closed his eyes for a second as if she pained him. Then he gave a resigned sigh. "My brother was killed two years ago."

Her heart softened. "I'm sorry."

He let his gaze glide over her body. His eyes narrowed. He put a disconcerting amount of heat into his voice as he said, "How about we go upstairs and you comfort me?"

There he went with the sexual-innuendo tactics again. She ignored the tingles that ran across her skin.

"How about we both act mature?" she suggested.

But he only grinned as he raised his piercing gaze to hers. "Have no worries, what I'm thinking is definitely for mature audiences."

She groaned.

His eyes widened, and she could almost swear that the desire she saw in their depths wasn't faked. But she'd be fifty shades of stupid to fall for it.

Would he take her to bed? Probably, because he was a man, and a horn-dog, and he'd spent the last week in the jungle. But it'd be nothing to him—scratching an itch he could just as easily scratch with Carmen from Brunhilda's or Margarita from the cantina, or any number of gorgeous women he probably had at his beck and call.

Whether she was physically attracted to him, far more than she'd been drawn to any other man, didn't matter. Clara wasn't interested. Unlike back in college, she now had something called *self-esteem*, and she knew she deserved better than a player like Walker.

***

He did use innuendoes to unsettle her. She was pretty sharp. In the beginning, Walker had acted like a jerk because he thought it would encourage her to leave. And now…He enjoyed the way her eyes sparkled when she was exasperated. Her sexy growls did something to him.

But he let her be as they finished their empañadas. Then he went back to her room with her and watched her pace between the window and her bed. He figured he'd let her exhaust herself before he told her of his plans. That way, she'd have fewer objections.

She said, "So we know that there are two major cartels in the area, the Tamchén and the Xibalba. And Carlos Petranos, the head of the Xibalba cartel, is Rosita's half brother. Would the Tamchén kidnap her as part of some power struggle?"

He nodded. "That's what I'm thinking."

"Why?"

"Maybe to trade. Maybe the Xibalba has one of their guys. Or maybe to use as leverage in a negotiation over territory. That's the good news."

She stopped at the foot of the bed to stare at him. "How is her being kidnapped by a ruthless cartel good news?"

"She's still alive. If they killed her, the Xibalba would have started all-out war on the Tamchén already. There must be ongoing negotiations as we speak."

She watched him as if trying to see inside him, her gaze sharpening. "You said cards on the table. So tell me how you're involved with the cartels."

Did he trust her enough to tell her? Would she cooperate if he didn't?

"I want them out of business," he said after a long moment.

"Why? Does this have anything to do with your brother's death?"

He nodded, and then he said, "Obviously, I can't take the cartels down single-handed. So I need to pit them against each other. But if the Tamchén has Rosita, it messes up everything. I don't want the Tamchén and the Xibalba at the negotiating table. I want them at each other's throats. I need to take Rosita out of the equation. Carlos Petranos isn't going to attack the Tamchén as long as they have his half sister."

She watched him carefully. "Why do I have this impression that you're on a timeline here?"

She was too perceptive by half and had way too many questions. He'd already told her more than he should have. He shook his head. In for a penny, in for a pound.

"In four days, the new pharma co in Mercita will start up full-scale operations. They're supposed to be making off-patent, generic drugs. In reality, they'll be making a brand-new designer drug. Some super pill. Looks like a harmless disco drug in colorful little pills, but it's more addictive than heroin, although that's the base. They've been sending small batches up to the US for the past six months with excellent results. It's a monster high and addictive after one pill. The income potential is tremendous. They have a delivery system for these small test batches that I can't figure out."

And at this point, it didn't matter. Large-scale production was imminent. He had to shut down the factory, the Xibalba compound, the Tamchén compound and jungle camp, find the noseless man, then find Ben's killer. Any one of these tasks could get him killed. So he set up a plan where the bad guys would take down each other, while Walker could focus on grabbing the bastard who'd murdered his brother.

"Why not let the law handle it?" Clara asked.

"Same reason you can't work on Rosita's case with the police."

This time, she stayed silent for several seconds before she said, "You want to start a cartel war that'll kill countless people. That has already killed people," she added, probably thinking of the cantina and the body bags.

"Only people that need killing," he told her.

Her eyes narrowed. "The excuse of vigilantes everywhere."

She waited, maybe for him to defend himself, so she could then counter, try to make him see the light, drag him from the "bad" column to the "good" column.

He felt strange every time he caught her doing that. The idea that she believed him to be redeemable caused a funny twitch in his chest.

He stayed silent.

Eventually, she asked, "You said gangs work with the permission of the cartels. So Jorge must have some connections. Could he make contact for us? I'd like to find out for sure if the Tamchén have Rosita."

"Jorge can't just call and ask something like that. He's too low on the totem pole. He answers to the cartel and not the other way around."

"Do you know where the Tamchén headquarters are?" she wanted to know next.

"In Torelmo, a town about the size of Mercita, but a little better off. Some major logging operations are headquartered there. They have a canning factory. Jobs. It's trying to become some kind of a regional center."

She walked over to her suitcase that stood by the wall, crouched to open the front pocket, and pulled out her laptop, carried it to the bed, went to Google Maps. "Torelmo is only twenty miles from here."

He closed his eyes for a moment and brought up the image of the Tamchén compound. He'd done a respectable amount of recon. But that knowledge was little use to him in this case.

"Rosita wouldn't be there," he said after a few seconds. "The head of the Tamchén is cultivating a gentleman-businessman image. He's running for

139

office in Torelmo. Over the past year or so, he's transformed his Torelmo compound into a business center for his aboveboard dealings, moving most of his illegal stuff to his drug-packaging camp in the jungle."

"You know where that is?"

He nodded.

She went back to pacing, deep in thought, her eyes growing unfocused again. But then they lit up suddenly as she stopped halfway between him and the bed. "I can ask the DEA for help. They have people down here. If they raided the Tamchén camp, we could go in and grab Rosita."

He shook his head, marveling how anyone could maintain such wide-eyed innocence. She believed in the freaking government. Because in some spreadsheet in her head, US government and the Drug Enforcement Agency were in a column under the header "good guys."

She believed in the basic goodness of people. She believed in everything. He believed in nothing.

And right now, her strange streak of innocence pissed him off, mostly because he knew with a dreaded certainty that it was going to get her hurt. But it also brought out his protective instincts. She made a man want to make the world a better place, just so she wouldn't have to be disappointed.

He couldn't believe he was thinking shit like that now. Clearly, the tropical sun had fried his brain.

"You can still decide to walk away from all this." His very last warning. Hell, there had to be a way for him to search the jungle camp without her help. He'd come up with something.

"No way," she said. "I need your cell phone to make a call. I'm going to get in touch with the DEA guys. We can't do this alone. There are drugs involved at that camp, so the DEA's involvement is natural. Professional help is the way to go here."

"I wouldn't advise it."

She searched his face, her expression growing suspicious, then disappointed as she stepped back and sank onto the mattress. "Are you involved in the drug trade? Is that who you hire yourself out to? The cartels?"

She paused. "You got involved with them thinking you'd take them down from the inside. Is that it? Is the DEA looking for you?"

He said nothing, just watched her pursed lips, wondering whether she'd draw on him if he tried to kiss her.

Oblivious to his thoughts, she said, "The DEA is our best chance. They have agents, weapons, and permission to operate down here. They're the only smart choice we have."

"Smartest choice always is to trust nobody." Since she didn't look like she was buying that, he added, "Let's go for a ride."

She wrinkled her forehead. "Where?"

"Torelmo."

"To look at the Tamchén compound?"

"To look at the DEA."

"Aye, aye, Captain."

He squinted one eye at her.

"Now that we're really working together, I'm trying to find a common denominator," she explained with a bright smile. "You know, navy talk."

"What do you know about the navy?"

She flinched. The smile withered. "Pretty much all I know about ships, I learned from Pirates of the Caribbean," she admitted. But then her face brightened again. "Wait. That's not true. I've been to several Army-Navy Games. Sailors are tough."

Her last sentence sounded bit off at the end. "But?" he asked.

"Not army tough, but close," she said with a hint of apology. "Really. I mean it."

He closed his eyes and shook his head. "Maybe it'd be better if we didn't get into the whole army-navy rivalry." He looked at her. "Let's just go to Torelmo."

Better to go and do something than stay in the room with her where he couldn't focus on anything but the bed, images of her in it, naked, filling his head.

***

Torelmo was roughly the same size as Mercita, but lay in the opposite direction from Furino. The houses were not quite as derelict, the streets better kept.

"I guess having a couple of major employers in town does help," Clara observed, glad that Walker was driving her to the DEA office.

Maybe she was making progress with him. If she could get him to give up his revenge...

She'd meant it when she'd said that he wasn't horribly terrible. Whatever he thought about himself, he did have principles. For one, nobody could escape serving in the military without having some principles drilled into them.

On the other hand, he'd been trained as a killing machine. And now he'd pointed himself at the people he held responsible for his brother's death. He was like a launched torpedo with the target locked in.

Could a launched torpedo be disengaged?

She had hope. He'd listened to her. He was taking her to the DEA to ask for assistance.

The Drug Enforcement Agency's Chiapas headquarters was exactly where she needed to go. If anyone knew about the Xibalba and the Tamchén, it was them. She needed information and a way into the Tamchén jungle camp, and the DEA could provide her with both. For all she knew, they had the camp under surveillance, and all she'd have to do was identify Rosita on the video footage. Holding a US citizen against her will would be enough probable cause for a raid.

They could help Walker too, since his brother's death was cartel related.

Clara watched the sleeping homes and businesses slip past the car window while she silently rehearsed the appeal she'd make to the DEA for help.

She was showing up outside of office hours, but she figured they'd have someone on duty, since crime never slept. She'd tell them she was looking for a disappeared US citizen. She would not share Rosita's connection to her department and her father. The link was immaterial. A young girl was in trouble, and she needed help. The DEA didn't need to know more than that.

As they reached the city center, Walker turned onto a street with bright lights where people were still out and about. He passed several small hotels and restaurants. Music filtered outside. On one of the corners, a drunk couple was slow dancing.

Walker pulled over to park, then turned off the engine. "Let's sit here for a minute."

She looked around but didn't see anything interesting. "What are we waiting for?"

"You'll see. Just watch."

"What should I be watching?"

He pointed to a two-story building between a cantina and a pawn-shop-looking place. All the lights were on, music pulsing from downstairs, liquor ad posters blocking the windows. The place could have been a nightclub, but it wasn't. Half a dozen young women loitering outside gave it away.

The women were much better dressed than Brunhilda's girls, but they were clearly prostitutes. Very young, early twenties at most, tall, slim, and beautiful to the last—enough so to be models. Oddly, they ignored men passing by who tried to cozy up to them.

"What are they doing?" Clara asked.

"Waiting."

"For what?"

"You'll see."

She stifled a growl. Just once, she would have liked a straight answer out of Walker. "How long do we have to sit here?"

"As long as it takes. But not long, I don't think. They're outside, which means the car is coming."

He was right. Five minutes later, a black limo pulled up, and the women disappeared inside the gleaming vehicle. Walker turned the key in the ignition, pulled into traffic, and followed them.

They didn't go far. Ten minutes later, they were in the business district, in front of an office building. Among the business logos on the side listing the occupants, Clara recognized the DEA's distinct round emblem: green field, blue sky, soaring brown eagle.

She sucked in her bottom lip, tension building in her shoulders as she watched. She had a bad feeling about this.

The limo idled in front of the building, and within a minute or so, six men came out.

Walker pointed at the one in the lead. "Michael Morgan, director of local DEA operations." He pointed at the next guy. "Greg Mensing, project manager." He went on and named all six, and added their titles.

143

His voice held no trace of deception. And, in any case, this was something she could easily confirm on her laptop. She didn't think he was lying.

Clara watched, sick to her stomach, as the men came down the steps laughing, then got into the limo, joining the prostitutes.

Walker followed the car again.

A few blocks later, the limo came to a fancy hotel, Grand Hotel Torelmo, and let out its passengers. Then the limo left, but Walker remained parked across the road.

Soon, another limo came. More men and women got out. The men wore suits, like the DEA guys, but not as fancy. The suits were wrinkled, as if the men had come here straight from work. These guys were clearly Mexican, judging by their features.

"Who are they?" Clara asked.

"The local top cops."

Shortly after they went in, another guy showed up, this one in an expensive suit, also Mexican, tall and distinguished, the flash of a gold watch at his wrist.

"The district attorney," Walker said quietly next to her.

The security guards at the door inclined their heads as they let the man in. One ran to take his car to the hotel parking.

"Is this what I think it is?" Clara asked, feeling nauseous.

"The Grand Hotel Torelmo is owned by the Tamchén. They throw a party a couple of times a week for their special friends. Booze, drugs, gambling, high-class prostitutes. Whatever the guests want, the Tamchén provides," Walker said matter-of-factly as he turned to her. "If you asked the DEA for a raid on the Tamchén, someone at the DEA would tip off the cartel, and you'd be found dead in an alley the next morning. The police report would cite a botched robbery. So tell me again. Who do you trust down here?"

She cleared her throat. "Nobody."

Walker nodded. "Now you're learning." He glanced toward the hotel. "You need to see more?"

She filled her lungs, feeling incredibly alone suddenly. "No."

The DEA had been her Hail Mary, her "if everything else fails." But her last line of defense had just evaporated. It was down to her and Walker.

Loose cannon Walker.

No allegiance Walker.

Cares about nothing but his own agenda Walker.

He turned the key in the ignition, then pulled into traffic.

She looked straight ahead but saw little of the street. She was too busy thinking.

She couldn't waste time on being disappointed. She needed to move forward. "So without the DEA, how do we confirm whether the Tamchén have Rosita?"

"Ready for the plan?"

She nodded. *Dear God, let him have a reasonable proposal.*

Walker flashed a quick grin. "We go and check for ourselves."

"That doesn't sound like a very good plan," she told him honestly.

In fact, it sounded more like a suicide pact.

CHAPTER
THIRTEEN

Traffic was light at this hour, so Walker had no trouble getting out of town. But instead of heading back to Furino, he was looking for an obscure old logging road that would take him where he needed to be.

"Are you sure the Tamchén would keep Rosita at their jungle compound instead of in town?" Clara asked next to him as they bounced over uneven ground.

"This is where they have the highest security. It's where they keep the things they want to hide. This is where they do all their dirty deeds these days. And this is where the well is," he added.

"What well?"

"Tamchén means *deep well* in Maya. Back in ancient times, the Mayans used wells to collect rain water. The Tamchén's jungle compound has one that's probably a thousand years old. They like tossing people down and letting them die slowly. Gives them time to ask questions."

She digested that for a few seconds before asking, "So if Tamchén means *deep well*, does Xibalba have any special meaning?"

"Xibalba means *place of fear*."

"Another Mayan word?"

He nodded.

"Why not something Spanish?"

He hadn't given that much thought, didn't see what difference it made. But, of course, Clara would want to know. She wanted to know everything about everything. He grinned. When you got used to it, it was actually an endearing quality.

"Maybe using an ancient name is a psychological thing," he said. "Sends a message that they've always been here and always will be. Establishing legitimacy."

"Resistance is futile?"

He turned to her. Did she just quote *Star Trek*? He didn't understand how flocks of men weren't following her moon-eyed in love with her.

Before he could examine why that thought sent a sudden flash of jealousy through him, his phone rang. He picked it up. One of Santiago's men was on the other end.

"Santiago says you can go back to Furino now. The banditos won't be after you no more." The guy slurred the words. Probably the whole Xibalba compound in Mercita was celebrating. "They didn't know what hit them. We were on them like a hurricane. Blew those banditos away."

"You found the lost shipment?"

"Not yet."

"How mad is Carlos?"

"He's off on some business. Haven't seen him in a week. We'll get the shipment before he comes back. We have a couple of Pedro's boys. I'm thinking they'll be talking before morning," the man said in a dark tone.

Santiago was a master of the blade. He'd come up from the cattle ranches, had spent his early years castrating bulls, then, later on, butchering them. But Pedro's men couldn't confess what they didn't know. Walker didn't envy the night they had ahead of them.

For a moment, maybe due to Clara's influence, he looked for remorse inside himself. He couldn't find any. He'd heard the banditos bragging at the cantina one too many times about what they'd done to people they'd robbed, women they'd raped.

"I'm not gonna lie. I'll breathe easier knowing Pedro's crew is not hunting me," Walker told the guy. "Thanks, amigo."

The man on the other end laughed. "As Santiago said, you've done the cartel a favor. He don't forget that shit."

After they hung up, Walker put the phone back into his pocket, thinking hard as he drove.

So Carlos had been gone for a week. What did that mean? Was he looking for his half sister personally? Maybe they were that close. Still, Carlos had men to send to do his bidding. He couldn't exactly go to the Tamchén camp and try to blend in. People knew his face. So what was he up to? Where the hell was he?

Maybe he'd been kidnapped too.

No, that didn't make sense. If the Tamchén managed to get their hands on him, they'd kill him and take over his operations. Maybe he was in the US, setting up large-scale distribution for his super pills.

Clara shifted next to Walker on her seat, peering out at the rainforest. Night had swallowed them. The headlights helped, but even so, the dark, towering jungle was probably unnerving for someone who wasn't used to it.

She showed every sign of alertness but few signs of fear. He wanted to pull over and kiss her. He wanted to pull her over into his lap.

His body stirred at the thought. Sadly, he'd bet pesos against papadzules—egg-filled enchiladas with pumpkin seed sauce—that she'd shoot him for manhandling her.

She was a fast draw. He needed to remember that.

As if to underscore his thoughts, she checked her gun. When she was satisfied, she slipped the Glock back into her boot.

"Almost there," he told her.

***

"Is this really necessary?"

Clara stared at Walker as he pointed up the tree they were standing under. They were in the jungle, the night pitch-dark around them. She could barely see the tree trunk let alone the higher branches. Rain began to drizzle once again.

"Surveillance," he said.

"This has *bad idea* written all over it."

Although, she was glad to be out of the pickup's cab. Spending time with Walker in tight quarters was getting to her more and more. His testosterone/pheromone cloud trapped her in an annoying state of physical awareness. The whole drive out, some insane part of her had been wishing that he'd pull over, draw her into his lap, and kiss her.

She didn't know what was wrong with her. It had to be the heat, or the exotic environment. Or maybe Consuela's chili peppers had strong aphrodisiac properties. Clara made a mental note not to eat those again.

Oblivious to her desperate state, Walker linked his fingers in front of him. "I'll give you a boost up."

She stepped into the boost with her right foot. Then realized she would have to put her hands on his shoulders, so she did—no way to gracefully back out now.

Her palms connected with solid muscles. Wanting to escape the situation as quickly as possible, she heaved herself upward, pushing down on him. But she lost her balance and pitched forward, slamming her breasts into his face.

He made a muffled sound while she scrambled like mad to extricate herself, straightening her knee so she could move her torso above his head. Then she let him go and reached for a handhold on the tree. Only when his nose knocked against her pubic bone did she realize that now she was mushing her hoo-ha into his lips.

She scrambled like a spider monkey on speed and caught the lowest branch, pulled herself up. Her heart hammered hard in her chest. Thank God it was too dark for him to see her flushed cheeks.

Given a choice, she would gladly have avoided him, say for a week, but under the circumstances, she reached down a hand to help him. He jumped for the branch instead and caught on easily, then went for the next branch above, pulled her up, then one more level, and one more, and one more, until they were at a juncture of multiple branches that created a spot where they could comfortably sit.

She took care so their bodies wouldn't touch. He made no reference to her trying to smother him first with her boobs then with her…She drew a steadying breath. She might have found the first thing she liked about him. The man could keep quiet if someone's life absolutely, positively depended on it.

He pulled out his knife. "Give me your boots. This rain is going to get in there. I'm going to put a couple of holes just above the soles to let water out. Staying wet hour after hour is not good for you. You get swamp feet."

Yay. Because things weren't bad enough already. She groaned. And handed him her left boot.

Up here, a little more moonlight filtered through, so they could see better.

He gave a wry chuckle as he set to work. "Some people think the jungle is romantic. Usually people who never spent a week in a rainforest. In reality, it's all about survival of the fittest."

She thought about the snakes and the spiders and the caimans and the bandits. "Scary."

"Not if you're the fittest." He grinned at her as he handed her the first boot, newly ventilated, then asked for the second.

While he worked on that, she looked around so she wouldn't have to look at him. A rucksack hung from a broken branch next to them. Obviously, he'd been here before.

"What's in that?" she asked, needing distraction.

"Some water, a backup gun, and binoculars with night vision." Walker handed her other boot back, then leaned against the trunk, spread his legs, and pulled her between them, her back to his chest, an arm loosely around her waist so she wouldn't fall. "We should be safe here."

Oh God. Her breasts and other parts were still tingling from the boost-up fiasco. He could *not* be embracing her!

Breathe. Not an embrace, she told herself. His hand on her was a safety measure, plain and simple. *Safety. Measure.*

He certainly didn't seem in any way perturbed. She followed his gaze to focus on whatever he was watching in the distance. If she acted normal, maybe her body would believe that this was nothing out of the ordinary.

They were close enough to the Tamchén camp to see the outdoor lights. She counted six buildings, one large hangar, the others smaller, flat-roofed storage buildings from the looks of them. The compound was fenced, but even with the lights, she couldn't judge the height of the fence. She guessed anywhere between eight and ten feet. "Is there electricity in the wires?"

"No." Walker reached for the rucksack, checked it for critters, retrieved a pair of clunky night-vision binoculars, then fitted them to his eyes. "The cartels are too powerful for anyone to seriously consider an attack. Everybody is scared of them, and they have the government in their pockets."

"You use this tree to watch them," she said.

"Studying the enemy."

"But you do jobs for them?"

"The best way to study the enemy is from the inside. In any case, like I said before, I work for myself."

She thought of Ben, his brother who'd died two years ago. Walker had said he'd come here two years ago. He'd said his hometown had gone to hell, gone to drugs.

"Did your brother die from a drug overdose?" Clara asked him.

"No. Although, not from lack of trying."

They sat in silence for a full minute before he added, "He OD'd once when what he shot up was unexpectedly pure. Basically, you have no way of telling how much the heroin has been cut, how potent it is. He was lucky. Quick intervention saved him. A guy I knew in the navy died because he was allergic to quinine, which was the cutting agent in the batch he got. I knew someone else who died just because he shot up someplace new. It's called environment-conditioned tolerance. The body associates the place where you are while shooting up with the drug, prepares you for the drug while you're in that place. But if you shoot up the same amount at a different location, the body is not prepared for it and can't take it."

"You know a lot about this."

"I looked into it."

They both fell silent, then she asked, "If your brother didn't die from an overdose, then how?"

Walker didn't answer.

"Cards on the table," she reminded him once again. She figured it wouldn't be the last time. He didn't easily volunteer information.

Clara didn't mean to be insensitive about Ben's death. But it figured heavily into what Walker was doing down here, and now she was involved. In her rule book, that meant she had the right to know.

And after a while, looking away from her, he said in a reluctant tone, "Ben was three years younger than me. I joined the navy. A few years later, he joined the Army Reserves. Even when we were kids, he always copied what I did. He looked up to me. And later, he wanted to be in the military like I was. Only he wasn't cut out for it."

He paused for a moment. "He shouldn't have reenlisted after he was done with the first four years. But I'd just gotten into the SEALs. So Ben figured a

Navy SEAL couldn't have a quitter for a brother. Like he'd be an embarrassment to me or something."

Walker looked out into the darkness, his voice tightly controlled. "He was deployed overseas. Straight into combat. The bloodshed did things to him. He came home with PTSD, got into drugs, then got into selling so he could afford his drugs. Then he got into trafficking. I was in the Middle East, clueless.

After a somber moment, he added, "Ben ended up down here somehow. Then he managed to get on the cartels' bad side. Someone decided to make an example out of him and a few others."

His voice was detached, devoid of all emotion. He wasn't raging or threatening but was all the scarier for it.

"They killed him," Clara guessed, her heart filling with sympathy.

"Torture and decapitation." His tone turned hard and dark. "I saw the crime scene photos. About a dozen men were killed at the same time. The main room had this Mexican tile floor in a checkerboard pattern. The heads were all scattered around, as if someone had been playing a board game. The bodies were in the basement. The cops wouldn't let me go down there. I had to match his body to his head at the morgue later."

The images his words painted overwhelmed her. She leaned against him.

His arm tightened around her. "I had his remains sent back to the States, but he disappeared en route. I couldn't even bury my little brother."

She could feel the pain that radiated out of him reach deep inside her.

"I'm still looking for him, have a bunch of requests out for records," he said. "I'm never going to give that up."

Suddenly, she understood why he'd acted so stiffly at the incinerator, as if he'd been holding something back. If Ben's body was lost and there was no record of it, he could easily have ended up in an incinerator somewhere, the same as all those other unidentified bodies in Mercita.

She understood Walker's need for revenge, but she also understood that it was going to get him killed, and everything she was rejected that thought. She stayed leaning against him and just breathed for a while. "Is there no way at all to work with the authorities?"

"I tried the local police first. Then I tried the DEA. You can guess how helpful they were. I even went as far as the top Chiapas politicians. Nothing. They prefer sweeping things like this under the rug."

Clara could imagine, after what she'd seen today. But..."You can't take out two entire cartels on your own."

His wide chest rose and fell at her back as he drew a deep breath. "Actually, I'm aiming for the bandits and the gangs too. Flash fire."

She turned her head as far as she could, trying to look at him. "I don't know what that means."

He shifted on the branch. "First time I was on a submarine, we had a flash fire. It's a combustion explosion. A flammable mist builds up in the air, then suddenly, *bam.* Think superhigh temperatures and a rapidly moving flame front. It kills by asphyxiation. Burns up all the available oxygen. It's devastating."

She tried her best to figure out what he was saying. A minute or two passed before she managed. "So you're trying to get the amount and ratio of combustible materials right to burn this entire region down?"

"Just the criminal element."

"Are you completely suicidal?" She wished he could see his expression better, but the shadows concealed his face.

He didn't answer. Instead, he handed her the binoculars. "Let's find Rosita."

After a moment, she turned back to take a look.

A dozen sentries moved around inside the fence.

"Let me know if you see a noseless guy," Walker said behind her.

"Voldemort?"

He didn't laugh at the joke but said, "He might have a bandana covering his face."

She wouldn't blame the guy, Clara thought, and kept searching. "Who is he?"

"I don't know his name," Walker said as if it pained him. "But he was there when Ben was killed. He can tell me who killed my brother. I need to know who held the machete." Walker's tone dipped into scary territory.

And yet, she still wasn't scared of him.

153

Some stupid part of her wanted to hug him, so she made sure not to so much as turn toward him.

Through the binoculars, she watched the cartel men out in the open, but everybody had a nose, so she refocused on the buildings. "How will we know where they're keeping Rosita?"

"Look for a door that's more heavily guarded than the others."

She did. "None of the buildings are guarded. I only see perimeter guards. Does that mean that Rosita isn't here?"

He wouldn't respond for several seconds. Then he said, "We are going to have to go in to make sure."

* * *

Clara brushed leaves and twigs out of her hair, grateful to be back in her room at the guesthouse after two hours of jungle surveillance, then another hour of a dicey nighttime ride through the barely there dirt roads of the rainforest.

Walker had said he had to set up certain things to infiltrate the Tamchén compound, and there wasn't enough time for that before daylight. Their infiltration op had to wait until the following night. Which gave them some time to rest and get ready, definitely a plus as far as she was concerned.

Not that she could think all that well at the moment, not when Walker was walking into the room, naked save a towel riding low on his hips. Drops of water glistened on his chest.

He was incredibly, unfairly attractive. Hotter than the equator. A bead of water ran down his rippled abs, and her gaze followed it helplessly as it disappeared under the towel.

One thing was sure, she hadn't known the meaning of lust until she'd met Light Walker. Actually, she used to think the whole blinded-by-irresistible-lust story was a myth people made up as an excuse to sleep around. She didn't believe in the existence of anything "irresistible."

When you wanted something you knew you probably shouldn't have, you simply listed the pros and cons, arrived at a well-reasoned *no*, end of story. You simply resisted. Not exactly rocket science.

Light Walker standing in front of her in a towel, however, ruthlessly drove the point home that lust was a real and nearly omnipotent force.

And then there was the fact that Clara understood him a little better now. Now that she knew his brother's story, her heart ached for him. Knowing something that personal created a level of intimacy between them that she wasn't prepared to handle. She was suddenly seeing him as more than an exasperating mercenary, and she was pretty sure that was a move in the wrong direction.

He cleared his throat.

She jumped from the bed without meeting his eyes. "My turn."

Then she shot out of the room as fast as if she'd been shot from a cannon. She was halfway down the hallway when she remembered that she needed clean underwear and PJs.

She walked back to her room and knocked. "Are you decent?"

"You can come in."

She opened the door as slowly and carefully as if expecting armed attack.

He stood by the window, the towel still mercifully around his lean hips. His phone lay in pieces on the windowsill in front of him, his attention focused on a small chip he was inserting.

"Giving the phone an upgrade," he said without looking at her.

Something to allow it to work in the jungle? A signal amplifier? She wasn't sure how that stuff worked. And she didn't want to hang around long enough to ask. She hurried to her suitcase, grabbed what she needed, then left the room lickety-split.

Light Walker's sex appeal was a living, breathing thing. She felt as if it could grab her by the shoulders and draw her to him. She was pretty sure that if she relaxed, if only for a second, she'd find herself plastered to his chest. Maybe with her tongue hanging out, looking for something to lick.

Not going to happen.

She repeated that to herself a couple of times while she took a cold shower. She only lost control once, when she was startled by a stray rooster. The little bandit crowed right behind her.

She screamed, slipped, banged her head on the stall.

The rooster fluffed his feathers, then pranced out, clearly satisfied. His work there was finished.

She was almost in complete control of herself by the time she walked back to her room—hair in a ponytail for sleep—wishing her PJs consisted of more than boy shorts and a tank top. Of course, back when she'd planned her trip to Mexico, she hadn't anticipated a roommate.

She felt fairly naked. Would he make a comment? If he did, she wasn't going to react. She wasn't going to let him get to her.

He was a reprobate. She was a woman blessed with a healthy amount of common sense. *Mind over matter.*

Then Clara opened the door and found him, eyes closed, in her bed.

The sheet was drawn to an inch or so below his bellybutton. He'd taken the far side, had his arms folded under his head, his splendiferous muscles on full display, as well as his scars and tattoos.

An insidious fog of testosterone and pheromones engulfed her. She closed the door behind herself and leaned against it, her body weak, her mind slowly working up enough annoyance to ask, "What are you doing?"

"What does it look like?" he asked without opening his eyes.

"No."

He turned his head and looked at her at last. "For most of last week, I've been sleeping in mud holes in the jungle with spiders and snakes and leeches. Not to mention scorpions," he added. "I'm not going to sleep on the floor now when a perfectly good bed is available."

"No," she said again and folded her arms across her chest for emphasis.

"I offered you my bed last night," he pointed out. "Technically, you owe me the same courtesy."

"No." She didn't seem to be able to form any other words. Which was perfect, because *no* was the most important word she needed tonight when it came to Walker.

But then, with effort, she gathered some remnants of her vocabulary. "Go get your own room."

"I think it'd be best if we stuck together."

"There's no danger here."

He drew a deep breath, which made his chest rise and expand. "Don't think all the banditos are dead."

She pressed her lips together.

"I'm not going to try anything," he promised.

She believed him. She really did. He had countless waitresses to sit on his lap, and, *hello*, he lived in a brothel. It wasn't as if she didn't trust him not to jump her. The thing was, she wasn't sure she trusted *herself* not to jump him. And then she'd have to die of embarrassment.

"I explicitly remember you lecturing me not to trust anyone," she said. "Especially not you."

He held her gaze for what seemed several consecutive lifetimes. At the very least, she was certain that seasons passed outside.

"There might be hope for you yet." He turned back to face the ceiling and closed his eyes again. "You can put your Glock under your pillow if it makes you feel better."

She couldn't go to him, but she didn't know where else to go. It was *her* room. She stood there, trying to think of what to say.

Her gaze drifted to his trident tattoo. "Did the navy kick you out? I'd like to know the truth."

She still hadn't been able to figure out if he was one of the good guys or the bad guys, and her brain craved the proper category. Not being able to pin him down left her off-balance.

Because...Navy SEAL defending the country: good. Mercenary to the drug cartels: bad. Trying to find his brother: good. Vigilante justice: bad. He drove her crazy.

She didn't understand gray. She liked things black-and-white, needed him to be one thing or the other. She needed to know before she did something stupid.

Two plus two was always four. She liked it that way. She'd chosen accounting as her college major for a reason. Her inability to see moral shades was also the reason why she struggled so hard with her father's confession. She thought about it a hundred times a day. *How could he? Why?* She couldn't understand him.

Walker interrupted that depressing line of thought by saying, "I wasn't kicked out of the navy. Ben disappeared around the time I was supposed to reenlist. I left the navy to find him."

She knew how that had ended.

"I would give anything to be able to turn back the clock so I could rescue him," he said.

She could feel her stupid heart soften all over again. She wanted him to be one of the good guys. At the beginning, before she knew him, since he'd been assigned as her facilitator, she'd assumed he was. Then he'd gutted Pedro, and her opinion of him had gotten revised in a hurry.

But now that she was beginning to understand his motivation behind his actions…He'd clearly loved his brother very much. He just as clearly carried a world of hurt he refused to acknowledge. He'd steeped himself in revenge so there wouldn't be room for emotions that hurt, like grief.

Blaming him would be pure hypocrisy. She'd immersed herself in finding Rosita so she wouldn't have to face emotions such as the overwhelming sense of betrayal and the anger that boiled inside her, and the guilt over the anger.

And, of course, above all that, the grief over her father's diagnosis, which half the time she pretended wasn't real, was a mistake, because she definitely couldn't face losing the person she loved most on this earth.

She could *not* think about that.

Even thinking about Walker was safer.

She watched him.

He was the archetypal wounded hero, irresistible to women, according to millions of movies and romance novels. And she felt the pull, even while her logical brain said giving in to the attraction would be the worst idea ever. She could resist, she told herself. She was a sensible, strong woman.

She walked to the bed and sat gingerly on the edge, with her back to him. She didn't want to be looking at him as she asked. "Are you naked?"

She was proud of herself for getting the words out without choking.

"I have the towel on," he said. "It's tied."

He was *mostly* a good guy—probably not irredeemable—she told herself, and lay down on the top of the covers next to him. She was paying for the room; she wasn't going to sleep on the floor with the bugs and the lizards.

The window was open, and a light breeze blew in through the screen, but it was just as hot as the air inside the room, improving nothing. She didn't mind sleeping on top of the sheets. She didn't need a cover. She suspected that he wasn't cold either, but covered himself for her sake.

If he tried anything, she had the skills to subdue him…Probably. Maybe. Okay, not really. She couldn't wrestle down an ex-Navy SEAL. But she *did* have enough skills to slow him down.

Not that she thought he'd try anything. He was a muscle-itious stud muffin and, let's face it, she was a recovering accountant and looked it.

But also, as she'd told him before, she was pretty sure there existed some distinct lines—however few—that Walker wouldn't cross, and pushing a woman into something she didn't want was one of them.

She comforted herself with that thought, and the secure knowledge that her Glock was in her boot, right next to her by the side of the bed. Her father didn't raise wimps, and her mother didn't raise fools. Light Walker could take that to the bank.

CHAPTER
FOURTEEN

Clara woke at dawn to an army of roosters crowing, inspiring murderous thoughts of chicken fajitas, which instantly vaporized when she realized that she was half sprawled over Walker.

She'd climbed him in her sleep. For some reason her Glock was trapped between her thigh and his body. She tried to remember how that had happened.

Her eyes flew wide-open when she realized it wasn't the barrel of her gun that she was feeling.

Her head rested on his sculpted chest. She stared at the smattering of golden chest hair and froze. Any sudden movement might wake him.

He had thrown a beautifully muscled arm around her shoulder, holding her to him, his fingertips dangerously close to the side of one breast. In fact, when she drew a deep breath, the very tip of his middle finger softly touched against her.

She did her best to keep her breathing as shallow as possible.

She needed to extricate herself slowly and carefully. She prepared herself for ninja-like stealth and bomb-squad-like care. But before she could make her move, he said above her head, "Good morning, Detective Cupcake."

Her gaze snapped up to his. His arm tightened around her, and then she couldn't breathe at all. Because from the corner of her eye, she could see his towel on the floor next to the bed.

It must have slipped off while he'd slept.

Which meant that there was nothing between his morning hard-on and her naked thigh but a very flimsy sheet.

***

He wanted her. Now. Hard and fast, no preamble.

He wanted her to smile at him, and say, "Yes," giving a clear go-ahead.

Walker wanted to roll her under him, bring her hands up, and trap them over her head. He wanted to see her eyes grow heavy-lidded with passion as he wrapped her lean thighs around his hips. He wanted her moaning his name as his body sank into hers.

Jeezus. He was so hard, he could have cracked nuts with his dick.

But instead of pushing for what his body demanded—for the past hour— he'd simply enjoyed lying with her like this.

He couldn't remember the last time he'd woken up with a woman in his bed. He looked in on Margarita now and then when he was in town. But neither of them expected anything from the other. If he never saw her again, he wouldn't think much about it, and he was pretty sure she wouldn't waste much time crying over him.

He'd never been the relationship type. Sure, if a beautiful woman threw herself at him, he took what was offered. But he avoided staying the night. He couldn't see himself chitchatting over breakfast. What would he say? Even back when he'd been legitimately employed, he couldn't talk about his work.

Yet he enjoyed waking up with Clara more than he felt comfortable with.

"We should probably get something to eat, then head out," he said while rubbing slow patterns on her arm, fantasizing about her sitting up and strad-dling him.

Her eyes turned the color of melting silver. Her breasts pressed against his chest. They were small but perfect. What idiot would ever think they weren't? A new wave of lust shot through him.

He cleared his throat. "We should probably get up before I do something you might regret later."

His words seemed to galvanize her, and she shot out of bed, leaving his arms empty. Was he stupid or was he stupid? Hell, he didn't know what he was. His brain turned to mush around her.

"Bathroom," she croaked, and was out the door the next second.

He looked after her and felt a smile tug up the corner of his lips. She did have *some* self-preservation instincts.

He got up, tied the towel back around his waist to disguise his hard-on as best he could, and went to take a morning shower in the other bathroom to cool himself off. The cold water got him halfway there. Thinking about taking Clara into the Tamchén camp tonight completed the job.

He wasn't the type for having second thoughts. Once he committed to a course of action, he saw it through. Yet now he was second-guessing himself, at the most crucial part of the game.

He had three days left to stop the Xibalba from launching the full-scale production of their super pills that would be shipped north by the truckload every night. At that scale, some would reach the competition within days. The pills would be analyzed by rival labs. Then, within a month or two, the new drug would be produced by a hundred outfits instead of one. The cat would be out of the bag, and nobody could stuff it back in again.

Those new drugs were going to be big business. Messing with them was a dangerous proposition.

He found that he hated the idea of Clara in danger.

Part of him still wanted to send her away. Another part reminded him that he needed her here. He would just have to protect her. Under no circumstances was he going to let her get hurt.

He toweled himself off, then dressed. The clothes that he'd washed out the night before and left in the washroom to dry were ready. He zipped up his fly, then returned to the room. She wasn't there.

He found her downstairs in the dining room, hanging up the wall phone just as he came down the stairs. She sat at the nearest table, and he went to sit with her.

Consuela was the only one behind the counter, soaking corn, probably for *masa de maíz*, dough made from fresh hominy. Maybe the rest of the family was at the market.

Walker's gaze slid back to Clara.

She was studying the tablecloth—striped, locally woven, all bright colors. She seemed distracted, her mind someplace else completely—probably on her phone call.

The dappled sunlight coming through the equally bright curtains painted her in a soft glow. At a distance of three feet—the width of the table between them—her eyes looked gunmetal gray, but now he knew that sometimes they turned the color of melting silver. He definitely wanted to see that again up close.

Her hair was back in its tortured bun, but now he knew the locks were silky soft. At night and this morning those locks had been spread over his shoulder.

She was dressed like a tourist in baggy khaki shorts and a flowery tank top that molded to breasts that had been pressed against him not that long ago.

He grabbed his glass of ice water and drank it down. Then he nodded toward the phone. "Anything important? Were you talking to Rosita's boyfriend?"

She frowned as she looked up. "I really don't think it was like that." She drew a slow breath. "I was talking to my father."

Consuela brought their plates and set them on the table with a smile, then pulled a bottle of hot sauce from under her arm and plopped it in the middle. "El desayuno." Breakfast.

"Gracias, Consuela." Clara smiled at her.

She had a good smile. Made a person feel like she meant it.

Walker nodded his thanks, his gaze still on Clara's lips. "Tell me about your father," he said, because he needed something else to focus on beyond the way she'd felt in his arms this morning, or his rearing dick would soon be lifting the tabletop.

Caution flared in her eyes. "Why?"

"I think in your world it's customary for people to have some sort of a conversation when sharing a meal." He dug into his breakfast burritos that were spicy and colorful, representing the essence of the country.

"And in yours?"

In his world? "People shoot each other over breakfast."

She gave a ghost of a smile that quickly disappeared. She rubbed the pad of her thumb over the handle of her fork. Her voice was a low whisper when she said, "My father has cancer. Prostate."

Okay, that sucked. He went still. "How bad?"

"He had it before, and he beat it. But now it's back." Her voice cracked. "The doctors say that this time..."

Since she couldn't finish the sentence, he was pretty sure he knew what the doctors said.

He didn't like the dejected set of her shoulders. The haunted look in her eyes squeezed something in his chest, although what, he couldn't fathom. He'd had nothing but emptiness in there for years.

Walker kept eating, but the food that should have felt like the flavors were dancing *jarabe tapatío*, the Mexican hat dance, on his tongue, felt tasteless. He watched Clara's clouded expression. "I take it you two are close."

She nodded.

And he asked, "Siblings?"

"None."

"How about your mother?"

"She's taking it hard."

Her mother would take it even harder if something happened to Clara down here and she didn't return home, Walker was willing to bet. With every passing hour, he hated the idea of her here more and more, and he hadn't liked it all that much at the beginning.

Clara said, "My grandmother has Alzheimer's, so that adds to things."

Oh hell.

He was beginning to understand her need for control and order. She'd been an army brat for starters, probably spent her childhood moving from base to base. And she'd spent the last couple of years with her father's possible death hanging over her head. While her grandmother was fading away...Walker was a man of action. He hated problems he could do nothing about.

They fell silent as they ate. He was almost finished when Consuela lifted the giant vat of soaked corn she'd been preparing behind the counter and headed for the back door, struggling with the weight. She was probably taking it to the outdoor pantry.

Walker set down his fork and pushed to his feet. "Let me help."

He needed a moment outside anyway, away from Clara, to think.

He didn't get that moment.

"I'll go out with you," she said, and followed him as he took the vat from Consuela and carried it outside.

Forty pounds of corn at least. No wonder Consuela had been bent over. Walker carried the weight easily, while the woman hurried ahead of him, thanking him over and over and showing the way.

The fenced backyard was the hens' and the roosters' dominion, the chicken coop in the back, under a forty-foot-tall tamarind tree that provided shade. Beyond that, another fenced-in area served as a sizable kitchen garden. Walker recognized the tomatoes and peppers, eggplants, onions, beans, but had no idea about some of the other greens.

Another world. He'd never known anyone who grew their own vegetables. He couldn't imagine the kind of steady, settled life that allowed a man to eat tomatoes he himself had grown. For a fleeting moment, the odd thought that he wouldn't mind trying came into his head, but he batted it away.

He followed Consuela to a shed and put the vat on a rough-hewn table that already held a dozen other covered containers. The woman thanked him again and busied herself, so he nodded and headed back out to where Clara was trying to coax a hen with baby chicks to come closer to her.

He smiled at her earnest expression, only half paying attention as a door in the fence opened to his right, and a young man appeared in the opening, wearing local garb and his best Sunday sombrero. For a moment, Walker wondered if the guy was here to court Consuela's oldest daughter, but the next second, the man pulled a weapon.

Ruger Old Army revolver, seven-and-a-half-inch barrel, .457 caliber, single action, six-shot cylinder. The information flashed through Walker's brain in a fraction of a second as he went for his SIG, swiping at Clara to push her behind him.

But then the darndest thing happened. Clara ducked under his arm in a fluid motion, put herself *in front of him*, and fired her Glock at the guy, three shots in rapid succession.

All three found their target, taking the guy down, but not before he managed to squeeze off a shot of his own that went wide—the four claps of gunfire coming in rapid succession.

The chickens were running in every which direction and clucking in panic, stirring up clouds of dust as they flapped their wings, immediately reducing visibility, which was no longer an issue, luckily, since the attacker was done for, shit out of luck—and life—by that point.

Unfired weapon in hand, Walker ran to the body. He didn't recognize the guy. He took the Ruger, stuck it into his waistband, then looked back incredulously at Clara, his jaw clenched so freaking tight—

She had blood on her side.

How the hell?

Jesus. Arctic cold spread through his veins. *Shit.*

The damn bullet had ricocheted off something.

He barely registered when Consuela, wide-eyed and pale, poked her head from the shed.

"Call the police," Walker ordered, then tackled Clara, picked her up in his arms, and strode inside with her, up the stairs as she beat his chest and protested.

"Put me down, dammit! This is not necessary. Walker!"

He carried her straight to the bathroom and set her down, pinned her to the wall with his hands on her shoulders. "What the hell was that?"

They were nose to nose, and he was yelling, because he couldn't help himself. His chest heaved. His mind was a black hole of swirling rage. She was hurt. "Why did you do that?"

She looked at him as if he'd gone mad. "He was going to shoot you. Who was he?" Then she said, "I'm fine. I swear."

"Probably one of Pedro's nephews." El Capitán had about a dozen. They were just the kind of little shits who'd ignore cartels orders in a hotheaded moment.

Walker sucked in air. Why was his chest so tight? *He* hadn't been hit. "You're bleeding. Dammit, Clara."

Then something occurred to him, so he checked the Ruger he'd taken away from the attacker.

He bit back a curse.

"Pure lead bullets. If it's in you, we'll have to take it out." He took a calming breath. "Do you want to go to the hospital? Or I could take you to the nuns at St. Lupe's."

He shoved the gun back into his waistband, then grabbed for the hem of her tank top and pulled it up. When the soft material slid back down, he yanked the damn thing all the way up and over her head.

She wore a simple sports bra that did nothing to settle him down.

Oblivious to his unsteady control, she was looking at the injury halfway up her rib cage, gingerly touching the tips of her fingers to the ripped skin. "It's just a surface wound. Didn't even break a rib."

That should have relaxed him, but it didn't. He had her inches from him, semitopless, pinned to the wall. Bleeding and not caring about it.

He wanted to shake her. Then he wanted to fuck her.

He couldn't go there. But he couldn't release her either. He put his hands back on her shoulders, pulled her flush against his chest, and sealed his lips over hers.

* * *

For all his innuendoes and come-ons, Clara had never thought that Walker meant any of it. He was an action-hero fantasy man, and she was…She wasn't the kind of woman action heroes ended up with on the silver screen.

She wasn't the lushly voluptuous type who inspired blind lust, or the fragile gamine who would bring out a man's protective instincts. She was average looking, in reasonable shape, nothing to drive a man wild, really.

But all the heat and humidity of the deep jungle was there with them suddenly in the room. She was so confused, she kissed Walker back.

His wide chest rose, and his hands loosened on her shoulders, his mouth gentled as he licked her lips, nibbled on her bottom lip, kissed his way across her mouth, then nudged her to open herself to him.

Like she had a choice.

Because, *sweet Jungle Jesus*, Light Walker could kiss.

She was by no means an expert in the kissing department, working from limited experience, but the way her knees wanted to fold, her nipples tightened and all the blood rushed to the V of her thighs…*wow.*

He…

Wha…

Wow.

He conquered, he plundered, he mastered.

And she let him. They might have struggled for dominance regarding her investigation, but she saw no reason to fight him on this.

He kept changing the angle, pressing hard, then gentling, then sweeping in again, as if he couldn't kiss her deeply enough, as if he couldn't get enough of her. Walker kissing her like this was a heady and unsettling experience for which she had not been prepared.

She was so dazed, she felt cross-eyed by the time he pulled back. They were both breathing hard.

That deserved a moment of consideration, actually. She made Light Walker lose his breath. She felt her self-confidence triple on the spot.

He kept his hands on her shoulders and watched her with a frightening intensity, like a lion or a jaguar might watch his dinner. His muscles were tightly coiled. *Ready to pounce* was the only description she could come up with for his body language. He pressed his lips together, relaxed them, pressed them together again, his gaze on her lips that felt tingly and swollen.

"Why did you do that?" she asked, weakly, but, hey, the fact that she could talk at all was a minor miracle.

"You needed to be kissed."

For some reason, the tone of masculine satisfaction in his voice needled her. "I *needed* it? Really?"

"Fine, I needed it." His gaze stayed on her lips.

She floundered, wanting to blame him for making her want him. "You can't just grab someone whenever you feel like it. You have to ask."

He watched her as if trying to puzzle her out. "I know you're not indifferent to me. We're adults. We could make each other feel good. Why not?"

"You don't just do things because they make you feel good. You have to consider all the consequences."

"I considered you. I would make you feel good too. I don't need to write columns of pros and cons about this. Sex is a natural human function."

Nonononono. They were *not* having sex!

She gave a warning growl. His eyes flared with heat in response. So she took a step to the side, which caused his hands to fall off her shoulders. She breathed easier with that connection broken.

Her reprieve didn't last long. He stepped right after her, and put his hands back on her. "Fine. Can I kiss you?"

Oh.

Her brain stopped working again.

He searched her face. She had no idea what he saw—blinding desire and bewildering confusion were her best guesses.

"I can't," she said while she still could.

He closed his eyes for a moment with a tortured expression. A groan rumbled up his chest. When he opened his eyes, his hands slid from her shoulders to her hands. "Okay, a no is a no."

All the air seemed to be gone from the room, which was strange, because the small window high up the wall stood open.

She let him draw her to a plastic stool next to the sink and push her down on it. Then he brought over the first aid kit that'd been hanging on the wall.

"I'm going to clean that wound," he said.

She barely heard the words. Light Walker had kissed her. He *needed* to kiss her. She still had trouble breathing.

"It's just the adrenaline," she tried to explain. "Shots have been exchanged. Blood has been spilled. It's natural to—"

"Bullshit." He held her gaze. "I've been wanting to kiss you for days."

He had to be exaggerating. How many days could it be? They'd only known each other for three—although, they'd been the three most intense days of her life, without contest.

She briefly considered that she was still sleeping and dreaming this entire episode, but then he dropped his gaze from hers and spread some kind of disinfectant on her torn skin, and the sharp sting convinced her that she was very much awake.

The air left her lungs in a hiss.

"Try to learn a lesson," he muttered, and reached for the gauze.

His massive shoulders this close to her, his arm brushing across her naked stomach as he moved, his hot breath caressing her side when he crouched to see better, were more than she could handle. She kept her eyes on the far wall and held her body motionless.

Unbearable, bewildering minutes clicked by like that.

When he finished, he picked her up and carried her out of the bathroom. Thank God for his T-shirt, or they would have been skin to skin. She had trouble breathing as it was.

"You don't have to carry me," she protested.

He didn't respond. He just kept going.

He carried Clara into their room and deposited her on the bed, then moved to her suitcase, rifled through it, discarding tank top after tank top, coming up with a modest blue T-shirt and bringing it back to her.

"Put this on."

She did. Fast. Because wearing nothing but a bra in front of Walker was seriously fraying her nerves. For good measure, she folded her arms across her chest, not even caring that her wound pulled and burned.

He cast her a grim, hard-eyed look.

"Don't you *ever* do that again," he said in a voice she'd only heard in movies, usually from hard-core assassins.

She had a feeling he wasn't talking about her turning down a second kiss, and he confirmed it by saying, "I swear to God, the next time you step between a bullet and me, I'm going to shoot you in the back."

She glared at him. She'd had no intention to step into the path of the damn bullet, but she'd seen the guy aim at Walker, and the next thing she knew, she was there. As much as he aggravated the living daylights out of her, she cared about him, and maybe even liked him, but she'd rather step in front of an entire firing squad than admit that.

When she'd seen that gun aimed at Walker, she'd acted as she'd been trained, as she'd practiced, and then the attacker was dead and—

Sitting on the bed, Clara suddenly felt as if a freight train hit her. She gasped for air, but she couldn't breathe. She cast a desperate, panicked looked at Walker who was next to her in a split second.

His entire demeanor changed. He dropped onto the mattress and pulled her onto his lap, smoothing his hand down her back without a single question, as if he knew exactly what was going on, as if he'd been expecting this.

"Hey. It's okay. You did what you had to. You saved my life, Clara."

She gasped for air. "I killed someone."

She'd trained to do just that. She'd thought she'd been prepared to do it. But thinking about shooting someone and watching her bullet slam into a real live person were not the same.

"The first time is hard." Walker held her, soothing her, kissing her forehead.

She sagged against his solid warmth, against his steady heartbeat, against the comfort that he offered. "God, I'm a horrible investigator. This is part of the job, isn't it?" she said into his neck. "I have to be able to handle it."

"You're a good person."

She heard his words, but all she could think was that she'd *killed* a man. Ended a life.

Minute after minute passed as she tried to process what that meant, how it changed her. The hundreds of hours she'd spent at the firing range, shooting at paper targets hadn't prepared her for any of the emotions that sliced through her now. Nothing ever could have.

She could see the guy's face in her mind—so young—and the way he'd crumpled.

Walker made reassuring sounds into her hair. Still, at least half an hour ticked by before she could breathe without struggle.

"He was no innocent," Walker told her. "He was going to shoot me down in cold blood. If you had to do it over, would you change anything?"

She thought about Walker crumpling to the ground instead of the attacker. "No. I know there was nothing else I could have done. But it doesn't mean I like what I've done."

He probably thought she was an idiot. He certainly had no trouble doing his job.

But his eyes held understanding.

"You're a hell of a quick draw," he murmured, sounding as if he was proud of her.

Clara pulled back, but only far enough so she could look at him more fully. She wasn't ready to leave the fortress of his arms yet. "I'm sorry. I can't believe I fell apart like this."

"You didn't fall apart. You had a panic attack. It's a pretty common response to this kind of stress."

"I bet Navy SEALS don't have panic attacks."

He held her gaze. "You'd be wrong about that."

She blinked at him in surprise.

"Nobody is invincible," he said.

But he sure seemed to be. He looked hard enough to be unbreakable. His body, anyway. His eyes, for the moment, were filled with warmth and tenderness. So much so that her throat tightened. She wanted to go back into his arms, burrow into his embrace, find shelter against his wide chest again.

Stupid. Stupid. Stupid. He was her *facilitator.*

All this was beyond unprofessional. The kiss had been a mistake. A momentary lapse of judgement. She needed to simply forget it. It was not going to happen again.

She slipped off his lap and made herself walk over to the window, stared out unseeing for a long moment before she turned back to him. *Okay. Better.* She just needed a little distance.

She bit back a groan. She did *not* want him to see her acting weak.

But his gaze held no judgment as he watched her. "Do you want to go back home now?"

"Do you want me to go back home?" Maybe he thought she'd be a liability. And maybe he was right. God, she hated that she was even thinking that.

"I'd prefer if you were safely away," he said without hesitation. Paused. Then added, "But I need you tonight to break into the Tamchén jungle camp with me and help me find Rosita, and to see if the noseless man is there. I have a way to get us in for about half an hour, but I can't search the whole camp in half an hour by myself. So we'd go in, then we'd split up. Your decision."

He needed her. Clara was pretty sure those were words Light Walker didn't utter often. "Are we a team right now? For this particular mission tonight?"

"Yes."

Good enough, she decided. No way was she giving up. She wanted Rosita, and right now, Walker was the only person who could help her get near the girl.

So Clara pulled her back straight and said, "I'm in."

CHAPTER
FIFTEEN

They had to go down to the police station to give statements. One skinny guy who looked like he had indigestion sat behind the front desk. He appeared less than happy to see them.

Walker figured there were probably three policemen on duty altogether this morning. The entire force had been called in last night, so most everybody would be sleeping, the station running with minimum staffing. The other two policemen were dealing with the dead body in Consuela's backyard. Worked for Walker.

He recounted the attack for Skinny, telling the guy almost word for word what Clara had just finished saying. Then they signed papers.

Then Walker had a sudden idea and said, "I have to make another report. I had my car parked at the cantina yesterday. I was out of town with friends for the day. By the time I came back, the cantina was burned out, along with the cars in the lot. I need some kind of official paperwork on that for the insurance company. I'm sure they'll be asking for a police report."

"Me too," Clara piped up next to him. "Mine was shot up."

Skinny didn't look excited, but grudgingly filled out an online form and printed each of them a copy. "Put your names and address on top, then sign on the bottom. Add your own license plate numbers on the dotted line."

Walker grabbed one sheet and gave the other one to Clara. They were done in two minutes.

"Actually, if I could ask you a favor." He reached into his pocket and slipped a hundred dollar bill under the sheet of paper before he slid it back across the counter for stamping. "I'm sure the insurance company is going to ask for photos. My camera was in the car. Any chance you could step out and snap a few pictures? If you could print just one or two and staple it to the report, I'm sure it'd make a big difference."

Skinny pried up the corner of the paper, looked at the hundred dollar bill underneath, then flashed Walker a pained look. "I'm not supposed to leave the desk unattended."

"We'll stay right here. If anyone comes, we'll tell them to wait. The cars are just a block away. Mine is the Jeep, hers is the Ford Fiesta parked in front of the guesthouse across the road."

Skinny nodded, pocketing the money. Then he grabbed a camera from his top drawer and headed for the door. "If anyone comes looking for me, I'll be back in five minutes."

As he hurried out the door, Clara looked after him. "Key?" she asked Walker as soon as they were clear.

He grinned at her. He figured she would know what he was aiming at. She was pretty sharp. Now that he knew her better, he actually liked having her on his team.

He vaulted over the counter, pulled a key ring that was hanging from a thumbtack pushed into the back of the counter, which he'd seen from where he'd been standing, but Clara couldn't.

She looked as if she could kiss him. A look a man could get used to, especially if she delivered on the promise.

By the time he was trying keys in the row of file cabinets lined up against the wall, Clara was over the counter too. When he found the right key and opened the first drawer, he left it to her to look through, and went for another.

"A through D," she told him. Stepped back. Pointed at the bottom cabinet. "Ruiz is probably in here."

He opened that drawer. She was right. The files went from P to T.

He let her quick, slim fingers do the work. In one minute, she had Rosita's file out and tucked into her waistband in the back, her shirt pulled over it.

"In case the Tamchén camp doesn't pan out," she echoed his thoughts. "Maybe this will give me a new lead."

"As long as we were here anyway," he said with a grin.

He locked the drawers back up while she slid across the counter in a hot, action-flick move, and hurried to sit in the chair she'd left just a few minutes ago. Walker hung up the keychain where he'd found it, then vaulted over the counter and went to sit next to her.

They needn't have hurried. They could have performed the whole exercise twice over before Skinny shuffled back.

He printed them the photos. They thanked him profusely, then walked back to the guesthouse. Grinning like a pair of idiots all the way.

***

Clara was appalled at how little breaking the rules at the police station bothered her. Maybe she didn't care because the cops were dirty. Or maybe it was Walker's influence. Heaven help her if he was rubbing off on her. She'd just broken Mexican law. She'd reached the slippery slope and slid down like a professional bobsled competitor.

Not something she was willing to waste time worrying about when she had Rosita's disappeared person report fanned out on the bed in her room at the guesthouse. A dozen measly pages—mostly detailing unproductive, door-to-door interviews.

She read the salient information out for Walker, who was watching the street through the window.

"She was reported missing immediately by the cousin. Nobody else was home at the time. No witnesses on the street."

"Fingerprints on the car?" Walker asked.

"The police didn't take any."

"There might not have been any, anyway. They could just have grabbed her."

"Okay, this is something new." She perked up. "A blue van was seen in the vicinity."

"License plate?"

"Nobody took the time to notice."

He turned toward her. "The van pulls up next to Rosita. One guy behind the wheel, another in the back. The one in the back opens the door, pulls her in. He closes the door, and they're off. She was gone in an instant."

Clara nodded, sympathy filling her. Given the circumstances, she wasn't Rosita's biggest fan, but she didn't wish harm on the girl. Rosita had to be scared to death. She was seventeen. And God knew where she was now, if she was even still alive. God knew what had happened to her since that afternoon on the street.

Clara wanted to find her, and not only to save the general's reputation and his marriage. She was going to find Rosita, would do her best to track the girl down even if Rosita wasn't personally linked to Clara.

For a moment, she considered checking in with her father, then decided against it. She didn't want to tell him where she was going tonight, didn't want to worry him. She'd call him if she found something at the jungle camp.

She *needed* to find something at the camp. The police report was a complete bust. There had to be a million blue vans in Mexico. Having that information helped them nothing.

She sighed. "I hope Rosita is at the Tamchén, and they're taking good care of her."

Walker glanced at his watch, "We'll soon see."

***

The truck's headlights cut through the night as Walker drove out of the jungle, ready to pick up Clara at the edge of the banana farm where he'd left her. He'd had her wait for him at a small cluster of workers' huts with friends while he'd gone to retrieve the Xibalba drugs he'd hidden after his ambush a few days ago. *Half the drugs.* He had different plans for the other half.

The truck he "borrowed" from Pedro's fleet—el Capitán wasn't going to need it again—rattled over uneven ground. Walker couldn't use the trucks the heroin had originally come in; they'd been shot to shit.

Not by him. He'd shot at Santiago's yahoos, and he hit what he aimed at, but the men—unable to see him—had been shooting all over the place. He was pretty sure at least one of them had died from friendly fire.

Walker put all that out of his mind as he pulled up by the jumble of huts that edged the road, a tiny community in the middle of nowhere, surrounded by nothing but banana trees. His gaze immediately found Clara. A head taller and several shades lighter, she stuck out from among the Tojolabal women who sat around the fire, husking corn for cooking.

Clara worked right along beside them.

A smile tugged at his lips at the sight. He liked looking at her. He liked kissing her even more. They'd be doing more of that in the future; she just didn't know it yet.

She turned as if sensing being watched, saw him. She said her good-byes and ran to him, got in, grousing as she snapped on her seat belt. "I don't see why I couldn't have gone with you."

Because he didn't want her to see the rotting corpses in the clearing. Not that he thought the scene would scare her off, since nothing had been able to accomplish that so far.

On one hand, he respected her fearlessness; on the other, it made him nervous. He'd never seen a woman so ready to face death to save someone else. He'd never seen a woman he wanted to keep alive more—a strange and frightening thought he wasn't prepared to examine.

"Let's run down our plan again," he said as he drove down the road, heading for an unmarked turnoff into the rainforest that waited just a short mile ahead.

"So you got everything okay?" She pulled out her camo hat and shoved it on her head, covering up all the blond.

She adjusted the hat in what might have been a nervous gesture. "I never thought I'd be riding through the night with a truckload of raw heroin. What if we get caught by the cops before we reach the camp?"

"The cops don't use this road. Even loggers won't use it. Nobody comes this way but the Tamchén. There's nothing at the end of this road except the Tamchén jungle camp and people who aren't invited don't go there. If they do, by accident, they don't leave."

After a moment of processing that, Clara said, "Okay. Let's talk about the plan. We go in, we split up, we search, we meet back up again. It's a pretty simple plan."

"All plans are simple until the first monkey wrench gets thrown," he told her, speaking from experience. "No op goes exactly as planned. For tonight, the main goal is to locate Rosita. We'll have half an hour to search the place. Once we know where they're keeping her, we make plans and come back to rescue her tomorrow night. I also need to find out if the noseless man is here."

If he was, Walker needed to make plans for the guy's extraction too, not just Rosita's. It would complicate things tenfold—not that any complication would stop Walker at this stage.

He'd been looking for the man everywhere. It'd be just Walker's luck if the bastard showed up at the most difficult place at the most difficult time. But there was no way Walker was going to let him slip through his fingers if they ran into each other.

He was prepared to succeed at his mission or die trying. Clara, on the other hand…

He looked at her as the truck bounced over potholes. "If something goes wrong, run for the jungle and keep running. Go north. I'll find you."

And if he couldn't come after her, by going north, eventually she'd hit a road that led out of the jungle and back to civilization.

She rolled her eyes at him. "You Tarzan, me Jane? Can we skip the swinging from lianas?"

"Are you kidding me? That's the best part."

The corner of her mouth lifted.

After a moment, she said, "Hey, while I waited for you, some medicine man fixed my side." She gingerly touched a hand to the spot.

"Baku was there?" Who was sick?

"Just for a while," she said. "He stopped in to visit with the head of the family to talk about some tribal ceremony. He was kind of freaky. He just looked at me and he knew that I was hurt. He rolled up a bunch of different kinds of leaves from his pocket and had me smoke it while he put some paste on the wound. I feel no pain."

Walker nodded. "That's good. Baku knows what he's doing."

"Looked questionable to me. I pretty much went along because I didn't want to offend anyone. I'm guessing the antismoking campaigns don't reach this far south."

He'd seen too much to make light of the shaman's talents. "I've come to learn that it's best not to question Baku's methods. For one, if you do, your next dose of medicine will be exceptionally nasty. And I mean boiled beetle brains."

She raised an eyebrow. "Spoken like a man who's eaten boiled beetles?"

He gagged just thinking about it. "Unfortunately."

She cleared her throat. "Do you think Baku is sweet on Brunhilda?"

Walker blinked. "You picked up on that?"

"Hard not to. He kept asking me about her."

"He's had a crush going for a while."

"And Brunhilda?"

"Sometimes I think it's mutual, but Brunhilda seems to be holding back for some reason."

"Because of what she does for a living? I don't think it bothers Baku."

"It's enough if she thinks it's a problem." Women were damn complicated, in every country and every occupation, a universal truth that needed to be acknowledged.

The truck rattled on. The night had closed around them, the twin headlights' attempt to keep the darkness at bay proving pitifully insufficient.

The dark night—the moon at a sliver—was in their favor. They both wore camouflage army uniforms he'd procured from Pedro's stash, and black army boots that would blend. Most of the cartel guys wore similar clothes, merchandise that walked off army bases. If anyone caught sight of Clara or Walker at the camp while they were snooping around, in the dark, nobody would think anything of it. They'd be mistaken for two of the guys.

Walker knew where the first sentries would be, so he stopped about half a mile before that point.

They got out. Clara climbed under the truck. He dropped to his knees, then to his stomach, holding the flashlight for her with one hand while he helped her with the other.

"Tie yourself up." He had a harness in place for her, and loops of rope set up for her feet so they wouldn't drop and drag.

She called back with, "Try not to drive like a maniac."

"Nobody can drive a jungle road like a maniac in the dark," he reassured her as he watched her securing herself into place and giving him a thumbs-up.

He would have preferred it if *he* was under the truck and her in the cab, but the sentries would never let her through.

He smiled at her. "You look like a spider monkey clinging to her mother's belly."

"That suspiciously doesn't sound like a compliment," came the response, and it made him smile again, despite the dangers that waited up ahead.

He pushed to his feet and left her with, "Hang in there," then climbed back into the cab.

He drove slowly and watched the road, made sure there were no fallen branches or rocks in the middle that would tear at Clara. He kept an eye on the road bed while pulling out his phone.

The Tamchén camp had some kind of a signal amplifier. He called Miguel, a connection at the Tamchén stronghold Walker had been cultivating for the past year.

Miguel was a low-level general manager at the camp. He kept an eye on the foot soldiers. He was responsible for anyone new brought into the operation. If someone didn't work out, it was his job to shoot the rookie in the back of the head. A 9mm bullet was all the severance package the Tamchén offered.

Walker had done a favor for him recently, by pure chance. Miguel had been one man short for taking a truckload of guns down to Guatemala. Walker had volunteered for the job, even dealing with the double-crossing buyer to Miguel's satisfaction. So they were good. For the moment. At least to the point where Walker had the guy's cell number and knew Miguel would take a call from him, and that was all Walker needed tonight.

"Hey, it's Walker," he said into the phone when Miguel picked up. "I'm coming up the road, bringing you something I think the boss will like. Can you call down so they'll let me through?"

"What is it?"

"The Xibalba shipment that Santiago lost last week."

Miguel paused for only the barest moment before his laughter came through the line. "I have to hear that story. Come on up."

From early on in the game, Walker had carefully cultivated a reputation for being an independent mercenary. He'd worked for both sides in the past, had been careful to swear no allegiances, although both sides operated under the assumption that he would join them eventually, if given half a chance.

He drove, thinking of Clara. She'd be all right. She was a tough customer.

He liked that about her more than was prudent. Liked her maybe a little too much. Good thing their association was nearly at an end. They just had to get through tonight.

He would have preferred if they had better equipment, radios and such, like a real SEAL op, but tonight was a simple recon mission. They weren't going to battle. *Half an hour. Look around. Get out.*

If Rosita or the noseless man was here, Walker would come back tomorrow for the extraction. Alone. No way would he let Clara anywhere near that.

He slowed the truck when he reached the forward perimeter. A palm-hatch shack stood next to the dirt road to keep the rain off the guards, nothing much, just enough for two rickety bamboo chairs.

After a quick look in the cab and the back, the first set of sentries waved him through. They clearly had gotten their instructions from Miguel. The second set of sentries acted much the same. Another three minutes later, Walker was at the final checkpoint at last.

The camp proper—a five-acre spread of carefully cleared parcel in the middle of the jungle—was fenced in with a ten-foot-tall double-strand chain-link fence with barbed-wire coil on top adding another foot in height. The gate was more of the same, with a bamboo gatehouse that sheltered two guards.

Miguel waited outside the half-open gate. He wore military pants and a drab shirt with the sleeves rolled up to above his elbows, the buttons open to the middle of his chest. Shaved head. Tattoos ran up his left arm, disappearing under his shirt, then continuing up his neck past the collar.

He was as tough as a log-splitter and about as attractive. He'd started his career in illegal logging, then moved up to more lucrative things until he ended up as a camp boss for the Tamchén.

He nodded to Walker, then moved to the tailgate and vaulted up into the back of the truck without waiting. Walker jumped from the cab and walked to the back, watched Miguel pan his flashlight over the cargo.

The bricks of raw heroin were dumped all over and now waited in a giant heap. Walker had lowered the pallets from the canopy in the jungle, then cut the wrapping loose that had held the small bricks in one huge block on each pallet. If he'd simply brought the pallets, everything neatly stacked, the truck could have been unloaded in ten minutes with a forklift, giving him no time to search the camp.

Miguel didn't seem worried about the work required. He laughed out loud, looking impressed with the load and gleeful in equal measure. "Is this really Santiago's lost shipment?"

Walker shrugged, giving a sly grin. "Half of it. I'll bring the other half when it's safe. Pedro stole it. I found it. Finders keepers."

"Law of the jungle." Miguel moved back to the tailgate but didn't jump down. He narrowed his eyes as he watched Walker. "How much do you want for it?"

Walker rubbed his jaw. "I'm considering coming under the Tamchén umbrella. But I'm not coming in as a foot soldier. So maybe Chapa will consider this as my buy-in for a higher position."

Miguel's gaze turned calculating. "When are you bringing the other half?"

"When I can." Walker pulled a cigar from his shirt pocket and lit it. "I should be able to get it here in a week, on the outside."

That second truckload was his only card in the negotiation. The first load was already the Tamchén's. Nothing to stop them from shooting him and taking his cargo right at this second.

"I'll need this truck back tonight." He puffed on his cigar as if he didn't have a care in the world.

Miguel nodded, then jumped down, waved at the guards to open the gate all the way and let the truck through. He hurried ahead. "Follow me."

Walker climbed back into the cab, started up the truck, and rolled forward slowly. He knew the layout of the camp like the back of his hand. He'd sat in the surrounding jungle for weeks at a time on surveillance with his military-grade binoculars, day and night. He had four different observation points like the one he'd shared with Clara the night before.

Now he took in the sight from a little closer. Five flat-roofed cement-block storage buildings, plus a hangar made of steel beams and aluminum sheet metal for sides and roof. Each building was draped with military camouflage netting.

Raw heroin came into the hangar, then was moved in batches into the storage buildings for processing and repackaging. None of the buildings had windows, no other opening beyond a steel-reinforced door.

The Tamchén had gone to that trouble in the middle of the jungle for a reason. When a full shipment was in, tens of millions of dollars' worth of drugs were housed here. The street price for heroin in the US fluctuated somewhere around two hundred dollars per gram at the moment.

To keep the camp hidden at night from planes passing over, it was minimally lit. Since all electricity came from generators, this also saved fuel, which was a pain to truck in. No sense in taking the trouble to light up the whole jungle anyhow. No work went on at night. Here in the middle of nowhere, they could work openly in daylight.

As expected, Miguel directed the truck into the hangar, then began shouting for men. By the time Walker got out again, half a dozen grunts came running from the darkness. Unfortunately, they all had their noses.

He was beginning to doubt if the noseless man even existed. But since it was the only piece of information he had that might lead him to Ben's killer, he found himself clinging to the hope that the bastard was real. If he existed, Walker was determined to find the son of a bitch.

Inside the hangar, only the truck's headlights provided illumination, washing the empty space in front of the truck with light, leaving everything behind the truck in shadows. Then the door rolled closed, and Miguel flicked on the overhead lights at last for the front half of the hangar where they'd be working.

Walker turned away from the men walking up to them. "I'd rather that nobody saw my face," he told Miguel. "Until I'm fully in. I don't want somebody tipping off the Xibalba before I have full Tamchén protection."

Anger tightened Miguel's face. "You think I work with men who'd talk to the Xibalba?" But then he gestured toward the dark half of the hangar with an exaggerated huff. "You go and wait over there."

Walker hurried away, toward the labyrinth of cardboard boxes piled at least eight feet high, and pulled into the shadows where Clara already waited, according to plan.

"We have about thirty minutes," he said under his breath, stomping out his cigar. He pulled his phone and surreptitiously snapped a couple of pictures of the men unloading the truck, then stashed the phone in his pocket again. "We'll go out through the back door."

She followed him. "And if your guy comes over to talk to you?"

"He's off to report up the chain of command. And he'll have to wait to reach Chapa, his boss. He won't be put through in a second. Chapa will have to be found first. He doesn't carry a cell phone out of paranoia. He doesn't want to be tracked through it. Then there'll be questions, then some time for deliberation on what to do about all this, how to distribute the extra merchandise. If Miguel comes looking for me, when I come back in I'll just say I stepped outside to take a leak. Right now, he's pretty damned happy with me. He's not looking to find fault. Since I brought in the drugs through him, he'll be getting credit for it."

They reached the back door in thirty seconds, and he spent another thirty on picking the lock with the piece of aluminum wire that he'd brought for this purpose.

Once outside, he scanned their surroundings. The nearest building stood forty feet away. Cover was minimal: a handful of cars, some bushes, then water and kerosene barrels in random spots, wherever they'd been dropped off by delivery trucks.

Perimeter guards watched the fence, but no guards stood stationed at the buildings tonight, same as last night. A serious piece of luck. As he'd hoped, the Tamchén were in between shipments.

Walker and Clara ran forward in a crouch, then split up as planned, each going to search a different section.

He didn't run toward the famous ancient well. The Tamchén wouldn't have brought Rosita here to kill her. If they wanted to send a bloody message to the Xibalba, they would have shot Rosita down in the street right outside her cousin's house and delivered that message publicly, a sign of power.

That she'd been quietly kidnapped meant the Tamchén wanted something from the Xibalba, or Carlos Petranos specifically, in exchange for her return. Either the Xibalba had some Tamchén men, or territory the Tamchén wanted. Or maybe they wanted in on the super-pill profits.

The kidnapping of the sister of a top-tier cartel boss like Carlos was a big deal. That Walker hadn't heard a thing, that nobody had breathed a word, meant either that Carlos himself kept it quiet, negotiating on his own to save face, or that things were kept quiet particularly from Walker, because word might have come down that he was not to be trusted.

Not a comfortable thought. The distance between a man's loyalties being questioned and that man being dead was pretty short in this part of the world.

His muscles tensed as he passed one building, then another. The storage buildings hugged the hangar in a half circle. He'd start searching on one end,

Clara on the other. The plan was to meet in the middle, at the building nearest to the hangar's back door, then slip back in unseen.

In another dozen steps, he reached the starting point for his search, the outmost building. He made quick work of the lock, stepped inside, and closed the door behind him before turning on his pocket LED flashlight.

Four rows of stainless-steel tables filled the space, some holding lab equipment, the rest holding scales. Unprocessed, grade one, raw heroin came in here, then grade three, "brown sugar" for smoking, went out, or grade four, white powder, the purest form of heroin that could be easily dissolved and injected.

He could see the entire interior from where he stood inside the door. No sign of Rosita. He turned off his flashlight, ducked out, locked the door behind him, then headed to the next building.

The second building was identical to the first. He moved on to the third, the one where Clara was supposed to meet him. He saw no trace of her. Since no alarm had been raised, he didn't worry.

Judging by the empty pallets piled next to the building, Walker figured this was where the drugs were packaged for distribution. The building had one steel security door and no windows, same as the others.

Not the same as the others, he saw as he went for the door. This one had a fancy keypad lock.

He didn't even try. He didn't know whether an alarm would sound if he punched in the wrong number.

As he stared at the lock, contemplating his next step, footsteps sounded from his left. One of the sentries was looping around.

Walker ducked around the corner of the building and hurried to the back, waited until the sentry passed, then got a running start and lunged for the roof. He made it on the first try, pulled himself up by his fingertips, lay flat for a moment and waited.

Nobody raised the alarm.

He looked toward the hangar where his truck was being unloaded. Nobody was outside looking for him.

Walker turned toward the last two buildings in his row. He saw no movement. Where was Clara?

He hadn't worked as part of a team in years. He'd gotten used to not having anyone to worry about. Having a partner all of a sudden threw him off his game.

Which he couldn't afford.

She could handle herself. He had to trust her. She *was* a DOD investigator. She'd had her training. She was an impressively good shot.

He stopped thinking about her and crawled to the ventilation unit on his stomach.

When the cartel had a shipment in, they had guards on the roof so nobody could get in through here. But now, nothing stood in Walker's way.

Only four screws held the ventilation unit in place. He took out his knife and unscrewed them. He hefted the fan box to the side and lowered himself down the hole, then dropped, landing on his toes, knees bent.

He stayed in a crouch and waited, only the moon illuminating the space through the hole he'd just created. He could hear no other sound but his own breathing.

He slipped the flashlight from his belt, turned it on, and panned it around as he straightened. More pallets, more scales—much larger here than the tabletop lab scales in the other buildings. Industrial-size rolls of plastic wraps lined the wall in the back.

And there were other rooms. He hurried toward the four doors neatly lined up in a row. Tried the first. The door opened to an empty three-foot-by-three-foot closet. He panned the light and saw bloodstains on the walls and floor. The space had been used as a prison cell before.

The second door led to a similarly small space, as did the third and the fourth. All empty. No sign of Rosita.

He hoped Clara had found the girl and was waiting for him outside with the good news.

He checked his watch. They had roughly ten minutes before the truck was unpacked and somebody would start looking for them.

They couldn't afford to get caught. First of all, he couldn't afford to get killed, not yet. He had to stay alive, and he had to keep up the pretense at both cartels that he was a friend. Only then could he nudge them onto a path of mutual annihilation.

When your goal was to move pieces around on a chess board, you had to be close enough to touch them.

And he wasn't willing to let anything happen to Clara either. He'd brought her in here, and he was going to take her back out. And then he wasn't going to let her around his cartel mess again.

He hurried back to the middle of the main room, stepped on the table nearest to the hole in the ceiling, jumped for the edge of the hole, and pulled himself up and out. As fast as he could, he screwed the vent back into place, then slid to the edge of the roof, ready to go and track down Clara.

But as he reached the edge of the roof, he found one of the sentries sitting right under him, having a smoke and a beer.

He checked his watch again. Five minutes left.

CHAPTER
SIXTEEN

Clara was in some kind of an armory. The door had been open a crack, so getting in hadn't been a problem. Looking around proved a tad more difficult. Two guards were having sex against the wall in the far corner.

She held her breath, her back pressed to the wall just inside the door. Rows and rows of gun crates towered between her and the lovers, blocking her view. She couldn't see them, and they couldn't see her, but when the men were done, they'd be leaving, so she couldn't stay by the door. She needed either to go back out and stay out until they left, or move away from the door and search the place while they were busy.

The clock was ticking. She had five minutes left—three to search the place, then another minute or two to run to the back door of the hangar and get in there. She had to hide under the truck again so she could leave the Tamchén camp with Walker.

She inched to the left, careful not to knock the crates.

Little light filtered through the barely cracked door, and the building had no windows. The overhead lights were off. The only source of illumination came from somewhere around the lovers, probably their flashlights dropped to the ground, two lit-up circles that left the rest of the space in darkness.

Clara waited until her eyes adjusted, then moved ahead a little faster.

Some of the crates had US Army stamped on the side, as if they'd come straight from an army depot. She frowned. That didn't seem right. But since she was here to investigate something else, she kept moving forward.

She stayed around the perimeter, checking three walled-off storage areas. One was empty, one held explosives, the other piles of MREs, packaged meals the military used. Rosita wasn't there.

Clara couldn't see the entire main room of the building since stacks of crates blocked the view, but having an empty room with a lockable door available, it wouldn't make sense to keep a prisoner out in the open.

She backed away, toward the door, the men in the far corner still moaning and growling, bodies slamming against each other. She was so focused on them, she didn't notice the new guy stepping in the front door.

"*Alto!*" the man shouted at her, going for his gun. *Stop.*

She was close enough to rush him, so she did, knocking him into the doorframe. Then she drove the base of her palm hard into his chin with all her strength.

His head snapped up, bounced off the cement-block wall, and he slid to the ground, but boots were already pounding on the ground behind her as the two lovers came running.

Clara darted outside.

Nowhere to hide.

A few bushes and a barrel here and there wouldn't hide her now, not when people were looking for her. Those would be the first places they checked.

The back door of the hangar waited a hundred feet away. The men chasing her would be outside before she reached that door. They'd catch her in the open. So instead of running for her rendezvous point with Walker, she ran in the opposite direction, around the armory, going toward the back.

The outdoor overhead lights came on. All of them. Men were shouting somewhere behind her.

Busted.

Her heart beating wildly, she ran for the scant shadows, half-blind from the sudden brightness.

Where was Walker?

Before she could panic, he appeared next to her. "This way. Toward the fence."

But two men came around the next building's corner with rifles in their hands, and immediately began shooting. Walker grabbed her wrist and yanked her right, darting between two storage buildings. They ran deeper into the compound, away from the gate.

An open area waited up ahead, some weird stone circle in the middle, then half a dozen open-sided bamboo huts on the other side, basically sleeping platforms with a roof, furnished with nothing but a couple of hammocks and mosquito nets.

Clara figured Walker planned on hiding under one of those huts, and she was cringing already at the thought of the plethora of spiders and snakes that probably lived under there.

But when they reached the stone circle, he stopped. "Jump!"

And because she hesitated, he grabbed her by the waist, lifted her over the edge, and dropped her into the abyss.

* * *

Walker had one foot on the well's lip to jump after Clara when someone slammed into him. The man must have been running from the sleeping platforms, checking his gun and not paying attention. For a moment, the two of them tangled.

Walker had the advantage. While the guy didn't know whether Walker was friend or foe, should be helped or attacked, for Walker everyone at the camp was an enemy, so he didn't hesitate.

He went for his knife to avoid the attention gunfire would bring. He grabbed the guy with his left hand, half turned him to gain access to his throat. But then, as the man's head came around, Walker cut a glimpse of the bandana that covered the guy's face.

The piece of fabric had half slid off. Because the man had no nose to hold it in place.

A sense of triumph shot through Walker, along with an extra shot of adrenaline.

He'd found the bastard!

But at the worst possible time. He couldn't interrogate the man right there. They were seconds from being discovered. And he couldn't take the guy out of the camp. He couldn't even get himself and Clara out at the moment. He only knew one thing: he had no time to think.

So he knocked the guy over the lip of the well, then jumped in after him.

* * *

One second, Clara was in a free fall, her stomach dropping out, then she hit water and she realized she was in a well. Definitely a well. She could see the stone walls now. Thank God, the moon was almost directly overhead, providing a little light. She would have been even more petrified if it'd been pitch-dark.

The water was stagnant and stank to high heaven. She didn't have time to so much as swear at Walker before he dropped on top of her, pushing her under.

She struggled up, fighting for air, blinking rancid water out of her eyes only to find herself staring into an unfamiliar face. And she shrieked, every zombie movie she'd ever seen pushing into her brain.

She desperately flailed back. Even with the moonlight, she could barely see the bottom of the well, but the eyes that glowed at her from the darkness, the ghastly face, and the weapon the man was pulling were way more than she needed to see.

Her brain barely had enough time to grasp reality and kick up the solution—*the noseless man*—before someone else dropped on top of them and pushed her underwater once again.

They all came up sputtering, breaking the surface together. Thank God, the new addition was Walker. He lunged at the noseless man without paying any attention to Clara, tangling with the guy for a second before disarming him and pushing him against the rounded wall, the glint of a knife at the man's throat.

He whispered a single word: "Quiet!"

Boots slammed on the ground above, men running and shouting.

The well was pretty large, about eight feet in diameter. Clara pressed herself against the ancient stone wall roughly three feet away from Walker, staying in the deepest darkness in case someone thought of looking down.

But the noises faded as the men ran by the well, heading toward the gate.

She stayed frozen in place, moving just enough to keep herself afloat, her gaze riveted on Walker and the man he'd captured, the brittle tension of impending violence filling the confined space.

Walker glanced at her, swore quietly but viciously, an undercurrent of desperation and resignation in his voice. For the barest of moments, he stilled, almost as if hesitating. Then the moment passed, and he turned back to his captive.

"Two years ago," Walker whispered to the man, "you were at an abandoned farmhouse about ten miles north of here. A dozen men were killed there."

The man struggled against Walker, but Walker held him pinned in place.

In the dark, Clara couldn't see if the blade had nicked the guy's neck, but she wouldn't have been surprised if it did. Since she couldn't think of a way to help Walker, she figured the least she could do was stay out of his way, so she hung on to a protruding stone, and kept quiet.

"One of those men was a tall American. Green eyes, blond hair. His name was Ben," Walker whispered to the guy. "All I want from you is to tell me who killed him."

The guy spat. Whether he hit Walker or not, Walker didn't react.

"Whose hand held the machete?" he asked, his tone colder than the well water and harder than the stone Clara was clinging to.

The guy struggled against him.

Quick movement. A muffled, pain-filled moan. She couldn't see enough to tell what happened, but then she noticed that the man's hand was at the side of his head, something dark dripping through his fingers.

Walker's knife was back at the guy's neck, but Clara was pretty sure that in that second of action she'd missed, he had cut off the guy's ear.

Her stomach rolled. On top of the panic from the sheer fact that they were trapped at the bottom of a well in a cartel camp with dozens of armed men looking for them above came the shock of bloody violence right next to her.

"Who killed the American?" Walker demanded again. "The Xibalba or the Tamchén? I want a name."

The guy spit expletives this time, hoarsely, in Spanish, sounding as if he was gasping for air. Maybe Walker's free hand was crushing his windpipe.

Another burst of movement. A flash of the knife. Another muffled scream.

Clara was pretty sure the man had lost his remaining ear, and she tried not to think of what he must look like. Nausea bubbled up her throat anyway. Fear squeezed her lungs, and it wasn't just the fear of discovery from above.

The man croaked a name, unintelligible. Then, probably at some prompting from Walker, he repeated it. "Santiago."

"Are you sure?"

The man spoke some more, but his voice was too shaky, Clara's Spanish not nearly perfect, so she didn't catch all of it. The gist of the few rasped sentences was that the man was certain, as Santiago had cut off his nose at the same time, for not catching the traitors sooner.

Then came an endless moment of silence, the tension in the well so thick they could have climbed it.

Then a violent, crunching pop.

Walker's shadowy form separated from the man's. After another endless moment, the man sank into the water, one dark shadow swallowed by another.

Walker hung on to the rock wall with one hand but was otherwise motionless.

She moved away, wary of the dead body somewhere under the surface. She couldn't tear her gaze from Walker. *This is who he is. He warned me.* But stupidly, she hadn't believed him. Because stupidly, she'd been falling for him.

Her mind felt like someone had taken an eggbeater to it, her limbs stiff, her breathing labored. She turned from him, needing to shut him out for a moment.

A hand touched her side.

She shoved her elbow back against what she thought was his arm coming around her, but whatever had bumped into her wasn't Walker. There was no resistance. The thing simply floated away.

She turned her head to see what was behind her, the smell giving away the corpse before the shape. A bloated body floated in the well next to her. The noseless man sinking to the bottom must have dislodged another corpse. Or maybe it had been floating around the perimeter all this time and she just hadn't seen it until now.

Past her breaking point, she lurched to the wall, blindly grabbing for rocks, trying to pull herself out of the water with every ounce of strength she had, slipping back over and over again because the rocks this close to the water were covered with some kind of slippery lichen.

Walker came to her, put himself between her and the floating corpse. "Hold on. Clara?"

But she just shook her head. She couldn't talk right now. She couldn't catch enough air, and what air she caught stank to high heaven. As they treaded water, all she could think of was all the other decomposing bodies below them.

Random gunfire shattered the silence of the night up above. Car motors came to life. Vehicles passed by the well.

Her heart hammered in panic. She was an investigator, not a super spy or special ops soldier. This was not how her cases usually went. She read case files and followed leads. She made phone calls and interviewed people. Mostly, it was very civilized. Investigations were about piecing clues together, not about bloody torture and going for midnight swims with dead bodies.

The difference between her being a government investigator and Walker being an ex-Navy SEAL turned mercenary came into sudden, sharp focus. The gap between them was a yawning chasm. The point driven home when, while she was grappling with the thought that she could be soon one of the well's corpses, Walker calmly said, "Moving on to Plan B."

They had a Plan B?

"I have a little distraction set up," he told her as he searched for a hand-hold in the rock wall.

He must have found one, because he pulled himself up, two full feet out of the water, then reached hand over hand and climbed up another two feet. "Keep transferring your weight from hand to hand, foot to foot. Make sure you have two points of solid support before you go for the next handhold."

He moved up another foot. "The slippery stuff is only on the bottom twenty inches or so."

She reached up as high as she could, felt the rock. He was right. No lichen there.

Okay. She had to get her act together. She had to focus on survival. "Should I go right behind you?"

"No. It's too dark for you to see where I grab on to, so you can't follow my grips anyway. Below me, you'll just be in danger if I slip. Come up next to me."

She was not a climber. At the gym, she spent most of her time on the treadmill. She lifted some weights for muscle tone, but that was it. While she was in good enough shape to have passed the fitness test required by her job, her usual workout routine wasn't exactly "hell week" on Coronado Beach.

But she reached for a handhold, and when she found a good one, tested it. She was grateful that the ancient well had been built with irregular fieldstones instead of smooth brick. She pulled her upper body out of the water. The floating corpse bumping into her thigh provided the motivation for her to go higher.

Walker climbed to her right, a full length ahead of her. He turned his head to check on her, then whispered over his shoulder, "Take your time."

She did. Because there was no way she was falling back into that water.

Coming down, she hadn't had a chance to notice how deep the well was, and when she'd been on the bottom, judging the distance up proved difficult in the dark. Only now, going handhold by handhold, did she fully appreciate how deep they'd dropped.

"When did you last have a tetanus shot?" Walker asked.

"What? Why?"

"You have an open wound on your side. That water was pretty nasty."

She winced. She hadn't thought about her side. Whatever the medicine man had put on the wound numbed the injury completely. She hoped the paste also sealed the broken skin. "I had a shot last year."

"Good," he said as he climbed.

Halfway up, he stopped and waited for her. They rested a few minutes side by side.

The sounds of men running around and shouting to each other filtered down, echoed around in the well. As she clung to the rocks, her muscles burning, she fervently hoped nobody would think of looking in there. She doubted anyone had ever voluntarily gone into the well before.

Walker reached out and pressed a hand against her back, supporting her weight partially so she didn't have to hang on so hard. "Are you okay?"

She drew a deep breath. "Not even close."

"You're doing fine," he said, then, after another minute, pulled his hand back. "Let's go, Clara."

The distance to the mouth of the well seemed endless, but they made it. She figured, altogether they'd climbed about forty feet.

They stayed inside, peeking out carefully. Although several vehicles had left to search the jungle around the camp, plenty of men had stayed behind, every corner now brightly lit, shooters on the rooftops with nasty-looking rifles.

Clara's stomach dropped. They couldn't possibly climb out without being noticed. And they couldn't hold on forever where they were. They'd fall back down again. Despite the chill of her wet clothes, sweat beaded on her forehead as she held on to the rim.

But Walker reached into his pocket and pulled out his rigged cell phone.

"Let's hope the water didn't kill it. Okay, here comes Plan B. Hold on tight. Ready?" He flashed her a grim look, then pushed a button.

An explosion shook the well, enough to have shaken them off if they were still clinging to the rock-wall side instead of hanging on to the lip of the well, a more secure hold.

"Now!" Walker shouted into her ear that was ringing from the explosion, then he vaulted out of the well, reaching back to pull her after him.

The hangar was burning, the roof and sides ripped open as if by giant claws. While everyone was looking at the fire and ducking from the debris falling from the sky, Walker and Clara ran for the fence, then followed it to the gate.

The guards had their full attention on the flaming hangar, shouting, "*Qué pasa?*" to each other.

While she tried to catch her breath, Walker put down the guards without hesitation, one bullet each to the head. As the men dropped, he ran for the gate. Clara ran behind him.

He shoved her through first. "Go!"

She didn't have to be told twice. In pure survival mode, she darted into the jungle that edged the dirt road, into cover.

"This way." Walker yanked her to the right after just a few yards, onto an animal trail he somehow knew was there.

The darkness around them was oppressive, a wall of black. She had no idea what was behind or in front of them. She tried to be careful of where she stepped, knowing that if she didn't twist an ankle or get skewered on a broken branch, it would be only sheer dumb luck.

And luck tended to run out eventually.

Every yard they moved forward seemed more nerve-racking than the one before. But Walker didn't go far. He stopped less than half a mile into the jungle. "We'll spend the night here. It's too dangerous to run through the jungle in the dark like this. And as soon as Miguel's men clear the compound, they'll be out, looking for us." He pointed up. "Remember this place?"

How could she remember something she couldn't see? Her mind was so freaked-out, it was numb.

"Up," he said, stepping to the nearest tree. And as soon as she moved next to him, he grabbed her by the waist and boosted her up to the lowest branch. "It's the surveillance tree from last night. Keep going until you reach the cross branch."

She had no choice but to obey, reaching up, hoping she would be grabbing on to a branch and not a poisonous snake. At least, the higher she went, the more she could see in the moonlight. She found the cross branch. She sat on the thickest part and waited for Walker.

He was up next to her within a minute, wedged his body against the tree trunk and made himself comfortable, then drew her against him to offer the support of his body.

She pulled away. She couldn't touch him. Not after what she'd just witnessed in the well. Her stomach was still rolling.

"How did you do that back there?" She asked the first question that popped into her mind, to distract herself. "How did you blow up the hangar?"

"Remember the C4 I got from that construction site?"

She closed her eyes. *Of course.*

He said, "I had a brick taped under the truck."

Her stomach rolled harder. The bomb had been next to her the whole way in? "So you planned to blow up the place all along?"

"I set it up as a contingency plan. In case of emergency."

She was gasping for air again. She slowed her breathing so she wouldn't hyperventilate.

She'd had about all she could handle in one night. "You know how you kept saying that I was in over my head? You were right."

"Try to relax." His voice was laced with concern.

Hysteria bubbled up her throat. "I just watched you cut a guy's ears off while I was swimming with a decomposing corpse. A seriously scary drug cartel is hunting us. And I'm in the middle of the jungle, in the middle of the night, sixty feet up a tree. For all I know, there are a dozen tarantulas and snakes up here next to me. I don't think I'll ever relax again." She shuddered. "Or feel clean."

Her skin was crawling. Her clothes stank of well water.

"The rain will help with the smell," he told her.

"It's not raining."

"Wait for it."

Because now he could predict weather?

But barely a couple of minutes passed before the downpour hit them. The rain truly did come as hard as a shower, then harder.

"How did you know?"

"The animals sounded different."

Oookay.

Rainwater washed over them, pouring out of the sky in a steady flow. They sat in silence. The rain kept coming down without slowing.

"Is it possible to drown in a tree?" she asked. She needed to talk, because when she wasn't talking, she was thinking about what had happened in the well.

"You're not going to drown."

"You don't know that."

"I've been through Navy SEAL training. First thing they do is try to drown you. Picture doing sit-ups on the beach in the surf with the waves washing over your head. We were under water more than we were above it."

"So Navy SEAL training lives up to the hype?"

"And then some."

"How tough is it?"

Maybe he knew how desperate she was for distraction, because he answered at length and with specifics. "Plenty tough. But it's not all about endurance. You start with eight weeks of Naval Special Warfare Prep School. Then twenty-four weeks of BUD/S training. Basic Underwater Demolition/ SEAL."

"Which is where you learned how to handle explosives."

He nodded. "After that, three weeks of Parachute Jump School."

"I don't think I could do that."

"Not to worry, they push you right out if you hesitate," he said. "Once you get good at jumping, you go to SEAL Qualification Training for twenty-six weeks."

"That's a lot."

"That's just the beginning," he told her. "You get the trident at that point, and you're officially a SEAL, you get assigned to a team, but the pain is not over. Next is ProDev, six months of Professional Development—Individual Specialty Training. Then six months of Unit Level Training. Then six months of Squadron Integration Training."

"How does anyone ever get through all that?"

"Over eighty percent drop out."

"But you didn't."

"I like to finish what I start."

"I guess that means there's no way you're going to give up your revenge mission here."

"None whatsoever."

"And if someone tried to stop you?"

"I wouldn't recommend it."

She closed her eyes for a long moment, let the rain wash down her eyelids before she opened them again. "Why can't you just stop fighting?"

"Fighting is all I've done, all my life." His tone roughened. "I killed people for my country. Now I kill them for my brother. It's the only thing I know how to do. Identify the enemy, kill the enemy. I have no other skills. I've gone too far to learn how to play nice with others."

He rubbed a hand over his face, then looked at her. "What am I going to do if I go back to the US, sell insurance?"

The stark finality of his words spread coldly through her. "So it's a suicide mission?"

This wasn't the first time the thought had occurred to her, and that she might be right scared her. "You take out as many people involved in your brother's death as possible until someone shoots you dead?"

"I've made my bed," he told her without taking his eyes off her. "I'm prepared to lie in it."

***

A good hour passed before the rain abated. The night was warm enough so Clara wasn't terribly cold even wet.

She didn't think she could sleep, but she must have, because she startled awake at dawn, facing Walker, straddling his lap in fact, her face buried into his neck while he held her to his chest with an arm looped around her waist. He must have pulled her onto his lap while she'd slept.

She yanked herself back, and the arm instantly tightened around her.

Walker blinked a few times, as if he too was just waking up at last.

"Easy," he said in a voice rusty with sleep. "You'll fall off backwards."

And her brain finally caught up with the fact that they were at least sixty feet up in the air.

She cleared her throat, trying to keep her balance while keeping a few inches of distance between them. "Why are we like this?"

He kept his arm around her waist. "Your legs kept slipping off the branch, and I was afraid they'd pull you down. You needed to be in a position so that your inert weight would pull you toward the tree, not away from it."

She didn't know what to say to that. She extricated herself from the situation and moved to a parallel branch.

"I scared you last night in the well," he said, his expression somber, his eyes filled with regret. "I'm sorry."

He *had* scared her. And he'd certainly made her see the truth. "We should go."

He nodded. "I'll go first. Watch what I do and step where I step."

She did, carefully holding on to the wet branches, catching herself every time her boots slipped.

Then they were almost all the way down finally, and Walker jumped from the lowest branch to the ground. He held out his arms. "I'll catch you."

She hesitated, but then let go. Walker breaking her fall was better than falling on her face.

He caught her. He checked her over. Then he quickly set her on her feet, respecting that she needed space.

"Anything hurt?"

She shook her head.

"Feel up to walking out of the jungle?"

"Try to hold me back."

He offered a ghost of a smile. "You're pretty tough for a civilian."

"I'm a DOD investigator."

The smile turned real, even if his eyes still held regret. "Yes, ma'am."

"What? No Detective Cupcake?"

"I was just trying to get under your skin with that," he admitted. "Some cupcake detective wouldn't have survived the Tamchén well. I'm going to have to start calling you The Indomitable Investigator."

That almost made her smile as she followed him down a barely visible game trail.

Since she was stiff, and sore everywhere, she slowed him down considerably. After a while, she gave up worrying about it. It couldn't be helped.

They reached a road midmorning, caught a ride with a priest who was headed to Mercita. He was an older, local man who'd seen a lot of things come out of the jungle in his long life. He didn't ask them any questions, just let them out at the edge of town as they requested.

"I need a shower with soap, possibly bleach," was the first thing Clara said when they reached Brunhilda's.

The house stood quiet, everybody asleep.

Walker pulled out his cell phone. Pushed buttons. Shook his head. "Looks like it survived the well but couldn't take the rain on top of that." He moved toward the front door. "I need to make a phone call."

"Who are you calling?" She went in with him.

His expression said, *That's in the when-I-want-you-to-know-something-I'll-tell-you column.*

She rolled her eyes then headed for the nearest bathroom. But then she stopped to look back at him. "So if the Tamchén don't have Rosita, where do you think she is? I really thought this was it."

"My best guess is that she's dead." He reached up and rubbed his fingers over the stubble on his chin. Regret sat in his gaze. "I think she was gone before you ever got down here."

"I need proof."

He shook his head. "I need to make a call. Then we'll talk," he told her.

CHAPTER
SEVENTEEN

Walker had two days left.

"I found your shipment," he said into the wall phone downstairs at Brunhilda's.

"Where?" Santiago asked on the other end, his voice sharp and demanding.

Walker had a feeling that if they were in the same room, he would have the guy's hands around his neck right now, amigo or no amigo. The feeling was mutual. Cold fury pooled in his gut at the sound of Santiago's voice.

"At the Tamchén." He paused for effect. "I was thinking where Pedro could have put it, since it wasn't found in Furino. I figured Pedro passed it on already, so I went looking for it."

"How the hell did you get in?"

"I did a small job for them back when. One of the guys knows me. I pretended I was looking for more work."

"Are you sure it was my shipment?"

"They were talking about it. They were unpacking it in the hangar. I took a picture, but my phone didn't make it." Maybe it'd work again when it dried out.

Walker waited a few beats, as if he was struggling with what he was about to say next. "I want to come on board."

Santiago didn't immediately respond. He took time to process the request. "Why now?"

"They caught me looking. I took a dip in the well. I barely broke loose. I shot a couple of grunts on my way out."

"No shit?" Santiago gave a startled laugh. "So you need protection?"

"It's time I clearly belonged to one side or the other. Makes things easier." Walker made it sound as if it was a simple matter of convenience. Santiago wouldn't respect a guy who admitted to *needing* anything. "Carlos around yet?"

"Yeah. But don't worry about it, all right? I'll put in a good word for you."

"Thanks, amigo. I appreciate it."

"Just come around when you're ready."

"I brought a small souvenir for you from the Tamchén. I'll be there later today," Walker said before he hung up. He couldn't go right away. War was about to break out. He wanted to get Clara out of town first.

If Rosita had been with the Tamchén, Walker would have returned to spirit the girl out. For Clara. But Rosita hadn't been there, and conditions were growing more dangerous by the minute—time for Clara to leave.

He filled his lungs. Shoved his hands into his pockets. *Fuck.*

She was scared of him.

She hadn't looked at him the same way since the well. He wished he hadn't taken her to the Tamchén. Not something he could change now.

He'd had no choice about the noseless man. He needed the information right then and there, no way to get the guy out of camp without drawing attention.

He'd promised Sister Sak Ch'up he wouldn't harm the guy unless absolutely necessary. In Walker's judgment, it'd been necessary.

But his broken word to the nun wasn't what bothered him the most.

Clara had seen him for who he was. And she'd recoiled. From the very beginning, he had tried to scare her. Now he'd finally succeeded, and he hated it.

She was right, of course. He was a dark-hearted, conscienceless bastard. But for some reason his chest felt even more hollow than usual at the thought of her loathing him.

Because he finally admitted to himself that he was falling for her—possibly the stupidest thing he'd ever done, and he'd done a couple of doozies.

He had feelings for DOD Investigator Clara Roberts.

The thought sent him reeling. How could something like that happen this fast?

Then again, what did he know about falling in love? He didn't have any previous experience.

Maybe it was always like this—a torpedo out of the blue, blowing you out of the water.

Jesus, she was magnificent. Tough and honest, and funny. Stood right up to him, something even rough men only did with extreme care. If ever.

Walker clenched his jaw. In the well, there'd been a moment of decision, whether to interrogate the noseless man or let go of the past, let go of his revenge, and maybe try to be the kind of man who could have a place in Clara's heart.

He'd made his decision. There was no going back.

He swallowed regret—more bitter than the shaman's boiled beetles—as he moved toward the stairs.

Clara had gone into the bathroom on the first floor, so he went up to the second floor and used the bathroom up there, stripped out of his clothes, washed off the stench of the well and the dirt of the jungle.

The rain had helped, but it hadn't been nearly enough. He used up half a bar of soap by the time he felt clean on the outside. On the inside…He was pretty sure he was past the point where he'd ever feel clean or whole again.

Clara deserved better. Letting her go, not starting anything with her, was his only way of loving her. Sometimes love was sending the one you loved toward something better.

He grabbed a bottle of iodine and a box of bandages from the bathroom cabinet and didn't bother going back down and around. He walked through Carmen's room—she was sleeping soundly in her bed—out the window, then up the fire stairs, wearing nothing but the towel wrapped around his waist, carrying his boots in his other hand, his gun inside one boot, his phone in the other.

Clara was already up in the attic and dressed, in a pair of old cargo pants and a black T-shirt from his stash. The pants were a little long, the shirt too wide in the shoulders. She had her arms up, drying her hair with a towel. The soft, worn material of the shirt clung to her uplifted breasts.

And just like that, a wave of instant lust cleared all other thought from his mind.

No bra.

She'd probably washed the one she'd had on. Her utilitarian sports bra was probably drying in the bathroom downstairs. Next to her utilitarian cotton panties, he'd bet.

Which meant she was naked under her clothes. His body tightened.

Then he thought, she was technically naked under *his* clothes. The idea that he was never going to see those breasts naked, let alone touch them, drove him a little crazy. He mumbled, "Lucky clothes," under his breath as he dropped his boots to the floor.

He wanted to make love to her more than he wanted to draw his next breath.

She blinked at him. "What? Do you mind? I didn't have anything."

He shook his head. "You're welcome to borrow whatever you need."

He sat on the mattress and placed the bottle of iodine on the floor next to him. He gathered up all the self-control he had. "Let me see your wound."

She hesitated. Just for a second, but that second killed him. Then she came over. She smelled faintly of papayas, probably from the scented soap in the bathroom. After another brief pause, she pulled up her—his—shirt.

The paste Baku had applied was brownish and viscous enough to stick, still covering her entire injury.

"I wasn't sure if I should rub off Baku's concoction in the shower," she said. "I didn't."

The wound looked no worse than it should have, no apparent sign of infection. He didn't reach for the iodine. "The paste looks to be an efficient barrier. I don't know if we should mess with Baku's work. How about if I put a bandage over the injury and leave it at that?"

The less he touched her, the better.

She nodded without looking at him, her head turned to the side.

Were things so bad that she couldn't even bear looking at him now?

He cleared his throat. "I'm sorry you had to see what you saw in the well."

"Do you regret doing it?"

He owed her the truth. "No."

"So you're going to kill this guy, Santiago, too?"

"Yes."

"When?"

"Tomorrow, if all goes well. He's Carlos Petranos's second in command."

She turned back to him, her gaze filled with sadness. "You took out Pedro. You took out the noseless guy. You said you shot some people in a clearing." She paused. "Did you have anything to do with the massacre in Furino?"

He hated the disappointment in her voice. He would have preferred if she railed at him, punched him, anything but this. "I set up the hit."

She flinched. "When will Ben be avenged? When is the killing enough? Do you think this is the life Ben would want for you? If the tables were turned, is this the life you would want for him? A suicide mission for revenge?"

He didn't want to think about it. "I've gone too far to turn back now."

"What anger wants, it buys at the price of soul," she told him. "Heraclitus said that back in ancient Greece."

Wise words from a smart woman. Her brain was one of the things he most loved about her. He said, "I guess the more men change, the more they stay the same."

She shifted back from him.

He hated even that small distance. He was going to hate her leaving even more, but there was no help for it.

He tamped down the strange ache growing in the middle of his chest. "I know the things I've done are not something you can look past. I don't expect you to understand. But just don't be afraid of me, okay? I would never hurt you."

She watched his eyes. "Not even if I got in the way of your mission?"

He drew a deep breath. "Not even then."

She nodded. "I guess I knew that."

She did? Some of the tension in his shoulders eased. For the longest time, he'd thought nothing would ever come before his mission. But the truth was, he'd been adjusting his plans to keep Clara safe from the moment she'd shown up in his life. And there were other hard truths here. That he was in love with her, and he was going to let her go, regardless.

"It's not that I don't understand why you're doing what you're doing," she said, "but it's still wrong."

"This is who I am."

"I know," she told him softly, as softly as if her heart was breaking. For him.

They stayed like that, immobile, inches apart, gazes locked.

Then Clara finally asked, "When can we go back to the guesthouse in Furino? I still don't have my suitcase. I'd like my passport and my wallet, at least."

He gave it to her straight as he moved to put on the gauze, then the tape. "Never. I've been seen there. And after last night, I'm a wanted man. The Tamchén probably has a price on my head. I don't want to bring trouble to Consuela's door. She doesn't need a shootout. I can't go there, and you shouldn't go there either. You've been seen with me. They'd grab you just to draw me out."

Clara's expression grew thoughtful as she lowered her arms and the shirt. "What will we do?"

"I'll be going to the Xibalba. I'll take you to the airport first. How about this?" He grasped at straws. "When I go to the Xibalba, if I see Rosita there, I'll get her out and drive her to the US embassy myself. Maybe she's just hanging out with her brother."

Clara's mouth pressed into a thin line.

He fully expected her to argue. But after drawing a deep breath, she said, "Okay. I'll go. But you don't have to take me to the airport. I can rent another car."

He nodded, relieved and pained at the same time. He was glad she was listening to reason at last and would be soon safe, but having to send her away just about killed him.

He wished they'd met under different circumstances. Hell, he wished for a lot of things. But she was out of his league. The plain truth was, she deserved better than him.

"I need to make a few more calls," he told her.

"I'd like to make some too," she said. "Then we should probably go to bed. Neither of us got much sleep last night. You shouldn't go to battle tired."

He *was* tired. But he found the idea of him and Clara in bed was an instant stimulant. Not that he was going to take advantage of her.

One more night. He just had to keep her safe for one more night, and that included keeping her safe from himself.

***

Once Walker returned from making his calls, Clara went downstairs to make her own. She called her father first. Her initial anger at him had lessened. Okay, he'd made a mistake. A *huge* mistake. But he was still her father. And he was dying.

The time she'd spent in Chiapas had driven home the point that life was incredibly fragile and fleeting. She needed to forgive him.

"Is everything okay?" was her father's first question.

"You first."

"I'm fine. I only had one chemo treatment so far. It's early in the game, and I'm a tough old buzzard."

"And don't you forget it. I don't care what the doctor says. I expect you to beat this thing."

"Hey, who's the general in the family? Who gives the orders here?"

Her lips tugged into a smile at their familiar banter. But then as she thought of what she needed to tell him, she winced. She hated to disappoint him.

"I don't think I can bring this mission to a successful conclusion. Things are getting complicated down here."

"Dangerous?" he asked, his voice immediately filling with concern.

"Rosita is Carlos Petranos's half sister."

Silence stretched on the line. "Are you sure?"

"Pretty sure."

"I want you to come home right away."

"I'll be leaving in the morning. Walker is going to see if he can track down the girl, although he thinks she might be dead already." She paused. "I'm sorry."

"Don't be. Just come home on the first flight. That's all I ask." She could hear him drawing a long breath. Then he said, "I'm ashamed to have asked you to go down there in the first place. I shouldn't have involved you in this. I love you more than I can say. I hate that I caused you pain and let you down like this."

She drew a long breath too. "I love you anyway." Her throat tightened. "We'll talk when I get back home, okay?"

"Okay. Until then, you make sure you stay safe."

"Yes, sir." Then she asked, "Is Mom home?"

"At a meeting with some nonprofit."

"Okay. Just tell her I'm on my way." She deliberated for a moment whether to say what she wanted to say next, but then she went ahead with it. "I think you should take some time off from work."

"I can't right now." He paused. "I'll talk to Milo again." His tone said: *but I can't make him do something he doesn't want to do.*

Milo would have been the perfect replacement. He'd been with the department from day one. Everybody liked him and respected him. He had an incredibly fast mind and could make connections everybody else missed. But he didn't want a desk job.

In his midforties, tall, wide-shouldered, skin the color of coffee, he'd been part of the FBI team that sorted clues prior to 9-11. He'd noticed some strange patterns and written a report, warned of imminent attacks. But the FBI had never passed on his report to the CIA. And Milo felt that he should have done more, should have raised holy hell.

Now, with the general's team, he was determined to save one life for each that had been lost in the attacks he couldn't prevent. He'd go into any hellhole, do anything at all, to bring Americans back home from danger. He was pretty much a legend in DC, and completely oblivious to it, too focused on the job to notice. Like he was too focused on the job to notice that Elaine, the office manager, had been in love with him from the moment they'd met.

"Keeping fingers crossed for Milo," Clara said, even while she knew that Milo was going to turn her father down again.

For someone, okay, slightly control freakish, accepting that she couldn't help people she cared about was difficult. She couldn't help Milo stop punishing himself and accept Elaine's love. She couldn't help her father undo his recent mistakes. She couldn't talk Walker out of his revenge.

"Life would be so much easier," she said, "if people would just do what I thought was best for them."

Her father gave a small laugh on the other end, a sound she hadn't heard in too long.

Her throat tightened. "I'll see you soon, Dad."

After they said their good-byes, she called her grandmother. The last time they'd talked, Grandma Lucy was in good spirits and fully cognizant, and since Clara didn't know how many good periods like that they'd have, she wanted to take advantage of every chance she got.

Especially after the dip she'd taken in the Tamchén well. That narrow escape drove home the point that her own life shouldn't be taken for granted either.

"Hi, Grandma, it's Clara," she said when the line was picked up.

"Hi, honey. Are you still in Mexico?"

Clara breathed a sigh of relief. "I'll be going home tomorrow. I'll definitely stop in to see you."

"Good, I want to ask your opinion about someone. I've been meaning to bring it up for a while."

"New nurse?"

"New guy. Antonio. Italian."

"Grandma!"

"He reminds me of Bud," she said wistfully.

Bud had been Clara's grandfather. Her grandparents had been married for forty years, had the kind of enduring love that was rare these days.

Her grandmother said, "He wants to go all the way."

Clara thought of the bowling alley in the basement, the farthest someone could walk within the facilities. "Be careful on those stairs." Then she gasped when she realized what her grandmother meant.

"I told him no," Grandma Lucy went on. "I told him we'd forget each other in a few days anyway." She sighed. "You know what he said? *Good, then every kiss will be like the first kiss.*"

Wow. Antonio had game. "Do you like him?"

"Hotter than pizza pockets," came the response. Then a long pause. "But I think I'll be seeing Bud soon."

"Don't talk like that. Have a wild affair."

Grandma Lucy laughed. "Maybe I will, if you will. You first. I don't want to die before I meet your young man."

Clara wondered what her grandmother would think of Walker.

Okay, that was stupid. Walker was definitely not Clara's *young man*. They belonged in different worlds.

The thought shouldn't have hurt, but it did.

Different worlds, different paths. She was going to drive away in the morning, while Walker rushed into deadly danger.

CHAPTER
EIGHTEEN

The temperature in the attic was bearable, thanks to the cooling rain outside.

As much as Clara hated to accept that her mission was a bust, she had to. Leaving in the morning was the smartest thing to do.

In the meanwhile, she needed rest.

After finishing the chimichanga Brunhilda had sent up, she went to bed. She was exhausted from their wild adventures of the previous night, and ready to pass out as soon as the hot food hit her stomach.

Walker rested on his back next to her, arms folded under his head. Clara was lying on her side on the mattress, facing toward the window. She expected to be asleep in seconds. But as the minutes ticked by, sleep wouldn't come.

She couldn't stop thinking about what had happened in the well.

She understood that Walker was desperate for answers about Ben's death. Back in the well had been his only chance of having his questions answered. He'd been waiting for that moment for a long time—he'd probably never have found the noseless guy again. So some of the rough treatment had been necessary.

But...God, she could still hear the sickening pop when Walker had broken the man's neck.

And yet, could she really judge him? She'd shot someone the day before. Except the young bandito had been a clear and present threat. While the guy in the well...They could have left him floating there.

Couldn't they?

Her eyes flew open. No, they *couldn't*.

Disparate emotions swirled through her as she turned toward Walker. The muscles in her chest tightened. "You killed the noseless man because of me."

He opened his eyes and looked at her but didn't say anything.

"He would have tried to pull us down, back into the water," she said. "You could have handled it, kicked him back, but I would have lost my grip. I would have fallen back into the water. He could have pushed me under."

He held her gaze. "I don't want you to think about that."

Because he knew how she felt about shooting Pedro's nephew the day before, and he didn't want to add to her anguish. He didn't want her to carry the guilt of another life taken.

The concept of Light Walker as a kind, thoughtful, caring man did a number on her brain.

She was going to miss him.

Not something she could have imagined when she'd first met him.

Light Walker was a complicated man. Lots of shadows in him, and some downright darkness, but he was also honorable, and had the capacity to be kind.

And the way he sometimes looked at her, with all the steamy jungle heat in his eyes…She had no idea in what spreadsheet to put *that*.

Or the fact that he was currently half-naked, lying next to her, within easy reach. Her thoughts about the well gave way to thoughts that took her into an entirely new direction.

Especially when the bed in the room below them started up its rhythmic creaking.

Little by little, tension filled the attic.

She bit her lower lip. "Have you ever—"

"No," he said before she could finish the question.

"I thought you and Carmen were friendly."

"I'm friendly with all the girls. And that's as far as it goes. I don't buy women."

No, he wouldn't. It'd been stupid to ask. He did have his lines that he didn't cross. "Sorry."

He nodded.

"Are you ever lonely?" she asked next.

He searched her face. "Are you offering to ease my loneliness?"

Was she?

"Clara?" His voice thickened as he said her name.

Her gaze dropped to his lips. He had great lips, supremely masculine and incredibly soft. She wanted to kiss him. She wanted more than a kiss.

Wait. What?

Oh God. Was she really considering a last-second fling with Walker? A one-night stand was stunningly, ridiculously out of character for her. And yet, here she was, just about panting for him.

Maybe he could read her mind because he reached for her.

She didn't know what to expect as Walker's mouth descended on hers in what would be their last kiss. Ravishing? The kind of plundering their kiss at the guesthouse had been when he'd told her he *needed* to kiss her?

But this kiss was respectful and gentle. As if he couldn't believe that he was kissing her. As if he didn't want to scare her away. As if not scaring her away was important to him.

He tasted her lips, nuzzled her, nibbled. He didn't push her to open up, but she found herself opening anyway. And even then, he didn't shove inside her mouth to conquer. The kiss wasn't what she'd anticipated. But it was a kiss that melted her completely.

He kissed her with so much longing, it caught her off guard.

Sweetness and longing weren't words she associated with Walker.

His kiss shot straight to the heart of her.

Her hands trembled slightly as they went to his shoulders. His muscles bunched and shifted under her palms, his skin warm under her touch. The kiss built heat so gradually, she got so lost in the feel of him, that she didn't notice the tsunami of desire roiling inside her until it was too late.

Suddenly, she was clinging to him, her blood rushing in her ears, her breasts pressed against his chest—aching for an even more intimate touch. In fact, she was aching for his intimate touch *everywhere*.

Her hands dipped to his chest, kneading their way down, settling restlessly at his waist as she pressed herself against him, against his hardness that reared between them.

At the end, he was the one to break contact first.

"I'd give anything to have you right now," he said in a thick voice. "I've wanted you since I saw you at that damned cantina, surrounded by slobbering wolves. I wanted you in the jungle. The first night we spent here. At the guesthouse."

He raised a hand, palm out, as if to ward off the objections he was sure would follow his words. "I know. It's a terrible idea. I've been telling myself that all along. But I can't stop the wanting."

She was a puddle of need, her heart a mess. But she had no idea why he would want her. His sudden confession confused her, which made her hesitate.

Normally, he came onto her to shut her up, to gain the upper hand, to scare her away. But she'd already agreed to leaving. He'd been right. She was in over her head. She knew it. She'd accepted it.

So why was he still amping up the seduction?

She gathered what little willpower she had left and moved out of the circle of his arms.

He let her go immediately. "Sorry. I don't seem to be able to help myself."

For real? She shook her head. "I don't understand why. I'm not the kind of woman men can't keep their hands off. For the record," she said, so he wouldn't think she was fishing for a compliment, "I'm okay with that. I like who I am."

His eyes narrowed. "So, to clarify, it's okay for you to like you, but it's not okay for me to like you."

Was he saying he liked her? "We don't match. If we were in a spreadsheet, we'd be in different columns." She'd be under *uptight/nerdy/homely girls*, and he'd be under *badass men with bodies of…um…Navy SEALs.*

He grunted. "Just so you know, I hate spreadsheets with a hot, burning passion."

She hurried on with, "I'm not remarkable on the outside, but I'm a strong, intelligent woman. I'm honest." She didn't want him to think that she had no self-worth. She wasn't hung up on beauty or craved it, or felt diminished because she didn't have it.

His eyes went back to narrow slits. "So you're strong, intelligent, and honest, but that can't be what men like me want and appreciate."

"Not in my limited experience."

"Then your experience sucks."

She couldn't argue with that.

But because she thought he still didn't fully understand what she was saying, she waved her hand in his general direction and added, "You are all shiny…muscly…stuff."

She groaned. He'd already robbed her of her self-control and ability to breathe. She resented him robbing her of her vocabulary.

"Maybe I'm shiny on the outside but a pit of darkness on the inside." His voice was suddenly somber.

She considered his words, because he sounded like he believed them. Yet she knew another side of him. He'd treated her injuries after she'd been grazed by that bullet. He'd saved her life at the Tamchén compound. He'd held her through the night so she wouldn't fall out of the tree in the jungle.

She sighed. "You're not without fault, but you're not rotten. Although you're very disorderly. You're pigheaded, cocky beyond bearing, arrogant." She stopped when she realized she'd just said the same thing three times over. "You have a troubling obsession with vigilante justice." She cleared her throat. "Well, I'm sure there are things you don't like about me."

"You're not naked, and you're not under me." His voice was thick with passion.

She lost her breath.

"I want you," he said. "I look at you, and I see your smart mouth that I want to kiss. As frequently as possible," he added. "I see your smart eyes that a man could look into all day long and not get bored. I see your hair that drives me crazy with the need to run my fingers through it. I see the sheer strength of your thighs and the softness of your breasts, and I want all of it."

She swallowed, her mouth suddenly dry.

"And that's just on the outside," he continued. "What's on the inside makes me even more crazy. Truth is, Clara, I love your orderly brain. And I love how you just suck it up when the going gets tough."

She tried to process that, but her entire body was tingling and the synapses in her brain were melting—not so orderly after all.

He seemed to like her. All of her. She swayed toward him. She might have braced herself with her palms on his naked chest. She might have tilted her mouth to his. With every passing second, she liked the idea of being naked under him more and more.

But he hesitated. He seemed to be fighting a silent battle with himself. So she brushed her lips against his.

With a deep, manly groan of capitulation, he kissed her. And again and again. He tasted her lips. He moved into her mouth and did wicked things with his tongue.

Her body burned for him.

Her fingers explored his warm skin, his seriously incredible muscles, his six-pack abs. Then she moved her hand lower, until his massive erection overfilled her palm. Even through his pants, he felt breathtakingly impressive.

He groaned again. In desire.

Then he rolled over her and fitted himself between her legs. He rocked his hardness against her center.

Her nerve endings sparked. *Oh sweet heavens, yes.*

He supported himself on one elbow, his other hand moving up to cup her breast. She arched into his palm.

When he tugged down her shirt, all that material bunched up and lifted her breasts straight to his face.

His pleased smile and the hot passion in his eyes stole Clara's breath all over again. Then his fingers…What his fingers did to her nipples was nothing short of magic. But they were only the harbinger of upcoming attractions, because next he used his lips on her, then his tongue, the heat of his mouth sucking her in.

The pressure between her legs increased as he pressed against her and moved in a rhythm that was pure perfection.

Below them, the bed stopped creaking, a short break, then creaking again.

"For the sake of my self-esteem," Walker said around her engorged nipple, "I'm going to pretend that's three different guys, not one guy for the third time in an hour. I can't take that kind of pressure."

She gave a startled laugh, and the vibration of that laugh inside her added to the sensations he was lavishing her with. When his hot lips closed around her nipple again, and he sucked hard while twirling his tongue around the sensitive nub, her body contracted, pleasure pulsing through her. Wave after wave.

She hung on to him, dazzled and dazed.

He moved up to kiss her gently. Held her until she returned to earth.

He smiled at her. She smiled at him.

She reached to unbutton his pants, but he moved her hand away.

"Clara. Wait." He squeezed his eyes shut, his expression pained. "You don't mean that. You're just being carried away by the moment."

He swore softly. "If I let this happen, I'd be taking advantage of you. I don't want to do that."

She stared at him, her mind too mushy to speak for several seconds. "You're protecting me from myself?" she asked when she could form words.

A rueful smile tugged at the corners of his lips. "I'm officially an idiot."

She swallowed and tried to gather herself. "No. You are right." Her mind swam in a sea of confusion. "I've never gotten carried away before."

She couldn't believe what had just happened was real.

Every cell of her body wanted him, clamored for more of his touch, for him to be inside her. But she'd never let her body rule her. She'd always followed her brain.

Granted, with Josh in college, she'd been a twit. But after that, she'd smartened up. Her decisions about sex had been calculated and conscious, after weighing cons and pros.

Sex was a big deal. A life-changing deal, not to be taken lightly. Sex could leave you pregnant or give you an STD. She was a serious, responsible person. She wasn't the kind of woman to throw herself into a man's arms on a whim.

He was still giving her that strained smile. Everything about his body language screamed that he wanted her. It was a heady feeling to be wanted this fiercely by someone like Walker. And the fact that he was holding back out of consideration for her was even more appealing. Stunning, and definitely doing a number on her brain.

The way he looked at her made her want to move right back into his arms and throw all caution—along with her panties—to the wind. The thought scared her more than a little. She wasn't the caution-to-the-wind type, never had been.

So why now?

Walker was somehow bending her will and common sense, no smaller feat than earth's gravity bending light. He was a scientific phenomenon. How was she supposed to fight against gravity?

She dragged her shirt back on.

"I don't understand what's going on between us," she whispered.

"There are things that can't be put in columns and charts, things that can't be tabulated and summed up easily. I didn't expect this either."

"But it can't go anywhere, can it?" she said more to herself than to him.

"No. We are headed into different directions. So I'm going to let you go." He held her gaze. "Listen, this is me, trying to do the right thing. Which doesn't happen often, believe me. Take advantage of it." Then he grew even more serious. "But if you come into my arms again, don't expect me to stop."

She felt as if all the air had suddenly been sucked out of the attic. She could barely say, "Duly warned."

He smiled at her—a torn, tortured smile filled with wanting.

She closed her eyes, because if she kept looking at him, she *would* go back into his arms.

The bed in the room below them stopped creaking. *Oh, thank the heavenly host.*

They lay in the silence that was now only broken by their breathing and the patter of the rain on the roof.

"Try not to get killed tomorrow," she said after a while, thinking it might be safe now to open her eyes, so she did.

She found him still watching her.

He gave a half smile. He was so incredibly handsome, it made her heart ache. His voice still had the rasp of desire as he asked, "If I disappear, will you come and find me?"

CHAPTER
NINETEEN

A million doubts bombarded Clara while Walker drove her to Mercita's one and only car rental office. They were standing outside the door when the place opened. He walked in with her and used his ID to rent a small sedan. She didn't need anything big. She had no luggage.

She wore the red shorts and a blue-striped sleeveless linen shirt Walker had found in a box in the attic. She felt underdressed compared to the young woman behind the counter—neat and professional in her gray suit, full of smiles for Walker. The woman had the paperwork done in fifteen minutes, then passed Walker the keys.

He walked out back with Clara, surprising her by taking her hand.

It was their first physical contact this morning. He'd been careful to be out of bed by the time she woke. He'd gone out and brought her breakfast and coffee. But as grateful as she'd been for caffeine, she would have preferred waking up in his arms.

At least, now he was touching her again, and she was determined to enjoy every second of his long fingers folded around hers in a secure but gentle grip.

He didn't let go until they got to her car, then he handed her the paperwork, the keys, and cash from his pocket, enough for gas, tolls, and for her to stop and eat when she got hungry.

He looked at her as little as possible, as if their gazes meeting might push him over some kind of edge, as if he found sending her away as difficult as she found leaving him.

Her heart thumped loudly in her chest. She put a hand on his arm. "Thank you."

219

Never in a million years would she have believed that she'd be attracted to someone like him. Yet here she was. She liked him. She more than liked him. Leaving him was hurting her heart.

Yes, he was a mercenary, but he was also a lot more. He challenged her preconceived notions of good and bad. She saw past the rough-and-tough façade now, to his scars, to his heart.

He leaned forward and brushed his mouth over hers.

Immediately, her body filled with heat.

He kept the kiss light. Then he pulled his mouth away and tugged her tightly against him, wrapped his arms around her in a hug of bands of steel. For a moment, she was frustrated with the brief kiss, then she suddenly understood. Anything more, and she might decide not to leave. Anything more, and he might decide not to let her.

"You think you'll ever go back to the US?" she asked, mumbling the words into the crook of his neck, against his warm skin, inhaling his scent, wanting to memorize the moment so she could take it with her.

"Probably not."

Her throat constricted.

He stepped back. Instead of his usual cocky smile, he flashed her a regretful, conflicted one. "Go save the world, one person at a time."

All she could respond with was, "Don't get hurt."

He nodded.

"When what you're doing is over, could you please somehow get word to me that you made it?" she asked. "So I don't worry."

"I will."

There was nothing more to say. Or maybe too much to say. But they'd made their choices. Except, she hated his.

Her frustration bubbled over.

"You know that this whole revenge thing is not for your brother, right? It's for you," she said, angry that she couldn't make him see it. "By being at war, you're distracting yourself from feeling the pain. You keep yourself in constant battle that requires your full focus. This way, you don't have to stop and think about how you feel."

She expected him to say something like, *I don't feel.*

Instead, he said softly, "This is me. This is what I do. You can't cut and paste me from the column where I am to the column where you want me to be."

Tears burned her eyes. She didn't want to cry in front of him, which meant she needed to leave. She blinked hard as she opened the driver's door and slipped behind the steering wheel. With one last nod, Walker turned and walked away.

She sat there for a few more minutes, familiarizing herself with the car, until she conquered the tears, and her heart and mind settled down a little.

By the time she drove out of the lot, Walker's pickup was gone from the front of the building.

She set the GPS for the Tuxtla Gutiérrez airport, then leaned back in the seat, ready for the trip. Except something hard poked her in the back.

The Glock.

"Dammit."

She couldn't go through airport security with a firearm. She couldn't leave the weapon in the rental either. The gun was linked to the US Consulate. If it turned up in a crime, it'd create an international incident.

Would have been nice to remember the damn gun ten minutes ago.

Of course, ten minutes ago, she hadn't been able to focus on anything but Walker.

She stifled a groan. Still, better to remember now than later. At least she was still in Mercita. With a small detour, she could leave the Glock at Brunhilda's for Walker, including a note for him to try to get it back to the embassy.

She turned the car left at the intersection instead of going straight.

Maybe Walker had to go back to the attic for something too. Then she could see him one last time. She held her breath for most of the drive, hoping. But when she pulled up in front of the brick house—forty-five minutes later, thanks to rush hour traffic—instead of his pickup, an ancient, light-blue Volkswagen Rabbit waited by the curb.

Brunhilda was squeezing in.

"Forgot something, Liebling?" she asked as Clara pulled up.

"I need to leave something for Walker, then I'm off," Clara said. "Where are you going?"

"To the market in Furino." The woman patted her crown of hair into place. "The small village markets are cheaper. Und the fruit ist frischer."

Clara paused.

"You need something, ja?" Brunhilda drew up a blond eyebrow.

And after a moment of hesitation, Clara asked, "Do you know Consuela's guesthouse?"

"Ja. Por qué?"

"I left my suitcase there."

"Und you want me to bring it? *No hay ningun problema.*"

"Are you sure?"

"I'll drive right by Consuela's place. You go und have a cup of coffee in the kitchen."

Clara hesitated. "When do you think you'll be back?"

The woman shrugged her pillowy shoulders. "*Dos horas.*"

Okay. Clara had two hours. She had plenty of time before her flight was leaving. Having her belongings was worth the wait. She'd called the embassy that morning and they were going to fax temporary papers for her to the airport security office, but she'd feel better having her passport. Her father had bought plane tickets for her online, but she would feel better having her wallet. At least she wouldn't have to cancel all her credit cards.

She thanked Brunhilda and headed into the house as the woman drove away.

The girls seemed to be sleeping, everything quiet. Clara carried the gun up to Walker's hideout and left it with a note, then went back down to the kitchen and started making coffee.

"Are you Walker's girlfriend?" a young woman asked in Spanish from the doorway, startling her. Carmen. She looked Clara over, her expression nothing but friendly.

"No. He was just helping me with something. Actually, I'm leaving today."

Carmen flashed her a dubious look. "He took you upstairs. He's never taken anybody upstairs before."

Before Clara could figure out what to say to that, Carmen launched into a long tirade about her dilemma whether to apply for a job with the pharmaceutical company that was opening, or stay here at Brunhilda's.

"I'd like to have a husband someday," she said, then her expression turned dreamy, "and children. Boys. It's hard to be a girl around here." She smiled. "I'd like to be rich, you know? Have a house with two bedrooms, one for the adults and one for the kids. And the kids would have a bed, so the snakes and the scorpions wouldn't crawl on them while they slept."

As they each grabbed a cup of coffee, she told Clara about the one-room hut she'd grown up in at the edge of a banana farm.

"I can read," she said with pride. "Brunhilda taught me. If I asked, she'd help me find a job. She's done it before for other girls. We don't give her money, you know. It's the other way around. Sometimes she helps out and pays for things if one of the girls gets sick."

Clara wasn't surprised.

They talked for a while, then Carmen went back upstairs. But then Julieta, another curvaceous beauty, popped into the kitchen, looking for a snack. Julieta wanted to know about Clara and Walker too, and stayed to talk for at least half an hour before she left to get some sleep.

Then Clara had nothing to do but wait, watching for Brunhilda, hoping for Walker.

Walker never came, but eventually, Brunhilda did return. With company.

Clara had her back to the window, making another cup of coffee, so she hadn't heard the car pull up by the curb. With the coffeemaker gurgling and sputtering, she hadn't heard anyone approach until the front door banged open, and at that point it was too late.

Four scary-looking thugs escorted Brunhilda into the house, guns in hand.

One of them wore a police uniform. He barked at Clara to put her hands in the air.

Brunhilda was swearing in three languages, blood dripping on her face. Her nose looked broken.

Bloody scratches decorated the cop's face. Brunhilda hadn't given in without a fight. Clara drew some satisfaction from that.

Adrenaline spiked through her as her mind raced. Hands in the air, she desperately scanned the kitchen. *Where was the knife drawer?*

The Glock was in the attic, dammit. But even if she had it…She was a fast draw, but not fast enough to take out four guys before one of them could shoot Brunhilda in the head.

As it was, Clara had no gun, and no other weapon in sight either. The game was over before it started.

***

Tonight was the night.

All Walker had to do was survive it.

The Xibalba compound in Mercita was a whole different matter from the Tamchén camp in the jungle. But even if the mansion looked a lot more civilized, it was certainly no less dangerous, something Walker tried to keep in mind as he drove there in another one of Pedro's trucks in the oppressive noon heat.

Pedro's fleet was scattered all over Furino. Eventually, the Xibalba would take over the bandits' assets, since Furino was under their control. The process had probably begun already, but it wasn't going to be finished anytime soon. First the Xibalba had to track down every last bandito hideout.

Walker had no scruples about borrowing another truck in the meanwhile. In the back, he had the second half of the drug shipment he'd stolen in the clearing.

D-day.

He rolled to a stop in front of the compound's gate. Since he'd called ahead, the guards let him through without trouble. Santiago was coming from one of the outbuildings, waving at him.

Instead of drawing his gun right then and there and shooting the bastard between the eyes, Walker parked the truck and got out, walked to the tailgate with Santiago, then yanked aside the tarp with a forced grin.

Santiago's chin dropped when he saw stacked pallets. He let out a low whistle. "Is this what I think it is?"

Walker shrugged, holding back the cold urge to kill. "A present for my new brothers. I managed to grab the truck on my way out of the Tamchén camp."

Santiago's eyes narrowed. "They still have the other half of the shipment?"

"They had it last night."

The man's gaze turned calculating. "People are talking about an explosion in the jungle."

Walker shrugged again. "I think their lab blew up. Not my doing."

Santiago waved a twenty-something guard over. "Take this to storage." Then he led Walker past the fountain in the middle of the courtyard, toward the mansion.

He kept clapping Walker on the shoulder. "You're the man, amigo. You're the man."

He had to be shitting himself with relief. He'd been responsible for the shipment. Carlos was probably ready to take it out on his skin.

Santiago was grinning like a jackass. Every time he touched Walker, Walker wanted to break the bastard's arm. Instead, he grinned too, and resisted. He could wait a few short hours to get to that part. Probably.

They stepped inside the foyer together.

Santiago clapped him on the shoulder one last time before hurrying up the stairs, calling back, "You wait here."

Walker had never been allowed on the upper level, not once during his half a dozen previous visits to the compound. The upstairs was Carlos Petranos's private quarters, his bedroom and office and who knew what else.

That Walker had gotten as far as he had was a minor miracle. He'd begun building his relationship with the Xibalba on the boxing circuit, making some members money, then by doing small favors for those members, backing them in a cantina fight, then providing muscle at shipment drop-offs and pickups.

Once he'd established trust, he met people higher and higher up in the organization. All the way to Santiago, the soon to be broken-armed bastard. But Walker hadn't been able to reach Carlos. Until today.

He scanned the closed-circuit cameras in the corners out of habit. He'd known that they were there. Since he knew he was being watched, he didn't attempt to sneak into the office on his right. He leaned against the wall and closed his eyes, wished for a cup of coffee. He hadn't gotten much rest last night.

Clara had been fast asleep. But Walker, who could sleep anywhere and anytime on command, had barely been able to doze off toward dawn.

He'd never held another woman through the night before. Had never wished he didn't have to let go.

Clara had snuggled against him in her sleep with subconscious trust. He'd kept his arms around her, feeling an overwhelming need to protect her, and other softer emotions he hadn't felt in too long, if ever. After Ben's death, he'd put himself on the search-and-destroy setting.

And now the search part of his mission was complete.

Of course, Clara was probably cursing him right now. Because he'd started a cartel war, it wasn't safe for her to stay and investigate. He was ruining her perfect record. She'd wanted to take at least Rosita's body home. But because of Walker's agenda, she couldn't. He had a feeling he wasn't one of her favorite people at the moment. He knew she was disappointed with how her mission had ended, disappointed with him.

But at least she was safe.

"Is this the man of the hour?" an unfamiliar voice asked at the top of the stairs.

Walker opened his eyes. He locked thoughts of Clara behind a wall in his mind.

Carlos Petranos didn't look like a crime boss. He was in his early thirties, wearing an impeccable suit, expensive watch, black hair neatly cut. He was polished in every way. He looked like a successful Silicon Valley entrepreneur. He could have been the CEO of a tech company, and Santiago a director. Except instead of social media platforms, they peddled in death and destruction.

Not exactly polished. Walker took back his initial assessment on second thought. Slick was a better word. CEO, but someone recently come into the title when his little startup took off, someone who in the past had done rougher work.

Walker could see the resemblance between the cartel boss and his half sister. From what he remembered of Rosita's photograph, they had the same eyes, the same mouth. The difference was, Carlos was taller, had a more pronounced nose and chin.

Walker pushed away from the wall. "Light Walker." He gave a small, deferential nod.

Santiago flashed him a look of approval from behind Carlos. Because of Walker, Santiago had been able to take credit for unmasking Pedro as a traitor. Now Santiago could take credit for having half the shipment back and having information on where the other half was. And by bringing Walker on board, Santiago would get credit for bringing in a competent soldier, an important asset.

The piece of shit thought he was having a great day.

Walker was eager to personally introduce him to grave disappointment.

Carlos looked Walker over from head to toe, his sharp gaze assessing, the same kind of look on his face as a stockbroker might have when analyzing a company for potential investment: detached, and determined not to miss any detail.

"Santiago vouches for you. I understand you have been a friend to my organization," the cartel boss said. "And now you're here to ask a favor."

Walker shifted from one foot to the other, as if uncomfortable in the presence of someone this high up the chain of command. He looked at his scuffed boots, then looked up at the man again. "People are looking for me."

Carlos kept watching him. "So I heard. It seems we have a common enemy." He paused, but not for long. He'd probably made his decision before he'd come out of his office. "You can stay at the compound. Santiago will see if he can find some work for you. Then we'll see."

A probation period. Walker nodded, putting plenty of relief in the small gesture. A way to stay at the compound tonight was all he needed. "That would be great. Thank you."

Carlos turned and walked away without another word. Santiago plodded down the stairs, looking pleased with himself. The sound of female laughter followed him, filtering down from upstairs, then Carlos's office door closed, and the sound was cut off. Walker stood a little straighter, straining his ears, but he could hear nothing else.

Santiago reached the bottom of the steps. "I'll show you to the kitchen. Word to the wise, if you want food, get there early. With all the trouble that's been going on lately, most of the guys are staying in the compound."

He was chock-full of friendly shit.

"Families too?" Walker made the question sound like idle curiosity. "I thought I heard a woman," he said without looking back as they left the mansion. Then he slowed and gave a suggestive wink. "I don't suppose I can bring a chica back to the bunkhouse every once in a while."

Santiago laughed. "Only if you're prepared to share."

Walker puffed out his chest, forcing himself to crack jokes instead of going for the jugular. "Once a woman had me, what would she want with the likes of those losers?" He gestured with his head toward the men in the courtyard.

"No woman would ever want a gringo when she could have a hot-blooded Latin lover." Santiago thrust his hips suggestively. "Maybe if you stick around, you'll learn some moves, amigo."

Weren't they just best friends?

They kept joking as they walked toward a long, single-story brick building in the back, but Walker's mind kept replaying that sound of female laughter. And kept going over the fact that Carlos had not looked as if something was troubling him. He certainly didn't look as if his sister was missing or dead.

Maybe he had no attachment to Rosita. Maybe they didn't even know each other. Or…

Was it possible that Rosita was hiding out at her brother's compound for some reason? Walker had briefly joked to Clara about that but hadn't really meant it. Nothing pointed in that direction. Still, he would keep an eye on the mansion, see if he could catch sight of the mystery woman.

Santiago slowed as they passed the bunkhouse. He checked out the SIG stuck in Walker's waistband. "You need something bigger?"

Walker shrugged. "A rifle would be nice. M14, AR-15, whatever you have."

He'd come with just the SIG. Showing up with his full arsenal would have been suspicious.

Santiago said, "I'll make sure you get something. A new shipment is coming up tonight. I want you to go and meet it at the border, give escort. What happened the last time can't happen again."

"Pedro's boys have been taken care of."

Santiago shook his head. "But the Tamchén seem to suddenly have a death wish. They might send their own people."

"Sure." Walker couldn't say anything else, even if he didn't want to go. He wanted to be at the compound when shit went down tonight. He wanted to be the one to take out his brother's killer. He rubbed his hand over his face, dropped it. He would just have to hurry back.

"You staying here?" he asked.

Santiago was a pretty big boss on his own. He had a nice place nearby, built with some serious drug money, had his own crew for protection.

The man's face clouded. "I don't like the look of things lately. It's as if everyone's gone crazy."

"Maybe it's the heat," Walker offered.

But Santiago shook his head. "We have good business here. Everybody from the coyotes to the banditos to the cartels. Why mess it up? Why suddenly? What did Pedro gain? And now the Tamchén? When business is disrupted, everybody loses."

"What can you do?" Walker said.

Santiago stopped as they reached the kitchen. "Wait and see if common sense returns."

Walker didn't like that sentiment. "Or initiate a decisive strike first. Instead of a prolonged war that'll do a lot of damage, start the war and finish it in the same hit. The sooner it's over, the sooner things go back to normal."

Santiago pulled a cigar from his pocket and ran his fingers over it in a distracted gesture, then pulled another one and offered it to Walker. "That's what Carlos said."

"Yeah? Soon?"

Santiago bit off the end of his cigar and spit it on the ground. "Just get the shipment inside the walls safely first."

"What time are they coming?"

"Should cross the border this afternoon."

Good. Then he'd be back by tonight. "I should head down there in a while, then."

Santiago pulled a lighter from his pocket, and they lit up. "I'll send a couple of men with you."

A couple of men.

No good way to refuse. Didn't matter. Walker couldn't take this shipment like the previous one. Another ambush would be way too suspicious. He was the one who'd found the scene of the massacre, supposedly, then the shipment, and now if the new shipment went missing while he was escorting it—he'd be the common denominator.

"There you go." Santiago ducked into the kitchen, puffing on his cigar, stashing away his lighter.

The first time he'd ever deigned to talk to Walker was when Walker had brought in a crate of Cubans to sell. They'd bonded over tobacco.

If only Walker had known back then that this was the bastard who'd killed Ben...

He knew now.

Cold fury had him clenching his jaw as he followed Santiago through the door.

A lot of places in this part of Mexico had the kitchen apart from the main building so the heat of the stoves wouldn't further heat the house, a practicality when temperatures regularly soared to a hundred and most houses had never heard of air-conditioning.

Food simmered on the stove in colorful pots, but the cooking women were someplace else, maybe out back, peeling or grinding something, or chasing a chicken. An industrial-size refrigerator hummed in the corner.

Walker watched Santiago go for a cold beer.

The two of them alone in the room. No witnesses.

Walker's hand moved toward his knife. He stopped himself halfway. *Not yet.*

He had a better plan that would provide him with more alone time with the bastard. He intended to have a long talk with Santiago about Ben.

Patience.

Santiago held the fridge door open long enough for Walker to see the piles of jammed-in food. "Grab what you want, eat, then come and find me. I'll have directions ready for you, a good rifle, and some car keys."

Walker nodded. He needed food to have energy for the fight that was to come. Before the day was out, the compound would be ablaze. And Santiago would pay.

The upcoming night would bring danger and death. Thank God, Clara was away and safe.

He'd sent her home.

In all this mess, he'd done one thing right at least.

CHAPTER
TWENTY

Walker wiped the sweat from his forehead with the back of his hand as the convoy rolled into Mercita at last, cutting through the sleeping town, following a prearranged path.

Nearing midnight, the streets were empty.

Although the police had night patrols, Walker hadn't seen a single cruiser as they passed block after block of dark-windowed houses and shuttered stores. Santiago had probably taken care of that. Carlos Petranos had plenty of cops on his payroll, same as he had border guards, DEA agents, and even politicians.

Walker's Land Rover led the convoy, then the two trucks, then a Jeep. He was the only one in the Land Rover, behind the wheel. The three men Santiago had sent with him had moved over to the trucks.

The convoy turned down the last street. The street lights were off. No lights on at all at the compound, not even at the gate. The convoy vehicles turned their lights off too and navigated with the help of men running to direct them with flashlights. Should there be any kind of surveillance, government or competitors, taking photos of the trucks entering the compound would be next to impossible, especially from a distance.

The gate opened when the Land Rover was halfway down the street. The convoy kept rolling, everyone eager to get out of the vehicles to stretch their legs and aching backs, take a piss, get a hot meal and a cold drink.

Once the small convoy crossed through the gate, the guards sealed the compound once again. Walker parked in the empty space to the left, right next to the gate. The trucks rolled into the oversized garage on the right where they'd be unpacked in the morning. The Jeep parked in behind Walker, blocking the Land Rover.

Fine with him.

The gas tanks were near empty, but both vehicles carried five-gallon cans of fuel for emergencies. No gas stations in the jungle. The gasoline would come in handy for Walker's plans later, increase the size of the fire following the explosion. And the tires he'd gotten from the dump, now in the back of the Land Rover, would burn with a thick, choking black smoke, nearly as good as tear gas.

Most of the men who'd escorted the shipment went straight to the kitchen. Walker followed, dropped into an empty chair, and shoveled in food without tasting it. Barely anyone talked. The original crew had been riding over washed-out jungle roads for days, through heat and bugs and rain, sneaking through multiple countries. They just wanted to eat then hit the sack.

Walker got up when they got up. But when they shuffled off to the bunkhouse to sleep, Walker stayed behind in the courtyard and pretended to be looking at the clouds drifting in.

Four guards at the gate, plus double the usual perimeter guards in position. Security was definitely beefed up, but nobody paid much attention to him. They were all watching for outside attack.

The streetlights came back on. Even at the compound, a handful of outdoor lights flickered on here and there.

Walker moved along, keeping to the shadows. He knew how to walk without making a sound, how to slip through tight places.

He wanted to know where all the players were so he could make an exit plan and figure out how to spirit Santiago out of the place. He wanted to be at least several blocks from here, preferably halfway across town in one of the boarded-up warehouses with the man when the Tamchén attacked. He had questions to ask and a score to settle.

He moved carefully and tallied everything he saw. One guard on the kitchen's flat roof, awake and moving. The gate guards had their backs to the courtyard. The perimeter guards were walking in slow circles along the wall. Santiago kept them moving like that all night, on the premise that falling asleep while moving was less likely than falling asleep while standing still.

When the opportunity presented itself, Walker darted to the nearest deep shadow—created by a pile of stacked pallets—and crouched there.

He could see a little more from his new position. He spotted another guard, smoking outside the oversized garage that housed the drug shipment. Most attention would be on that area tonight, so Walker identified his next possible hiding spot in the opposite direction.

He darted close to twenty feet in a crouch and dove under an empty truck. He pulled his body into a ball and hid behind the front driver's side tire, stayed motionless. He could see the main house's front steps from there. One man stood guard on either side of the door.

Santiago was in there, so Walker would have to get in and find a way to drag the man out unseen. The relative dark of the courtyard, the sliver of moon that kept hiding behind clouds, were in his favor.

A loud truck rattled by on the street on the other side of the wall. All the guards turned that way, stiffened. They were probably wondering if the Tamchén were coming. Let them wonder.

Walker darted behind the mansion. Here, only a thirty-foot-wide gravel strip stood between the house and the wall. A security camera stood on the top of the wall, but it faced outward. The perimeter guards would walk by regularly and monitor the inside.

Walker pulled into the cover of a bush and waited.

He didn't have to wait long until a guard strolled by. He appeared alert, looking around, walking at a pace that allowed him to take careful stock of his surroundings. One full minute passed before he disappeared from sight.

Walker stayed where he was and waited for the next guard. Fifteen minutes passed before the man appeared. He walked slower than the first guy and didn't look much at anything, shoulders slumped, eyelids at half-mast. Only moving around kept him awake. He'd be asleep the second he sat.

Once he passed out of hearing distance, Walker reached for his phone and dialed his Tamchén connection. Now that his cell phone had dried out, it was working again.

The man on the other end of the line picked up with, "You're fucking dead, gringo."

"I didn't know the truck was rigged, I swear. They set me up. I bet the guy who tipped me off to where the drugs were is working for the Xibalba. They were watching me when I took the truck to you and blew it with a remote. I could have been in the cab, man. I swear, I had nothing to do with this."

"Then why did you run?"

"Fucking people were shooting at me!" He put as much righteous indignation into his voice as he could while still keeping the volume down. "I step out the back to take a piss, next thing I know, some idiot guard is pointing a gun at me and shouting. I moved to pull up my zipper. Idiot thought I was going for a gun, started shooting. Of course, I ran."

He drew a breath. "Then the freaking hangar blew, and everyone was shooting at everything. I got the hell out of there before somebody decided to blame me."

A reasonable story that explained the preexplosion gunfire. If anyone had seen Clara, they'd likely mistaken her for one of their own in the dark in that getup she'd been wearing. If Walker had any luck at all, the men who'd seen him and Clara running from the storage buildings had been blown up in the explosion.

"I figured once things calmed down," he said, "you'd see that I couldn't have anything to do with this. I could have been blown to pieces."

But the man on the other end just kept shouting at him, promising death that would be slow and imaginative.

"Let me make up for my mistake," Walker begged. "The Xibalba just got in a shipment. Two new truckloads. Plus they have the other half of the shipment I took to you."

Originally, he'd planned on enticing the Tamchén with that single load, but being able to add a whole new shipment was even better. The sheer size of the bait made it irresistible.

"I'm tipping you off so you can come and grab the whole jackpot," he said." And I'll get you in, too. I'm going to blow the gate."

More swearing sounded on the other end, but not as heated.

"I'm in position right now," Walker added. And then he told the guy the number of people at the compound, the location of the sentries. "It'd be a quick hit."

Silence. Then a tense, "I'll call you back." Then the line went dead.

Walker waited. The phone buzzed in his hand in five minutes. He'd talked for about three minutes to the guy before, so he had seven more minutes before the next guard would walk by.

He spoke fast. "Are you coming?"

"One hour. When you hear the trucks, blow the gate. If this is a trap, I'm personally going to hunt you down to the ends of the earth."

"The gate will blow before you're halfway down the street. The trucks are in the garage on the right, ready for unloading in the morning. You grab them. Drive them away. Done deal."

He hung up. He had five more minutes. He called Jorge.

"Hermano, want to stay on the right side of history tonight?"

"Got something?" Jorge sounded sleepy. With the gang war, he'd probably not had a lot of restful nights lately.

"I know where Hernandez's crew is hanging out these days. But I have a favor to ask."

"Whatever you need." Excitement pumped up Jorge's voice as he came instantly awake.

"They're guarding the new Xibalba drug company. The Tamchén are taking out the Xibalba tonight. The cartels will be busy. You can get Hernandez."

"You threw in with the Tamchén?"

"Just the way it played out."

The line went silent for a moment before Jorge asked, "And the favor?"

"I'd appreciate it if the factory burned to the ground."

"That's it?"

"It'd be a big help."

"Consider it done, hermano," Jorge said with full confidence, and then Walker had to hang up because the next perimeter guard was coming.

As Walker tucked away his phone, he glanced at the time and thought about Clara, glad that by now, she was on her plane.

***

Clara sat on the ground in some kind of a storage room, alone, her hands bound behind her back with coarse rope that bit into her skin when she tried to free herself.

She'd been waiting for hours for someone to come for her so she'd know what enemy she faced, so she could negotiate.

She doubted they knew she was with the DOD.

She wanted to tell them they were messing with an official of the United States.

But nobody came.

The room was around ten feet by ten feet, brick floor, adobe walls, no window, relatively cool, which made it ideal for storage. A dozen sacks of corn were stacked in one corner, leaving the space otherwise empty. The handful of shelves nailed to the wall held nothing.

Clara was grateful that the men who'd kidnapped her had at least taken off the blindfold before they threw her in here. At least she could see. Sitting here blind would have been a hundred times worse.

Judging by the distance they'd driven, she was at the Xibalba compound in Mercita. They'd only spent maybe twenty minutes on the road. The Tamchén compound in Torelmo and the Tamchén camp in the jungle would have been farther.

Of course, she based her speculations on the assumption that the men who'd grabbed her were cartel men. But they weren't dressed like the banditos. They were older than the teens and twenty-somethings she'd seen with Jorge, and they weren't American, so not corrupt DEA agents either.

And there'd been a cop with them. Walker had said the cops worked for the cartels. God, she missed Walker. But missing him wasn't going to conjure him, so she focused on how to save herself.

She was finished with waiting.

Okay. Xibalba. What did she know about their headquarters?

The place was in Mercita. *Good.* If she escaped, at least she'd be in the middle of a town, wouldn't be swallowed up by the jungle, going from one hostile environment to another.

She put her hands on the ground behind her back, lifted her butt, pulled her hands forward, and looped them around her legs until her bound wrists rested on her lap. *Better.* Now at least she could see what she was dealing with.

The knot wasn't anything fancy. She brought it to her mouth and bit into it, trying to pull the individual strands apart. She spit out some fiber that came loose in her mouth, then went back to work, thinking of Brunhilda as she strained.

The men had left Brunhilda bleeding on her kitchen floor, unconscious from being pistol-whipped. Hopefully, the girls had come down and taken her to the hospital by now. At least Brunhilda had definitely been alive the last time Clara had seen her.

She spit out more fiber, then looked at the rope with chagrin. She was making no progress. And if she was right, and she was at the Xibalba compound, then there'd be a major attack here tonight—orchestrated by Walker. She needed to get out before that happened.

She scanned the room again. She couldn't find a use for the corn. The empty shelves were held up by brackets, however, the brackets nailed to the wall. One of those nails might come in handy to open the lock. But first she had to get her hands free.

Other than the corn and shelves, she had nothing but the floor and the walls. She scanned every nook, her gaze catching on one of the floor bricks in front of her that had an uneven edge and stuck out from the others.

Here we go.

She scooted forward and ran the pad of her thumb over that edge. Hard enough. The bricks had been fired. She angled her wrists and rubbed the rope over that edge. Then, when the first strand of rope broke, she grinned in triumph.

Of course, the next second her hand slipped, and she managed to cut her skin. She wiped the welling blood on her shirt, then went back to working on the rope. She alternated between sawing strands and pulling them apart with her teeth. Her muscles were burning by the time she freed herself about twenty minutes later.

Step One: Complete.

Step Two: Get out.

She went straight to the door. Locked. So she took apart one of the shelves, lifted the wood off, then yanked on the left bracket as hard as she could, worked it back and forth until she eased that nail out of the brick wall.

But with that, all progress stopped. She couldn't open the lock with the nail, no matter what she did. She sweated, swore, kicked the damn door. Nothing.

Before they'd broken into the Tamchén camp the night before, Walker had taught her how to pick a lock. But the piece of aluminum wire she'd used then was a lot more bendy than the nail she had now. Having the right tool mattered.

Walker could find a way, she'd bet. And if Walker could, so could she. She was no damn cupcake detective.

Breathing hard, she smiled, despite her frustration, as she remembered Walker calling her the Indomitable Investigator. *Damn right.*

She stepped back. *Reevaluate.* She scanned the room again, picked up the metal bracket she'd dropped onto the floor earlier. Then she attacked the lock with that, simply beating off the doorknob. Once she managed that, she was able to finagle the tongue of the door into the open position with a finger.

She didn't bother being careful when opening the door. She'd made enough noise so if anyone was out there, they would have come running by now.

She scanned the area outside the door. She was at the back of a building, at the back of the compound, a twelve-foot stone wall maybe twenty yards from her.

The rumble of truck motors filled the air. That explained why nobody had heard her. The noise had come in handy, but now it worked against her. She wouldn't hear if anyone approached.

Where was Walker? *How long would it take to find him?*

Probably too long. Bad idea. No way could she search the compound without someone seeing her. Her best course of action was to leave as fast as possible.

Step Three: Go, go, go. And don't stop running.

She pulled the door closed behind her. But as she contemplated making a dash for the fence, the shadow of a guard came around the corner. Clara darted into the gap between the building she'd just escaped and another larger one next to it.

She was looking at the main mansion, she realized once she was in the shadows, pressed against the wall.

The guard said something. She held her breath. A different voice answered. There were at least two of them. She was outgunned and outnumbered.

If they continued on their path, they would see her in the gap. And she couldn't go in the other direction, or she'd end up in an open courtyard, from what she could tell. She would be seen there for certain.

On one side of her was a blank wall. On the other stood the mansion with dark windows, each with bars over them. But only on the lower level. The upper floor had no bars. Up there, a narrow balcony ran the whole width of the house, with potted palm trees that could hide her.

Without wasting time, she scaled the nearest window, using the bars as the steps of a ladder, and pulled herself up onto the balcony, crouching between two large pots while the guards talked about a shipment that had come in earlier. They were planning out how to spend their paychecks. Women and tequila played a large role in the conversation.

From her higher position, Clara had a better view of the wall that surrounded the compound. Few lights were on, but they provided enough illumination for her to see glittering glass where broken bottles had been embedded in the mortar at the top of the wall. Above that, coils of razor wire stretched.

She winced. A couple of her fingers were still bleeding from prying off the rope. But she'd do what she had to.

She stuck out her head and tried to look around the buildings. Could she somehow cause a distraction and get through the gate? But she couldn't see the gate from here, had no way to tell what the best way would be to approach it.

She turned to crawl to the other side of the balcony to check if she could see something useful from there. Then she gasped when what she saw was beyond anything she'd expected.

A night-light had been left on in the room behind the next set of French doors she passed. Rosita lay on the bed.

The girl's face was toward Clara, toward the light, so her features were clearly visible.

Clara stared, dumbfounded.

Was this why the cousin hadn't been worried? Had Melena known that the girl's own brother had taken her? Why would he do that?

Clara's thoughts stuttered, a fresh wave of adrenaline hitting her. She'd found Rosita. But Walker had been right. She wasn't playing some DEFCON video game. She was in over her head. How on earth was she going to get the girl out of here? One wrong move tonight and they could both be killed.

The realization was underscored by an explosion somewhere in the courtyard.

The balcony shook under her. On the other side of the mansion, flames lit up the night.

She pressed closer to the potted palms. Thank God, she was in the back of the building where nobody could see her. But then a light came on below the balcony.

"Turn off the light, you idiot!" a man shouted in Spanish, and the next second, the back of the house was shrouded in darkness again.

Inside the room, Rosita had come awake, looking around. She probably couldn't figure out if the explosion had really happened or if the sound had been in her dream.

Then she blinked the confusion from her eyes and hurried to the door on the other side of the room. She banged on the wood, shouting to be let out, but nobody answered.

Why was her brother keeping her captive?

Clara moved to the balcony door in a crouch and tried the handle. Locked.

She knocked on the glass, quietly at first, then louder, so the girl would hear her. And, at last, Rosita turned. She stared at Clara, a look of incomprehension on her face while Clara madly gestured for her to open the balcony door.

The girl stayed where she was, in her pink shorts and tank-top pajamas, looking startled.

Maybe she didn't have the key. Made sense. If her brother had ordered her locked up for some reason, they wouldn't want her to escape through the balcony.

Clara backed up and kicked the balcony door open with one well-aimed kick. Then she was in. "I'm here to help."

Her heart raced. She needed to get the girl and herself out of the compound before the real fighting began outside.

She barreled toward Rosita, who still stood frozen to the spot. Clara figured her disheveled look and the blood on her shirt probably didn't inspire too much confidence, so she said, "I'm here to take you home to your aunt. I'm Clara Roberts, DOD Investigator. I'm going to take you back to the US."

She grabbed the stunned girl by the wrist and dragged her to the balcony, but armed men were lining up below to reinforce the perimeter. *Dammit.*

Clara scrambled for a solution. She'd heard trucks earlier in the courtyard. If she could take one of those, she could bust through the gate.

She rushed back into the room, scanned it again, then grabbed a can of hair spray from the dresser. Not exactly pepper spray, but better than nothing.

"Put on your flip-flops." Then she was pulling the girl after her.

She kicked at the door, grateful for the combat boots Walker had given her. She prepared to duck and roll, but the door banged open to an empty hallway.

A few steps forward showed her the layout of the upper floor, the stairs, the foyer below, the open front door, and beyond it, the chaos in the courtyard.

Clara grabbed the girl's wrist again and dragged Rosita down the stairs. "Keep behind me."

They made it to the landing, the front door less than ten feet ahead. *Almost there.*

Then a man rushed toward them from a room to her left, and Clara let Rosita go so she could use both hands in the fight.

She punched with her right and sprayed with her left. And missed, dammit. Then the hair spray flew from her hand as the guy smacked her wrist.

That really freaking hurt.

She fought on anyway.

She used every bit of her training and then some, gave as good as she got. She ducked as fists flew toward her. She kicked, elbowed, punched. But when a second, then a third thug came running, fear cut through her.

One man grabbed her left arm, another her shirt. As she twisted, the shirt ripped, and she let it, pulling to get away. She couldn't. Before she could get in even one more punch, something hard and heavy connected with the back of her head, and her world went black.

CHAPTER
TWENTY-ONE

Walker kept glancing toward the mansion as he helped the others fight the fire. Blowing up the pickup in the middle of the courtyard hadn't been difficult. A strip off the bottom of his shirt, stuck half-in, half-out of the gas tank, then a lighter. *Boom.* The perfect distraction so he could go inside and grab Santiago.

"I saw earlier that it was leaking oil," he shouted to the men next to him. "I bet somebody flicked a freaking cigarette."

He wanted the men busy, but not hypervigilant for attack. Technically, oil was difficult to ignite, a cigarette shouldn't have done it, but he banked on these guys not knowing that.

Santiago rushed from the mansion and called out. Walker couldn't hear the words over the men shouting all around him and the fire cracking and popping.

He dropped his empty bucket and ran to Santiago, along with two others whom Santiago had probably called by name. But by the time Walker reached the front steps, the two men had gone inside. Santiago was pulling the door closed.

Walker called out. "You need help in there?"

"Just deal with the fire," came the response, and then the door clicked shut. *Shit.*

He hurried back toward the burning pickup, grabbed the empty bucket, but didn't run for water. Instead, he ducked between two buildings, abandoned the bucket, then rushed toward the back of the mansion.

He climbed the window bars up to the second-floor balcony, where he figured he could easily kick one of the French doors open. Except one had already been busted.

242

His focus sharpened.

He checked inside—nobody in there. He pushed in. The bed looked slept in. By a woman. A purple dress lay on a chair, makeup on top of the dresser. He strode to the door that connected the room to the rest of the house. This door too, had been broken. His instincts prickled.

He didn't like mysteries or surprises on an op. He'd planned for contingencies, but this was something that simply didn't fit into known parameters. Who had been kept in the room? Why had she been locked up? Where was she now?

He stepped out into the hallway, gun in hand. He could hear people downstairs, Santiago's voice one among half a dozen. But something else captured Walker's attention.

A small pile of familiar fabric lay on the landing—a blue-striped linen shirt.

He knew that shirt. He'd found it in the attic box that morning. He'd given that shirt to Clara, and she'd smiled at him and thanked him. The blue was grayish, the perfect shade to bring out her eyes.

Clara's shirt. Torn and bloody.

Walker's blood ran cold.

He forced himself to breathe. Waves of hot rage alternated inside him with waves of icy panic. *Not Clara, dammit.* He'd been prepared to give everything for his revenge, but *not* Clara.

He pushed away images of her bloody and broken. He'd seen too many times what cartel men were capable of. The farmhouse with the severed heads flashed into his mind. He gritted his teeth. *Not* Clara.

In the light of the foyer's wrought iron chandelier, the blood still glistened. *Fresh.*

Clara had been here, maybe just minutes ago.

All of Walker's senses sharpened. Where was she now?

Downstairs, Santiago was talking to Carlos. "I don't like it. How the hell did that pickup just blow like that? You need to go to the safe house. I'm driving you. Right now. No sense in taking risks."

Carlos didn't argue. Even as Walker moved quietly to the top of the stairs, the two men were already through the door, their entourage behind them.

Walker had no idea where the safe house was.

So he had a choice: follow them and avenge Ben's death at long last, or stay and look for Clara—who, judging by her shirt, might already be dead.

***

Clara woke naked, tied to a table, in what looked like a basement turned into a morgue. Three dead bodies lay on other tables, all men of various ages. White. American-looking. They all had the standard autopsy Y-cuts, all stitched up, as if the coroner had already processed them.

The room stank of death.

Cold fear rushed up her spine as she struggled against the ropes that bound her ankles and wrists. A moment of blind panic took hold of her, and she writhed and fought, hard enough to lose skin in the process. In the overwhelming adrenaline rush, she barely felt the burn and pain.

What happened? Her panic-flooded brain struggled for answers, even as the ropes bit into her harder.

Calm down. Fear makes every situation worse. Her training slowly resurfaced. *Breathe. Assess.*

Okay. Okay.

If she gave into panic, she had no business being an investigator.

She forced herself to go still, to draw a long breath instead of the rapid panting that was making her lightheaded. *Breathe.*

That helped. At least, she was beginning to remember. She recalled finding Rosita, trying to escape the mansion, the guards. Then pain. She'd been hit on the head from behind. Probably why her head was pounding now.

She cranked her neck, trying to block the bodies from her mind and notice the rest of her surroundings. She squinted against the harsh light the neon tube threw from the middle of the low ceiling. Cement floor, cement-block walls, no window, a single metal door. Her clothes and boots lay in a pile by the door.

Where was Rosita?

Before Clara could start worrying about the girl, the teenager appeared at the door, slamming it shut behind her.

At the mansion, she'd been stunned and confused. Now she was staring daggers. And carrying one. Or rather, a twelve-inch kitchen knife.

Not an encouraging sign.

"You should have stayed the fuck home," she said, still in her pink pajamas, looking jarringly out of place in a morgue with that knife. She could have come straight out of a horror movie.

Clara stared at her—not exactly the lost and desperate seventeen-year-old she'd expected. She didn't bother telling the girl again that she was here to rescue her. Rosita didn't look in need of rescue. Just the opposite.

The dark, unhinged light in her eyes was definitely on the scary side. Rosita might be just a kid, but she was a kid with a sharp knife, and Clara was as vulnerable as she'd ever been. *Hello. Naked. Tied.*

"How did the old witch know I was here?" the girl demanded.

By old witch, she probably meant her aunt in the US. Rosita seemed to have no desire to reunite.

Clara fought to keep her voice calm. "I'll explain everything. Could you please cut the ropes? You don't have to come back with me if you don't want to. Your aunt was just worried about you. She thought you might be in trouble."

The look in Rosita's eyes only turned fiercer. "I hope the dumb hag chokes to death. She wanted me to freaking help her scrub other people's toilets. My brother's like major rich, and she didn't want me to be with him. She wanted me to go to school." The girl sneered. "Screw that."

"Just let me go, and I'll leave. If you don't want me to tell her where you are, I won't."

But the girl sneered again. "Jesus, you're stupider than her. You should never have come looking for me. Once we heard that you were asking questions all over the place, we started looking for *you*. You think my brother would ever let you leave?"

"I'm not here for him or anything that has to do with him," Clara said reasonably even as her heart pounded madly. "I'm not with the DEA."

Rosita stepped closer. "Whatever. We need your body."

If there had ever been a sentence to knock the air completely out of a person, that had to be it. *We need your body.*

Clara broke out in a cold sweat. She had to work to force out her next words. "What for?"

The girl flashed a taunting smile. "You'll be a drug mule."

Clara's gaze flew to the bodies, to the red lines running down the men's chests and abdomens where they'd been cut then sewn back together.

"We need more Americans," the girl said.

And the puzzle pieces came together in Clara's brain in a flash. The marine corporal at the US embassy saying that they'd seen an uptick in repatriation of bodies this summer. Walker saying he didn't know how the samples of the new designer drug were getting into the US undetected.

Drug mules.

Bodies of US citizens who died abroad. Expedited through customs.

She lost her breath. Then lost it all over again when the girl stopped next to her and placed the tip of the knife against Clara's breastbone. Rosita drew the knife down, without breaking the skin, mimicking a ruthless gutting, while Clara lay frozen motionless. *Don't panic.*

"Why were you locked in?" she rushed to ask.

Was there strife between the girl and her brother? Could Clara exploit it?

The teenager flashed a sullen, baleful look. "Carlos told me I had to stay in my room tonight. I snuck out to see one of the boys. I got caught." She swore in Spanish, worse than Walker.

Where *was* Walker?

He hadn't been in the mansion. If he'd seen Clara being dragged away, he would have come to her aid. Was he in this building, wherever she was? Could he hear her if she screamed? Could he save her? Or would Rosita stab her in the heart before Walker had a chance to reach her?

The second scenario seemed more likely.

Clara filled her lungs. She was an investigator. Her job was to find and save people. She had to be able to save herself. *Think!*

Her hands were tied too tightly. She couldn't move them at all, couldn't grab for the knife. The girl stayed too far for a head-butting. *Think.*

"Ready?" Rosita asked, full of glee, lifting the blade.

Oh God. She was a teenage psychopath. Desperation washed through Clara, drowning her. She felt herself being pulled under, like in the Tamchén well.

"Wait!" She tried to distract the girl. "I'm General Roberts's daughter. I know you like him. He's worried about you. He sent me, not your aunt."

God, she hated saying the words.

And they didn't have the desired effect either. Rosita laughed in her face.

"Screw that old idiot. Oh my God, how freaking lame! You think I like him?"

"I thought you—" Clara fell silent as the knife pressed against her sternum.

"I set him up, bitch," Rosita crowed. "For Carlos. He knew from Melena that my aunt worked for the old fart."

Clara stared.

"Carlos is going to grow the gun trade," Rosita bragged. "He needs someone at the DOD to ease his way. He needed pictures of the general so when the time comes, the old fart will do whatever we tell him."

Rosita flashed a look of teenage superiority. "I roofied his beer, then I took my top off and took pictures with my phone. His too."

Clara tried to comprehend the utter nastiness of the whole plan, and the utter futility of it, since her father wasn't going to live long enough to be blackmailed. She wanted to reach out and smack the girl.

But before she could as much as respond to the whole vicious story, before she could come up with the slightest spark of a plan for escape, the door opened and a scarred-faced, twenty-something man lumbered in, wearing a butcher's apron.

Clara really, *really* wished she wasn't naked.

He was about the same height as Clara, heavy-set, but with fat instead of muscle. Fleshy chest, fleshy arms, fleshy lips. Eyes that were flat brown, holding no emotion, no spark, and very little sign of intelligence.

He had a ten-gallon galvanized-steel tub in one hand, an eight-inch-by-twelve-inch, plastic-sealed brick of drugs in the other, which he tossed onto the tabletop above Clara's head. He dropped the tub on the floor and kicked it under the table.

Rosita grinned at Clara with dark malice. "Your guts will go in there."

Scarface scowled at the girl. "Go back to your room."

"You don't give me orders," the teen snapped back. "Where's my brother?"

"Went to the safe house with Santiago. Raúl is looking for you."

That the man was talking openly in front of Clara, confirmed he didn't plan on letting her live long.

Clara's heart banged in her chest.

Scarface held out his hand to the girl. With a few choice swearwords, Rosita handed the knife over, then stomped out, swearing some more as she went.

Who the hell was Raúl? Her boyfriend?

But Raúl's identity didn't truly matter, only that mention of him had called Rosita away. One on one was better than two against one.

Not that one attacker still wasn't one more than Clara could handle under current circumstances. The breath got stuck in her lungs when the guy kicked the door closed behind Rosita.

His gaze livened up as it slid appreciatively over Clara's exposed body.

She couldn't look away from him either. The two dozen scars that criss-crossed his face were evenly spaced, as if they were not a result of an accident but systematic torture. She wasn't in the mood to feel sympathetic.

He licked his fleshy bottom lip as he stepped up to the table.

Clara's gaze dropped to his right hand. The way he held the knife, at a certain angle, with a certain grip, elbow loose—like the master chefs on one of those TV shows—did not bode well.

Clara's heart pounded so hard, it hurt.

Rosita had just been playing. *This guy* was the real butcher.

***

Walker searched the upstairs of the mansion first but found no other sign of Clara. He didn't waste time wondering how in hell she had gotten into the compound.

He'd ask her later. Because he *was* going to find her alive.

He tried not to think about her shirtless and bleeding. Or how she got that way.

He clamped down on his emotions, in robot-soldier mode. He was going to go through this place and kill every bastard who stood between him and Clara until he found her. It was that simple.

And if they'd hurt her...*Hurt* wasn't a big enough word to describe what he would do to them.

He had free rein of the rooms. The house guards were fighting the fire in the courtyard.

By the time Walker checked the last room downstairs and made it outside, Carlos and Santiago were long gone. The men, still wrestling with flames that had spread to a carport, paid no attention to him. He was heading for the building that housed the kitchen and food storage when he heard the sound of approaching trucks on the street.

He slowed for a second.

Shit. He'd planned to be outside the compound by now. *With Santiago.*

To blow the gate or not to blow the gate, was the question.

Hell. The more distractions the better, right? He reached into his pocket, then pushed the remote.

The Land Rover he'd parked by the gate blew the next second, blowing the gate right off its hinges, chunks of metal flying through the air like shrapnel.

All around in the yard and the guardhouse, men screamed and ran for cover. Then the Jeep that had parked behind him burst into flames.

Walker ran toward the outbuildings.

He couldn't remember the last time he'd prayed. Couldn't remember how to do it. So all he said was, "God, please, don't let me be late." And then he said it again and again.

If something happened to Clara...

The thought was a frozen black hole that threatened to swallow him. He refused to let it.

As the first of the Tamchén trucks burst through the open gate and gunfire erupted, Walker ducked into the kitchen.

He'd tipped off the Tamchén about how many men were in the compound, so they'd likely brought more. Which meant they'd overtake the Xibalba in the courtyard in short order. Then they'd move to take the buildings.

He only had minutes to find Clara and get her out of here. He *would* find her. He refused to accept the alternative.

But she wasn't in the kitchen or the pantry.

He rushed back outside. The first man who charged him, he shot in the face. The second man he shot in the chest.

Walker strode forward, not letting anyone stand in his way. When he ran out of bullets he snapped in his backup magazine. When that ran empty, he started pistol-whipping people and breaking necks.

He refused to acknowledge his own injuries.

In his mind, he was back in the fighting ring. Boxers didn't fight to win over their opponents. They fought to win over themselves, win over their own doubts, the exhaustion, the pain. Boxing was as much a mental game as it was physical. Just like Navy SEAL training.

His mind was locked on a single thought. He would save Clara.

He kept going.

CHAPTER
TWENTY-TWO

Clara looked up at the man who loomed over her, leering at her as he held the knife. Blood rushed loudly in her ears, but she fought back the panic.

Do. Not. Pass out.

If she blinked out now, she'd never wake up again.

Scarface had ignored the explosion outside and was now ignoring the gunfire. Apparently, he'd been given the job to gut her, and he was good at focusing on the task at hand, minding his own business.

Normally, Clara appreciated goal-oriented people. This one time was the exception.

She was tied spread-eagle to the table, naked, as vulnerable as she'd ever been. She desperately wanted a weapon, or at least to be able to use her hands, but none of that was going to happen. Her mouth was the last line of defense left to her.

"I work for the US government. I'm not a random tourist you can pretend died in a car accident."

Carlos Petranos probably had a deal with the local coroners. All deaths were ruled accidental. By the time the embassy sent someone to collect the bodies, they were stuffed with drugs. The sewed-up incisions wouldn't be suspicious, as they were the standard autopsy Y-cuts.

Then the bodies would go through rapid repatriation, in deference to the families. The cartel likely had someone on the US side who followed the bodies and removed the drugs either before or after the families received the remains. Possibly even after burial, via exhumation.

"If I disappear, the US government is going to look for me," Clara promised, filling her voice with confidence and warning.

Scarface simply shrugged as he reached out and thumbed her nipple.

Revulsion and fear mixed into a cold, sticky mud inside her, a dark swamp that threatened to swallow her.

His eyes stayed focused on her chest.

Clearly, he wasn't the one making important decisions here. He'd been told to gut and stuff Clara, so he would gut and stuff her. The only thing left up to him was what he would do with her body prior to slitting her stomach open.

He caressed one breast with his hand, the other with the flat side of his blade. She held herself still and didn't react. Maybe he got off on fear. She wasn't going to cry and make him any more excited.

Then his hand slipped to her belly, moving downward.

Not reacting became increasingly difficult.

"Could you please at least untie my legs?"

He didn't seem to hear her.

She tried to squeeze her thighs together as much as possible. He forced his hand between them.

"No!" She kept her voice strong. "Stop!"

His flat gaze did snap to hers then. The humorless laugh he gave said he'd do with her as he pleased, with or without her approval.

He pressed the tip of the knife between her breasts. Then pressed down harder.

Blood welled up.

She caught her breath at the piercing pain.

"Don't." She turned to begging after all. "Please."

All she could think of was how el Capitán at the cantina had held in his own guts. She wouldn't even be able to do that.

Scarface drew the knife down, scoring her skin, blood beading up. It stung like hell. For a panicked moment, she thought she was going to watch him open her up. Her hands were tied. But even if they weren't…She was frozen in terror, could barely breathe, let alone move.

But he kept the cut light, little more than a bloody scrape, as if to mark out where he'd slice her later. He watched the blood well up. He licked his lips again, his other hand suddenly restless between her thighs. Then he gave a low grunt and shoved his fingers inside her.

The new wave of terror and the pain between her legs snapped Clara out of her frozen state.

"I didn't break out of the storage room on my own," she lied in a rush—inspiration born of desperation. "There's someone else."

Scarface's gaze snapped to hers, his eyes narrowing as he breathed heavily. He slid the knife up to her neck.

The blade pressed against her madly pulsing carotid artery.

"I could never have managed to get out earlier by myself. You know that, right?" She kept going. "One of the men helped me."

"Who?" Scarface barked the single word as he pulled his fingers out of her and fisted his hand.

"I want to talk to Rosita." Clara put as much steel in her voice as she was capable. "I don't care what you do to me. I'm not going to talk to anyone but the girl."

Scarface, not nearly as sharp as the knife he was holding, watched her for a moment, trying to decide what to do.

"Carlos will want to know who the traitor is," Clara pushed.

Her plan was just to delay the moment when the knife would slice into her for real. But then, for the first time since she'd begun the investigation, something finally went right.

Scarface laid the knife between her breasts, the blade touching the underside of her chin, before he lumbered away with a last dark scowl at her.

Her stomach felt like a nest of squirming eels. Nausea washed over her. *Do. Not. Throw up.* Tied down lying on her back like this, she'd probably choke to death.

The door closed with a thud. Clara listened for the key scraping in the lock. The sound never came. Scarface probably didn't see any way for her to get away at this stage. And maybe there wasn't a way, but she wasn't about to just lie there and wait for death.

When she figured he was too far to hear, she began throwing her body from side to side, until the table started rocking.

The knife slid off, first to the tabletop, then to the floor with a clatter. Nobody came to investigate.

Clara kept rocking, the ropes burning her tender, scraped-up wrists, then ripping her skin. She didn't stop. Instead, she gritted her teeth and put all her strength into the effort.

Then her momentum finally tipped the table to two legs, and she strained, grunting, tears springing to her eyes. And at long last, the table fell over with a crash. It landed on its side, her shoulder slamming into the tile floor.

Oh sweet Jesus.

Her bones rattled. Pain shot through her. If her collarbone wasn't broken, it was probably cracked.

She'd worry about that later.

All she cared about now was the knife that lay closer to her foot than to her hand. She had one chance. If she kicked the knife out of reach, she was done here.

She swiped upwards with her toes, connecting with the handle. The knife skittered across the tile. Toward her, thank God, not toward a distant corner. But it stopped short of her fingers.

She wiggled, rocked again, trying to slide the table on its side as she strained to reach the weapon. "Comeoncomeoncomeon."

And then the tip of one finger touched the blade, then another. But she wiggled too much as she tried to get a better grip. The table tilted, then crashed over, trapping her facedown underneath.

That *hurt.*

The weight would have broken her nose if she hadn't had her head turned to the side. Maybe it'd broken her cheekbone. Her face pulsed with pain.

But she didn't let go of the knife. She positioned it at the right angle—nearly dislocating her wrist—until she could use the blade on the rope, with the weight of the table as added pressure.

Minutes ticked by as she sawed through strand after strand. *Hurry.* Scarface could be back any second. *Dear God, let Rosita be difficult to find in the chaos outside.*

Sweat beaded on Clara's forehead. She nicked herself more than once. Blood made the rope slick. But then the last strands finally gave.

Having her right hand free was a tremendous help. She freed her left hand in just a minute. Then she half crawled out from under the table and freed her legs.

She tested her limbs. She was scraped, bruised, and bleeding, but as she yanked clothes on, she gave thanks that nothing was broken. *Underwear first, then jeans.* Her blouse was missing.

She put on her bra, had no time to worry about modesty. She would have run naked.

She pulled on her boots, then picked up the knife, listened at the door—couldn't hear anything beyond distant gunfire. She cracked the door open an inch. An empty corridor stretched before her, lit by an overhead light, no windows here either. She was definitely in the basement.

How far was the gate?

She hurried forward and almost reached the stairs at the end of the corridor when the door opened above and Scarface appeared. This time, he had a gun. And the second he saw Clara, he aimed the weapon at her.

***

Chaos swirled through the compound. Everyone was running around, shooting at everything that moved, the scene apocalyptic.

Walker rushed from building to building. Then a heavy-set guy in a butcher apron hustled across the courtyard, catching his eyes. On instinct, Walker followed him, taking out anyone who got in his way, grabbing a new weapon every time the one he was holding ran empty.

Butcher Boy hurried into the next building, down a short hallway, then opened a door to stairs that led down. But he didn't move forward. Instead, he swore and raised his gun.

Walker was quicker. He shot the bastard in the back of the head.

Then he ran forward, ready to jump over the body when he spotted Clara darting up the steps.

She was a bloody mess and nearly half-naked. But she was moving. Air rushed into his lungs. He could breathe again.

"How bad are you hurt?"

She had steel in her gaze as she dropped the knife she'd been holding, and grabbed the dead guy's pistol. And shot him in the dick. Then she turned to Walker. "Nothing serious. I can make it."

She was alive. Without life-threatening injuries. *Thank you, God.*

He reached for her hand. He needed to be touching her. "Time to get out of here."

They ran down the hallway, and were at the door in less than a minute. Then they stepped out into an inferno.

"The Tamchén are attacking," he shouted over the din, and darted around the building with her.

"What's all the black smoke?"

"I set some tires on fire."

Even in their mad rush, Clara took the time to flash him a withering look. "Do you know how bad that is for the environment? Why don't you just stab a fork into a dolphin's eye?"

God love a woman who could keep a sense of humor in a situation like this.

He grinned at her, but then his good mood dipped when they had to step over a lifeless body. A young girl. *Aw, shit.* He checked closer. "Rosita?"

She'd caught a half-dozen bullets in the back. Walker glanced at Clara, but Clara didn't seem surprised to see the teenager there. She didn't seem heartbroken either.

He shot a man running toward them, but he kept one eye on Clara. Her mission was toast.

He shot another guy who got too close. "Looks like Rosita's recovery will be a body retrieval. I'm sorry."

But instead of chagrin, a fierce expression sat on Clara's face, a kind of *fuck-the-bitch* look. She moved forward, past the girl, without a backward glance. "How do we get out?"

He suspected there was a story there, but his questions would have to wait.

"Through the back." He ran, spraying bullets.

She followed him without hesitation.

As they rounded the corner of the next building, he grabbed a discarded cement block and headed for a parked truck. "Stay here."

He jumped into the cab, turned on the engine, aimed the truck at the wall, then dropped the cement block on the gas pedal. He made sure the truck would hit the wall, then jumped out at the last second, rolled, while the ground shook with the impact of the crash.

The wall didn't exactly come down, but the top did collapse.

"Up!" he shouted to Clara.

They climbed the truck's crumpled front. From the roof of the cab they could reach the top of the half-toppled wall. The barbwire had snapped, a definite bonus. One leap over the jumble of wires, then a jump down onto the other side. Then they were in the clear.

"Run as fast as you can."

But even as they dashed forward, toward the houses, more Tamchén were moving in, arriving in the backs of pickup trucks.

"The jungle-camp crew, coming to provide reinforcements."

Walker grabbed for Clara again and dragged her into the nearest doorway, kicked the door in, slammed it shut behind him.

Nobody in sight, but a kid was crying somewhere. The family was probably huddled in the pantry or basement. They'd seen turf wars before. They knew to run for cover the moment the first gunshots sounded.

Walker darted through the house with Clara, out the back, then ran through backyard after backyard, scaling fences. He didn't have any specific destination in mind, so he simply ran in the opposite direction from the sounds of gunfire and explosions.

He only slowed when Clara could no longer keep up.

He picked her up and carried her through a gate, back out to the street, to the nearest car. He kicked in the driver's side window, brushed the glass off the seat, then reached over and opened the passenger-side door for her. "Get in."

By the time she limped around, he had the car hot-wired. "Do you need to go to a hospital?"

"A bottle of peroxide and some bandages will do."

"Brunhilda will have that."

"Brunhilda was hurt when I was taken." She sounded a lot more stricken about that than she'd been about Rosita.

"Is that where they grabbed you? Why did you go back to Brunhilda's?"

"Couldn't take the Glock to the airport. I forgot to give it to you before you left."

Shit. He should have remembered to ask for it.

He turned the car in Brunhilda's direction. But then gunfire sounded somewhere ahead of them.

A building burned in the distance. Fighting had probably broken out all over town, gangs joining in on the sides of the cartels, his best-case scenario coming true.

He turned onto a quiet side street. "Forget Brunhilda. She's tough enough to take care of herself. I'll check on her later. We need to get you out of here."

When they reached the end of town, he could see the drug factory in flames a few blocks away. *Thank you, Jorge.* But Walker felt little satisfaction. He just wanted Clara safe.

While he scanned the road ahead, Clara was watching him. "This is what you wanted, isn't it?" Her tone turned subdued, with a hint of shaky. Her adrenaline high was crashing. "This is what you came here to do. Did you get Santiago?"

He shook his head. "I'm taking you to the airport."

For once, she didn't protest. Her hands shook. She shoved them under her armpits. The move smeared more blood on her torso, but she didn't seem to notice.

Seeing blood on her kept shorting out his brain. The shiner she was sporting didn't help. Her face was bruised, as if she'd been punched in the face, maybe more than once.

They were out of immediate danger, but the tension in the car didn't abate. He kept his eyes on the open road in front of them. He filled his lungs, and then he let himself think the thought that he hadn't allowed himself to think while they'd been in the thick of the fighting.

Clara shot Butcher Boy in the crotch.

That seemed like a very specific shot.

The blood she had on her was mostly on her wrists, except that bright red line down the middle of her chest. And she'd had her jeans on when Walker had found her.

Yet that crotch shot...

He could think of no easy way to ask the question, so he asked it straight. "Were you raped?"

"I'm fine." But her voice was too damn tight and suddenly brittle.

Cold fury spread through him. His knuckles turned white on the steering wheel. He wanted to turn the car around, go back, and pound those bastards into a bloody pulp with his bare fists.

"They had me tied naked to a table." Her quiet words reached him through his fury, through the blood roaring in his ears.

Jesus. He couldn't breathe.

Maybe he shouldn't have asked. But if she wanted, needed, to talk about it, he would damn well listen. "It's okay. You can tell me."

And then she told him the rest: Rosita, Butcher Boy, and their plans.

Walker pulled over, drew Clara into his arms, and held her as tightly as he could without hurting her. It was just as much for him as it was for her, maybe more. Butcher Boy had died way fucking easy. If Walker had known, he would have definitely spent more time on the sick bastard.

"Thank you, for coming for me," Clara whispered into his neck.

He held on to her.

He never wanted to let her go.

But he knew he had to. He knew he did. Even if it was killing him.

Adrenaline still coursed through him, his body aroused from the fighting. He sported an impressive postbattle hard-on, a common male biological response to violence.

Except, an overload of testosterone filling his brain with images of her moving over onto his lap and stripping was the dead last thing she needed.

He held his body still.

But she kissed his cheek.

God, she had soft lips.

He turned his head to catch her gaze and talk her out of whatever she thought she was doing, but instead, their lips met. And held.

She deepened the kiss first.

But he let her.

And then he kissed her back. Not gently. Not nicely. He kissed her back like crazy.

She responded with instant heat.

Oh man.

He didn't trust himself with her. He *could not* be trusted with her. Except, she didn't seem to realize this.

Thank God for the blaring police sirens, for the half-dozen cop cars that zoomed by. The ear-busting noise brought them both back to sanity.

He pulled his lips from hers and buried his face into her soft neck so he wouldn't kiss her again.

He held her for as long as he dared. Then he drew away and pulled the car back onto the road.

She had to leave so she would be safe.

He drove north through the night, stopping at a gas station only to gas up the car and buy a small first aid kit, along with food and water and a T-shirt for her. After they ate and he treated Clara's wounds, they kept going.

He drove her straight to the airport. He didn't walk her in. She had on a clean T-shirt, her wrists bandaged, but Walker was covered in blood. He stayed next to his car in the shadow of the parking garage, watched her walk away from him, into the light of the airport entrance.

Just over the line where the light and shadow met, she stopped and turned back to him.

"I want you to come with me," she said instead of heading inside. She stepped back toward him. "Walker—"

She hesitated for a moment, then seemed to make up her mind and came all the way back.

He didn't wrap his arms around her again so he wouldn't dirty her clean shirt. But he wanted to feel her one last time. So he kissed her.

He kissed her so that if she forgot everything else about him, she would still remember their last kiss. He kissed her to brand himself on her brain, as she was already branded on his. He was so hard, wanted her so much, he probably would have lost it if her hands dropped and brushed against the bulge behind his zipper. To prevent just that, he gathered them and pressed them against his heart.

He held his lower body away from her, when all he wanted was to grind himself against her, to switch their positions and push her up against the car, hook her legs around his waist, and pump himself into her sweet heat.

Which was really fucking sick, because she'd just been traumatized. He had to stop reacting to her in a sexual way.

The shadows hid her bruises, but he knew they were there. And that knowledge ripped him to shreds.

He tore his mouth from hers and backed away.

"I'm never going to see you again, am I?" Her voice thickened. Her eyes filled with tears. "Come with me."

He didn't respond.

He loved her. So he had to let her go. So she would be safe.

What had happened to her at the compound only cemented his resolve. She'd gotten hurt because of the war he'd started. She'd almost become a casualty of that war.

He had a hard time living with that thought.

She searched his gaze. "Are you going after Santiago right now? Are you just going to head back into the fray?"

He nodded. And then he turned and moved away from her to the driver's door, putting the car between them, because he needed a physical barrier to keep from reaching for her.

If he reached for her, he wasn't going to be able let her go again.

"Please try to stay alive," she said, because, of course, she was worried about him the Navy SEAL, not about herself, even while she was covered in bandages.

"Don't punish yourself for Ben's death," she kept going, unstoppable. "Because, you know how guilty you feel about Ben's death? That's how guilty I'm going to feel about leaving you here alone if something happens to you. Do you want me to live my life like that?"

That nearly got him smiling. He shook his head. She was blackmailing him into being careful. God, he loved her.

"I'm not going to die here," he promised. "I wouldn't give these bastards the satisfaction."

Her smile of relief wobbled toward the end. "Thank you."

He didn't trust himself to say anything.

What if he opened his mouth and all that came out was, "Please stay."

He watched as she finally turned and walked into the bright lights surrounding the airport. He watched her until she passed through the doors and disappeared.

And suddenly, he felt like a ship that had lost its anchor. He was adrift. Waves of emotions he'd never felt before and couldn't identify battered him. He reached up and rubbed his chest where a heavy pain spread with alarming speed.

He was never going to see her again.

The thought nearly dropped him to his knees.

He slammed his fist into the car's doorframe and welcomed the pain.

Then he got behind the wheel and rode off to battle.

CHAPTER
TWENTY-THREE

Five months later, Washington, DC

Clara watched from the kitchen door as her coworkers mingled around the Christmas brunch buffet her mother had set up on the kitchen island. Brunch at the general's house Christmas morning was in its second year, on its way to becoming an office tradition. Not that they were having much of a party. Other than Clara, only three investigators could make it, everyone else overseas on various cases.

Milo Davis, Finn Carter, and Jackson Turner were talking with her father, analyzing a past case that had gone wrong and ended up with the recovery target's death. At her mother's slight frown, Clara's father smoothly transitioned the topic to what everyone's plans were for New Year's Eve.

The three guys were packing away serious amounts of food while they talked, all three bachelors who normally existed on microwave dinners.

Milo strode off to grab a drink. He always cut a solitary figure somehow, even in the middle of a party. He had a kind of Lone Ranger vibe to him. Clara could see why Elaine Fisher, the office manager, would be attracted.

"When's Jill coming home?" Finn asked Jackson, a twenty-nine-year-old ex-Marine.

Jackson flashed a sailor-on-shore-leave grin. "Tomorrow. Man, I can't wait."

Jill, Jackson's girlfriend, was deployed in the Middle East with the Air Force.

"I guess we won't be hanging out over the holidays." Finn smirked.

Jackson flashed his pearly whites. "Don't call. Don't come over. No offense."

Finn shook his head and almost smiled as he said, "Make sure you keep hydrated."

Finn had his usual air of tragic mystery around him. He was in his midthirties, handsome enough for Hollywood, but could never act, because for that he would have to show emotion, and Finn's emotions were locked down tighter than Fort Knox. And maybe that worked for him, because his success rate for target recoveries was phenomenal.

The rumors at the DOD had it that a decade or so ago, when he'd been a CIA spy, he'd spent some time in an Asian prison with the woman he loved. She'd been executed—death by firing squad. He'd been sent to labor camp, escaped, and eventually made it back to the US. A very different man than when he'd left.

Behind Finn and Jackson, Elaine, the office manager, was chatting with Grandma Lucy over Christmas-tree-shaped French toast sprinkled with powdered sugar.

While Grandma Lucy talked about making maple syrup when she'd been young, Elaine cast longing glances toward Milo, who, still oblivious to her feelings for him, was staring into his coffee. He didn't like being between assignments. He would have traded Christmas for being in the field in a heartbeat.

Clara felt the sudden sensation of being watched and turned toward the living room, caught Bjorn, the department's resident IT guru looking at her with an expression that resembled Elaine's. He was a six-foot Viking with dirty blond hair and ice-blue eyes, in his late twenties, quick to joke, easy to smile. He was smiling at her now.

He'd been smiling at her quite a lot lately.

He was seriously hot. Smart. One of the good guys, the kind who would send flowers after a date. He'd been hinting for the past month or so that he was open to an office romance.

"Hey, want to go outside and make snow angels?" Bjorn asked with a playful glint in his eyes. A glint that said he wouldn't mind a round of the ancient Viking game *hide my war club* either.

"Too cold." Clara felt a pang of guilt at the undisguised disappointment on Bjorn's face, so she tried to soften her words with a smile, but even she didn't buy it.

He flashed her a look of, *I like you and I don't mind waiting.*

Her next smile was more sincere, but she couldn't make it encouraging.

What's wrong with me?

A hundred out of a hundred other women would have jumped for joy at the thought of rolling around in the snow with Mr. Sexy Viking. He was a great guy in every possible way. Except for one major, crucial fault that Clara couldn't get past.

He wasn't Walker.

And she was in love with Walker. Which she'd realized too late, and now she couldn't tell him, because she couldn't find him. He'd disappeared off the face of the earth.

She turned back to the kitchen and forced herself to pick up a cookie, so her mother wouldn't frown at her for being empty-handed. She didn't need another you're-not-eating-enough speech of motherly concern.

If she didn't feel like eating, she didn't feel like eating.

She swallowed a groan. God, she was like a lovesick teenager. She hated being this miserable, missing Walker still with every breath. She hated the longing that filled her up and wouldn't let her sleep at night.

Walker had obviously gotten over her. He hadn't called or emailed. He hadn't tried to reach her once since they'd last seen each other at the airport in Tuxtla Gutiérrez. She only knew that he'd survived the cartel showdown because her father had told her. But even her father didn't know more than that.

Clara had told him about Baku, the Tojolabal shaman, and his strange ways of healing various illnesses. She had begged her father to go and see the man. She couldn't stand the thought of not trying absolutely everything, no matter how remote the chance of success.

The general was now drinking some "jungle juice" three times a day he insisted tasted like ground-up snake skin mixed with slug slime and eyeball of caiman. The mix certainly smelled revolting. The second he pulled out his bag of green powder, all the Roberts women usually fled the kitchen.

He'd met Walker briefly while visiting Baku, but Walker disappeared right after that. Rumor had it he'd crossed the Chiapas border and went even farther south, into Guatemala or possibly beyond.

Clara bit into the cookie and resolved to chew it with full Christmas cheer if she choked on it. She was *not* going to ruin the mood of the party for everyone else.

She walked over to Elaine and Grandma Lucy and joined in the conversation that centered on nursing-home love triangles. She tried not to think of the fact that she was envious of her eighty-year-old grandmother's love life. Seriously, Grandma Lucy had a better love life than three-quarters of the people in the room.

Clara settled in to listen to Grandma Lucy's advice on how to best avoid a jealous catfight in the cafeteria line.

But, of course, Clara's thoughts kept drifting back to Mexico, to Walker, as always.

She was in love with Walker.

But she had to face the fact that Walker had serious self-destructive tendencies. She didn't judge him. She loved him with all his shades of gray. But he had to stop living for revenge. Or they would never have a future together. Not the kind of future they both deserved.

Until he could let go, all Clara could do was pray for him from afar, which she did on a daily basis.

She desperately wanted to talk to him. She couldn't stop thinking about him as the party buzzed on around her.

Then brunch was over, the guests gone, the family retiring to the living room where the angel on top of the sixteen-foot tree touched the cathedral ceiling. It reminded Clara of being up in Walker's surveillance tree in the jungle, him holding her through the night so she wouldn't fall.

God, she missed having his strong arms around her.

Don't think about that tree. She dropped her gaze.

Opened presents covered the carpet from that morning. Christmas lights glinted off the discarded wads of wrapping paper. All she'd wished for last night was Walker under that tree come morning—wearing nothing but a ribbon.

Probably for the best that she hadn't gotten her wish. Her parents would have been pretty startled. And Grandma had already been through her share of No-Undie Mondays.

"A lovely brunch, Meredith. Thank you for doing all that work." Clara's father led her mother to the sofa, holding hands.

Ever since her father's condition had been upgraded, the two of them had been acting as if they were on a second honeymoon, touchy-feely to an embarrassing level.

He had come clean about Rosita, Clara's mission, and everything that had happened. The only thing his wife did was hug him and tell him she loved him and trusted him.

"Where is Bud?" Grandma Lucy asked from her recliner, looking toward the door. Apparently, the lucid part of her day was over, which brought another pang of heartache to Clara's chest as she sat in the armchair next to her grandmother's. "He always takes me skating on the pond on Christmas morning after we open presents."

William "Bud" Roberts, her husband, had been gone for twenty years.

Grandma Lucy narrowed her eyes at the general. "Are you my father?" She looked to the door again. "When is Bud coming?" Then she glanced at her bare fingers. Frowned. "I thought we got married. Didn't we?"

Her rings were upstairs in the drawer of the nightstand. Since she'd lost so much weight, she couldn't wear them any longer. They slid off her finger.

"Have you heard from Antonio?" Clara asked, hoping to bring her grandmother back to the present. Grandma Lucy and Antonio were having a "courtship."

Since Antonio had no children, he'd been invited for the holidays, but he'd broken his hip the week before, falling off the pool table, so he had to stay at Serenity Acres. What he'd been doing on the pool table, Clara had no idea. Probably singing.

Apparently, he'd been a crooner in his youth, determined to follow in Sinatra's footsteps, and now had a tendency to claim high ground as his stage every chance he got, to serenade Grandma Lucy.

But Grandma Lucy just furrowed her forehead at the mention of his name. "Why do you think Bud is late? Is the weather bad?"

While Meredith began talking about the tree to distract her mother-in-law, the general was watching Clara.

"Are you all right? You look a little pale."

Was she all right?

"It's the sweater." She forced a smile. "Christmas sweaters never look flattering on me."

But the truth was, she did feel off-kilter this morning more than usual. She'd dreamed about Walker last night. They were back in the river, fleeing from the banditos. But this time they didn't make it to shore. The current

267

washed them farther and farther apart, while she fought desperately, without success, to reach him.

Clara blinked away the remnants of the dream. Anger filled her suddenly. She *had* asked Walker to come back to the US with her. But she hadn't been important enough for him to do that. The truth was harsh, but it had to be faced.

Thousands of hearts have been broken at thousands of airports all over the world. Hers hadn't been the first. Airports were for departing, leaving behind people and places.

She'd left her heart in Mexico. The empty hole inside her felt no less real, no less painful than if Scarface had gutted her.

"I swear, I'm okay," she told her father, because he was still watching. "Just chillin'. I think I'm in a sugar coma from the cookies."

Her father was about to say something, but his phone beeped. He glanced at the screen, then put the phone back on the coffee table. They had over a dozen active cases, since a lot of people travelled outside the country for the holidays. He'd been getting updates all morning.

Clara had taken the holidays off. Her father felt much better these days, but she was still determined to spend as much time with him as possible, make as many happy memories as they could. Both with her father and her grandmother.

He cleared his throat. "One more present for you, Clara." Then he exchanged a secretive smile with her mother, who seemed suspiciously perked up suddenly, struggling to hide a grin. "It's out in the driveway."

Clara rolled her eyes. "Like I'm going to fall for that."

When she'd been sixteen, she spent the entire year lobbying for a car for Christmas. Then the big day came, and after each gift, she asked, "And one more present in the driveway?" Which became a family joke.

She never did receive a car. She had to work and buy one for herself from her own savings. But the "one more present in the driveway" turned into a family tradition. Her parents got a kick out of giving her an annual gag gift, something inexpensive, but something that would make everyone laugh as a capstone to their Christmas morning.

She rolled her eyes, but she pulled a blanket around her shoulders and shuffled outside in her house slippers.

She looked around from the front porch. She didn't see anything. She turned back for her boots. "You hid it in the snow again, didn't you?"

But strong arms folded around her from behind.

"Hey—" She turned, startled, and found herself staring into jungle-green eyes.

Her world tilted. For a long moment, she couldn't talk. Her heart beat so hard, she felt dizzy.

Walker's hair was shorter than when she'd last seen him, in a neat cut. He wore a gray sweater with camo pants and combat boots. God, he smelled good—some übermasculine aftershave, but light, not overpowering, just enough to make her want to bury her nose in his neck. As if she didn't want to climb him like a tree already.

His presence swept away her heartache and anger over their parting.

He was here. Nothing else mattered.

He was alive. He was alive and well. Relief should have made her laugh, but instead, her eyes were burning.

She had trouble finding her voice. "What are you doing here?"

"I came to tell you that your trip to Chiapas wasn't a failed mission."

"I didn't save Rosita."

"But you saved me." His voice turned low and raspy. His eyes ate her up.

Her heart stuttered. Heat spread through her, and tingles, and flutters. And then all the Christmas cheer found her all at once. Her inner elf was doing backflips. And pirouettes. While throwing Christmas confetti.

Her mind was silently screaming: *He's here! He's here! He's here for me!* She could barely string words together into a coherent sentence. "I thought you moved south from Chiapas."

"That'd been the plan, but somehow, I ended up working for the DEA."

He's here! Then she caught up with his words. "What are you talking about?"

"After the Chiapas cartel war, the DEA caught a lot of grief for not preventing it. Half the crew was fired. The powers that be want to start with a clean slate. They reached out to me. Apparently, they had some kind of file on my 'activities' in the region."

He shook his head with a half smile. "Hell, when they grabbed me, I thought they were taking me to prison. Instead, they offered me an undercover job to clean up the place."

She could only stare, her brain feverishly trying to process the implications.

"What happened to Santiago and Carlos?"

"I caught Santiago and turned him over to the new and improved DEA. He'll spend the rest of his life in prison." He kissed the tip of her nose. "Carlos escaped to Honduras. For now. That's why I wanted to go down there. But I'm pretty sure Santiago will give up his boss's whereabouts sooner rather than later for some prison perk."

She narrowed her eyes. "You let revenge go, just like that?"

"I realized I had to have my hands free if I wanted to grab on to you."

She stared at him.

He said, "You can't cut and paste people from one column into the other. But I realized that people can get off their stubborn asses, and move themselves. You were right. The revenge was for me. Ben wouldn't have wanted it."

God, she loved him.

"I cleared up the cartel problem," he said with a touch of pride but without any detail. "Then I asked for a desk job at the DC office."

"Desk job?" She squinted. "Who are you again? Walker never mentioned a twin."

He laughed, a lovely sound to hear. Then he paused a beat. "I wish you'd mentioned that General Roberts was your father. Imagine my surprise when I ran into him in Baku's village and he told me."

She sucked in her lower lip. Let it go. "I couldn't. Due to…circumstances."

"He said as much." Walker didn't move his eyes from her face. "I'm sorry I haven't been in touch before now. I had plans for us, but I wanted to wait with contacting you until I had my act together. So I'd have something real to offer."

That made her heart beat way too fast, so she moved the conversation into another direction to give herself a chance to catch her breath.

"How is Baku?"

"He hooked up with Brunhilda, believe it or not." Walker grinned.

Clara was grinning too, picturing the two together. "I believe it."

"How about you? How is work?"

Who cared about work? She wanted to drag him to her car in the driveway, into the backseat and…Probably not a good idea, with her parents and grandmother in the house. *Work. Okay.* She could talk about work. "I'm on vacation. The last couple of cases have been pretty standard. Tracing credit cards to track people."

He raised an eyebrow. "What, no cartel wars?"

"No open war, explosions, or crazy people who want to gut me."

He grabbed the edges of the blanket she had around her shoulders and drew her closer. "You must have been bored."

She looked into his eyes that held all the heat of the equator. "To tears. I had to help a couple of friends with their taxes for entertainment. Quarterly estimated tax payments from self-employed taxpayers are due on January fifteenth. People who fall in that category must calculate what they should pay so they don't underpay and get hit with a fine later." And now she was babbling. She pressed her lips together.

His gaze dropped to her mouth, then he dragged it back up to her eyes, slowly, as if it took great effort. "How is your father?"

"The cancer stopped progressing. His diagnosis has been upgraded. He's in good spirits." He wasn't cured, but the six-month prognosis had been extended to a year, and even more time wasn't outside the realm of possibility.

"Anything else to report?"

She flashed him a questioning look. He was so close, she could feel his body heat. She wanted his arms around her, but his hands were still clutching her blanket. She wanted him to kiss her, wanted it so badly, she was going to die if he didn't. Her gaze dropped to his chiseled lips.

A soft groan escaped him, sounding like, *I give up.* And then he *was* kissing her.

Oh God. She sagged against him in relief. His chest was wide and hard with muscles, his strong arms around her at long last. His warm mouth was tasting her, their lips saying hello to each other. Then his tongue swept inside her mouth to deepen the kiss, to take fully, and to give everything she needed.

Liquid desire and heat spread through her all at once, blew through her like flash fire. She let her hands explore his chest, and she pressed her whole body against him, thrilling at the feel of the hard ridge behind the zipper of his pants.

He groaned into her mouth. But then, to her disappointment, he pulled back, breathing heavily.

Okay. Right. They were on her parents' front porch, in view of the entire street. *Jesus, Clara, get yourself together.*

"Boyfriend?" He watched her closely for the answer.

"Shouldn't you have asked before you kissed me?"

"I was going to kiss you either way. If there's someone, I'm going to run the fucker off. Fair warning."

She rolled her eyes with a breathless laugh. "When would I have the time for a boyfriend?"

"I want you to make time for me," he told her. "Why do you think I took a desk job?"

"Temporary insanity?"

The corner of his mouth turned up. "I'm done with mortal combat." Then he added, "I took a desk job because you travel. Both parents can't be traveling. Somebody has to stay around for the kids."

Kids? With Walker?

Just when she'd nearly regained firm footing, solid ground disappeared from under her once again. It felt like falling into the well. But a *lot* more pleasant.

"We are from different worlds," she said, a little faint, having no idea why she was arguing. Maybe she had some deep-seated thing about not looking too easy.

"Maybe." He held on to her. "Or maybe we're both drowning in the same sea."

She definitely felt like drowning as she looked into his turbulent gaze.

"Maybe we need to hang on to each other," he said. "That's my plan. Hang on to you, and never let you go again." He brushed his lips against hers. "Do you think you could hang on to me?"

For some reason, her eyes filled with tears. "Like a wet suit that's two sizes too small."

"Do you think you can love me?"

"I kind of, sort of, have grown fond of you in a way." She was *not* going to blurt out *I love you*, not when he was probably going to say something infuriatingly vague just to torture her.

"I love you, Clara," he said unequivocally.

He dipped his lips to hers again and kissed her, softly at first, then more thoroughly, making up for the long months they'd been apart. His tongue swept into her mouth, licked hers.

The starch went out of her knees. Then Walker murmured, "I love you, Clara Roberts, again," and her heart did a double lutz, wobbly on the landing.

CHAPTER
TWENTY-FOUR

Walker walked into the house behind Clara and surreptitiously adjusted himself, hoping to make his 'condition' a little less obvious. No need to completely embarrass himself in front of his future in-laws. Ideally, he would have preferred spending a week or two in bed with Clara before meeting her family, to take the edge off his hunger, but the general had extended an invitation when Walker had contacted him to day before to ask where he could find Clara.

The general stood to greet him, shook his hand. "Walker."

"General. Thank you for the invitation, sir."

Next to Walker, Clara grinned. "All the lame in-the-driveway presents are forgiven," she said, and her father laughed.

After Walker shook hands and introduced himself all around, Clara dragged him to a love seat. Because the love seat was close to the fireplace and the heat the burning logs radiated, he pulled off his sweater.

The grandmother perked up immediately, leaning forward in her seat. "Bud! There you are. I've been waiting."

Walker looked at Clara. She pointed at his T-shirt that had BUD/S written on it. From Basic Underwater Demolition/SEALs training.

"Bud was my grandfather," Clara explained under her breath. "Grandma Lucy is having a rough day with her memory."

Grandma Lucy smiled at him with such love on her face. Walker couldn't help but smile back at her. She looked like a nice old lady. Clara resembled her. The gunmetal-gray eyes had clearly come from that side of the family.

"How is the DEA?" the general asked, and followed up with a few more work-related questions.

Walker answered and soaked up the warm family atmosphere. He hadn't participated in a traditional Christmas morning since elementary school. He hadn't realized he missed it.

Although, the whole family thing was a little intimidating now that he was in the middle of it. The house too was impressive. He couldn't offer Clara anything like this. For now, he was little more than a DEA bureaucrat, on a bureaucrat's salary.

He took her hand. Just sitting like this with her was more than he'd dared hope for in these past few months while he tried to create a life for himself that could include her. He figured since the general had participated in setting up this visit, maybe the man wouldn't shoot him for the handholding.

The general pretended not to notice. *Good enough.* Walker could work with that.

Meredith Robert beamed with approval. "How about I go and make some fresh coffee?"

"I'll help." The general stood with her, looking between Clara and Walker. "You two catch up. I'll take kitchen duty."

Grandma Lucy kept watching Walker. "When are we going skating?"

He looked at Clara, who gave a small nod, so he said, "A little later."

"I'd like to sit in the sunroom and look at the snow," Grandma Lucy said next, lifting a stack of old letters tied together with a ribbon from her lap.

"I found Grandpa Bud's old letters from Vietnam in the back of a closet when I was looking for Christmas decorations," Clara whispered next to Walker.

The pleased smile lighting up her face went straight to his heart. He wanted to kiss her again more than he wanted to draw his next breath. But they were in full view of the general and his wife in the kitchen. So Walker was going to take things slow.

Some things were worth waiting for. Clara was worth everything.

He stood and offered his arm to escort her grandmother, following Clara, who walked in front of them. At least he could look his fill. She wore jeans and a bulky Christmas sweater, but to him, she was hotter than a Victoria's Secret model in nothing but lace and wings.

They passed through the French doors into a spacious sunroom that looked over the snow-covered backyard. When Grandma Lucy settled into a wicker sofa, Clara tucked a blanket around her.

Since Grandma Lucy didn't let Walker's hand go, Walker sat next to her. Clara sat on his other side, close enough so their thighs touched lightly. He shifted until the contact became more solid. She seemed to relax, as if she needed to touch him as badly as he needed to touch her.

Grandma Lucy passed him the letters she'd been holding in a hand that was liver-spotted but as elegant as a piano player's. Which she probably was, considering the gleaming black baby grand in the foyer. "Could you read them to me?"

He took the stack, pulled the letter on top, and opened the faded envelope, unfolded the wrinkled, stained paper. "My Dearest Sweetheart, I miss you more every day..."

He wasn't a sentimental man, but his eyes were burning by the time he was done with the first letter. The only thing that kept him going was the way Grandma Lucy and Clara beamed at him. When Clara looked at him with such admiration, he would have drained oceans and battled sea monsters for her.

He read on.

Obviously, Clara's grandfather had been to some seriously bloody battles. He'd suffered staggering losses, among them the loss of his twin brother in a chopper crash Bud had barely recovered from. He'd done dark things to survive. He hadn't spelled it out in his letters to his sweetheart, but Walker could read between the lines and felt a connection to the man.

He liked knowing that Bud *had* survived to return home. He had not let the past claim him. He'd married his Lucy and started a family. A life like that *was* possible. Maybe even for Walker.

Grandma Lucy fell asleep on the third letter.

Clara tucked the blanket tighter around her, then took Walker's hand, led him out of the sunroom, through the living room, and into the library.

"So is this where the hot monkey sex happens?" he asked on a note of hope. But she didn't laugh with him.

A quiet, thoughtful look came over her face. "I have something for you. I got it two days ago. I've been trying to find you."

She walked to the fireplace and picked up a copper urn from the mantel, holding the urn as carefully as if it were a priceless treasure. She hesitated.

He stepped closer. "What is it?"

Her expression turned tender. "I need to tell you something." She held his gaze, letting her love and concern show in her eyes undisguised. "I found your brother." She paused. "US Customs had him. The box hadn't been correctly stamped as remains."

He felt as if the floor had dropped out from under his feet. For a moment, he could only stare at her. All the air left his lungs. He struggled to draw some back. Then he reached for the urn and cradled it in is arms.

Ben.

Walker's throat tightened.

Clara had found Ben for him. His little brother hadn't been lost to the incinerator. Ben was here.

Walker blinked moisture from his eyes. His cheeks felt wet. He was holding on to the urn so tightly, it was a miracle he didn't dent the metal.

He turned from Clara, too embarrassed to cry in front of her. He couldn't remember the last time he'd cried. Not even when he'd found out about Ben's death.

Ben.

And then, *oh great,* Walker couldn't see.

He was definitely crying. Like a big giant baby. But suddenly he didn't care. Nothing mattered but that he had Ben back.

Then Clara wrapped her arms around Walker and pressed herself against his back, laid her cheek against his shoulder, and just held him. Held him up. Held him together.

"Thank you." His voice was so thick, he barely recognized it. "You don't know what this means to me."

She held him tighter, her arms strong and steady. Man, it was a good feeling. Best feeling ever.

Ben before him, Clara behind him. Surrounded by the two people he loved most. Feelings he couldn't begin to identify spread through Walker's chest and threatened to drop him to his knees. A vast, stormy sea of emotions threatened to wash him away. But he had an anchor: Clara Roberts.

When they'd first met, he'd thought she was about as soft as a fishhook in the eye. But if something got hooked, it was his heart. Truth was, she *was* soft, and warm, and kind. Which didn't stop her from being pretty damn kickass when she needed to be.

As she held on to him, his dead and empty heart filled with life again.

* * *

Walker couldn't sleep.

He couldn't believe the day he'd just had. Clara's family had treated him as if he was one of them. Before dinner, they'd taken Grandma Lucy to look at the ice-skaters. Putting those old bones on ice was not the best idea, so they kept her on the sidelines. But she seemed satisfied with watching, her arm hooked into Walker's on one side, Clara's on the other.

After the visit to the frozen pond, her memory seemed to return. The old gal was a hoot and a half. Walker liked her. A lot. And not only because Grandma Lucy seemed to wholeheartedly approve of him.

For dinner, they took her to her favorite restaurant, where Bud had proposed to her, and she was so happy, she squealed like a young girl.

While she napped in the afternoon, Walker played cards with Clara and her parents. He'd been a little unnerved by the general, but he liked to think he stood his ground in Uno against the man. Then Clara took him for a walk in the park, a winter wonderland, very different from the jungle where he'd fallen in love with her.

He kissed her every chance he got and hoped for more, but after dinner, Meredith, the general's wife, set up the guest bedroom for him.

Where all he could think about was Clara somewhere down the hall, way too far away from him.

Walker loved her so much, he could barely breathe when she was in his arms. Which was where he wanted her right now. But he wasn't going to push her. He was going to wait patiently, even if it killed him, until she arrived to the same page where he was.

He turned onto his back, folded his arms under his head, and stared at the ceiling in the semidarkness. No way was he going to be able to sleep while under the same roof with Clara.

He settled in for a long night, but when he heard furtive footsteps in the hallway, he turned back toward the door and held his breath in hope.

Clara stuck her head in. Her gaze met his in the dim room. "Can I come in?"

"Does your father have a gun collection?"

"Nothing bigger than a grenade launcher." She flashed him an is-my-big-bad-navy-SEAL-scared? look.

Then, before he could respond to the unspoken challenge, her gaze dropped to the comforter, making it clear that she wasn't asking to sit in the armchair by the window. She wanted to come into his bed.

Hell, yeah.

God, he loved her. "When did I ever not offer to share a bed with you?"

He shifted to the side, making room for her, his heart thrilling at the sight of her, his body immediately ready to go as far as she would let him. Preferably, all the way. As many times as possible. Tonight, tomorrow night, for the rest of their lives.

He held her gaze. "Remember what I said the last time you were in bed with me?" *If you come into my arms again, don't expect me to stop.*

She just smiled as she hurried over, wearing the skimpiest black nightgown he'd ever seen. She slipped under the covers.

An answer, right? A definite yes. He hardened even more, which seemed impossible.

And then, the wonderful, amazing woman that she was, she spelled it out for him. "I was promised a present in the driveway. You were in the driveway. I'm here to unwrap my present."

Full green light. Okay, then.

Her warmth and soft scent enveloped him—the scent of chocolate, peppermint, and cinnamon. Maybe she hadn't been able to sleep either and had tried the hot-chocolate treatment first.

He desperately wanted a taste.

When he reached for her, she didn't resist.

But she did say, "Oh, you're naked."

"I live in hope. It's my new motto."

She pressed herself into his embrace, laid her cheek against his chest. He caressed the velvety skin of her back, barely able to believe that she was in his arms at long last.

She tasted like Christmas, and hope, and future—everything he'd never thought he could have. She tasted like an impossible dream. He was determined to make that impossible dream his. He'd waited too damn long for this moment.

When they came up for air, he told her, "I'm in this for the long haul. Just so you know." It needed to be said.

"Okay." She nibbled his earlobe.

Heat shot through him. "Okay?" The single word came out in an uneven tone.

He turned his head on the pillow to force her to look at him. He wanted to make sure that she meant it. "I've done some seriously bad shit in the past."

"I know," she said patiently. "I was there."

He winced. Searched her gaze. "It's possible that I'm messed up. You know, in the head. Maybe I'm not just part-time nuts. I could be full-on crazy."

"You mean like PTSD?"

"I don't know. But I have some pretty nasty baggage from my SEAL days, and after." He filled his lungs. "I'm seeing a shrink over at Walter Reed."

From the way her eyes flared, he knew that he'd surprised her.

A smile flashed onto her face. "Really?"

"You deserve a good man. Better than me, for sure. So I want to do whatever I can to be as good a man as I can be." He paused. "I kept thinking about what you said, that quote from Heraclitus."

"What anger wants, it buys at the price of soul."

"Yeah. Thing is…you are my soul. Or a big part of it. And I'm not going to let my anger touch you, or hurt you. That just can't happen. So I'm letting it go." He offered half a smile. "I'm working on letting it go," he corrected.

Her gaze softened. She worked off her nightgown and pressed her naked body against his. "I love you, Walker."

His heart swelled with emotion. He tasted her lips over and over again, then swept inside and explored her fully, just in case there was something he'd forgotten. There wasn't. She was just as sweet as he remembered.

Then he kissed her neck, her collarbone, nibbling his way to her pebbled nipples. He circled them with kisses.

He laid his head between her breasts. When he stuck his tongue out, her nipple was at the perfect distance for licking.

Every man needed a bosom for his pillow, indeed.

He hummed the song as he grinned.

Damn straight.

By the time he sucked the nipple into his mouth, she was writhing under him.

He'd been waiting for this for too long. He was tired of dancing the blueball shuffle around her. If he didn't get to bury himself in her sweet body and soon, his dick was going to fall off, hit the floor with a clang, and roll off into some dusty corner. After all the years of fun they'd had together, he figured he owed his dick a better fate. He was done with trying to keep his distance.

He moved over her and fit his erection against her. She moaned in approval. He was so freaking ready. But a torturous thought jarred him out of his lust haze.

He lifted his head, and swore. "I don't have a condom. I have them at the hotel."

He'd gotten a room, hadn't expected that he would be invited to spend the night. He was close to grinding his teeth with frustration.

Clara blinked. "I put some in my robe pocket." She groaned. "But then I was so distracted by the thought of sneaking in here, I left my robe in my room." She closed her eyes for a moment. Opened them. "Try the nightstand."

When he did, he found a brand-new six-pack. Relief slammed into him pretty damn hard.

She grinned. "My mother. My father is a general and could organize the occupation of a large country. But he pales next to my mother when it comes to planning ahead."

He decided that he really, really liked Meredith Roberts.

"I'm going to do something very nice for your mother in the near future. Say, she needs closet organizers put in, or whatever women go crazy over these days. Whatever it is, I'm there."

He rolled the condom into place, then moved back over Clara as her thighs parted to welcome him. *Ahhh.*

He did *not* give any further thought to closet organizers.

Nothing had ever felt as right as their two bodies joining together—every moment pure bliss.

He thrust into Clara's tight heat.

The headboard hit the wall.

Shit.

The general slept on the other side of that wall with his wife.

Walker held still. Sweat beaded on his forehead. He couldn't stop. No way. He pulled back, thrust again, slower this time. But the headboard knocked into the wall anyway.

In the other room, the general coughed.

Shit.

***

Clara had a romantic night in mind for their first time together—something sweet and poignant she would always remember. And great sex, of course.

She knew her body. Certain parts had to be touched in a certain way, for a certain length of time. She wasn't afraid to ask for what she needed. She was a twenty-first-century woman. She was in charge of her own orgasms.

Except, one second, they were in bed, the next, Walker was on his feet, and she was somehow wrapped around him, the comforter wrapped around both of them. He evacuated the room as fast as if bombs were falling.

"Headboard. Wall," he whispered into her ear, his voice unsteady and strangely guttural.

Okay, she could be flexible. Even if her small, twin-size bed wasn't nearly as nice as the queen mattress in the guest bedroom.

But as she thought about pointing him toward her room, the mountain of evidence to her childhood geekiness held her back. Wall-to-wall Mathlete trophies didn't exactly make for a nest of romance. And how did one explain a life-size portrait of Einstein in boxer shorts?

While she hesitated, he was already carrying her down the stairs, his movements as stealthy as if sneaking through enemy camp. He headed for the couch.

They were almost there when Grandma Lucy called from her downstairs bedroom in a sleep-laden voice, "Is that you, Bud?"

Walker turned from the couch. Then they were at the back door, then outside.

The cold didn't even touch Clara. The heat of his body radiated through her.

Her brain screamed: She was about to have sex outdoors! Against the house. Like in a movie. *Okay.* Maybe she could stretch her comfort zone this far.

But the next step they took forward turned on the motion-sensor floodlight.

If her father looked out his bedroom window…

Walker must have thought the same, because he crossed the deck in a few strides and dove off with her.

Lying in the ditch sheltered them from the motion sensors. The lights clicked off.

She lay on top of the comforter in the snow, Walker on top of her. And then he was inside her again.

Okay, so Navy SEALs were known for being highly adaptable to their environment, but…

In a ditch?!

Their first time making love was going to be in a ditch?

This was *not* how tonight was supposed to happen. She'd had plans.

She was a twenty-first-century woman. She knew what she wanted. She knew what worked for her. She was in charge of her own—

Then he moved inside her, claiming her lips at the same time, and suddenly she was in charge of nothing.

Mad tingles ran through her body with his every move. Her response to him was spiraling rapidly out of control. The best she could do was hang on to his wide shoulders while she arched her back and tilted her hips on instinct to take him in even deeper.

Then she was close. So close…But every time she came to the edge, he pulled back. Then he built the pressure again. And again, and again. Until he finally pushed her over, and she flew apart in his arms.

As she slowly returned to earth, she became aware that the comforter under her was wet from the snow her body heat had melted. When she squirmed, Walker noticed.

He pulled back. "Are you cold?"

Well, now she really was, since he took away his heat. But she shook her head. She didn't want him to stop. He hadn't…

"Hang on." He picked her up again and dashed across the deck, back into the house with her. Into the downstairs bathroom, into the shower, which he turned on before stepping under the warm water with her. "Better?"

She wasn't sure. *Shower sex!*

Not that she was completely against it, but shouldn't their first time be something more reserved? Didn't people save shower sex for later, when they were more comfortable with each other?

She didn't get to ask those questions, because Walker set her on her feet, turned her around, and spread her legs with his knee. His palms came around to massage her breasts while his erection nudged her opening, then reclaimed its earlier spot inside her.

She melted against the shower wall.

Water sluiced down her face. Too much, really. She made a choking sound, which he must have misinterpreted, because he asked, "You like that?" in a tone that said he was mighty proud of himself.

Okay. She was seriously loosening up here, but relationships had to be built on truth. "Feels like I'm being waterboarded."

"Sorry." He laughed and turned her, repositioned her. "Better?"

Her legs were once again wrapped around his waist, her back against the tile. And suddenly it was not just better, but *perfect*. She hung on to him as her body contracted around him all over again. *Wow*.

One more thrust, and he followed her over, a deep groan reverberating in his chest.

They were both breathing hard as warm water washed over them.

Beyond her body flying apart for the second time in ten minutes, she felt as if her brain had just exploded. How was this even possible?

She felt as if every spreadsheet in her head had just been set on fire.

He kissed her. "Marry me."

She stared at him, overwhelmed. "What if we just—"

"It's a yes-or-no question. Marry me. I don't just want to date. I don't just want to live together."

She brushed wet hair out of her face. "Now you start thinking in black-and-white?"

"It's a black-and-white issue. I want you to be my wife. No gray areas."

"And if I'm not ready?"

She couldn't believe she was arguing him while she still had her legs around his waist, while he was still inside her.

He looked like he couldn't believe it either. "I'm willing to do whatever it takes. Up to and including kidnapping. I'll run off with you to the jungle. Your future will include loincloths and swinging from lianas."

"Are we really back to Tarzan and Jane?"

"Damn right. I'm going to find a monkey and train him to be our butler."

"That's completely against animal rights," she said, dazed. Then felt bereft when he slipped out of her and set her on her feet.

He held her gaze. "I'm willing to hold you hostage for as long as it takes for you to admit that I'm the only one for you."

She snorted. "Do you know what kind of workload my department deals with? I can't in good conscience add another disappeared person case to the list."

His lips broke into a wide grin. "Does that mean you'll marry me?"

"To keep you out of prison. Consider it a humanitarian mission."

"You're a saint."

"And don't you forget it."

He turned off the water and wrapped her in a large towel, then took care of the condom and wrapped a towel around his own waist. He lifted her into his arms. "Let's go to bed."

She leaned her head on his wide shoulder, dazed. *Flash fire.* The right mix of combustible materials. *This is what it feels like,* she thought. She felt scorched by him.

She kissed the strong line of his jaw. Lingered.

He groaned and said, "We have to be good until morning now, or the general will hear."

She hated the idea of being "good" with Walker. Before she could tell him that, he stepped out of the bathroom with her. Froze.

Grandma Lucy was standing in front of the fridge, the open fridge door the only thing between them.

"There's a pool table in the basement," she said without closing the door, without looking at them.

Clara was so used to strange comments from her, a moment passed before she realized what her grandmother was trying to say. As Walker headed for the basement door, Clara buried her face into his neck and half groaned, half laughed.

"What?" he asked once the door was closed behind them and he was heading down the stairs with her.

"I think I just figured out how Antonio broke his hip," she said, then told him the whole story.

Walker looked impressed. "Fifty years from now, when we're in a retirement home together, there'll be no pool table safe from us," he promised.

And then he gave her a preview of upcoming attractions.

-THE END-

Thank you for reading my books! To be notified when my next title comes out, please sign up for my **New Book Alerts** at www.danamarton.com. I send out a one-page note, once a month at tops (and sometimes not even that frequently), so I promise not to overwhelm your email! I also always notify my readers of upcoming sales and giveaways.

Would you have a moment for a quick review? Authors live and die by their online reviews. **Would you, please, consider leaving a review** on Amazon or Goodreads? Just your honest opinion. Even a single sentence would make a real difference to me. The more reviews, the more visibility some retailers give the book. Thank you!!!!

And if you are online, please **come chat with me** on Facebook. I'd love to 'meet' you.

Wishing you all the best,
Dana
Author

ABOUT THE AUTHOR

New York Times bestselling author Dana Marton writes about smart, strong women and the alpha heroes they love, especially when those heroes are cops and military men. Luckily, her secret research source is always close by—her husband has served in the US Army, has been an EMT, and a fireman, a hunter, a trapper, and a number of other things he won't admit to in public.

Dana's small-town romantic suspense series set in Broslin Creek is based on her real life home in Pennsylvania, and has over one thousand positive reviews. Book one in the series, DEATHWATCH, is currently free.

She also writes an international romantic thriller series full of intrigue, danger and exotic locales, based on the investigators of the Civilian Personnel Recovery Unit. FORCED DISAPPEARANCE and FLASH FIRE are the first two books in this series.

Kirkus Reviews calls her writing "compelling and honest." RT Book Review Magazine said, "Marton knows what makes a hero...her characters are sure to become reader favorites." Her writing has been acclaimed by critics, called, "gripping," "intense and chilling," "full of action," "a thrilling adventure," and wholeheartedly recommended to readers. Dana is the winner of the Daphne du Maurier Award of Excellence, the Readers' Choice Award, and Best Intrigue, among other awards. Her book, TALL, DARK, AND LETHAL was nominated for the prestigious Rita Award. DEATHSCAPE reached the #1 spot on Amazon's Romantic Suspense Bestseller list.

Beyond being a bestselling author of romantic suspense thrillers, Dana also writes a popular fantasy romance series, Hardstorm Saga. Book 1, RELUCTANT CONCUBINE, spent 6 weeks at #1 on Amazon's fantasy romance list.

When not writing, Dana loves to browse antique shops and enjoys working in her flower garden, while fighting her addictions to reading, garage sales, coffee and chocolate. If you know a good twelve-step program to help her with any of that, she'd be interested in hearing about it!

Keeping in touch with readers is Dana's favorite part of being an author. Please connect with her via her web site (www.danamarton.com) or her Facebook page (www.facebook.com/danamarton).

37111351R00166

Made in the USA
Middletown, DE
19 November 2016